MW01075318

Titles by Todd Borg

TAHOE DEATHFALL

TAHOE BLOWUP

TAHOE ICE GRAVE

TAHOE KILLSHOT

TAHOE SILENCE

TAHOE AVALANCHE

TAHOE NIGHT

TAHOE HEAT

TAHOE HIJACK

TAHOE TRAP

TAHOE CHASE

TAHOE GHOST BOAT

TAHOE BLUE FIRE

TAHOE DARK

TAHOE PAYBACK

TAHOE SKYDROP

TAHOE DEEP

TAHOE HIT

TAHOE JADE

TAHOE MOON

TAHOE FLIGHT

TAHOE FLIGHT

by

Todd Borg

THRILLER PRESS

For Kit

ACKNOWLEDGMENTS

Last year, a friend of mine, Shelby Swartz, invited me to go flying with her. Shelby is an accomplished acrobatic pilot. She picked me up at the airport in Palo Alto and flew me down near Monterey to have lunch. How cool is that?! As we cruised above the Pacific, Shelby treated me to some acrobatics! (It was a good thing we had lunch after our four-G maneuvers instead of before!) The plane she flew was a Super Decathlon. Shelby even let me take the stick for a few moments. That was the first time I'd flown in a taildragger. The experience inspired me to feature a taildragger in this book, and to name the book Tahoe Flight.

In this book, I was confident I'd need very little editing. I knew my prose was nearly perfect. Nevertheless, I thought it would be a good exercise for my editors to see if they could find any problems. Ha. Ha. Liz Johnston, Eric Berglund, Christel Hall, and my wife Kit saved me again.

For the cover, Keith Carlson managed to mix the beauty of Tahoe's natural landscape with an unusual plane that telegraphs danger and excitement. The result is magical. But then, he is a magician.

Thanks so much to everyone.

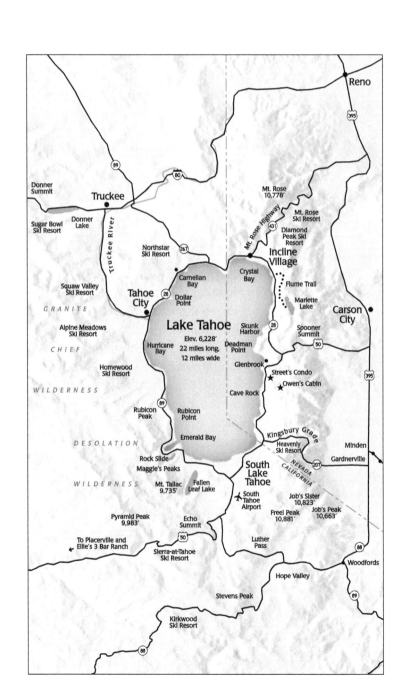

PROLOGUE

On a chilly evening in November, Avery Kingsley strolled along the sidewalk on the boulevard in Tahoe City on Lake Tahoe's northwest shore. It was dusk, a good time for escaping notice because there were crowds of people out, and it was too dark to be easily recognized.

Avery's friends up ahead knew Avery was there, although they only knew Avery's real name and real personality. When Avery's friends glanced back to look at Avery in the darkness, they saw only what they've always seen. The familiar face and gait, the rumpled dark clothes and hat, the happy smile.

But when Avery's friends turned forward to check out the restaurant and bar ahead, Avery cocked the hat sideways and pulled it down low, adopted the practiced limp with the ever-so-slight drag of the left toe, and made the subtle back rotation of the right shoulder with each step. Avery replaced the standard smile with a grimace, and moved the jaw to the left.

The result was that Avery's friends only saw the friend they knew. Anyone else who looked at Avery Kingsley saw a fictional construct so different from reality, it was as if Avery was invented and perfected by a theater major.

Avery's goal was simple. If a crime should take place that the cops would investigate, they would quickly focus on a fictional person who seemed to vanish. If the police conducted extensive interviews of people who were in the area, they would at best learn that their "person of interest" was following close to a group of people who were chatting and laughing and enjoying a night out in Tahoe. The police would get only a vague description of a dour individual with a limp and wearing a hat pulled down low. And if several people could be found to describe Avery Kingsley, they would likely disagree on all major aspects of the person, including the person's gender.

Of course, Avery Kingsley had no intention of telling anyone the fake name. It was part of the theatrical invention. When a person wants to become another, it helps to create a full picture of the phony individual including the name. And if the small possibility arose that a stranger asked Avery's name, well then the name Avery Kingsley existed.

The bottom line was that the person acting as Avery was only Avery when it was time to commit a crime. The rest of the time, the actor was just one of the friends, one of the group.

Up ahead, people were spilling out of restaurants and bunching up at the entrances to bars. From their boisterous voices and movements, it was clear their dinner drinks had loosened their moods, and they were eager to expand the feeling.

Across the lake, 25 miles to the south, a moon glow lit the early-season snow on the top of Heavenly Ski Resort. The white dome of snow looked vaguely like a pale hand resting palm down on the top of the 10,000-foot mountain with the ski runs spreading down like white fingers.

Another group merged from the side. The people made a lot of noise as the groups met. Most of them appeared to know each other. The people exclaimed their hellos and hey dudes and good to see yous. The women gave each other gentle hugs that were more about decorum than affection. The men shook hands and slapped each other on the backs and shoulders.

Somebody said they couldn't believe it had been a dozen years since medical school.

"Remember those days, man? Those were good times, huh? Busted our bodies and brains from no sleep. But now the honeys are seduced by our careers, and the other kind of honey flows into our bank accounts. Stress of the job balanced by the sweet elixir of success."

"Right on, dude."

Avery remembered those days as well. But they weren't good times.

A memory returned from years before, when Avery's class sat in on an autopsy.

The doctor was a pathologist, and he was very thorough. He began with a lecture, going back 2,500 years to the Hippocratic Corpus, the written summation of Hippocrates' studies of evidence-based medicine, the very beginning of the practice of medicine as a science as opposed to a collection of myths involving gods and demons and shamans who could talk to spirits. From there, the doctor explained the purpose and history of autopsy, and he listed the standard components.

After his brief lecture, he turned to the body on the table. The body was blue white, its clothes removed, male, mid-twenties in age, muscular, about six feet in height, with short, black hair. The pathologist began the external anterior examination, talking as he worked.

"The identity of the deceased is unknown. The body was found without identification. So we have no access to medical history. With no hints of disease or information about past medical problems, our work today will be more of a treasure hunt than normal as we try to find the cause of death."

The students were quiet, no doubt gripped by this dramatic exposure to a side of medicine they hadn't much contemplated.

The pathologist seemed to use his hands for discovery as much as his eyes, the blue latex-gloved hands touching and poking and stroking the body. He noted that the deceased appeared to be fit with no obvious scars from injuries or surgeries.

When the doctor rolled the body over for the posterior examination, he paused at a small reddish dot on the body's back, to the left side of the spine. He touched his blue fingertip to the dot, continued his examination, then turned the body over and began the interior examination. He used a scalpel to cut into the abdominal cavity and a rib shears to open the thoracic cavity. He described his activity as he inspected and removed organs.

The person who would eventually use the name Avery remembered that there were no remarkable aspects to the doctor's interior examination, yet a powerful wave of nausea had made Avery's stomach clench. Avery had choked back a gagging reflex, swallowed, shut eyes hard, and took deep breaths. Eventually, control returned.

The doctor was saying something about the pericardial sac around the heart and the pericardial fluid, the details of which Avery had missed while struggling to control nausea.

"There are many types of tests," the doctor said during the autopsy, "that can reveal diseases, toxins, and physical problems. But I started with a radiological examination, which showed none of the common problems, such as cardiomyopathies, that can lead to death."

As the doctor spoke, he was spending a lot of time on the thoracic cavity, transecting arteries and veins.

In time he said, "Let's now consider the heart." The doctor removed the heart and held it up for all to see.

Avery immediately wondered if the pathologist was following standard autopsy routine or if he was deviating to make certain points more obvious to his students.

"The heart looks healthy, and the aorta and other arteries of the heart are normal." The doctor turned the heart over and around, looking at it closely. "Yet it appears this little heart muscle has an interesting story to tell. And that story will probably explain why the heart quit quite abruptly. We'll get to the reasons in a minute. Regardless of the reasons, a heart that gives up quickly presents an interesting circulatory situation."

The professor looked at the assembled students. "Let's revisit the basics. You bleed from a wound because there is blood pressure in your arteries and even a little in your veins as well, right? Take away the blood pressure, a wound doesn't bleed very much. Without blood pressure, a wound oozes. Nothing more. Where does the blood pressure come from? The beating heart, of course. Each time the ventricles squeeze, they shoot a pulse of blood through your arteries. The right ventricle sends pressurized blood to your pulmonary arteries, which go through the lungs, where the blood does the important stuff of releasing carbon dioxide and absorbing more oxygen. Then the blood returns to the left atrium, gets pushed down into the left ventricle, which sends pressurized bursts of oxygenated blood into the aorta and on through all the other arteries of your body. That blood pressure is what causes a wound to bleed."

The professor casually set the heart on the body's forehead, balancing it so it wouldn't roll off.

Avery gagged again. There was no doubt that Avery's fellow students thought the move was grotesque as well. But there was also no denying that not a single student was dozing or looking at his or her iPhone. Everyone stared at that heart sitting where a heart is never seen. Against the body's pale forehead skin, the heart was a deep purple orb, giver of life in the minds of doctors, yet closer to a symbol of obscene violence to the casual passerby.

The doctor was on the far side of the body and the table. He lay a towel on the table, then placed his blood-coated, blue latex-covered hands on the towel. He leaned forward toward the students, his masked face directly over the body.

Avery could barely contain all the emotions coursing through. Just the smell off that body must have been asphyxiating to the doctor. It certainly was to Avery back in one of the rear chairs.

"Let's consider the ways of stopping the heart," the doctor said. "Certain drugs and toxins will do it, but most of them take a relatively long time. A lightning bolt or even household electrocution will do it, but it is very hard to be in the right place at the right time and connected to electricity in just the right way to be electrocuted. No, the fastest way to stop a heart quickly and easily is with sufficient physical trauma, my friends. A bullet to the heart stops it quickly, but bullets are messy. And bullets make relatively large holes that will ooze a lot of blood even if the heart isn't beating. Furthermore, acquiring a gun isn't always easy, especially here in the city of San Francisco."

The pathologist gazed at the naked, cut-open body. "This young man died in a much cleaner way. However, the method requires some precision."

The man picked up the heart from the body's forehead and set it in a specimen bowl on the table. Then he rolled the man over once again. He pointed to the tiny red mark on the back.

"This dot is on the medial side of the left scapula, meaning between the shoulder blade and the spine. At first, I thought it was a surface mark, like what you get when you accidentally scratch at a raised mole and cause a skin abrasion that brings blood to the surface. But now that I've examined the body's organs, I think it is something else entirely."

He turned the body over once more and—with great care and no small difficulty—he explored at length in the thoracic cavity. Then he straightened up and addressed the students.

"Well, well," the doctor said. "It turns out that the red dot on the victim's back is a tiny puncture wound. I've followed the path from the puncture wound on the body's back, through the back ribs to the center of the thoracic cavity. I now understand why the heart and the pericardial sac that surrounds it have a small hole in them."

The doctor paused and took a deep breath that indicated great weariness.

"I began this autopsy thinking I'd find that death was caused by a drug overdose or an undisclosed disease. Now I see that death was almost certainly caused by a stabbing assault. It appears that a long and very narrow implement was thrust into the victim's back. Based on tiny tears in the tissues along the path of the weapon, I believe the weapon did not have a sharp point that would cleanly separate the tissues and was instead likely to be a long, very thin screwdriver."

He lifted the heart out of the specimen bowl and held it in his palm.

"So let's consider this unlucky fellow. We have very little bleeding. The fact that blood didn't flow out of the puncture wound on the victim's back may simply be because a long thin hole through the tissues tends to squeeze shut as soon as the weapon is pulled out."

He brought the heart toward his face and looked at it closely.

Avery nearly gasped. It looked like the doctor was sniffing it to see if it might make a nice meal.

The doctor continued. "After a wound like this, the heart might continue to beat, albeit with great struggle and much pain. However, once the weapon—screwdriver or otherwise—

was removed, blood would flow through the newly-created hole in the heart and into the pericardial sac around the heart, creating what we call cardiac tamponade, which is when the sac around the heart fills with blood or other fluid. This gradually puts pressure on the outside of the heart and makes it difficult for the atria to fill. Eventually, cardiac tamponade kills the victim. But because I see no signs of cardiac tamponade, I think that the reason there was no bleeding is because the heart simply stopped beating when it was initially pierced. We don't know why this little muscle sometimes gives up the ghost, as it were. It could be that its electrical trigger patterns were severely disrupted by the stabbing. Or it could be that the shock of trauma was so significant that it simply spasmed like a cramp in your calf muscle and never regained its pumping task.

"Whoever inserted the screwdriver knew what he was doing. The driver was angled slightly up and aimed at a point just to the left of the center of the chest. Once the heart was punctured, the screwdriver was removed. As I already said, my guess is that the heart stopped then and there, and the victim collapsed, dead by some measures before he hit the ground."

The doctor stood back and gazed at the body, which was still opened wide.

"Because the cause of death wasn't discovered until this autopsy, the killer has gained a great deal of time after committing this murder. And as we all know from watching TV and reading crime novels, the more time that passes after the commission of a crime, the less likely that crime is ever solved. This body was delivered to me yesterday, not long after it was found on a sidewalk in the Tenderloin. However, I'll be calling law enforcement to report a homicide as soon as this class is over. The killer is no doubt long gone. But one positive result of this crime is that you have all revisited the heart and blood circulation in such a way that you will never forget the basics. Yes, I can see the horrified looks on your faces. However, horror is a close cousin of fascination. And fascination helps to create long-lasting memories and a successful education."

The doctor gave the students a tight grin that bordered on

a grimace.

"We all go into the doctoring business to provide health care and, when possible, to save lives." He gestured with the heart, which was still in his palm. "Welcome, dear students, to the other side of doctoring, dealing with the dead."

The person who was now acting as a character named Avery Kingsley could not get out of that class fast enough. Avery had certainly been both horrified and fascinated during that instructional autopsy years ago. More than a dozen years later, the memory was still fresh.

Avery slowed to watch the group of people who were now between streetlights, one of which flickered. Large areas of dark shade seemed to pulse on the sidewalk and street. Avery recognized one of the people toward the rear of the group. The flickering streetlight caused the shade pool to splash over the person who Avery recognized. Light, then darkness. Light, darkness. The staccato darkness seemed, to Avery, as if it portended a calamity.

Avery reached down, hand sliding into the right front pocket, and felt the screwdriver. The driver's handle fit comfortably in the hand. The driver's long thin shaft poked down through a small hole at the very bottom of the pocket. The cool metal shaft brushed against the thigh, smooth metal rubbing the skin. The screwdriver had a narrow slotted end designed for reaching very small screws in hard-to-reach places, manufactured to be quite sharp in order to fit tiny screws.

Avery gripped the handle of the screwdriver and walked faster.

It was time…

ONE

My ringing cell phone woke me up. Because I had commented on the basic ring of my phone, Street had changed the ring tone to the voice of an ancient cartoon character named Elmer Fudd, who couldn't make the R sound. He was speaking about Bugs Bunny as if the rabbit were a rapper. 'That Wappa Wabbit' over and over. I squinted at the red letters on the clock. 6:10 a.m.

"That Wappa Wabbit. That Wappa Wabbit."

"McKenna," I answered, my brain filled with images of Bugs Bunny, the object of Fudd's antipathy. Maybe my enunciation wasn't clear.

"This is your morning wake-up call," Sergeant Diamond Martinez said. "You sound so groggy, you worry me."

"My phone was saying, 'That Wappa Wabbit.'"

"You're mumbling like you can't pronounce your Rs."

"It's so early it's not even light out."

"Time of year, not time of day," Diamond said. "Back in June, the sun would have been up a long time. Anyway, we law enforcement types keep our communities safe without regard for the time."

"You got an emergency or what?"

"Just wanted to talk to you about an unusual death last night. Will you be at your office later?"

"Yeah." I was about to ask, "What death?" when Diamond said he had to go and hung up.

So I checked the news on my laptop while I drank my morning coffee, and I learned that a doctor had died the previous evening in Tahoe City. The woman's companions, who were also doctors, reported they'd been out enjoying the evening when the woman collapsed to the sidewalk. They administered CPR but hadn't been able to revive her.

The deceased was identified as Veronica Eastern from the Mission District in San Francisco. I'd never heard of her, but thinking about the Mission brought back a series of notable memories for me.

I tried to recall the details as I sipped coffee.

The Mission was where my partner and I caught a murderer when I'd only been on the job for two weeks. Although I was a rookie kid of 24 on the police force, my partner was a seasoned old man of 30 and he deserved credit for giving me a guiding example of courage under stress.

We'd been on foot patrol when we heard a woman's screams coming from a building. My partner called it in and then shouted instructions as we climbed multiple flights of stairs until we got close to the screams on the fourth floor.

There was a gunshot, and a big man seemed to burst out of an apartment door. He gripped the arm of a skinny kid. The boy was about 16 or 17 with large striking eyes that were haunted with fear. The man had a gun pushed into the kid's side.

"Stay back or I'll kill him!" the man shouted at us. "I swear to God I'll kill him just like I killed his mama!"

We stayed back. The man ran the kid down the hall, out a door, and onto the fire escape.

We followed.

My partner shouted the standard warnings at the man, who seemed unaffected by them.

We all pounded down the metal steps.

When the killer got the kid to the bottom, I thought to yell something different.

"Look out on your left!"

The man turned toward his left, then tripped and dropped his gun. As he bent to pick it up, I leaped forward and kicked it away. The kid jerked free of the man and ran. The man tried to get his gun, but I tackled him to the ground and held tight. My partner jumped on as well, and the two of us got him cuffed.

Later, the kid, Benito Diaz, got a threatening call from one of the killer's friends. As a result, Diaz was afraid to testify, assuming, reasonably, that he might be killed like his mother.

So I got to know Benito Diaz a little, periodically stopping by at his aunt's apartment where he'd moved after his mother's death. I didn't know if my uniform would make him feel better or worse. But after the first two visits, I managed to find out he wrote some poetry and that he'd written some kind of a long poem about his mother who'd had a hardscrabble life. So I went to City Lights Bookstore and bought him an anthology of San Francisco poets.

Benito Diaz decided to testify, and the killer, a stupid street tough who tried to make Benito's mother into his personal servant, was sentenced to 25-to-life.

Catching a killer was an auspicious beginning to a good law enforcement career that I, nevertheless, gave up when I killed someone in the line of duty. Life is short. People who want a second act need to close the curtains on the first before they can move on.

My second act was being a private investigator in Tahoe, and my off time involved a woman named Street Casey, a brilliant entomologist who was currently in the complicated process of adopting a girl whose guardian grandfather had died.

Time for me to check in on them.

TWO

Spot and I left my little log cabin and headed down the mountain on the private road that I share with my wealthy vacation-home neighbors. I turned into the condo lot at the bottom. We walked up to the door of our favorite companions.

Before I could knock, there came an excited, high-pitched bark of greeting from inside. There were no uncovered windows that allowed easy viewing of our approach. There was no strong wind to drive our scent through any leaky weather stripping. We hadn't made any sound, and my Jeep, despite its advanced age, didn't make any more noise than the other cars. Unless, that is, the bullet holes whistled at a pitch that only dogs can hear.

But dogs have sixth-sense sensory abilities when anticipating a ride, a run, a walk, or a visit from someone who might take them to do stuff. Dogs want action, and they can tell when potential action approaches.

The door opened, and Blondie raced out. She did a leap, smacked both her front paws on Spot's chest, bounced away, and shot off into the forest. Spot ran after. Compared to a 45-pound Yellow Lab, a 170-pound Great Dane is slow to accelerate. But like a long-hood Kenworth big rig, he can eventually get his bulk cruising faster than most dogs. Just don't expect him to do a quick U-turn.

Spot would never intentionally hurt Blondie, but if he caught her, he might body-slam her for fun, which wouldn't be fun for her as she raced between tree trunks. So Blondie had perfected the art of feinting and dodging to avoid a collision, and she was doing it at high speed as they disappeared into the woods.

I looked inside the open condo door.

My girlfriend Street Casey had turned back toward Camille Dexter, her 9-year-old adoptee-in-waiting. From their words,

I quickly realized that Street was trying to set a non-sugar breakfast example for Camille, who apparently had some kind of addiction to Honey Nut Cheerios.

"But I like Honey Nut Cheerios," Camille said, signing as she spoke. And then, in an insightful moment of childhood inspiration, Camille added, "Honey Nut Cheerios is how I get my energy." Camille signed with much emphasis as she spoke. She could see me standing in the doorway, but she paid me no attention. Compared to the importance of Honey Nut Cheerios, I was of no account.

Although I'd known Camille for a few weeks, I was still amazed at her fluency with spoken English, something most of us take for granted, but something that stood out as an amazing skill for a person who'd been deaf since birth.

Using her nascent sign language skills, Street signed as she spoke. She explained that the whole point of regular Cheerios was that they had almost no sugar and that a sugary version was practically a contradiction in terms. Street then explained that added sugar was bad by every measure.

The look on Camille's face made it clear she wasn't buying it.

Street, ever the persistent scientist and tutor, held up a glass measuring cup. She explained that the cup contained steel-cut oatmeal with cinnamon, sunflower seeds, almond slivers, and dried wild blueberries for excitement. Street smiled and moved the cup around in the air like some kind of TV cooking show demonstration. She grinned at Camille as she extolled the virtues of healthy eating.

Camille shook her head. Her mind was made up. Case closed.

Despite feeling a solidarity with Camille, I said nothing. Even though everyone knows that sugar is one of the direct paths to happiness, my face was stone. I too liked the sweetened version of Cheerios, but I was loathe to weigh in on the wrong side of a discussion with a child. Some preferences are best left unspoken.

I caught Street's eye, pointed to my chest, then pointed

outside the open door. It wasn't American Sign Language, but it worked. Street made a single nod as I walked outside.

When Blondie and Spot's impromptu race course brought them near the door, I stopped Blondie, then looked back into the condo. Street and Camille were still in a kind of sugar stalemate. I directed Blondie inside, made a wave at Street and Camille, and chose that moment to make an exit. I shut and locked the door with the key that I carry and drove off with His Largeness for a guys' breakfast.

We stopped at a breakfast cafe for two takeout orders of cheese omelets and bacon and hash browns and brought our food to the office, where we could savor the dangers of our misguided nutritional excesses in private. However, the only questionable ingredients that I could see in our breakfast were the fried potatoes and the bacon and the salt packet I emptied onto my omelet and hash browns. I was pretty sure that eggs were still approved of. I loaded the coffee maker to brew while we ate.

Spot did his Shop-Vac impression with his food. If the Shop-Vac marketing people witnessed the spectacle, they would want to talk to Spot's agent about making Spot their cover boy for TV commercials.

I enjoyed my meal at a vastly slower pace, taking an entire minute or two to eat.

As I sipped coffee, Spot turned, stared at the door, and wagged. Seconds later, it opened, and Sergeant Diamond Martinez walked in.

THREE

Diamond's left hand held both an open, plastic baggie and a closed, waxed paper bag. I couldn't see the sandwich bag's contents well, but they looked like variegated chunks of green.

Diamond left the door standing open and used his free hand to pull Spot's head against his hip and give him a hard rub.

Diamond pulled a green chunk from the baggie and popped it in his mouth.

"What's that green stuff?"

He was still chewing as he gestured with the bag of green. "This is my donut points reward program. Raw broccoli. Makes a healthful snack." He popped another piece in his mouth. "Each broccoli floret is worth a bite of donut. Maybe two bites."

For some time I'd been getting unrequested advice from my girlfriend Street, who was on guard for best food practices. Now Diamond had caught the habit. Spot and Camille and I were the last creatures left on the planet who ate according to what we liked rather than according to what was good for us.

"You like raw broccoli?" I said.

Diamond shook his head. "Didn't say that. I used to pick this stuff in the fields when I was a migrant farm worker. I don't think I could ever really like it. But I like the reward points."

Spot turned his head toward the window just as we heard the screech of braking tires in the parking lot down below.

"What does raw broccoli taste like?"

Diamond shrugged. "Like what a rabbit would eat."

I heard my new ringtone in my mind. That Wappa Wabbit.

"You're eating rabbit food because it mitigates the guilt that comes from enjoying donuts?"

A car door slammed. There was a thump. Someone dropping

a bag of trash into the dumpster?

Diamond shook his head. "Ain't about guilt. It's about eating healthy. Operant conditioning says that if I do something that's good for me and follow it up with a reward, I'll be more likely to do the thing that is good for me."

"And the paper bag has the donut rewards."

"Sí," he said, nodding. He set the bag on my desk. "Help yourself." Diamond was still chewing on a chunk of green that appeared much too large and rubbery to be anything but unpleasant survival food.

"What if I wanted to simply sit down some morning and relish an entire donut or two with my coffee?" I said.

"Only way to work off that level of sugar-and-fat assault would be adding carrots to your broccoli. But you could live to the ripe old age of seventy even on your sugar diet."

I wondered if Diamond had been reading the same science journals that Street read.

"Only seventy?" I said.

Diamond shrugged. "Maybe you can ride that diet all the way to seventy-four or five. It would take some luck. And maybe a half-dozen stents. 'Course, they don't yet have a pill for the dementia that comes from all that sugar."

Tires screeched as a car raced out of the parking lot. I would have walked over and looked out the window, but Diamond held out the paper bag.

"What I don't get," I said, "is how you can judge my diet when you can inhale donuts almost as fast as Spot."

"'Cuz I've got broccoli to make it all better."

I reached into the bag and pulled out an old-fashioned donut. Spot had been staring alternately at the window and at the door, his ears turning forward then backward. He refocused his attention on my donut.

I took a bite.

Diamond said, "These are made by a tiny Vietnamese immigrant woman named Linh, with an H, who works in the bakery. Good?"

I nodded. "A solid ten."

"If you'd just eaten broccoli, it would be an eleven."

"No doubt."

We heard the muffled thud of the downstairs entrance door opening too far and hitting the stop. Then came the slow, heavy footsteps and labored breathing of the computer repairman in the end unit.

Spot turned back and looked at the opening where Diamond had left my office door open.

"Broccoli will help you live long and healthy like your mother in Mexico City?" I said.

Diamond shrugged. "Her health comes from walking all her errands. Every day she walks to get her groceries and then carries them up multiple flights of stairs to her apartment. You know Mexico City is very high, right? Her apartment building is on a hill, so her kitchen table is at about eight thousand feet. Lotta exercise in that grocery trek."

I had finished my first donut. I reached for another.

Diamond gave me a disapproving look. "You are unabashed at eating food that's bad for you, but you're not compensating with any rabbit food. Or walking all your errands."

I remembered Camille's line. "Donuts are how I get my energy," I said.

Spot turned to look toward the open doorway. The thumping noise was now in the upstairs hall and getting closer.

Diamond's broccoli was gone. He took a donut out of the bag and gave it a long, intense sniff, and took a big bite.

"The reward points work?" I said.

"Heaven is probably a place named Linh's Donuts."

A hand appeared at the door, bloody fingers gripping the wood like red hooks. Next came a person, pulling himself into the opening. The person was male, thin, bloodied across his face and down the left side of his neck. One eye was swollen shut, the tissue puffy and dark blue. The man looked at me with his single open eye, large and haunted. I still remembered him from more than two decades ago.

"Benito Diaz," I said.

FOUR

Benito Diaz, the bloodied man who appeared in my doorway, began to sag as if about to fall to the floor. Diamond dropped his donut on my desk, made a quick step to the man's side, and grabbed his elbow and opposite shoulder to support him. Diamond guided the man to one of my client chairs. Spot, his brow furrowed so deeply it looked like a network of arroyos seen from miles up, was on the man's other side. Spot's nostrils were flexing, but he kept a little distance. Maybe it was the smell of blood reminding him of the bad guy's blood-bath death in my last case when Camille Dexter came into our lives. Diaz was wearing bright yellow bicycling shorts. The blood that had dripped onto them was as dramatic as a red Rorschach test.

"Sit here, man," Diamond said.

The man sat, his head lolling as if he were about to pass out. It seemed he could see out his good eye, but he didn't react to my dog, whose head was level with his own when he sat. Spot sniffed the air near the man's wounded face. Most people would pull back in startled surprise if not fear when they saw the head of a dog up close, especially a dog's head that was twice the size of a human head. Because this man didn't, I thought he was not aware of his circumstances.

"Benito Diaz," I said again, leaning forward in my desk chair. "Do you remember me?"

"You're the reason I'm here." His words were thick and somewhat garbled. "You caught the man who killed my mother."

"I remember. Tucker something…"

"Tucker Dopple."

"Right. Your testimony helped convict him, and he went inside on a twenty-five-plus ride."

"He was granted parole after twenty-one years, and was released from Pelican Bay State Prison three days ago. He's on a mission to kill both you and me."

"What makes you think that?"

"He…" Benito's head wobbled again. "He told me. He said his job was to kill us."

Benito Diaz was slurring his words. He got his elbows on his knees and leaned his head forward onto his hands.

Diamond still had his hand on the man's shoulder. "I'm going to check your pulse," he said. He reached one hand to Benito's neck, fingertips sliding to the carotid artery. After a moment, Diamond held still.

"Weak pulse and fast," Diamond said. "About one twenty, one thirty. Probably from stress and climbing the stairs. It will slow." Diamond took his hand off of Benito's neck, then squatted down in front of him. Diamond's face was directly in front of the man. "Look at me," he said, his words soft but firm.

Benito lifted his head from his knees and looked at Diamond with the eye that wasn't swollen shut.

"Now look at the window." Diamond pointed toward my office window, which was bright with sunshine.

Benito did as told, turning. The bright sunshine coming in the window was like a spotlight on his eye.

Diamond nodded. "Pupil response is good. At least, in the eye that isn't swollen shut. Can you breath okay?"

"Yes. My chest hurts, but yes."

Diamond reached his hands forward and gripped each of Benito's hands with his own. "Squeeze my hands."

I could see Benito's hands tightening. Diamond nodded.

Diamond said, "You walked in here relatively okay. Can you still move your feet?"

Benito pushed down with his toes, raising both knees in turn.

"Tell me how you feel," Diamond said.

"The man beat me up. Hit me in the face, in the stomach. Swung his elbow at my chest. So everything hurts. My ribs even more than my eye. But I don't think they're broken."

"Do you think you're bleeding anyplace other than your face?"

"I don't think so."

"I could take off your clothes and check."

Benito kept his open eye steady on Diamond. "I know I'm not very lucid. But I don't think I'm bleeding. Not externally. Bruised, but not bleeding. As for internally? I'll probably know in the next hour or so."

"Headache?"

Benito said, "Not more than a beating would justify."

"Dizziness?"

"Not especially."

"How do you feel other than the pain?" Diamond asked.

"Okay. Weak, but okay."

"My concern," Diamond said, "is that you probably don't have experience getting beat up. So you might not be a good judge of the situation."

"Actually, I once got beat up worse than this, and I survived."

"How did you get beat up?" I asked.

"I was putting some money into an investment group. After several months, I realized the manager was stealing money from the general fund. When I confronted him about it, he told me not to tell the authorities. When I said I had to turn him in, he attacked me. Luckily I got my hand in my pocket and hit the emergency dial button on my phone. The cops came as he was still pummeling me. He went to prison for both assault and financial fraud." Diaz took a breath. "That beating was bad. This beating isn't that bad. So I think I'll be okay."

Benito took a deep breath and shut his eyes for a moment. "I smell coffee. I could use some coffee."

"A man who wants coffee is likely going to live," Diamond said in a sincere voice.

I stood up, poured a mug, walked around my desk, and handed the coffee to Benito. "Sorry, I don't have a nearby table. You can hold it or lean forward and set it on my desk."

Benito made a slight nod. He sipped coffee. Rested the mug

on his thigh. Sipped some more. Didn't spill a drop.

We waited. He would talk when he was ready.

"Is that donuts that I smell?" Benito asked.

"Sí," Diamond said.

"May I have one of those, please? I'm feeling hypoglycemic."

Diamond reached the bag off my desk and held it out. Benito angled his head so he could see it with his unswollen eye. He pulled out a donut, took a bite, sipped some more coffee.

"That was a good assessment," Benito said.

"What's that?" I said.

"Airway, Breathing, Circulation, Disability, Exposure."

"I made a few adjustments that the sheriff's office likes," Diamond said.

I spoke to Benito. "You know this stuff because…"

"I'm a doctor. A geriatric oncologist. We don't have much need in our department for the ABCDE assessment. But it's always useful to know. I should look at my eye." After a moment, he said, "Why are you looking at me like that?"

"I'm just trying to match a kid whose mother was murdered to a geriatric oncologist."

"I spent some time working for Doctors Without Borders. A wonderful organization. And I learned some critical field techniques. But I also learned that I could be more effective helping people in a clinical setting. Cancer seemed a good match for my aptitude."

When I didn't immediately respond, he said, "Do you have a mirror?"

I walked over to the 8-by-10 mirror above the micro sink. It hung on a picture hook. I lifted it off and brought it over to Benito.

He took it and angled it and his face to get some light on his eye. He reached up and palpated the orbital arch. He winced.

"It seems my eyeball will be okay. But the orbital arch might be fractured."

"My friend Doc Lee is an ER doc at the hospital on the California side. I can see if he can make a house call." I picked up my phone.

Benito shook his head. "I'll need an X-ray or whatever imaging equipment they have. So I should go in."

"I'll give you a ride," Diamond said. "Is timing critical?"

"No. I shouldn't dawdle. But it's no emergency."

"What brings you to Tahoe?" I asked.

"A twelve-year reunion. Our UCSF Medical School class."

"University of California San Francisco," I said just to clarify.

"Right. I decided the reunion was a good excuse to bring my nephew Damen up to Tahoe. He lives with me in the Bay Area. But we could still use some quality time together."

"Your nephew…" I was trying to remember. "When your mother was killed, I thought you were an only child."

"No. I had an older sister who was already out living on her own. Danielle was divorced a few years after mom died. Danielle died from internal hemorrhage a year ago. She had hemophilia." He seemed to mouth a few silent words. It oddly reminded me of when a Catholic crosses himself at the mention of the death of someone close.

"Hemophilia is the bleeding disease," Diamond said. "It's hereditary, right?"

"Yes. She was a heterozygous carrier of hemophilia. The genetics cause men to be affected more than women. Unfortunately, Danielle was one of the minority of women who suffer the effects of full-blown hemophilia. She died from undiagnosed abdominal bleeding."

"Sorry to hear it," I said.

Diamond was frowning. "Are you saying most women with hemophilia don't have as many bleeding problems as men?"

"That's true. It's one of the sex-linked diseases. Caused by a defect on the X chromosome that reduces the clotting factor in the blood. Because males only have one X chromosome, that has to come from their mother. So any son who receives the affected X chromosome gets the disease. Whereas women have two X chromosomes. If one chromosome is affected, the other usually prevents the problem from being severe. But that wasn't the case with Danielle. Her son—my nephew Damen—also got a severe version of Type A hemophilia. So he has to be very careful not to get injured. He's now thirteen. I've been trying to help him lead an injury-free life. But he's a real handful. It's hard to keep him safe."

"Sorry to hear it," I said. "But you can't always keep him safe, right? Kids have a mind of their own. You can't watch over him every moment."

"I know that, of course. And I regularly repeat those very words to myself. But keeping him safe is my desire as his friend, his guardian, and his uncle, and it's a huge part of my oath as a doctor. It's imbued in us from the moment we decide to become doctors. Whenever possible, if a life needs saving, we try to save it, no matter what it takes."

"I understand. But I have another question about hemophilia. What about you? Did you get the affected hemophilia gene?"

"No. Our mother was unaffected. So my X chromosome was unaffected."

"Then how was it that your sister was affected?"

"Like me, the X chromosome she got from our mother was unaffected. But of course, where men only have one X chromosome, women have two. Danielle got her other X chromosome from our father, and it had the defective gene."

"I don't remember hearing anything about your father," I said.

"He was absent without leave."

"AWOL dads, what a surprise," I said sarcastically.

"Yeah. My mother raised us by herself."

"From what you're saying," Diamond said, "it sounds like a lot of women might live a fairly normal life if they get the problem chromosome."

"That's right. But a few, like Danielle, have major bleeding problems."

Benito took another bite of his donut. "Despite my pain and stress, this donut tastes amazing."

"Linh's donuts," Diamond said.

"Linh's donuts," Benito repeated, as if committing it to

memory.

Diamond said, "With an H on the end of Linh."

"Linh with an H sounds Vietnamese," Benito said.

"Medical school didn't cramp your learning too much," Diamond said.

"I don't know about that. But I can say that a doctor's donut radar is right up there with that of cops."

"How did you find out about Tucker Dopple being released?" I asked.

"I'd been aware that his release was coming up. But I didn't know exactly when until he tracked me to Tahoe, found me an hour ago, beat me up, kidnapped me, then took me in his van to your office. He told me he'd just been released, and he said his mission was to kill both you and me to pay for him losing twenty-one years in prison."

"But he didn't kill us."

"Right. He saw a police car in your lot. Or a police SUV. Whatever. It had the emblem on the door and those lights on the top. That spooked the guy. He said he didn't get paid enough to deal with cops, so he'd come back. Then he kicked me out of the van and sped off." Benito Diaz frowned, then turned and looked at Diamond's clothes.

"You're wearing a cop uniform. So that was your cop car."

Diamond made a single nod.

"Your cop car saved my life. Maybe Mr. McKenna's, too."

"Good to know cop cars are useful," Diamond said.

"You are here because Mr. McKenna used to be a cop?" Benito said.

Diamond nodded. "So I had to bring him some donuts."

"Not just any donuts. Linh's donuts," Benito said.

Diamond nodded. "If Linh FedExed you a dozen donuts each morning, you could put them in your waiting room. Your morning patients would start showing up on time."

Dr. Benito Diaz made the slightest hint of a smile, his purple swollen eye looking especially ghastly. "No doubt about it," he said. "If you knew what doctors call chronically late patients…" He let his words trail off.

"Tucker Dopple told you he didn't get paid enough to deal with cops," I said. "Do you think someone hired him to kill us?"

"No. I think it was a figure of speech. Otherwise, why would he also say he wanted to kill us as punishment for putting him in prison?"

I nodded. "You said Tucker Dopple tracked you to Tahoe," I said. "How did he know you were here?"

Benito looked embarrassed. "I posted it on my social media pages."

"For all the world to see," I said.

"I know. I willingly forego any semblance of privacy."

"Don't get me wrong," I said. "Even if I'm reluctant to give up my own privacy, I still know that lots of people have to post their schedules for work and other reasons. And they put down where they're going on vacation."

"But I don't have to," Benito said. "So why do I do it? I suppose I'm too full of myself. It's like I'm telling the whole world, 'Guess what, I'm going to Tahoe, and I'll be living large at the lake while the rest of you are stuck in traffic jams.'"

"You said you brought your nephew Damen up here. Where is he now?"

"There's some special game at the arcade in one of the Stateline hotels. I should call him." Benito frowned. "I know my speech is a little blurry. Do you think I can sound normal enough to not worry Damen?"

I looked at Diamond. "Seems doable to me."

Diamond nodded. "Tell Damen to stay in a crowded spot. The arcade. A cafe. The slot machines. You and I will pick him up on our way to the hospital."

Benito seemed surprised, as if at a sudden realization.

"Oh, what have I gotten us into?"

FIVE

Benito got out his phone, dialed his nephew Damen, and spoke. Even from our distance, Diamond and I could hear the bells and rings and beeps of arcade games. Benito told Damen he was checking in and that he would be gone another hour. Maybe less. "Are you okay with that?" Pause. "No, don't leave the arcade. Not even to use the bathroom. Stay where it's crowded." Another pause. "Okay, I'll tell you. The man who murdered your grandmother? He went to prison because I testified against him. He just got out of prison. He says he's coming for me. He kidnapped me at the door of the hotel. Luckily, we ran into a cop, and I got away. There's a possibility he might try to grab you and use you to get at me." Pause. "No, it's just a possibility. I wouldn't tell most kids. But I'm telling you because you're tough. Will you promise me to stay in the arcade? Good. And if anyone, even a little old lady, wants you to go with them, don't do it. Not even ten feet out of the arcade. The cop and I will be there soon." Pause. "That's a promise? Okay. Thanks, Damen. You know how I worry. It helps when I can count on you. What?" Another pause. "Another twenty minutes? Okay."

Benito clicked off. He looked very afraid. He said, "Damen promised he will stay in the arcade until we show up. And he doesn't want us to come right away because the game he's playing has timed moves. He's almost at a record score and he wants to finish it out, which takes twenty minutes. He says not to worry because there's a good-sized crowd of kids and a hotel security guard in the hallway."

"I know that guard," Diamond said. "Steve Liborn. He's an off-duty deputy in our office. I can get his number and call him. First, can you give me a description of Tucker Dopple?"

Benito nodded. His breathing seemed to have sped up to a

pant. "White male, late thirties, about six-two, heavily muscled, about two hundred forty pounds. He moves with a natural athleticism. He's covered with tattoos of knives and guns and dragons and naked women. He's got brown hair cut short and spiky but with his head shaved on the sides so you can see the tattoos on his temples. The temple tattoos are some kind of quotes about Hitler and death. I'm not sure how cops would describe him, but he's a very unsavory man."

"We might have trouble describing him with clean language." Diamond glanced at me. "A dirtball?"

"An idiot dirtball," I said.

"Oh, one more thing I remembered. He has a long sparse goatee that hangs down like a mini horsetail."

Spot took three steps over to his Harlequin Great Dane camouflage bed. He stepped onto it, made two turns to the left, stopped, made another turn, then lay down. He rested his jaw on one of his front paws.

"By the way, that was a good physical description," Diamond said.

Benito shrugged. "Doctors have to size up patients. An animal's appearance predicts much about the kind of medical issues it faces."

"Lemme get that guard's number." Diamond dialed, waited for the phone to be answered. "Hey, Clark. Diamond calling. Post a BOLO for a white male named Tucker Dopple. Six-two, two-forty, muscles, tatted up, spiked hair cut close on his temples. Got out of prison a few days ago."

Pause.

"Tucker Dopple kidnapped a doctor at the Stateline hotel where Liborn moonlights as a guard and carried the doctor off in a white van. What? No, the doctor escaped near Owen McKenna's office. Next, can you look up Steve Liborn's number? Thanks." Diamond pulled his pen and pocket notebook out of his shirt pocket. After a moment, he wrote, said thanks, then clicked off and dialed the number he'd just gotten.

"Steve, Sergeant Martinez calling. You're on your hotel shift, right? Are you near the arcade? Good. There's a kid in there named Damen… hold on." Diamond turned to Benito.

"Damen Diaz," Benito said. "Same as me."

"What's Damen look like?"

Benito said, "Thirteen years old, sandy hair cut below his ears. Five-five, slight build, maybe one hundred ten pounds. Wearing black jeans and black high tops and black sweatshirt."

Diamond passed on the description to the man on the phone. "You see Damen? Good. Don't let him out of your sight. He's being stalked by a violent predator who just got out of the pen and just kidnapped the kid's uncle." Diamond gave the hotel guard the description of Tucker Dopple.

"Dopple wants to kill the uncle and Private Detective Owen McKenna for putting him away on a murder rap twenty-some years ago in San Francisco. I'll be there with the uncle to pick the kid up in about half an hour." Diamond hung up.

Benito said, "Thank you both so much. I'm hoping you can find Tucker Dopple. Find him and get him off my back. Maybe get him arrested for assault? I'll pay whatever you need." Benito looked at me. "Would that fit in your schedule?"

"I'll see what I can do."

Dr. Diaz turned to Diamond. "How does this work? I want to pay you. Is that possible?"

"Not under these circumstances. I'm paid well by the county. So we're covered."

Benito nodded. "Thank you again. Does Nevada have a three strikes law?"

"Yes, but it doesn't always kick in at three."

"A man like that shouldn't be out on the street." Benito's stress was morphing into anger.

"You won't get disagreement from cops," I said. "So you came to Tahoe for the medical school reunion?"

"Right."

"Where is it being held?"

"It's a group of activities held all around the lake."

"Who organized this?"

"I think it was mostly the Brontë sisters."

"Brontë, like the writers?" Diamond said.

"Yes, but contemporary. They were our class's defacto leaders. Still are. They've got that leadership quality. And they certainly know how to organize stuff." Benito looked off, frowning. "As you may know, a lot of doctors are not that smooth in the social skills arena. Our strengths are more limited to science topics. But the Brontë sisters are social champions. They excel across the spectrum. Science, business, and the arts. Probably comes from them being identical triplets. They had to excel to survive in the womb, even just to get along with multiple copies of themselves, and they've carried that ability into every aspect of life."

"When do these reunion events happen?"

"The first was the kick-off dinner last night. Which I missed because I couldn't get here in time. The events don't happen every day, but the reunion goes for something like ten days. There are hiking and biking events during the day, several dinners, a couple of performances in the big showrooms, and then a send-off breakfast."

"Where was the kick-off dinner?" Diamond asked.

"Tahoe City."

"Any chance you know a doctor named Veronica Eastern?" Diamond asked.

"Sure. She was in our class the first couple of years. Then she left to get a Ph.D in psychology and become a clinical psychologist. But I don't know if she's coming to the reunion. Nice lady. Very smart."

"I'm sorry to tell you she died last night."

Benito's tawny complexion paled, his purple, swollen eye looking even more horrific. "Oh, my God. Veronica died? How?"

SIX

"We don't know how Dr. Eastern died," Diamond said. "She was walking with a group of other doctors—your group, maybe—and she collapsed to the ground. She couldn't be revived. We won't know cause of death until the ME does the autopsy. Maybe not even then, if they have to wait for toxicology test results."

Benito's look of horror morphed to fear. "There's too much dying. All around us. That's the problem with my medical specialty, too. Too much. Sometimes I don't think I can take it."

He used his fingertips to rub his temples. "Could her death be connected to Tucker Dopple?" He glanced from Diamond to me.

"Maybe," I said.

"Because you're an ex-cop, do you have access to police reports? Maybe you could look into Veronica's death when you look up Tucker Dopple. I can give you an advance retainer."

"That won't be necessary. Benito, you're here in my office because Tucker Dopple threatened to kill the two of us, and he dumped you in my parking lot. So the subject of dying is front and center in my life as well."

I remembered something Diaz did earlier. "I don't want to pry," I said. "But when you mentioned your sister dying, you seemed to mouth some words to yourself."

Benito nodded. "I was at her bedside when she died. When I think of her, I say her last words to myself. It's just ritual, between my sister and me. I suppose it's kind of like a little secular prayer for her."

I waited.

Benito said, "'He kindly stopped for me.'"

After a moment, I said, "Those were her last words? 'He kindly stopped for me?'"

Diamond spoke up. "Isn't that from an Emily Dickinson poem? 'Because I could not stop for Death, He kindly stopped for me.'"

"I guess cop school didn't cramp your learning too much," Benito said, rephrasing Diamond's earlier comment.

"Basic stuff any poetry fan would know."

"A cop who's a fan of poetry?" Benito said, surprise in his voice.

"Cop interests are broad," Diamond said. "We've got a deputy who can play all twenty-one of Chopin's nocturnes by memory, and she's performed them on stage in San Francisco."

"Point received. Please pardon my parochial view. I live in a very narrow world."

Diaz turned to me. "Will you please keep me informed of any developments in Veronica Eastern's death?"

"Yes. Can you imagine any possible connection between Tucker Dopple and Dr. Eastern?"

"No."

"Probably, there's no connection," I said. "But when a bucolic community like Tahoe has a sudden death, and the very next morning an ex-con threatens two murders, it raises the possibility." Benito looked first at Diamond, then at me.

Spot flopped over onto his side and made a big sigh, his exhalation making his jowls flap.

Diamond looked at the time. "Damen's game will be over in fifteen minutes. We gotta pick him up, get Dr. Diaz to the hospital, find Tucker Dopple, maybe figure out why the doctor lady died in Tahoe City, and while we're at it, reestablish law and order in Tahoe."

"Before you go," I said, "a question for Benito." The man had been sagging into his chair. He lifted his head to look at me.

"Can you think of any reason your doctor colleagues might have some antipathy for Veronica Eastern?"

Benito looked alarmed at the thought.

I said, "You asked me to look into her death. Obviously, you wondered if her death was not from natural causes."

Diaz should his head. "I won't say Veronica was a sweetheart. But she was a kind, normal woman. I can't imagine why anyone would want to hurt her."

As he said it, his speech got softer. A bit hesitant.

"You sound like you're having a second thought."

"No." He paused. "I'm just processing the enormity of a woman dying in her prime."

"Benito, cops learn early that hesitations and pauses reveal concerns worth looking into."

He nodded and looked serious. "She had a drinking problem," he said. "Back in med school, anyway. I imagine she got control over it. How else could she go on to have a good career? And anyway, a problem like that would make people want to help her, not hurt her."

"Drinking manifests in many ways. I'll keep it in mind."

My turn to look at the time. "I'd like to ask you a couple of quick questions about Tucker Dopple."

Benito nodded.

"Did you had any contact from him while he was in prison?"

"No direct contact. But my personal lawyer knows Tucker's defense attorney, who kept getting calls and mail from Tucker after Tucker was convicted. I don't know how attorney client privilege works in this situation. But the defense attorney told my attorney that Tucker continued to make threats against me because I testified against him."

"Was there anything specific in the threats?"

"He just said things like I was going to pay, and I was going to be sorry for ruining his life."

"Tucker murdered your mother, but you were ruining Tucker's life."

"Right. My lawyer also told me that, like a lot of prisoners, Tucker underwent a change in prison. He was radicalized by prison rituals. He took steroids and bulked up, got a bunch of tattoos, joined a gang. Tucker also started rapping and going by a new name."

Diamond was shaking his head. "For what it's worth, felons aren't allowed to change their names until ten years after they have been released from prison."

"I don't think it was a legal name change. More like his rap handle. He was rapping about the Harley festival in Sturgis, South Dakota. And he insisted that everyone in prison use his new name. My lawyer told me about it. I remember the line.

'I'm Sturgis The Chief, jus' so ya knows
Call me sumpin else, I break y'nose.'"

"Sturgis The Chief. How inspired," I said.

Benito said, "He claimed that his great grandmother was Lakota Sioux, which made him a bona fide Indian Chief."

I looked at Benito. "How did Tucker Dopple kidnap you?"

"I'd dropped Damen off at the arcade at the hotel. Tucker saw me, followed me out of the hotel lobby, and grabbed me in the parking lot. He said, if I made a noise, he would kill my nephew. So I kept my mouth shut. He walked me over to a panel van that was parked at the corner of the lot. He opened the side door, punched me a bunch of times, pushed me into the van, shut the door, then drove off. He headed directly here."

"Did he say anything while he drove?"

"Yeah. He said he was going to kill me and that jerk cop who tackled him years ago because we ruined his life. When I said he didn't need to kill anyone, he said it was a ceremonial killing to please the gods. Apparently, his cell mate in the prison told him about how some past civilizations had ritual sacrifice. So Tucker adopted the idea that he wasn't going to murder us. He was going to sacrifice us, as if sacrificial killing were somehow more legitimate."

I was trying to imagine how such a conversation would go. "He said all this in the van."

"Yeah. It was a kind of delusional rambling. I'm in back trying not to vomit from his beating, and he's driving and carrying on in a kind of soliloquy about ceremony."

Diamond said, "He's one of those dumb guys who thinks he's smart. I've met guys like him. It's more exasperating than dealing with dumb guys who know they're dumb."

"Exactly," Benito said. He looked at me with his one good eye. "So now I have to worry that he's going to kill me and you. Worse, he might hurt Damen. Or kill him, too." Benito's voice went up in pitch as he pleaded, "Is there anything you can do to catch a guy like that?"

"Maybe. I'll let you know what I find out."

Diamond stood and said, "Time to go. We'll pick up Damen and get the doctor to the hospital. But I'm concerned leaving you here and there's a guy who's threatened to kill you, and he's wandering the street."

I said, "I don't have a lot of options. I could make the case that Benito and I shouldn't stay together as we'd make a group target." I looked at Benito. "I think the best approach is for you and me to follow basic caution. Stay alert, keep our doors locked, look before we get into or out of our vehicles, don't go anywhere alone, especially at night."

Diamond reached for Benito's elbow, helped him stand up, and walked to the door.

"Check in now and then."

"Sí, mi amigo," I said.

Diamond nodded, and they left.

I called Doc Lee and left a message about Dr. Benito Diaz coming in. Whether Doc Lee was on his shift or not, he would make certain that Benito would get good help.

SEVEN

I thought about the death of Dr. Veronica Eastern in Tahoe City. I called Sergeant Santiago of the Placer County Sheriff's Office.

He answered, "Santiago."

"Hey, Jack. Owen McKenna calling to ask about the doctor who died."

"Yeah, last night was a sad one."

"Any idea what happened?"

"Not much other than the woman, Veronica Eastern, had dinner with her friends, some other doctors. Afterward, she keeled over. They couldn't revive her. Unfortunately, I won't know anything more until we get a cause of death. Got our little town buzzing, though."

"Does her death look suspicious?"

"Not in any specific way. But anytime a healthy young woman drops dead, it makes you wonder. And there was something about her companions that stood out." He paused before continuing. "They didn't seem as upset as one might think. I would expect them to be a little freaked out about it. But they took it in stride. Maybe that's just a doctor's reserve. They work in a business where people are always dying. So what's one more death, even if the deceased is one of their own? It could be nothing, but it made me wonder. Why do you ask about it?"

"I just had one of her fellow doctors in my office. Benito Diaz. He was badly beat up by an ex-con that Diaz and I both knew from my San Francisco days. I was one of the cops who caught the man after he killed Diaz's mother. Diaz testified against him, and he was convicted of murder. He was sent inside and was just paroled after twenty-one years. The man came to Tahoe, kidnapped Diaz, beat him up, and brought him to my office where he intended to kill both of us. Then he saw

Diamond's patrol unit and fled."

"Diaz knew Dr. Eastern?"

"Yes, but not well. He went to med school with her, but he hasn't seen her in the twelve years since school. Diaz came to Tahoe for a reunion with his classmates. Apparently, these doctors all went to UCSF Medical School. Diaz was supposed to be with that group last night."

"Do you think the Diaz beating could be connected to the death of Veronica Eastern?"

"I can't imagine how. But you never know. What can you tell me about Veronica Eastern?"

"Only that she was a clinical psychologist from San Francisco. I spoke to her friends. Or maybe I should say colleagues. There were eight in the group not counting the deceased. One unusual aspect is that three of them are identical twin sisters. I guess you would call them identical triplets. Anyway, as I realized they were sort of casual about Eastern's death, I started asking more questions. Let me grab my notes."

I heard some background noises.

"I interviewed all the doctors the deceased was with," Santiago said. "Three men and five women. The triplets are all named Smythe. Charlotte, Emily, and Anne Smythe. But here's something different. Two of the men referred to the triplets as the Brontë sisters. Like the writers from way back."

"The beating victim, Benito Diaz, also referred to them that way. Diaz said the Brontë sisters were their class's defacto leaders. But he didn't explain the Brontë moniker."

"Maybe they write stuff. There's a writer under every rock, far as I can tell. Placer County Sheriff's Office even has a lieutenant who's writing some kind of thriller novel."

"I remember that Charlotte Brontë wrote *Jane Eyre*," I said. "But I don't know what the others wrote. Did you ask the triplets about it?"

"No."

I was making my own notes as we spoke. Maybe an online search would turn up something.

"What about the other doctors?" I asked.

"Another woman with them was…" Santiago paused. "Dr.

Janice Mitchell," he said. "A General Practitioner in Irvine. Then there was Dr. Cheryl Wright, a neurologist from Chicago."

"And the men who were with them?"

"Let me see. Nicholas Taylor, an anesthesiologist from Sacramento. A big guy with a big beard. Raymond Lopez, a radiologist from San Jose. He peers at you with his thick glasses, and you think of a mad scientist from a fifties' horror movie."

Another pause.

"Anyone else?"

"Kyle Brown, a dermatologist from Carson City. One of the sunshine capitals, right, along with Sacramento? Good place to be a skin doc."

"Anyone else in the group? Non-doctors? Like spouses?"

"Let's see. There was a woman who was with Taylor, the anesthesiologist. I don't know if she's a spouse. But she sure is a character. Daria Cazacu. Dramatic eyebrows. Moves them up and down with everything she says. And everything she says is dramatic. Like some kind of stage actor in a melodrama."

I was making notes. "How do you spell Cazacu?"

"That's what I asked her. She said it was Romanian. C-A-Z-A-C-U."

"And the other doctors' spouses?"

"The husband of Janice Mitchell was there. Luke Walker, a biology professor at USC." Another pause. "The other docs all seemed single to me. Why I think that, I don't know. But I didn't think to ask outright. Oh, I just remembered. One of the Brontë sisters mentioned another guy who isn't a doctor and isn't a spouse. She said something like, 'We're hoping our friend Heathcliff will join us as well. He was in our class the first year, and he lives in Tahoe."

"Any information about him?"

"No. Except he wasn't with the group last night."

"Which of the sisters mentioned him?"

"I think it was…" Santiago paused. "Come to think of it, I don't know which one said it. It's hard to tell. If you meet them, you'll understand. Except for one of them who has a scar on her face, they all look alike. They all talk continuously. They finish each others' sentences. And they keep moving. Like they've got some kind of fidgeting syndrome. You're talking to one of them, and she moves, another takes her place, and then they rotate as a group. It's like a human shell game."

"Then how did you tell them apart?"

"I didn't," Santiago said. "You'd see that if you looked at my notes. I just wrote down B for Brontë and noted what was said. I have a bunch of notes next to a bunch of Bs. I couldn't attach any statement to a particular one of them."

"Maybe I should talk to these people. Dr. Diaz hired me to find the man who beat him up. When he learned that Veronica had died, he asked me to look into that as well."

"Does Diaz think her death might not be natural?"

"No. But he's probably wondering about how unlikely it is that an ex-con comes to kill him in Tahoe and at the same time a former classmate dies in Tahoe. I'm wondering the same thing."

"I'd love it if you talked to these doctors," Santiago said. "Then we could compare notes."

"Does it seem curious to you that more of these docs don't have spouses with them?"

"Kind of. But it also makes sense, in a way. If any of the docs were married, would their spouses want to join in at a reunion and talk shop with a bunch of other doctors? Maybe they invited other doctors to join them at the reunion, but the married ones didn't show. I think single people would be more likely to go to a reunion. Just my thought, anyway."

"Makes sense. Those doctors you spoke with last night, can you email me their contact info?" I said.

"Sure. But I'm no good on this phone. I'm heading back to my office and will do it from that computer."

"After talking to them, did any of them seem like potential suspects if it turns out that someone dropped poison into Veronica Eastern's drink?"

"No."

"Then who do you recommend I talk to to learn more about Eastern's pals?"

"I'd talk to the Brontë sisters."

"Thanks."

EIGHT

I had bills to pay, paperwork to file, and when I was done, it was late afternoon and beginning to get dark. I called Street to see if she and Camille had plans for dinner.

"Yes. Camille already asked if you and His Largeness would like to join us because she is cooking."

"A deaf nine-year-old who is fluent in American Sign Language, English, a little bit of Spanish, and is an expert longboard skateboard rider is also a chef?"

"Apparently," Street said.

"What's she cooking?"

"Homemade vegetarian pizza with her secret sauce."

"Interesting. Do you know what's in the secret sauce?"

"If I did, it wouldn't be a secret, right?" Maybe Street's voice was a little reproachful.

I said, "I'm glad you are so respectful of a little kid. What time should Spot and I arrive at your place?"

"You won't. We're coming there."

"A pizza delivery?"

"More like a pizza truck. You just haven't seen it as such."

"You mean Camille is going to cook in the pickup camper in my driveway."

"That camper is where she grew up learning to cook."

I was picturing three of us and two dogs in the camper, a space that Spot fills so thoroughly by himself that he has to back out to turn around. But I didn't want to sound like a downer. "I don't remember an oven in that micro galley."

"She says that Grandpa Charlie bent cookie sheets to make some of kind oven that sits on the stove top."

"Like a toaster oven where the heat comes from the stove?"

"I don't know. I've never seen it. But it's supposed to make good pizza."

"With secret sauce. What time were you thinking?"

"Seven."

"Okay. But I should pick you up. I had a doctor in my office today who'd been beat up by a guy who was just released from prison a few days ago. The ex-con blamed me and the doctor for his lengthy prison sentence many years ago when I was an SFPD rookie."

"I don't like your business."

"I understand."

It was a moment before Street spoke. "You're warning me in case the guy tries to get to you through me."

"Right. Typically, a thug like this will only focus on me and the doctor. But you and Camille will want to use extra caution."

"Don't open the door unless I know who's knocking. Be vigilant in parking lots. Don't go out at night. But now we're planning to go to your cabin tonight."

"I'll pick you up just before seven?"

"Okay. Thanks."

We said goodbye and hung up.

"Time to go, Largeness. We need to pick up the abode before the women visit. There might be a taste of pizza in it for you."

Spot got to his feet at speed, and we left.

Spot was on full alert when we walked out the front door of the building. He scanned left and right, his ears turned back and forth, and his nostrils flexed. Was his attention because he was naturally looking out for me?

The parking lot had just four vehicles in it.

We got in the Jeep, went down the hill to Highway 50, and turned north to head home. In that area of Stateline, 50 is four lanes. I was probably cruising a bit over the limit when I sensed a vehicle coming up behind me at high speed.

I stayed in the right lane so he had room to go around me on my left. But he didn't immediately move over. Instead he came up close and tailgated me as if to send the message that I was a road hazard for my reasonable speed.

I had the brief thought that tailgaters are probably suffering from testosterone deficiency or worse. Their need to make other drivers feel pressured and intimidated speaks volumes about their insecurities.

I let my speed drift lower. Partly, it was an enticement for him to go around. We were the only cars on this section of road. Partly, it was behavioral modification. Tailgate me, and you end up going slower instead of faster.

The driver's headlights disappeared behind my tailgate, he was so close. Then he jerked into the left lane and raced to go past me.

Except he didn't go past. When he got next to me, he braked hard to slow down and match my speed. As a former cop, I recognized the threat.

I hit the brakes as the first gunshot flashed, the bullet shattering my driver's window but luckily missing me.

When someone shoots at you on the highway, the first instinct is to turn away and flee and hide. Which is a fine option if you have the opportunity and a good place to go. But my opportunities were few. There was no immediate place to turn off. And my cop training from way back had given me a strong, ingrained strategy for how to deal with conflict. The first rule of which was to do what your aggressor least expects.

There was a second gun blast as I continued to brake hard, then turned into him. The Precision Immobilization Technique is a tactical ramming maneuver taught to cops. You veer in from the side and hit the other vehicle at its rear corner behind its rear axle. As long as the other vehicle isn't too heavy, the PIT technique will turn the suspect's vehicle sideways, which sends it off the road.

So I rammed the left front corner of my Jeep against the right rear corner of his vehicle.

Because it was dark, I couldn't see what model of vehicle he drove. But it clearly wasn't the van he'd used to kidnap Benito. It was a sedan, which was lighter weight and more vulnerable.

When my Jeep struck him, the rear corner of his vehicle was pushed to the left, which made his car point to the right. I steered harder to the left and accelerated to maintain contact, forcing his vehicle perpendicular to the traffic lane. His car still had some momentum. It shot across the road in front of me and hit a tree. The rule of cars and trees is that trees always win. But the moron didn't realize it. As I rolled to a stop twenty yards away, my left front tire squealing, wobbling, and rubbing on the fender, I heard him revving his engine, trying to back up. But his vehicle seemed to be attached to the tree. After several seconds, the man realized he wasn't going to drive away. He got out of the car, saw me some distance away, raised his gun and fired a shot toward us. I didn't even bother to reflexively duck because I knew there was no way he could hit us with a hand gun from that distance in the dark.

Then the man turned and ran away toward the trees.

I didn't know if Spot was traumatized by the gunshots and my shattered window. I turned, reached back, and rubbed him. "You okay, boy? That was loud."

Spot pushed his muzzle against my hand. He seemed fine.

So I stayed in the Jeep and called 911 as the man ran away.

I went through the routine with the dispatcher, explaining who I was and where I was and why I was calling. I concluded with the suspect's last known position on Highway 50 and said that he was on foot, heading east into the forest, and that he was armed and prone to use his gun as he'd already fired at me three times, breaking my window with one shot.

While I waited for cops to show up, I thought I could rent a car. So I called a guy I'd once helped with an extortion squeeze on his rental equipment agency.

"Craig Fahrman? Owen McKenna," I said when he answered.

"Hey, McKenna. You ready to take me up on the favor I owe you?"

"That's why I'm calling. I need to rent a car."

"I do heavy equipment, remember? I've got cats and front-end loaders and backhoes. Oh, and I just took delivery of a Kubota tractor with a hydraulic rotary plow attachment."

"I was hoping for something that would haul three people and two dogs."

"That's funny," he said. "You talk quantity, but with your dog you should be talking weight. Something that would haul three dogs would be the right size for you. But all I've got is my personal six-pack Silverado with dual rear wheels and a Meyer Super Blade for plowing snow. You're welcome to use it, but I should warn you it only gets about three miles a gallon."

"That might be a bit much. How about a referral to..."

"Hold on," Craig said. "My wife wants to say something."

I waited. I heard talking in the background.

"Well, what do you know," Craig said. "Remember my wife Shelley? She's going to visit her sister in Oxnard for seven days. She's flying tomorrow, so she says you can use her Prius."

"Tell her thanks. But I couldn't bear to put dogs in her nice car. If they could even fit."

"She's got the big model. You'd be surprised by its size."

"Dogs are dirty, and they shed."

"Trust me, McKenna, it's no problem. She's been hauling hydraulic parts in that car. We'll drop it off at your office in, say, fifteen minutes. See you then."

"Wait. Craig I'm not at the office. I'm on Highway Fifty, between Kingsbury and Round Hill. My Jeep is damaged, and I'm on the side of the highway. You can bring the Prius here."

"We're on our way." He hung up.

I next called a tow company to have the Jeep hauled to the repair shop. When I was on the phone, the first responder to arrive was a Douglas County Sheriff's Patrol Unit, its light bar flashing. It parked behind the car that crashed into the tree. The spotlight illuminated the crashed sedan, which was a Nissan. The bright light revealed that the driver's air bag had deployed. The light swiveled to shine on Spot and me next to our Jeep. I waved.

The cops stayed in their vehicle. Probably running the plate on the crashed car.

After a minute, a young deputy got out on the passenger side.

I walked over. "I'm Owen McKenna. Thanks for coming."

"No problem. You're the guy who called this in. Friend of Sergeant Martinez," he said.

"Yeah."

"Sarge wants you to wait until he gets here. He says he's just leaving the hospital, taking a doctor to his lodging, then coming here."

"Got it," I said.

Another cop got out of the driver's side. This one was only

slightly older.

The two men had me go through Tucker Dopple's motions and how the crash came about.

"You caused the crash on purpose?"

"Yes. A PIT move."

"They talked about that! But I haven't taken the driving class, yet." The younger cop was excited. "Precision Immobilization Technique. So it really works?"

"Yeah. Quite well. But my Jeep is damaged on the left front. And the driver's window is shot out."

"We'll note that on the police report, right Oliver?"

"Yeah. I'm not sure the right wording…"

"Sarge will know?"

"Yeah." He looked at me. "Looks like the air bag kept him from getting hurt?"

I nodded. "Last I saw him, he took a wild shot at me and then ran into those trees," I pointed. I gestured at the crashed car. "If the suspect is the guy Diamond and I are thinking of, the car is probably stolen."

"I checked," the older guy said. "It's not on the list. Probably the owner doesn't yet know it's missing. A vacation homeowner who isn't around."

The men gazed at the dark forest. One of them said, "If he goes far enough up the mountain, he could end up at houses off Kingsbury Grade. If he looks long enough, he'll find an open garage door. The sheriff has told us that garages are the easiest way into a house because people often don't lock the inside door to a garage."

The other cop said, "Somewhere up there will be a Mercedes with a key in it. He could upgrade his ride."

Diamond pulled up in his Sheriff's SUV. He left the light bar flashers on and jumped out.

He turned to me. "You look impatient. You need to be somewhere?"

"I've got an important dinner date."

"And you don't want to keep her waiting."

"Nine-year-olds aren't used to waiting."

Diamond looked at me.

"Camille invited me."

Diamond nodded. "I assume you didn't see Tucker Dopple's piece. Assuming the shooter was Dopple."

"I'm quite confident it was him. His piece was covered by his hand. But if I had to guess, I think it was a revolver. Small, but louder than a pistol."

Diamond nodded. "Revolvers are louder than pistols, true. Could you see the round as it whistled by?" Diamond didn't grin, at least not enough that I could see in the dark.

"If I had to guess, I'd say a thirty-eight special. In days past, I would take one to the range in the Bay Area. This man's sounded the same."

Diamond nodded. "You better go. Don't want to keep your hosts waiting."

"Why don't you join us for dinner?" I asked Diamond.

"Sounds good. But you should ask Street and Camille."

"It's at my place. Camille likes you. Street thinks you are the best there is. It'll be fine. Come when you're done here."

A tow truck pulled up to my Jeep, followed by a Prius and a huge Silverado pickup with dual rear wheels. The pickup had even more rust than my Jeep. Craig and Shelley got out of the vehicles.

"This is very kind of you," I said.

"No sweat, Owen," Shelley said. "A day from now, I'm going to be walking the beach in SoCal, and my car needs exercise to stay limber."

Craig was looking at my Jeep and the crashed Nissan.

"Looks like you pulled a PIT on this dude."

"Yeah. It worked pretty well."

"Dangerous criminal?"

"A danger only to me, I think."

"I hope he doesn't shoot up the Prius."

"Me, too. I can give you some payment up front if you can take a credit card."

"Hey, I said I owe you a favor."

"Can't thank you two enough."

We said goodbye, and they drove off in the pickup.

NINE

I picked up Street, Camille, and Blondie. The dogs and Camille squeezed into the back of the Prius, which turned out to have more room than my Jeep. Street carried a large cardboard box that smelled of veggies and cheese and pizza crust.

"Where's your Jeep?" Street asked.

"I had mechanical trouble on the way home from my office. The Jeep got towed to the shop, and I called Craig Fahrman's equipment rental. They didn't have cars, so they're letting me use Shelley's car."

We headed up to my cabin. Camille and Street got busy inside Grandpa Charlie's pickup camper where he and Camille used to live.

Diamond drove up a half hour later and parked his Douglas County Sheriff's patrol vehicle near the entrance to my drive. He walked over to where Spot and I stood near the camper. We heard murmurs through the camper's thin walls and from the skylight vent.

Spot took a step forward, and Diamond gave him a rough head rub.

"No appearance from Tucker Dopple?" Diamond said.

I shook my head and spoke softly so my words wouldn't be heard inside the camper. "My biggest worry is that he tries to get to me through Street. And now through Camille."

"Could happen," Diamond said. "But let's hope he's one of those guys who just focuses his animosity on you. Some scumbags automatically think of getting to a target through their loved ones. But it doesn't occur to others. Could be that Tucker Dopple is one of those. We'll probably know soon."

"You mean," I said, "if he is currently hiding in the forest out there…" I gestured toward the dark trees across the road, "we'll find out soon enough, if he starts shooting."

Diamond shrugged.

I said, "You're a great guy, Diamond, but I've never gotten over your ability to separate emotion from your 'just the facts, ma'am,' rationale."

"Guy shoots you from some convenient spot doesn't make it less terrible. Recognizing the terribleness doesn't make it less likely. But being prepared for the possibility—even a casual preparation—might make it less difficult to cope."

"Like I said…"

"So I'm out here with my sidearm and my backup. You're out here with the wonder hound. Guy would be stupid to come after us."

"He's already demonstrated stupid," I said. "Your patrol vehicle put the stop to him last time."

"Why I parked it on the road. He can't miss it. 'Course, a lotta idiots decide suicide-by-cop is an acceptable result if they can hurt the people they want to hurt." Diamond gazed toward the forest. He gave Spot a solid smack on the side of his neck. Spot wagged. Blondie crowded in to get her share of attention. Diamond rubbed her as well. "The best thing we've got going here are these two hounds."

"If they alert, we hit the deck."

"In the meantime, do you need to check on the food prep? Three adults and two dogs are staking their lives on the skills of a nine-year-old whose kitchen consists of a propane stove in a camper."

"I'm not worried." I stepped over to the camper and did a soft rat-a-tat on the door. "Checking in on Julia Child's masterwork…"

Without opening the door, Street called back through the camper wall. "The chef is monitoring the ovens. She is aided by a little wind-up timer and periodic glimpses into the blue flame caverns invented by Grandpa Charlie, caverns that look like a miniature sci-fi movie set. What could possibly go wrong?"

"Let us know when we can help."

Ten minutes later, the camper door opened. Camille was standing there in an apron with a painted picture of a large purple moon over Lake Tahoe. I remembered that Camille was a painter of moons, and that her new business, which Street had helped her start, was already making sales online.

"La pizza esta…" Camille said tentatively, then turned and looked back at Street.

"Yes," Street said.

"La pizza esta lista para comer." Camille signed as she spoke.

"Eso es fantástico," Diamond said. He turned to me. "It's ready to eat."

Diamond, Blondie, Spot, and I stood crowding the back door of the camper. Camille and Street had plates on the little fold-out dining table, which was even smaller than the fold-out table in my cabin's kitchen nook.

They put pieces of pizza on them and handed them out the door.

Street set bottled beer on the end of the little counter to the left of the stovetop, which was nearest to the open door.

We ate. Spot watched.

"Gotta cool first, Largeness."

Camille and Street ate standing up in the micro space.

After Diamond and I had each eaten two pieces, Camille handed out two more for each of us.

"Esta pizza es extraordinaria," Diamond said.

I got the gist of his meaning. "Secret sauce," I said.

Camille grinned.

After we ate four pieces each, Camille said, "Do you want more?"

I looked at Diamond. He turned to Camille.

"I could have another piece. But I don't understand how you cooked so much pizza in such a small space."

Camille made the 'I don't understand' sign next to her ear.

I said to Diamond. "Move in closer to the camper light so she can see your lips."

Diamond did so, and repeated himself.

Camille said, "I'll show you the oven Grandpa Charlie invented." She pointed to a large metal box made of bent cookie sheets. "The lower compartment is for cooking. The upper two compartments are for warming."

"I get it. You cooked three pizzas in a row. Each time one was done, you moved it up to the warming compartment. That invention is almost as good as your secret sauce." Diamond pointed to Camille's apron. "And your art keeps getting better. Someday the museums will come calling."

Camille grinned.

When the pizza was thoroughly cool, I broke up two pieces, stirred them into Spot's and Blondie's sawdust chunks in their two separate bowls, and then, when Spot's saliva flood got dangerous, gave them the okay.

Camille shrieked as Spot set a new world record. When Spot was done, Camille watched Blondie, who was no slouch when it came to eating, but who was much more civilized.

"They like it," Camille said in one of the year's great understatements.

I turned to her and said, "It's the secret sauce."

Camille gave me a big grin as if she were about to reveal a huge secret. "Do you know what's in the secret sauce?" she said.

"No. What?"

"Love." And then she nearly fell over giggling.

TEN

The next morning, I got a call at my office, but not on the landline.

"That Wappa Wabbit. That Wappa Wabbit."

I answered, "Owen McKenna."

"Santiago, here. The pathologist determined that Dr. Veronica Eastern was murdered," he said.

"How?"

"Stabbed in the back with a long thin instrument. She thought it might have been a narrow screwdriver. The weapon was aimed perfectly, because it pierced the victim's heart."

"It sounds," I said, "like a type of murder suited to someone with medical training."

"It sure does," Santiago said. "Time to reexamine the deceased doctor's companions,"

"I can help, if you like."

"I like."

I said, "Do you have a preference regarding who I talk to first?"

"I'd like you to try those triplet sisters."

"The ones they call the Brontë sisters," I said.

"Yeah. They don't fit my idea of doctors."

"How is that?"

"I don't know. Too much personality? More like entertainers than scientists."

"Do they know that Dr. Eastern was murdered?"

"No. The only people who know outside of our office are Sergeant Martinez and now you. I thought Diamond should know because he is dealing with the assault on the other doctor." Santiago paused. He was probably consulting his notes. "Benito Diaz."

"Do you want me to inform the Brontë sisters of Eastern's death?"

"You've had more experience with these things than I have. So, yeah. Do the honors. Report back when you get a chance."

"Will do. I'm looking for the contact list you emailed me. What were the Brontë sisters' names again?" I dug around in my desk. If I ever got organized, I wouldn't know what to do with all my extra time.

"Charlotte, Emily, and Anne Smythe," Santiago said. "I'm curious what you will think of them."

I found the list Santiago had emailed me, which I'd printed out. "I'll let you know."

I took Spot out for a run in the forest. Then I called Street to check in on her new busy life with Camille. Street said things were under control, and that Camille was occupied with reading Amor Towles' A Gentleman in Moscow.

"Isn't that book over the head of a nine-year-old?"

"Some aspects, sure. But it's not racy. She likes it. It even has a little girl."

I told Street what I'd learned from Santiago.

"It sounds like the woman was killed by a doctor," she said.

"Indeed. My next stop is talking to the Brontë sisters."

"Sounds appropriate. Good luck."

Next to the phone numbers on the list, Santiago had written that the sisters were staying at a vacation rental on the North Shore. Charlotte's number was the first of three. I dialed.

"This is Charlotte Smythe, MD," a pleasant contralto voice answered. I didn't realize it was a recording, and I was about to respond when the voice continued, "If you have an emergency, call nine, one, one. If you want to make an appointment or have medical questions, please press five to speak to the office manager. If you have a personal message for me, please leave it after the beep."

There was a beep.

"Good morning, Dr. Smythe. My name's Owen McKenna. I'm an investigator working on behalf of the Placer County Sheriff's Office. Sergeant Jack Santiago gave me your number and asked me to call you about your colleague, Dr. Eastern. Please call back at your earliest convenience. Thank you."

I clicked off. The phone rang almost immediately. "That Wappa Wabbit. That Wappa Wabbit." It's only when you get a standout ring tone that you realize how often your phone rings.

"Owen McKenna."

"Charlotte Smythe calling. Have they figured out what happened to Ronnie?" The woman sounded casual as if she were asking about the weather.

I tried to think of a response that wouldn't reveal the truth but also wouldn't create too much curiosity.

"We're working on it. I'd like to meet with you and your sisters. When would be a good time?"

"Let me ask my sisters."

I heard background voices.

She came back in my ear. "This morning would be good. Could you come by our Airbnb at ten o'clock?"

"Sure."

She gave me an address in Kings Beach, a little town near the state line at Crystal Bay but on the California side.

At the appropriate time, Spot and I got into the Prius loaner and headed up the East Shore. We went through the town of Incline Village, into California at Crystal Bay, and in another mile came to Kings Beach, an impossibly cute little town right on the water. Because November is "shoulder season," the myriad of restaurants, coffee cafes, T-shirt shops, and sporting goods stores were not overwhelmed by the crush of summer tourists. The multiple beach and park areas actually had a parking space or two.

I turned off on a narrow side street. The address was a newish house with Craftsman architecture. The siding was gray and the trim was white. It had a broad front porch with a six-foot overhang that sheltered a wicker couch painted white but with red cushions and several wicker rockers with red cushions held on by string ties. The second floor had two dormer windows. Because it was only two blocks from the beach, it probably rented out for a four-figure nightly sum, even in November.

I left the Prius on the far side of the street.

The house's front door opened as I walked up. A 40-ish woman walked out. She was dressed in clothes that were designed to look casual but had probably been professionally tailored. The woman fit the L.L.Bean, rustic model look. Her red flannel shirt was tucked in and showed that she had a narrow waist, and her chocolate jeans were tight enough to be uncomfortable. She wore a sheepskin vest that hung open such that its warmth would be lost, but it matched her sheepskin boots.

She had a plain oval face. I didn't get the sense that her cheeks and neck were rounded by baby fat, but if she clenched her teeth, you probably wouldn't see her jaw muscles bulge. Whatever her physicality, it was upstaged by the way she radiated intelligence.

She called out, "Owen McKenna?"

"That's me."

"I'm Anne Smythe." She looked past me to the Prius, where Spot had his head thrust out the rear window. "Bring your dog, hon. No dog owner can visit the Smythe sisters and leave a hound in the car." She gave me a broad grin that showed teeth that were white but had a little overlap at 2 o'clock. For a moment, I wondered why a doctor wouldn't pursue orthodontia. Then I liked her more for it, the same way I liked Street Casey for not covering up her acne scars.

"Thanks, he'll love that."

I fetched Spot, holding his collar as I walked up. He strained forward, his tail held high, anticipating meeting yet another woman who'd already fallen in love with him from a distance.

We climbed up three steps to the porch.

"Oh my, look at the size of this guy. And you've got such a small car you stuff him into."

"Yeah," I said, not seeing any point in discussing how I ended up with the Prius.

"What is this boy's name?"

"Spot to most. His Largeness to his closest friends."

"Ooooh, Largeness, you are so…"

She bent over and hugged him. "...large. And beautiful!" She had curly strawberry-blonde hair cut just below her ears so that it swung and bounced.

"Can I take the reins? Wait, he has no reins. Oh, he's one of those ponies you control with your knees and your hands on his neck."

She reached for his collar. "Come over here, Largeness. I've been waiting all morning to do some lounging with you on the couch. I make a mean batch of popcorn. Do you eat popcorn?"

Spot yawned and then broke into a pant, his giant tongue flopping.

"Oh, my," she said again, staring at his tongue and fangs.

She turned and called through the front door, which was still standing open.

"Girls, come experience what Captain Ahab felt when he stared into the maw of Moby Dick!"

ELEVEN

Anne Smythe sat down on the porch couch and tugged at Spot to bring him up close. But he knew about couches.

Instead of coming close, his nose to her face, he rotated until his rear hit the couch cushions and sat down next to the woman, his tail folded under, his butt on the couch, rear legs bent, front paws on the porch floor.

I heard movement. Another woman came to the door. Then another. Both appeared to be copies of the woman sitting next to Spot, although one of them had a faint-but-wicked scar that ran down her forehead, across the outer corner of her eye, and back to her ear. It had probably been lessened by plastic surgery, but it still revealed that she had been in a nasty accident years before.

The women stepped outside and saw Spot, who was being smothered by Anne's hugs. One merely made a pronounced inhalation. The other gasped.

"I get to be Ahab," one said.

"We'll both be Ahab," said the other. Their voices were all the same. "C'mon, Anne, your turn is up. Make way for your elders." The woman grabbed Anne's hand and pulled. Anne reluctantly stood up.

The other two sat on either side of Spot and hugged and caressed. Spot was dutifully patient.

"Elders?" I said, staring at three identical women. There were small differences from the one named Anne. The other two had hair that was possibly less curly, possibly cut shorter. One, when she grinned at Spot, revealed that she didn't have the tooth overlap. The other had a lop-sided smile, and she held one eyebrow slightly raised. Other than the one with the big scar, the differences between the women were so slight that it required careful observation. And when they changed position, any sense of who was whom was lost until I relocated the scar.

"They call themselves my elders because I was born last," Anne said. "Charlotte was first." She looked at the woman with the raised eyebrow, who grinned at me.

"And I am Emily," the one with the scar said. "Not too old, not too young, just right."

I was already having trouble keeping them apart.

"Birth order is, of course, important with triplets," one of them said.

"Especially if you're Emily," said one of the ones who wasn't Emily. The one with the curlier hair? Anne, I think it was.

"Of course, in a world of big problems and grand puzzles, birth order is nothing," said another.

"I'm sorry, I can't keep track," I said.

"We'll make it easy." The woman held up her hand in the shape of a C. "I'm Charlotte." The one with the raised eyebrow.

"I'm Emily." Emily flashed a quick E. The one with the scar.

"And I'm Anne." She made an A shape. The one with the tooth overlap.

I frowned. "Now I remember. From American Sign Language."

"Oh, you know ASL. Girls, we have an educated man in our midst. Imagine that."

"Tough concept, huh?" I said.

"Maybe we should give him a test to be sure." She made some signing motions with her hands.

Spot turned and watched.

I said, "I don't know ASL."

"But your dog is watching."

"That's because someone who knows ASL has been teaching my dog and rewarding him with treats."

"The magic of food treats," one of them said.

"Dogs and men being the same," said another.

The comments were so rapid fire, it was like watching a stage play with fast-talking actors.

"Help me out, here," I said. "Emily, you sit there." I pointed to the right side of the couch. The woman with the scar sat. "Anne, there." The woman with the tooth overlaps sat. The woman in the middle had the raised eyebrow.

They grinned as they sat, musical chairs to help the visually-challenged.

"Now you're in alphabetical order," I said. "Anne, Charlotte, Emily."

"You forgot His Largeness," one of them said.

I nodded. "I'll have to be careful not to confuse him with one of you."

I remembered being in a play back in high school. Maybe it would help fix the women in my mind if I thought of their character names in upper case letters like in the script book from way back.

EMILY signed something, holding her hands in front of Spot. Spot seemed interested.

I said, "It doesn't help if I know your order but can't understand what you're saying."

CHARLOTTE, her tone very dry: "It looks like your dog can learn ASL, but you can't?"

I said, "That might be true. I'm trying, but I'm slow."

ANNE: "At least the man has good intent."

CHARLOTTE: "The dichotomy of intent versus action."

My turn to raise eyebrows.

EMILY: "Conundrums we've experienced. Do men with good intent ever act on it?"

ANNE: "They act on their bad intent."

EMILY: "He is kind of cute if you ignore his lack of education, intent or not."

ANNE: "Excessive size could be an issue. I have a Fiat."

CHARLOTTE: "But I have a Range Rover. Insufficient mileage combined with more-than-sufficient space."

EMILY, glancing at Charlotte, gave her head a small shake: "The world has always suffered the excesses of the first born."

ANNE: "A shame. The last born are always better adjusted." She signed as she watched Spot.

EMILY: "You've come to tell us about Ronnie."

"Ronnie?" I repeated.

CHARLOTTE: "Veronica Eastern."

I said, "First, a question," I said. "Are you all doctors?"

ANNE: "Yes. UCSF Medical School. We're all internists."

Spot pushed back with his front paws, shifted sideways so he could get his elbows up on the couch, sighed, then flopped over toward Anne, his head landing in her lap.

ANNE, running two fingertips over the crest of Spot's head and down his nose: "My God, this brute's head must weigh fifty pounds."

I said, "I'm here to tell you that your colleague Veronica Eastern was murdered." They had no reaction, no surprise.

EMILY: "We figured as much."

I said, "Really?"

CHARLOTTE: "Ronnie was dishonorable."

ANNE: "Low standards."

EMILY: "Lots of people might want to do her in."

I repeated her words. "Do her in?"

CHARLOTTE: "We heard that in an old movie. It became a thing for us."

As they spoke, I realized that they were more interested in their own repartee than they were in Veronica Eastern's murder. If Eastern's murder was actually no surprise for them, that meant they already knew it. Or at least suspected it.

I said, "Were you all nearby when she collapsed?"

ANNE, shaking her head: "We weren't especially near. I was over to the left of the group. Veronica was kind of in the center, but toward the rear. Charlotte was in front of her, I think. Is that right, Char?"

CHARLOTTE: "I must have been because when someone called out that Ronnie had fallen, I turned around and looked behind me."

I said, "How about you, Emily?"

EMILY: "It's all a blur. One moment we were all walking along. I was talking to Luke about cars of all things. He's into electric cars. The next moment, Ronnie was on the ground, and people were exclaiming. 'Call nine, one, one!' and such."

I said, "What about the others?"

EMILY: "Nick and Ray were together. And Kyle was in front of them, doing that thing where he would turn back and talk to Luke and the other guys behind him."

I said, "These men are doctors?"

CHARLOTTE: "Yes, Nick Taylor, Ray Lopez, and Kyle Brown. But Luke is a biology prof at USC. They were together, just in front of Ronnie. I remember that they were talking football. How predictable is that? Does no guy realize that if you want to bed a woman, you don't get there by talking football? Books or movies or theater, maybe. The only thing worse than football is hockey. Or maybe ultimate martial arts or ultimate fighting or whatever it's called."

ANNE: "Beautiful celebs. Talking about beautiful celeb hotties is worse than talking about football or hockey or UFC fights."

I said, "Men probably know this but would rather talk about sports than pursue bedding women."

CHARLOTTE: "Yeah, you're probably right."

ANNE: "Has the ME determined how Ronnie was killed?" More signing. For Spot? Or just practice?

I said, "She was apparently stabbed from behind." I didn't describe the weapon as a matter of standard strategy.

CHARLOTTE, turning to look at the others, her eyebrows raised, eyes huge: "Like the autopsy in med school!"

EMILY: "Yes, the Tenderloin art platter!"

I said, "What?"

EMILY: "Gallows humor, doctor-style. Our pathology professor was a stuffed shirt. All about Hippocrates and the lofty principles of medical science. Afterward, we ridiculed the experience by talking about art."

ANNE, explaining further: "The class the pathologist taught was about autopsy. He performed his act on a young man who'd been found dead in the Tenderloin."

CHARLOTTE, interrupting: "If you don't know, that's an area in San Francisco."

I wanted to keep them talking with abandon. So I told them more than I normally would. "I was a cop on the SFPD for twenty years. I thought I've heard it all. But why is talking about an art platter a kind of ridicule?"

ANNE: "Not art. ART in caps. It's doctor slang for a person who died. An ART platter is a recently-dead body Assuming Room Temperature on the table."

Two of the women looked amused. The third, Emily, with the scar, did not. In fact, Emily looked stressed.

I said, "This autopsy was on a man who was stabbed in the back like Veronica Eastern?"

CHARLOTTE: "Yes! Isn't it exciting?"

ANNE: "Makes you wonder if there's a connection!"

I said, "Back to Veronica Eastern. Can any of you think of a reason why someone would want her dead?"

The sisters seemed to share a glance, back and forth.

EMILY: "Blackmail?"

CHARLOTTE: "Good call, Em. Ronnie blackmailed a professor back in the day."

"About what?"

CHARLOTTE: "Veronica walked in on him with another student. Nothing illegal about it, of course. But he must have been worried about ending up as an ART platter, because he paid Ronnie real money to keep quiet."

I said, "How would you know he paid a lot?"

ANNE: "References about this stuff end up in a subsection of a subsection of a social media company that we all love to hate. This particular section features med school gallows humor."

I said, "I'm surprised that anyone cares about those things these days."

EMILY: "You mean professors and med students getting it on in the autopsy specimen closet? Brains in jars to one side, kidneys and livers on the other?"

I shrugged. "Does this blackmail mean we've established motive? Could it be that the professor finally killed her as payback for blackmailing him?"

ANNE: "That's one possibility, anyway."

I said, "There's more than one?"

CHARLOTTE: "There are some people who didn't like Veronica even if they were never blackmailed by her."

"Such as?"

Charlotte looked at Anne, who looked at Emily.

EMILY: "He didn't dislike her. He just felt burned by her."

I said, "Who is this?"

CHARLOTTE: "Heathcliff."

TWELVE

"Who is Heathcliff?" I asked.

ANNE: "It goes way back. Almost to when we were born."

I said, "Because I'm officially investigating the death of Veronica Eastern, we better go back as well."

The three identical women looked at me. No one spoke.

I said, "Is your beginning secret?"

ANNE: "No, but it's not that interesting."

I said, "What I've heard sounds interesting. For example, your colleagues refer to you as the Brontë sisters. What's that about?"

CHARLOTTE: "That's because our parents named us after the Brontë sisters."

EMILY: "Our father especially had pretensions of us being creatives, writers of some kind. But we severely disappointed him by becoming doctors."

ANNE: "And our mother died when we were young. So our fates, linked to our father, also became linked to *Jane Eyre* for Charlotte, *Wuthering Heights* for Em, and *The Tenant Of Wildfell Hall* for me."

I said, "Those were books the Brontë sisters wrote?"

CHARLOTTE, ignoring my question: "In addition to the Brontë sisters, Dad also loved Joseph Campbell. The hero's journey and such. Dad was so focused on character that he divined our essential traits before we could talk."

EMILY: "Before *you* could talk. I was practically quoting *Wuthering Heights* when I started talking."

ANNE: "I don't think he divined our traits so much as he prescribed our traits by assigning us our names."

I said, "Joseph Campbell was a writer?"

All three of them looked shocked at my question. Such

ignorance. Such naivete.

EMILY: "Campbell is the guy who discovered the basic types of characters that are in practically all stories."

CHARLOTTE, shaking her head: "He didn't discover them. There were people before him who did that. Otto Rank, Lord Raglan, and others. Campbell wasn't the greatest scholar. But he had a serious gift for packaging."

EMILY: "Oh, come on. Packaging? How cute is that?"

ANNE: "I think she's got a point. Campbell's Hero With a Thousand Faces didn't break new ground so much as come up with the catchy idea of the Monomyth. Catchy is sticky. George Lucas used the Monomyth when he wrote Star Wars. That was a sticky movie. And dad loved it."

EMILY: "Dad was mostly in love with Campbell's characters, not Lucas's characters."

I said, "Campbell didn't create Darth Vader, did he?"

ANNE, while signing: "No, Campbell didn't create any characters. He merely identified character types. The hero. The villain. The wise woman. Character types you find everywhere."

"I don't mean to interrupt," I said, "but your signing is fascinating."

ANNE: "I don't mean to look like a showoff, but I had a deaf patient. I saw him almost continuously for over a year while we dealt with a liver issue. I learned some ASL. I've tried to maintain some pretense of fluency."

EMILY, signing back: "We all learned signing basics. I think the shapeshifter is the most interesting character."

ANNE: "No, the trickster wins hands down. In every story." More signing.

Spot lifted his head off Anne's lap to look at their signing.

I said, "You're using sign language to be inscrutable. Like the Mexican kids here in Tahoe who switch to Spanish when they don't want adults to know what they're saying."

CHARLOTTE: "Inscrutable. I knew you were smart down in there somewhere." She glanced at her sisters. "Don't forget Dad's favorite character type."

ANNE: "The anti-hero."

EMILY: "A character I didn't used to understand until we met Heathcliff."

ANNE: "Yes, Heathcliff. Who could have known?"

I said, "I've heard that name before. Is that an actor?"

ANNE, looking off across the street: "The bad boy in *Wuthering Heights*." Was her tone exasperation? Or wistfulness?

I said, "You don't need to accept the depth of my ignorance. You can educate me. Set me on the straight and narrow path to knowledge."

CHARLOTTE: "See, more smarts." Then, in a correcting tone: "Heathcliff was the classic anti-hero."

EMILY: "The *iconic* anti-hero in all of literature."

"What exactly is an anti-hero?" I asked.

CHARLOTTE: "Heroic style combined with bad actions."

ANNE: "Yet good intent."

I said, "Did this man Heathcliff act on his good intent?"

CHARLOTTE: "I think so. But it could just be street smarts."

EMILY: "The answer is yes and no. Yes, he sometimes acted on good intent. No, he sometimes didn't. But it happened through no fault of his own."

I said, "His actual name is Heathcliff?"

EMILY: "Horatio Harris is his given name. But he was Heathcliff to us."

I said, "Because of the *Wuthering* novel."

CHARLOTTE: "Yep. Total bad boy."

ANNE: "But dashing in a nineteenth century way."

CHARLOTTE: "Handsome beyond words, I'll give him that."

I said, "How is it you all know him?"

ANNE: "He started out with us at UCSF Medical School."

I said, "But he didn't finish with you?"

EMILY: "Nope. He had to drop out."

"Had to?"

ANNE: "A tragic story. His girlfriend Isabel DeMille died

in a fall. Then he tried to kill himself. He lived, but gomered his brain."

CHARLOTTE, explaining: "As doctors, we religiously use accurate medical speak."

I said, "Like gomered."

ANNE: "There's lots of different medical speak. But gomered is definitely on the list."

EMILY: "Some think Heathcliff's suicide attempt was a kind of self-punishment for not being able to keep his girlfriend safe. Heathcliff was very chivalrous."

I said, "Do you mean, as opposed to suicide as a sincere attempt to end one's life and thus one's depression?"

CHARLOTTE, nodding: "That's a good way to put it."

I said, "Did he witness Isabel's fall?"

ANNE: "No. He was studying late at the med school library. When he came home, he found Isabel at the bottom of the stairs. It pretty much freaked him out when she died. He jumped off the Golden Gate Bridge three days later."

EMILY: "A fishing boat was nearby. They saw him fall and fished him out. They thought he was dead until they saw his fingers moving. So they gave him chest compressions and got him to the hospital."

I said, "Did the fishermen see him jump?"

ANNE: "Wow, you are a natural cop. Looking for murder here, there, and everywhere."

CHARLOTTE: "No, they didn't see him jump. And no one up on the bridge ever came forward, either."

EMILY: "The ER docs did the scans, found out his brain was severely bruised, and sea water had been forced into one ear canal so hard it blasted a walnut-sized pocket of water into his brain. So they put him in an induced coma to help his brain heal. Eventually, they brought him back."

CHARLOTTE: "But he lost his cutting-edge mind. Couldn't keep up with med school."

I said, "Did he lose his good intent? You said he felt burned by Veronica Eastern."

ANNE: "Burned, yes. After Isabel died, and then he almost

died, Heathcliff pursued Veronica. We thought he was getting over Isabel's death. But Ronnie was just leading him on, dishonorable woman that she is."

ANNE: "Was."

CHARLOTTE: "When Ronnie found out he had lost his brilliance, she dropped him."

I said, "Do any of you think Horatio Harris Heathcliff is the kind of man who could murder years after an insult?"

They looked at each other as if assessing.

ANNE: "The Heathcliff I knew could never murder."

EMILY: "Agreed. But the current Heathcliff is probably nothing like the Heathcliff we knew."

CHARLOTTE: "It could be that years of simmering pain eventually boils over. If he found out that Ronnie was in Tahoe for a reunion, maybe he saw an opportunity to put the pain behind him."

I said, "You think that kind of thing actually happens?"

CHARLOTTE: "Sure. Where does the cliché 'nursing a grudge' come from?"

ANNE: "But he pretty much went back to Isabel."

I wanted to be sure I heard her correctly. "The woman who died."

ANNE: "Right. A dead woman can never spurn you. And when he reconnected with Isabel, I think he got past Ronnie and was able to rekindle his good intent."

CHARLOTTE: "You may be onto something. I agree he's still got his good intent. In fact, most of Heathcliff is still there. Based on the last time I saw him, anyway."

EMILY: "The part that is fixated on airplanes is still there."

I said, "What does that mean?"

EMILY: "After his fall, when he came out of the coma, he was talking about planes."

"Why planes?"

ANNE: "You'd have to ask Heathcliff. He said it always was about planes."

THIRTEEN

I said, "Airplanes must be very important to Heathcliff if he talks about them a lot."

CHARLOTTE: "He also talks about his girlfriend."

I wanted to clarify. "The one who died."

ANNE: "There might have been something about Isabel that was connected to planes. Something important, but we never knew what it was."

CHARLOTTE, nodding: "Eventually, Heathcliff decided she maybe didn't die."

I said, "Would this be the Heathcliff in the *Wuthering* novel, or the Heathcliff whose name is Horatio Harris?"

ANNE: "The Horatio Heathcliff. Not the real Heathcliff."

"I thought…"

CHARLOTTE: "The real Heathcliff is the fictional Heathcliff."

EMILY: "In *Wuthering Heights.* The Heathcliff who dies after being haunted by the older Catherine's ghost."

It was confusing. "But the girlfriend of the Horatio Heathcliff did, in fact, die, right?"

CHARLOTTE: "Oh, yeah. We were there after Isabel took the stairway dive. Heathcliff called us after he called nine, one, one. We went right over. We knew that Isabel had a serious work ethic. No job was ever left unfinished by that girl. And sure enough, she died all the way."

"Pardon me if I'm out of line. But you sound quite brusque about her death."

ANNE, with a dismissive wave of her hand: "That's just more doctor humor. You can't get through life in our business without putting the horrors at arm's length. We don't just make a few jokes about life and death. It's a constant POV."

I repeated the letters. "POV?"

EMILY: "Point of View."

I said, "I've met doctors who are always serious and earnest."

CHARLOTTE: "Those kind are out there, but they're rare."

ANNE: "The ones whose marriages fall apart, whose kids won't talk to them, who quit to become writers."

EMILY: "Either that, or the earnestness is a facade."

I said, "Do you think Isabel's fall down the stairs was an accident?"

CHARLOTTE: "We'll never know. But if it wasn't, a fall is not a reliable way to kill someone, even if they break their neck. Nevertheless, Isabel DeMille was the kind of woman who would perceive the extent of her injuries and give up the ghost through shear brain power. No veggie life on a machine for her."

I said, "Was Isabel DeMille a med student?"

EMILY: "Everyone in our world back then was a med student. Now everyone is a doctor."

I said, "Except for Heathcliff, who thinks Isabel didn't die."

ANNE: "In my philosophy-of-life class in college, some of their definitions of life might consider Isabel to still be alive merely because Heathcliff thinks she's still alive. Maybe Sarte was wrong. Maybe essence does, in fact, precede existence."

The concept sailed over my head. "They teach philosophy of life in college?"

CHARLOTTE: "They do at Stanford."

I said, "Is that where you all went to college?"

ANNE: "It was part of the unwritten agreement when dad paid for their new medical building."

I said, "You can buy college admission with buildings?"

CHARLOTTE, looking at Anne, then at Emily: "He's not that naive. Trust me. It's a conversational ploy."

I said, "Nevertheless, Isabel didn't die in Heathcliff's mind."

They all nodded.

I said, "Did he decide she didn't die because the real, fictional Heathcliff was focused on the ghost of a woman who died?"

ANNE, shrugging her shoulders, then nodding: "If the real, fictional Heathcliff found sustenance in the ghost of Catherine, then the non-fictional Horatio Harris Heathcliff might find equivalent sustenance in an Isabel DeMille who is alive, even if we can't see her."

I had many questions. "Why does he talk about planes?"

EMILY: "We don't know. But every time he sees an airplane, he watches it."

ANNE: "Studies it. Always did from way back."

CHARLOTTE: "He analyzes airplanes. Equations. Geometry of structure. Propulsion. Aerodynamics. Weight. Lift."

EMILY: "Don't forget beauty. He studies airplanes for their beauty. Science meets poetry."

This seemed a new direction. "There's beauty in planes?"

CHARLOTTE: "Of course. Like sailboats on Lake Tahoe. Science and art go together. Employing wind is an art. Wind is beautiful. Ask Columbus or Magellan or Sir Francis Drake. Ask a physicist. NASA has demonstrated that you can use solar wind to power space ships."

EMILY: "Only if their mass is light enough and their sail is large enough."

"You doctors are drawn to the Age of Enlightenment."

CHARLOTTE, nodding: "Yes! More smarts. I'm taking this man home."

I said, "Spot and I go home to my girlfriend and her new daughter."

ANNE: "Who's that?"

I wondered if it was safe to give out personal information. My gut instinct was yes. "Camille is nine years old. My girlfriend is in the process of adopting her."

EMILY: "And your girlfriend's name?"

"Street Casey."

ANNE: "Oooh, very intriguing. And what does Street Casey do when she isn't adopting children?"

"She studies bugs. Entomologist. Ph.D. from Berkeley."

CHARLOTTE: "I'm taking their whole family home. Think of the conversations, bugs, and the enlightenment."

EMILY: "Where would His Largeness sleep?"

CHARLOTTE: "Where do all unattached males sleep when they stay at my house? In my bed. Street and Camille and Mr. Enlightenment get one of the guest rooms."

I said, "The Enlightenment thing was just something I heard.

I thought it would make me sound educated."

CHARLOTTE: "I'm not fooled. You are."

EMILY, turning toward the others: "You think Heathcliff is still smart enough to consider planes in terms of science and beauty? Maybe he simply never had the intellectual fire power for med school. Maybe we've been bamboozled by his beauty."

ANNE: "The bamboozlement was your reaction. You're just saying that as a reaction to falling in love with him."

CHARLOTTE: "Come on, girls. You both know that what he lacked was drive and focus, not smarts."

ANNE: "He was a natural playboy."

EMILY: "Gorgeous, with rakish charm, a larcenous heart, and impulse control problems."

I asked, "Would impulse issues come into play when he felt burned by Veronica?"

EMILY: "Probably."

I said, "Enough that he could backstab her?"

All three of them seemed to consider the possibility.

EMILY: "Probably not."

CHARLOTTE: "It's clear you should meet Heathcliff and decide for yourself."

ANNE: "Yes, the professional cop should interrogate the delusional anti-hero and see if he is sufficiently anti-heroic." Then, looking embarrassed, she added, "Is it okay that I refer to you as a cop? You might be one of those Assistant Deputy Chief Commissioner Special Task Force Superintendents and have the title embroidered on your boxer shorts."

"It's okay. We're all cops. But I like the embroidery idea. How would I find this Heathcliff fellow?"

CHARLOTTE: "It's said he lives in Incline Village."

I gestured to the east. "In Tahoe? Just over there? Who's saying this?"

ANNE: "A woman Charlotte met in the Bay Area. But the woman doesn't know where in Incline Village."

EMILY: "Word is he hangs out in coffee shops with his girlfriend."

I said, "Would this be Isabel or a new flesh-and-blood girlfriend?"

ANNE: "Gotta be Isabel."

CHARLOTTE: "I can only visualize Isabel DeMille."

I said, "Her name when she died."

ANNE: "Probably her name still. Unless Heathcliff has married her postmortem and they changed her name." She turned to look at her sisters.

EMILY: "Find Heathcliff and ask. I'm sure he's still hanging with her, whatever her name."

I said, "Is there any remote chance she's really alive?"

EMILY: "Like we told you, she got all the way dead. She only lives in Heathcliff's mind."

I said, "And he has coffee with her."

CHARLOTTE: "So says the woman I recently saw." She signed something in front of Spot's face.

I had to ask. "May I ask what you're telling my dog?"

CHARLOTTE: "I'm asking him if he thinks blueberry scones go best with black Arabica coffee or latte Arabica. He doesn't seem to have an opinion."

"He struggles with differentiation. He thinks a scone is good regardless of libation."

ANNE: "You say that as if he drinks alcohol."

"He loves beer."

EMILY: "I suppose dogs who are home schooled have to jump extra hurdles to keep up with modern scone-and-coffee trends."

I said, "That's funny. Can you please tell me how I might find Heathcliff? The actual, non-real, non-fictional version."

ANNE: "I thought it would be fun to see him when we came to Tahoe. So I did a little research, but I wasn't successful. Charlotte knows more."

CHARLOTTE: "Just what the acquaintance told me in The City. She knew Heathcliff back when he jumped. The woman still works at UC San Francisco, and I bumped into her at the supermarket in Haight-Ashbury."

I said, "Is that the one with the produce section that practically glows when you see it from out in the street at night?"

CHARLOTTE: "Yes! Okay, I'll up my offer. Your own bedroom and your own office space. I've got a mini fridge I could put in your office…"

I raised my eyebrows but didn't speak.

CHARLOTTE: "Anyway, the woman and I talked about old times. The subject of Heathcliff came up, and the woman said she thought he lived in Incline Village at Tahoe. I wondered how Heathcliff got around because he hadn't been able to drive since his fall and Incline is not a very walkable town. The woman said Heathcliff told her he went everywhere on his bike, even in the winter. And with the new bike trail out to Sand Harbor, Heathcliff's favorite place, he was happy when the weather was nice."

EMILY: "Great concept, nice weather in Tahoe."

I said, "Best weather in the world when it's not snowing."

ANNE: "How long is that? Four months of the year?"

"About."

EMILY: "The woman said Heathcliff told her he'd found several coffee shops in Incline and nearby towns, and that's where he went to write."

I said, "The only other town near Incline Village is here. Kings Beach."

CHARLOTTE: "We know. And we've already looked in the coffee shops here."

I was curious. "What does Heathcliff write?"

EMILY: "Poetry, what else?"

"Poetry and coffee shops go together," I said. "In your research, did you get any hint of where Heathcliff might live?"

ANNE, shaking her head: "No. Nothing shows up in public property records. Not that he could afford a place in Incline, anyway. So I assume he's made a friend or two or simply responded to a roommate ad on Craigslist."

I said, "Any other place you can think of that I should look?"

CHARLOTTE: "Poets go to libraries, right?"

"Do any of you have a picture of Heathcliff?"

The three sisters looked at each other. After a long moment, Emily stood up and went inside the house. She came back holding a small leather purse. She opened it up, unzipped a miniature pouch, pulled out a photo that was an inch or so across, and handed it to me.

CHARLOTTE: "Emily! We never knew."

ANNE: "Em, you are such a surprise."

The photo was too small to show much detail. But the general picture of the man revealed why the sisters were focused on him. He looked like the movie great Clark Gable with disheveled hair and a curled lock that came down over one eye. He would be easy to recognize if I saw him, and if he hadn't changed his look.

"May I borrow this photo?"

EMILY, thinking carefully as if it were very valuable, "Yes. But can I have it back when you're done?"

"Certainly. Thanks," I said to them as a group. "I'll let you know if I have more questions."

CHARLOTTE: "If you do find him, please tell him he's invited to our reunion party on the South Shore tonight. For that matter, you are invited, too."

EMILY: "And bring His Largeness."

ANNE: "And Street and Camille."

I said, "Street and Camille also have Blondie, a Yellow Lab. Spot will stay home to keep Blondie company."

CHARLOTTE: "His Largeness has a girlfriend? And he's chivalrous! How sweet."

I said, "A girl who can out-run him, out-maneuver him, and out-smart him."

ANNE: "You mean like all women and men?"

"No argument," I said. "Where and when is your shindig?"

CHARLOTTE: "We have an oncologist colleague who is staying on the South Shore. His name is Benito Diaz."

ANNE: "Benito is a truly great guy. If only…"

EMILY: "Anyway, the party is at the vacation house Benito is renting."

"I met him," I said. "I'll be talking to him again. Maybe I'll see you all at the party."

ANNE, to the others: "Did you know Benito adopted his nephew?"

EMILY: "I suspected as much. There are men who act on good intent."

CHARLOTTE: "There are good men everywhere. Just not in my bed."

FOURTEEN

I forcibly separated Spot from the three doting women, and we drove three short miles to Incline Village.

Because the weather was so beautiful, I thought I'd try Sand Harbor first.

Unlike Kings Beach, with its great public beaches, Incline Village is a classic example of how bad city planning can make it so there are no decent public beaches or parks. The gorgeous natural sand crescent that lines Crystal Bay is mostly available only to the wealthy who own the zillion dollar homes on the boulevard known as Billionaire's Row.

But Sand Harbor State Park, a couple of miles south of town, makes up for the lack of beach access in town. The park has beaches and scenery that invite comparison with any in the world, and there is a great bike and walking path connecting Incline Village to the park. It would be an obvious place for Heathcliff to visit and spend time.

I paid the parking fee and drove into the parking lot, which, as in Kings Beach, showed the shoulder season advantages of increased parking availability.

Spot and I did a thorough search of the area, on the lookout for men who looked like movie stars. Sand Harbor has several beaches, large and small, a stage and amphitheater where they hold the Shakespeare On The Beach festival, areas of giant boulders, and some secluded wooded areas. An hour later, I was satisfied that Heathcliff was not there.

We drove back to Incline Village and stopped at the Sierra Nevada College campus, which was in the process of merging with the University of Nevada, Reno. The school library is a beautiful building with wooden posts and beams and tables with old-fashioned lamps with lamp shades. There were multiple students at tables and in chairs, but all looked to be in their early 20s or younger. Heathcliff would be closer to 40. I walked up to the counter and waited while a middle-aged woman was working. She dragged a computer mouse, clicked a few times, then turned to me.

"May I help you?"

"Yes, please. I'm an investigator looking for a man named Horatio Harris who may be able to help us in solving a crime."

Her eyes widened with concern.

I held out the photo and said, "He's not a suspect of any kind. But he may have some knowledge about a person who is. He's a poet who spends time in libraries. Can you please tell me if you've seen this man?"

She took the photo and studied it for a brief moment. "No, I haven't seen him." She looked a little longer. "I would remember if I had." She handed the photo back.

"Thank you for your time."

We drove through town and stopped at the public library. I said the same thing to a young man working there.

He looked at the photo and said, "I'd be interested in meeting this guy. Especially with him being a poet. But no, I haven't seen him."

My next stop was the Starbucks. Same response.

A block and a half down was a coffee shop with no major brand name. Same response.

Spot was snoozing when I got back to the Prius. Fresh air at the beach does that to both of us, but I didn't have a place to nap. I left him in the Prius and walked across the highway and found another coffee shop, this one also local. It didn't have the large selection of Starbucks, but it smelled even better. I walked up to the counter to show them the photo of Heathcliff and to maybe get a coffee and pastry when I noticed a man sitting alone at a table in the corner. His appearance was unchanged from the photo. I put the photo back in my pocket.

I stayed back for a bit to assess his situation. His clothes looked slept in, his hair was messy and unwashed, his forehead was creased with worry. Yet somehow he telegraphed charisma.

A pair of large binoculars hung from his neck. There were two cups of coffee on the table. He sipped from one. The other cup was across the small table. His cup had been partially drunk. The other cup was full. The other chair was empty. Heathcliff mumbled as if talking to an imaginary person. I went to the counter, ordered my own cup, and walked over.

"Good morning," I said. "May I join you?" I reached for the other chair.

The man reached out his hand and waved me away from where I stood. "That's Isabel's chair."

"Oh, sorry. Is this side okay?"

He seemed to consider the position. "Yes. That's okay."

I pulled a chair over from another table and sat down.

I said, "Isabel is…"

He hesitated. "Isabel DeMille. My friend. Special friend. A poet."

"She writes poems?"

He nodded.

I knew nothing about poetry, but I wanted to get him talking. "A particular type of poetry?" I said.

"Like the poet Elizabeth Barrett Browning, if I had to find a comparison. But I think Isabel's poems are more inspired. And her meter is more innovative." His eyes moistened. He ran the back of his hand across them. "Of course, many would think it blasphemous what I say about Barrett Browning."

Maybe I frowned. The man could probably tell I didn't know Barrett Browning.

He said, "'How do I love thee? Let me count the ways.' The truth is, it's catchy stuff. But I'm a heretic for calling serious poetry catchy."

"Oh," I said, though I wasn't sure what he meant. "I've heard that How do I love thee poem. I suppose everyone's heard it."

Heathcliff made a single nod. "Isabel isn't famous like Browning. Unlike Browning, Isabel has never shown her poetry to anyone but me. Isabel is more like Emily Dickinson, another follower of Barrett Browning and a hundred plus years before Isabel. Theirs is an intensely private life. A need to create."

I'd never thought much about such things. Heathcliff probably sensed it. But I recalled that Benito Diaz had quoted Dickinson, and now Heathcliff had brought her up.

"There's huge value in creation," he said. "Not so much value in audience."

"Doesn't an audience help the world remember the creation?"

"Probably. But do we need the remembering? Dickinson didn't think so. She made Lavinia promise to burn her papers after her death. Correspondence. Poems."

"Lavinia…" I said.

"Emily's sister. In the end, Lavinia didn't burn the poems, and the world is glad for that. But Emily would have been conflicted. She organized her poems as if to save them. But in the end she asked that they be destroyed."

"Does Isabel have a sister?"

"If only," Heathcliff said. "All Isabel has is me and my dreams and hallucinations. And she's known me long enough to know that my hallucinations provide no pleasant companionship."

"But your hallucinations aren't obvious here."

"No. They stay away when I have coffee with Isabel."

I glanced at the empty chair and the undrunk coffee.

"Do lots of people write poems?" I asked, trying to make conversation, yet also curious.

"I don't know. I think many poets are private about it. Maybe like Dickinson. Very private."

I thought about how Benito Diaz mentioned the poem his sister quoted just before she died. 'Because I couldn't stop for death, he kindly stopped for me.'

I also remembered that the Brontë sisters said Heathcliff was originally one of their medical school classmates. Before he attempted suicide.

"Do you remember a former medical school classmate named Benito Diaz?" I asked.

Heathcliff gave me a blank look that morphed into something more specific.

"I think so. His sister died from bleeding, right?

Hemophilia."

"He talked about Emily Dickinson," I said. "Now you mention her. That seems unusual."

He shook his head. "It would seem unusual for anyone not to mention her every now and then," he said. "She was probably the greatest American poet. We even had a professor in med school who would read one of her poems before class every morning."

"That could add up to a lot of poems."

"She wrote almost two thousand poems, but no one knew until after she died."

"Sorry if this seems like a dumb question, but what makes her poems so special?"

"A poem is often about your deepest feelings. Sometimes, your darkest feelings. The point of a poem is considering ideas in a metaphorical, rhythmic way. Dickinson could crystallize those feelings. That's what made her great. She could immortalize those feelings in words. Some poets write fancy. Dickinson wrote simple. 'Hope is the thing with feathers.' You never forget such a metaphor about birds or hope."

"Why did she write so many poems, if she didn't want to show them to anyone?"

"Sometimes the whole point of writing poems is to put down private thoughts and not show them to anyone. Something that private… Privacy disappears when you've told someone you've written something private. It's like telling someone you have a secret. The point of the secret is destroyed. Of course, some secrets are merely puzzles. Dickinson used puzzle secrets. She referred to people by pseudonyms. My Master. My Philadelphia. My Dearest. Guess who."

"Is Isabel private about her poetry?"

"She's private about everything. Sometimes I ask her about her past, but she doesn't answer."

"More privacy," I said.

"That kept me from knowing her better. Even so, I know her so well. So completely. I couldn't live without her. Now, all we have left are the chairs she likes."

I waited for him to continue, but it seemed like he'd stopped.

"Which chairs are those?" I asked.

He looked down at the chair he was sitting on.

"She wrote a poem about them. It's called 'These Chairs.' I can't remember all the words. Something about 'Way stations and Journey's punctuation.' But mostly it's slant rhymes. Like Dickinson. 'Troubled pace, Twisted past, Transferred pains.'"

He paused, then continued. "They're in this coffee shop. In my apartment. And there's a bench not far from here. It has a view of the lake. The plaque on the bench says, 'in loving memory of Francis Johns.' But to me it's Isabel's bench. I could add a plaque to it. Isabel DeMille. Put it on the bottom side where I'd be the only person to see it."

"More privacy," I said.

"You understand. I like that." He looked out the window. "We used to get sandwiches from the Raley's deli and take them through the woods to that bench. But we don't do that so much anymore. We come to these chairs in the coffee shop. I sit across from her. Her presence in her chair is palpable. She exists."

I didn't know what to say. I thought of the comment Anne Smythe made, something to do with Sarte, a name I'd heard but didn't know. Maybe essence does, in fact, precede existence.

Heathcliff looked as if he was submerging into darkness.

I said, "I'm reluctant to change the subject, but I wanted to ask you something. I was talking to the Brontë sisters. They told me about you."

The man looked puzzled. "I remember. The triplets. In med school."

"Right. They said you knew Veronica Eastern."

The man seemed to look into another world.

"I'm sorry to tell you that Veronica Eastern was murdered."

His eyes made a kind of flash. Widened but with the lower lids raised. "The poem ebbs," he said. "The page ends." His eyes went back to normal. Almost a blank look. Dull.

Was he acting? I doubted it. But I wasn't certain.

"The Brontë sisters said you were burned by Veronica."

He nodded slowly, remembering. "She thought I was rich. She thought I was smart. When she found out I couldn't stay in school, she flew away. Like an airplane. She could have had the most devoted companion. But she threw it away. Isabel told me it was Veronica's loss."

He looked out the window and up toward the sky. "Planes are magic." He waved his hand through the air. "Imagine floating on this stuff. There's hardly anything there."

"I'm a pilot, so I think about that a lot."

"You're a pilot?" He sounded excited. "What do you fly?"

"Small planes that I rent. Like a Cessna Skyhawk. Or a One-Fifty."

He recognized the names but didn't say anything. Maybe saying those aircraft models to Heathcliff was like telling an auto enthusiast that I drove an old, rusted Jeep.

I wanted to move the conversation back to the doctor who was murdered.

"Have you seen or heard from Veronica recently?" I asked.

"I saw her in med school. I saw her at the library after Isabel fell. Then I woke up. They said I fell, too. How long ago was that? Twelve years? I contacted Veronica. Wrote her a poem. But she had gotten involved with some other guy. So I went back to Isabel. Isabel's poetry could fly. Like airplanes."

"Was it upsetting that Veronica stopped seeing you?"

"Of course. It made me very..." The man took a deep breath, held it, breathed it out slowly, the classic technique for cooling down when one was angry. "It was frustrating," he finally said.

"You haven't seen Veronica since med school?"

"No." He looked down at his coffee. Frowned. "I don't want to see her. Isabel doesn't want me to see her." He pointed up toward the sky. "I saw a biplane up there."

"Fun," I said. "I've never flown a biplane. Like a little flying sports car."

"This one was big. Real big. And silent. I saw it twice."

"You saw a large silent biplane." It didn't make much sense because biplanes were generally small and, because they were often tuned for aerobatic performance, their engines made lots of noise.

"Interesting. Tell me, have you had any contact with the doctors from medical school?"

He shook his head.

"The Brontë sisters wanted me to invite you to their reunion party. It's being held tonight on the South Shore where Benito Diaz is renting a vacation home."

Another head shake. "Thanks, but I don't want to go."

"They would love to see you."

"But they wouldn't like Isabel to come."

"I think they'd like her to come." As I said it, I thought it was true. But it felt awkward that I was inviting an imaginary person on behalf of the Brontë sisters.

"No," Heathcliff said, "they would look at me funny. They would think, 'He used to be smart with words. Now he talks but isn't good with words. And he spends his time with a poet who's good with words, but she's silent.'"

I realized that anything I said would sound like a protest. It wouldn't change his mind. And I didn't see anything good that would come of him attending the party unless he revealed something about Veronica Eastern.

"I understand. Before I go, you knew Veronica Eastern better than most. Do you have any thoughts about her murder?"

Heathcliff frowned as if thinking hard.

"Look for the plane," he said.

That was a surprise. "The biplane?"

He gave me a somber nod. "When an unusual plane comes into Tahoe right around the time that Veronica came to Tahoe, and she dies…" He drank the rest of his coffee, which must have been cold.

"You think there's a connection? It's not just a coincidence?"

"I'm not a doctor. But I know that when a patient suddenly develops different symptoms at the same time, they are probably connected. The doctor should search for that possible connection."

It was a clear statement that stood out from other things

he'd said, things that suggested the presence of a woman who died over a decade ago. It was the same approach that law enforcement officers use. Assume there are no coincidences.

"Is there a way I can contact you if I have other questions?"

He looked around at the other tables in the coffee shop. "I usually sit here." He pointed to a far corner. "Sometimes over there."

"I was thinking about a phone number."

He shook his head. "I don't have a phone."

"Email?"

"No."

"Perhaps I could have your physical address?"

Another head shake. "My roommate said I can only stay if I don't tell people where. He doesn't like strangers knocking."

"Okay. I can look for you here. Do you have regular hours?"

"I usually come here for breakfast, but sometimes lunch. Eight a.m., or one p.m., but sometimes not."

"Okay. If I want to see you, I'll try here, morning first."

He nodded.

We both stood up. I thanked him. We went outside where he unlocked a mountain bike. I made a little wave, but he ignored me as he rode off into the nearby forest.

I went back to the Prius. Spot was groggy with sleep. I'd read that lions sleep 17 hours a day. Even if it was a huge exaggeration, I had no trouble believing it. Spot wasn't far behind. Have some breakfast. Take a nap. Go for a short run in the forest. Take a nap. Meet some ladies who hug you until your skin feels like you have rug burns. Run on the beach. Take another nap.

"You ready to go have a late lunch?" I asked.

He looked at me with droopy eyes. Which meant yes. And after lunch, it would be time to take another nap.

FIFTEEN

I parked the Prius in my office lot and let Spot out of the back seat. Compared to my old Jeep, the Prius was quiet and smooth and probably got great gas mileage. But it seemed to have no personality. Was I nuts to think about whether machines had personality? Probably. We climbed up to my office on the second level.

I'd just loaded the coffee maker, and Spot had just made two complete turns before lying down on his Harlequin Great Dane camo bed when we heard two sets of footsteps coming up the office stairs. Dr. Benito Diaz walked in my door. With him was a boy just on the cusp of starting his teenage growth spurt. The boy looked vaguely like a young version of Benito but with lighter coloring.

Spot jumped to his feet and pushed forward with more enthusiasm than normal. Life experience had taught him that women and girls were all in love with him, and he responded in kind.

But he hadn't known many boys, and he was very curious. What are these humans with loud voices and uncoordinated moves like men but who obviously aren't men?

The boy seemed delighted and put on a huge smile. "Whoa, this dog is huge! Huge and awesome!" He reached his hand forward. Spot sniffed it, his tail on slow wag.

"Meet Spot."

"I can pet him, right? He's like, you know, safe to pet?"

"Yes. I can almost guarantee you'll leave with as many fingers as you walked in with."

Benito said, "I vaguely remember meeting this dog before, but I was pretty out of it."

"That's an understatement. Until Diamond gave you the

ABC assessment, I wasn't even sure you were going to live."

The boy put his hand on the top of Spot's head, carefully slid his hand back in the gentlest of pets, then ran his hand down the side of Spot's neck. Then down the other side. "Awesome," he said again. "Spot, you're awesome." The boy's moves were nothing like the solid, heavy rubs and smacks that Spot got from men. More like soft touching as if he were learning about an entirely new kind of creature.

"Owen, I want you to meet my nephew Damen," Benito said.

"Hey, Damen." I raised my hand in a largely pointless gesture.

The boy was completely occupied by my dog, and he ignored me just as he ignored his uncle.

Damen was a thin lanky boy with blue eyes and a rock-star mop of sandy-colored hair that probably made the girls think he was hot stuff. Damen had a smile to match the hair. His teeth weren't especially straight, but they were very white. He smiled a lot, and he had charm, despite a goofy quality that would probably go away after another year or so.

Eventually, Damen turned toward me and shook my hand with the kind of enthusiasm that made it seem like he really liked meeting new people. "So good to meet you, Mr. McKenna!"

"You, too," I said. "But you can call me Owen."

He shot Benito a concerned look as if asking for his approval.

Benito made a single nod, smooth and understated.

Damen said, "Okay, Owen." He grinned.

"Benito, you are looking better. Your swelling has gone down. I hope you're feeling better."

He gave me a tired smile. "I only look better if you think green bruises look better than blue bruises." He hesitated. "I wanted to ask if you've had any success with finding Tucker Dopple?"

"I've learned some things and gotten close to catching him once. But he slipped away." I didn't want to explain that Dopple had shot at me while I was driving, and I survived largely by being lucky.

"Maybe this is a stupid idea," Diaz said, "but on TV they always show how they track crooks by their credit card use."

"Yeah, that's sometimes a possibility. Unfortunately, Dopple isn't using a credit card that we know of. So he's likely staying with someone he knows. Don't worry. We'll find him."

"You sound confident. What gives you confidence?"

"Because Dopple's stupid yet cocky. When you were in the van and he spoke of sacrificial ceremonies, and his Chief Sturgis moniker…" I shook my head. "Guys who think of things like that are not focused on the here and now. They make lousy criminals. They're impulsive. Distracted. Successful criminals have to make a coherent, careful plan. That's not Tucker Dopple."

Benito nodded thoughtfully. "Thanks for your effort and the info. I'll remain hopeful." He glanced at Damen. "We also wanted to invite you to a party we're having tonight for the UCSF doctor reunion. Most of the docs are coming. Some are on the South Shore. Some are driving down from the North Shore."

"Thanks for the invite. Where is the party?"

"It's at the rental house where we're staying on Keller up by Heavenly Ski Resort."

"It's awesome," Damen said. "You can walk to the ski run at Heavenly and ski down to the lift. I'm trying to talk Uncle Benny into renting it again in March during spring break."

"As you can see, Damen has a large appetite for the finer things in life."

"It's your fault I'm getting… What do you call it?" Damen paused, remembering, "Habituated to quality. Because you always demand the best."

"Let me check with my girlfriend and her daughter," I said.

"Oh, you have a daughter," Diaz said.

"I do now. A stepdaughter, Camille Dexter. May I bring them if they're up for it?"

"Yes, of course."

He gave me directions and time, and they left.

That evening, we left Spot and Blondie together at Street's condo. Before we left, Camille brought Spot over to the couch. She kneeled on the cushions, then lifted one leg over Spot's back in a horse-riding posture. But she didn't coax him to go anywhere. She just sat on his back, then leaned forward and lay on him, hugging him.

Street looked at me and frowned. I shrugged. Both of us recognized that the behavior was unusual. Neither of us knew what motivated it. But it was probably nothing more than affection before she went off to a new, strange experience. Then the three of us left the dogs and drove in Street's VW Beetle to the party. Instead of sitting on my lap, Camille wanted to sit in back. She seemed low key.

As Street parked on a dark street, she flipped on the interior lights and turned around to look at Camille in the back seat so the girl could read her lips. "You are so quiet. Are you okay?" she said.

"Um, yes," Camille said. Her normally high-pitched voice was even higher than normal. "But I've never been to a party. I don't know what to do." She signed as she spoke.

Now we understood.

"Oh, hon, I didn't realize that Grandpa Charlie never brought you to a party," Street said.

"He baked cupcakes for my birthday. He called that a party. He lit candles in the camper, and the two of us listened to music." Camille's voice was thick with emotion.

I was facing back toward Camille as well.

Street glanced at me, then said, "There will be several people here. They are mostly doctors, mostly very nice. So here's what we'll do. When we walk in and meet some people, Owen or I will stay with you the entire time."

"I don't need a babysitter," Camille said, her voice sounding shaky.

"No. We won't be babysitters. We'd just like your company." Street turned to me. "Right, hon?"

"Right. I'm not good at dealing with lots of people, Camille. So I was going to ask you to stay with me. Will you be my party buddy?" I reached my hand back and gave her a little fist bump.

She met my fist with hers. We got out of the car. I took Camille's hand and walked with her to the house.

The front door had a large gable overhang, and standing underneath it were three women and one man, all well-dressed, all seeming to speak at once. The front door was very wide and stood open. Beach Boys music spilled out.

"And who is this?" one of them said, leaning over toward Camille.

Camille said, "My name is Camille Dexter." She signed as she spoke, using just her left hand because I was holding her right.

I realized for the first time that she didn't sign because she thought a stranger would understand ASL. She signed because it communicated that she was deaf. I also realized that she appeared to be an ambidextrous signer, able to use either hand.

"What's that?" a woman said. "Speak up girl, it's hard to understand your words. Oh, wait, you're signing. I get it. Sorry, girl. I'm slow off the mark."

Camille repeated herself, then added, "It's hard for you to understand me because I'm deaf."

"Oh, Camille, you're adorable. We don't care if you're deaf. I'm Bev. Come with me. I'll show you to the food and introduce you to Nanna."

The woman took Camille's free hand and pulled her. Camille let go of my hand.

"Are you sure?" I said.

Camille nodded. She and the woman walked away from me.

As the woman pulled Camille through the front door and inside, I turned, wide-eyed to Street. "Is that okay? Should I go pull her back?"

"I think it's okay," Street said. "Camille is sometimes insecure. But she's enormously competent. She nodded that it was okay. She'll be fine."

"She'll charm them, too," I said.

Benito appeared at the door. I introduced Street to him.

"Ah, the entomologist. You went to Berkeley."

"Owen told you that?" Street said.

"No. But I Googled you. I hope that's okay."

"Oh, yes. I'm a reluctant internet subject, but I'm getting used to it, as I spend much of my day on a computer."

"Come in. I want you to meet Damen, my nephew. He has thoughts of pursuing science. It would be great for him to meet an actual entomologist."

We followed Benito inside. The foyer was large and built in a kind of Tahoe Rustic design with big timbers holding up high roofs. On the stone floor was a huge rug in a Native American design. There was a kitchen off to one side, and it seemed that bedrooms stretched off in the other direction.

The main room had opposing walls of high windows. One window wall faced up toward the ski runs of Heavenly resort. The opposite wall looked out at the lake a mile away. A side wall had a huge cobblestone fireplace. A sparkling fire crackled behind a tall, fireplace screen.

The centerpiece of the room was a black grand piano. Benito's nephew Damen sat on the bench, playing a soft Boogie Woogie, his left hand running the bass line, his right hand playing chords. It was a simple version, but very fun. Bev, the woman who pulled Camille into the party sat next to Damen. She tried to add a treble duet line above Damen's chords.

Camille was standing next to the piano, her hand on the wooden case. She may have been shy attending her first party with multiple people. But she'd found a good place to be. Her eyes were half shut, her head was moving to the beat. In the short weeks I'd known her, I'd learned that deaf people absorb sound through their bodies even though their ears don't process the vibrations. I knew that, even though Camille was deaf, she was absorbing the music by feel.

The woman's efforts at a duet crashed and became discordant, Damen lost his groove and stopped, and the two of them laughed with gusto. It was a pleasure to see, a woman—a doctor, no doubt—in her late thirties having fun with a precocious boy at the piano.

Benito brought Street over to meet Damen.

Bev put her arm around Damen. He stopped playing.

As the music stopped, Camille opened her eyes.

I walked over and stood next to her. I put my hand on her shoulder. She saw me and seemed reassured and more relaxed, and that made me feel better than I had in a long time.

Bev turned to me and spoke as if Camille wasn't there. "That girl of yours is a sweetheart. It seems like she loves the music even though she can't hear it. Or maybe she can hear better than she lets on?"

In my peripheral vision I saw that Camille was watching the woman's lips and no doubt understood what she said.

At that moment, I understood something of Camille's dilemma, of all deaf people's dilemmas. Dealing with people who act as if a deaf person doesn't exist must be one of the most exasperating human interactions. And suggesting that a deaf person might overstate the extent of their deafness was very rude. No wonder that deaf people sometimes keep to themselves or other deaf people.

I tapped Camille's shoulder and gestured for her to come with me.

She took my hand, and I walked her over to the buffet. I picked up two plates, handed one to her, pointed at the food, and said, "Help yourself to whatever food you want."

"But I shouldn't take too much." She signed with her free hand.

"Don't worry about it. This is common at parties. When a party host puts out a buffet, they want to know that people enjoyed it. You show that by eating."

Camille nodded understanding and put a small selection on her plate. I followed, and we went over to a sitting area that looked out at the deck. The party was quite loud, but it was quieter where we sat. As we ate, we looked through the windows at the partygoers under the heat-lamp reflectors out on the deck.

The people were illuminated by a hanging string of lights that arced along the deck's perimeter like cables on a suspension bridge. The Brontë sisters were among the people under the heat lamps.

"Those three ladies are twins," Camille said, looking at the sisters.

"Yes. Identical triplets are quite rare."

"Triplets," Camille repeated. She'd probably never seen triplets before. She may not have heard the word before, either. "Do they happen the same way as twins do?"

"Yes. Street can explain the science to you."

I ate. Camille nibbled as she watched the triplet sisters.

"They're talking about someone who died," she said.

That shouldn't have been a surprise to me, but I hadn't anticipated it. Of course, Camille could read lips on people outside almost as easily as with someone close and inside. It reminded me of a super-power story. The ability to understand what someone is saying even when they are out of earshot…

I didn't want to encourage eavesdropping in general, but Camille had certainly piqued my curiosity. The Brontë sisters had been with Veronica Eastern when she died.

I tapped Camille's shoulder so she would look at me. "That's curious," I said. "I wonder what they are saying."

Camille looked back out the window, then spoke. She was translating yet another language, the language of lip movements. "'Ronnie probably dessert it. It not an I for…' something. 'It's pree ven… mur death.'"

Ronnie probably deserved it. It's not an eye for an eye. It's prevention of more death.

That was more than I could have asked for. It was only an editorial comment. Not any kind of evidence of crime. But it was revealing.

Benito came over.

"Benito, please meet Camille," I said.

"What a pleasure," he said. He reached for her hand, then smiled and nodded at her.

"I'd like to introduce you to the others who came for the

reunion," he said.

"Camille?" I said. "Are you okay here for a bit? Or do you want to meet all these people?"

She nodded. "I can meet people."

Benito took us through the crowd. I came to understand that about half of the twenty people were doctors. The rest were a couple of spouses, two or three friends, a neighbor from next door and also one or two from the Bay Area.

"Here's the most important person in the house," Benito said. "Nanna Hansen? I want you to meet Owen McKenna and Camille..."

"Dexter," I said.

"Camille Dexter," Benito corrected. "Owen McKenna is the private detective I told you about."

Nanna Hansen turned toward Camille. "This delightful girl is Camille?" She reached down and took Camille's hand in both of hers. "I'm so happy to meet you."

"Hi," Camille said. "I'm sorry I couldn't hear your name. I'm deaf."

Nanna immediately started signing as she spoke. "My name is Nanna Hansen. I used to teach ASL to one of our employee groups at Apple. I have several friends who are deaf. You are now one of them."

Nanna pulled Camille close, then spoke and signed. Camille smiled and nodded. Then Nanna turned to me.

She was a small, fine-boned woman in her mid-seventies. She had short white hair and intense green eyes that suggested equally intense intelligence.

"Pleased to meet you, Owen," she said. "Your reputation, by Benito's telling, puts you in league with Sherlock Holmes. And from what Damen said about your dog, he could out-do the Hound of the Baskervilles."

I grinned. "Except that his teeth don't glow. Unless, maybe, he thinks he's about to eat steak."

"One of Conan Doyle's oversights," Nanna Hansen said. "Phosphorus is quite toxic and even dangerous. You'd think a doctor would be more careful researching luminescent chemicals to paint on a fictional dog's teeth."

"I didn't know Conan Doyle was a doctor."

"Like lots of writers," she said. "Probably some of these doctors in this room are writers."

"I'm curious how you know about phosphorus."

"She's an industrial designer," Benito said, "and they think about every possible use for various materials. She worked at Apple these last many years before she retired." Benito paused, then said, "Nanna is our adopted mother, grandmother, all-around guide to the universe. Everything about life I don't know, Nanna knows. And half of what I've learned about life, I learned from Nanna."

"Then I need Nanna in my life," I said.

"Industrial design," Nanna said, "is all I really know. That and a little bit of common sense."

I thanked them both and explained it was time to go.

Camille looked back through the windows at the Brontë sisters.

I made a little tug on the shoulder of her jacket.

I took her hand, and we walked back through the party. I stopped by the piano where Damen was still noodling around, this time with a different older woman sitting next to him and fawning over him.

If I didn't have Street, I'd have to take up the piano.

I said hello and goodbye to Damen.

"It was so nice of you to come, Mr. Mc… Owen. And you, too, Camille."

"You and Benito and I will connect up another time," I said.

Damen waved goodbye at us, and Camille made a little wave back. She seemed comfortable even though this was her first large party. I chalked it up to a solid constitution. It was as if she knew herself well, her abilities, her knowledge, and those areas where she didn't have either.

We found Street.

I said, "We just said goodbye to Benito and Nanna." Then to Street, I added, "Camille and I are going to move toward the door."

"I'll meet you there in a few minutes," Street said.

I tapped Camille's shoulder. She looked up at me. "Do you want to wait for Street inside or out."

"Outside," she said and made a sign with her free hand.

We stepped outside and sat on a little built-in bench by the front door.

"What did you think of the party?" I asked Camille.

"It would be hard to be around so many people for very long."

"I agree. I'm fine for a bit. Then I need fresh air and, especially, silence." As I said it, I realized that could come off as a loaded comment to a deaf person. But Camille just shrugged and made a little nod.

After a minute or two, Camille said, "Do you know people who fly airplanes?"

"Yes. I know several, including myself."

"You fly planes?"

"Yes. It's very fun. Maybe I can take you up sometime."

Camille did not say yes. She seemed to think about it.

Eventually, she said, "Is it hard to fly a plane?"

"Not generally. Each plane is a little different. But most of them work in similar ways. Why do you ask?"

"I was just wondering. Those twins… The triplets. They fly planes."

There was another surprise. "Do you remember their words?"

"It was kind of like, 'When I'm flying, I always do a full pre something."

"Preflight?" I said.

"I think so. I don't know what that means."

"It means carefully checking out the plane before you fly. Was it just one of them who spoke?"

Camille shook her head. "Another one said, 'You don't have to if you just watched the same plane land. Just make sure it has gas."

"Two of them talked about flying?" I said.

Camille nodded.

"Did you hear... Did they use names? Any idea who was speaking?"

She shrugged. "One has a big scar."

"Yes."

"It was the other two."

"That's interesting, Camille."

I was going to give her an enthusiastic thanks, but I didn't want to give her the impression that listening in on others' conversations was a good thing.

I thought about going to ask the sisters about what Camille had told me. But I didn't want to make Camille uncomfortable. I could leave her with Street, but she was not in view. I also realized that the sisters were smart and savvy. If they had anything to hide, they would continue to keep it well-hidden.

Street drove home and invited me to stay at her condo. I accepted, and we had a quiet thoughtful evening, talking with Camille about her reaction to her first party, which she thought was fine but nothing special.

But in the night we were awakened by her cries.

Street ran to her bedroom, scooped her up, and sat with her while the girl woke up and explained her dream, which was about Grandpa Charlie dying.

I stayed in the living room, not sure what was appropriate regarding a child's nightmare.

"Is Owen here?" I heard Camille say.

"Yes," Street said. "Would you like him to come in here?"

Camille's response was too soft to hear.

"Owen," Street said, "Camille wants you to join us."

So I went in and sat on Camille's bed with them.

"My dream was about a man with a gun," Camille said.

"I'm so sorry," Street said.

Camille turned to me. "Street told me that after you stopped being a cop, you stopped using a gun."

Camille's phrasing made me wonder if Street had actually said that I stopped carrying a gun. But maybe Street was presenting things in a way that would make the most sense for a girl who had only known the two of us for a little more than a month. And maybe it didn't matter at all.

"I used a gun as a cop. But when I quit, I didn't think I'd need one."

"Why? Now someone is trying to hurt you. What if he shoots at you?"

I didn't think I'd spoken about Tucker Dopple around her. But she'd heard somehow.

As for him shooting at me, it had already happened, but it wasn't an appropriate time, if ever, to point that out.

"Guns are dangerous," I said. "I thought it would be more comfortable to go through life without a dangerous weapon."

"Why did you quit being a cop?"

"I had a case that was very stressful." There was no point in saying that the case was a bank robbery where I'd shot and killed the robber, a kid who was not that much older than Camille. "So I went on a long sabbatical. During that time…"

"What is a sabat…?"

"Sorry." I turned to face Camille more directly so she could see my lips better. I tried out my weak sign language skills and signed the letters of the word sabbatical while I spelled it.

She giggled.

"Why are you laughing?"

"Because your signing is funny."

"Are you making fun of my sign language skills?"

She laughed some more. Street was on Camille's other side, grinning.

"I don't think you could get a job using sign language," Camille said.

"I agree. You've taught my dog more sign language than I know."

Camille said, "What is a sabbatical?"

"It's kind of like a long vacation, only not for play. It's for study. In my case, I studied the job of being a cop. In the end, I decided I no longer wanted to be a cop. Twenty years was enough. So I quit and moved up here to Tahoe."

"Are you glad you did that?"

Another insightful question. "Yes."

"And you met Street."

"Yes. Best thing that ever happened to me."

Street squeezed my leg.

"Why?" Camille asked.

"Because she cares so much about every little living thing. Including bugs. And she is adopting you."

"Will I make things not as fun for you and Street?"

"No, silly. You make everything better!" I reached over and gave her a hug and then gave her the finger poke on the sides of her waist that makes her laugh.

She giggled again. "You make things better, too."

I thought, how could I not love a kid like that? I stopped moving and just looked at her.

"Why are you looking at me?" she asked.

"Because you're a good friend to me. A friend can make everything better. Street and I always want you to know that. It helps when you get scared."

Camille was suddenly serious again. "What if I forget and I get scared again?"

Street and I looked at each other for a moment.

I reached for Camille's hand. I turned it palm up and used my finger to draw a circle on her upturned palm. Then I closed her open hand. "This is how you will remember. A circle represents the three of us being connected, being friends. Any time you feel like you need a friend, you draw a circle on your palm and hold it. That will help you remember that Street and I will always be there."

Camille looked at both of us and then lay down on the bed, turned sideways, held her closed hand near her face, and went to sleep.

SIXTEEN

The next morning, Street had Camille help serve up breakfast. A frittata with grilled onion, fresh asparagus, tomato, green pepper, both cheddar and feta cheese, and spinach. The veggies were so numerous, it seemed more like a cooked salad with an egg binder. On the side was dry toast made from some kind of heavy, coarse bread. There was no jam or butter for the toast.

I was very pleased to be served good food by sweet loving people. But I had a private longing for bacon and hash browns and a big stack of pancakes with butter and syrup. I wisely kept my thoughts to myself.

I said, "It's very smart that you're eating such healthy food, Camille."

"No big deal," Camille said with a shrug. "Anyone can be smart."

Maybe I looked skeptical.

"Even a dog can be smart," she said.

"Sure." Did I telegraph doubt?

Camille looked at me like I had no clue. She lifted her hands up and clapped them together twice.

Both Blondie and Spot lifted their heads to look at her.

Camille looked at Spot. She signed with several fast movements.

Spot jumped to his feet and trotted over to the refrigerator.

Camille walked over, opened the door, and pulled out a treat. She gave it to him. He chomped once and swallowed it down.

"That's amazing," I said. "My dog just understood sign language." As I said it, I recalled that when we practice suspect takedowns or rescue searches, I drop my hand next to his head and point toward the suspect. Still…

"He knows more," Camille said. She clapped again and signed some more.

Spot took three steps to Street's laundry nook. He looked at Camille, then looked up at the cupboard door where Street kept the detergent.

Camille raised up on tiptoes, opened the door, pulled out a little bag. She reached in, got a treat, and gave it to him.

"Unbelievable," I said. "My dog is bilingual."

Camille made some more signing moves. This time, Spot just watched her, his brow furrowed as if he didn't understand.

Blondie jumped to her feet and ran over to the guest bathroom. Camille went inside, fetched a treat, and gave it to Blondie.

I turned to Street. "I already knew that Camille was a Rhodes Scholar-type kid. But Rhodes Scholar dogs? Have I been depriving Spot all these years by not teaching him other languages? Maybe I should teach him German, where his ancestors were originally bred. He might want to know his roots."

"Maybe. But to do that, you'd have to know German."

"Good point. Anyway, Spot's not like a border collie, smart as a seven-year-old kid. But Camille is teaching me that he's smarter than I thought."

"That's what scientists keep discovering, right?" Street said. "All animals are smarter than we thought."

"So why do we make that misjudgment?"

"Because people are arrogant," Street said. "We think we're so special. I read about an African Grey Parrot who uses the voice-recognition 'Alexa' computer to order treats from Amazon. He says, 'Hey, Alexa, I want the bulk pack of graham crackers.' And it shows up on the doorstop two days later."

"No wonder I'm a Luddite. I don't like that technology."

"But you adapt well," she said.

"Adaptable but resistant. Give me a dog, maybe a horse, and old fashioned books to read during long winter nights by the fire or by a kerosene lantern. I've already got the log cabin and wood-burning stove."

"Yes, but would you adapt well to hunting deer for food, and slaughtering chickens you raised yourself, and digging up wild onions and carrots, and…?"

"No."

"Time travelers don't get to bring supermarkets back in time," Street said, grinning.

"It must be hard to be a scientist, always logical," I said.

After breakfast, Spot and I headed to the office in the Prius. As I entered the southbound tunnel at Cave Rock, the driver's window and windshield shattered simultaneously. It took me a moment to figure out what happened, my thoughts starting with the idea that rocks had fallen from above the entrance to the tunnel, before progressing to an understanding that I'd come under rifle fire.

A bullet had come from behind my left side, gone through the side window, missed my head, then exited through the windshield. The windshield had cracked in a big spider web, but no glass had fallen into my lap. I slowed inside the tunnel, coasting to a near stop, then realized there was no point in stopping. The tunnels at Cave Rock are one-way.

I also realized there was no point in trying to turn around once I was out of the tunnel. Even if I raced back through the northbound tunnel to give chase to the shooter, I had no idea what kind of vehicle to look for or even if I was looking for a vehicle. Tucker Dobble could have been on foot, shooting from the forest on the northeast side of Cave Rock.

As for giving chase in the Prius, it wouldn't be possible. The windshield was too fractured to easily see through.

I continued on and turned off at the entrance to Cave Rock State Park, which is a thin strip of land with a parking lot, boat launch, and picnic tables. I pulled over, got out, and looked at the car. The windshield cracks all emanated from a single hole in front of the passenger seat. When I sighted through to the hole in the driver's window, it appeared the bullet had just missed the tip of my nose.

Tucker Dopple almost got me.

It was a good plan from his point of view. He probably

parked near the exit of the northbound tunnel and fired at me as I came from the other direction. He might not know if he hit me or not. Either way, he could easily drive off to the north, knowing there would be no way I could chase him when I was stuck in a one-way tunnel going the opposite direction.

I opened the back door and let Spot out. He didn't show his normal enthusiasm.

"You okay, boy?" I said, giving him a brisk rub.

He seemed okay, but only just that. He was in a strange car, and strange things were happening to it, and I was breaking my normal pattern of activity. Nothing wrong with that from a dog's point of view, but it made Spot wary. What strange thing was going to happen next?

I checked my phone, saw that I had cell coverage, and made calls. The first was to Diamond. I explained what had happened.

"Probably no point in asking, but do you think there's any chance of recovering the bullet?"

"No. From the angle of trajectory and my sense that it came just as I was entering the tunnel, it could be lodged in the tunnel, or the dirt near the tunnel entrance, or maybe it missed all that and ended up in the lake."

"And you don't recall seeing anything of note—vehicle or person—on the northbound side of the tunnel."

"No."

"I should still make a proforma visit to the crime scene. Can you stay there for a bit? I'm up here at the lake. It won't take me long."

"Yes. I'm just inside the entrance to Cave Rock State Park."

Five minutes later, Diamond appeared from the south. He turned into the park, stopped near the Prius, and got out. He gave Spot a rub, then walked around the car.

"Rental company ain't gonna be happy."

"I borrowed it from friends."

"Ouch. Whyn't we get in the patrol and look at the north side of the tunnel and see if there's anything we haven't thought of."

"There's a sentence I never thought of," I said.

"Churchill said proscriptions about ending a sentence with a preposition are the kind of errant pedantry up with which he would not put."

"I didn't mean 'thought of.' I meant the word whyn't," I said.

"Ain't nothing wrong with whyn't."

Knowing that Diamond's command of his second language, English, was beyond my command of my first language, English, I said, "Forget it."

We drove to the north side of the tunnel, got out and looked around. Diamond pulled out his phone and took some pictures.

"Let me turn on the recording app, and you give me your statement." Without a hint of a smile, he added, "Include all the prepositions and uncommon contractions." He tapped a button, and I gave him my statement of what happened.

Diamond dropped me back at my car. I drove slowly and carefully to my office while Diamond followed. Once in the parking lot, Spot and I walked over to Diamond's vehicle. He had his phone plugged into the patrol computer.

"Your friend's insurance company will want a police report of your… Let's call it an accident," Diamond said. "I've transcribed your statement, inserted it into my crime report and added the sheriff's office details." He tapped on the computer, moved his fingers on the track pad. A printer under the computer whirred. Out came two sheets of paper.

Diamond handed them to me.

"Thanks much."

"I'll call the tow company. After your last tow for your Jeep, they've probably got you on their VIP list. Maybe you'll get the frequent tow discount. And I know a rental company agent. Want me to call her and get a car delivered to you?"

"Please."

He got on the phone and made some official-sounding comments that would generate a very fast response from whomever he was talking to. Every business wants to keep law enforcement happy.

When he hung up, he said, "I've got a meeting and some other business to attend to. Then I'll stop at your office and we will design a trap for Tucker Dopple. What did Dr. Diaz say Dopple called himself?"

"Chief Sturgis."

"Right. We'll trap the chief and teach him it's not polite to shoot at people in our lovely resort area."

Diamond drove off. Spot and I waited.

Ten minutes later, a flat bed truck with a Ford on it pulled up. A tow truck came a minute later.

I signed the papers, got the Ford key, and walked up the stairs to my office.

I made a pot of coffee and poured a mug. Drinking black coffee with no donuts made me feel more like a monk than a PI, but we make do with what we have. I left a message on the voicemail of Craig and Shelley Fahrman, the people who'd loaned me their Prius. There were no good words to explain how their car got shot up, but they would probably understand as well as anybody. They'd been around long enough to know the common counterpoint to Karma. Do someone a good favor and you will be punished for it.

By the time I finished my second cup of coffee, I knew how to trap Tucker Dopple.

SEVENTEEN

Diamond showed up at my office later that morning. He perched on the corner of my desk. Spot rested his head on Diamond's angled lap. Diamond rubbed him.

"You were here when Benito Diaz explained how Tucker Dopple found him in Tahoe," I said.

"Sí. Diaz had posted his Tahoe plans on social media. Dopple did some online stalking and tracked Diaz to Tahoe. Probably Dopple had already looked you up, knew you were in Tahoe, and thought he could kill both of you on one trip."

"Which leads to how we could trap him."

"Ah, with social media, of course."

"Right. Tell me what you think. What if Benito were to post some information about an exciting event he's going to attend? Something at night. In the forest. Something where Tucker Dopple could go where he would think he could maybe kill us both."

"A night sky star seminar," Diamond said.

"That's good. That's ideal. People go to Tahoe for romance and romantic ideas and subjects. Like stars. It would be like an elder hostel. Except we can't put other people at risk."

"So make it a private meet," Diamond said. "I've seen stuff like that. 'I'm having dinner with a fashion designer. I'm so excited.' Everyone knows the person is just bragging and no one else is invited." He paused. "This is a good time to look at stars. The moon is now in its last quarter and doesn't rise until just a bit before the sun. So the stars are out and dramatic."

"I can get Benito to word it that I'm just taking him out on a hike to look at stars from a great viewing spot. Castle Rock, up near the top of Kingsbury Grade, for example. If Benito puts that on his social media pages, that might entice Dopple to sneak out in the forest and shoot from a distance. But I would need to make Dopple think I was out there with Benito. I could go out alone, but I'd have to trick Dopple into thinking I'm not alone. I need a full-size blow-up doll or something to impersonate Benito."

"I'm about his height. We both have black hair. Diaz's skin isn't as dark as mine, but it's darker than many Norte Americanos."

"I could never ask you to take that risk," I said.

"You didn't. I'm volunteering. You and I will both wear Kevlar vests. It'll be at night. We'll keep moving. If you never stand still, you make a difficult target, even for someone with a rifle."

"Not a pleasant thought. And how would we wear Kevlar vests without tipping him off?"

Diamond didn't immediately respond. "The day Benito came to your office, he was wearing tourist clothes. Those tight, bright yellow bicycling shorts. And he had the matching shirt, dark blue body with yellow sleeves."

"That's right. The blue portion looked like a vest. If you're playing Diaz, you would wear something that makes the kevlar vest look like sports gear."

"It's even easier for you," Diamond said. "You've got lots of dark frumpy clothes. Put one of those windbreakers over the vest. No one will notice."

"Frumpy?" I said.

"Your normal clothes are baggy. Frumpy. Stuff that makes you look homeless. Take your pick."

"I expect Doc Lee to impugn my fashion sense. But now you?"

"Ain't no impugnment. You're just a professional when it comes to frumpy, homeless, plainclothes, undercover presentation."

"I didn't know there was a word called impugnment."

"Me neither," Diamond said. "Sounds good, though, huh?" After a moment, he added, "I could get some other bodies from our county to help," He paused. "They could stay out in the woods and catch Dopple as he approaches. But they would have to be very good at being incognito."

"Catching Dopple as he approaches wouldn't be enough," I said. "Unless he shoots at us, the most he could be charged with is possessing an illegal firearm."

"Which would put an ex-con felon back inside."

"Right. However, if we could get him to take a shot, then we have attempted murder."

"Sí, that would be better. 'Cept if he succeeds."

"Right. Actual murder would be a bit more serious." I thought for a moment. "I think we should go in lean," I said. "Just the two of us."

"If we prepare, we could catch Dopple unaware."

"How would you prepare?" I asked.

"I don't know. But based on his two previous attempts to attack you, we know he's a sloppy planner. It shouldn't be that hard to catch him. I'll think on it."

"Okay, here's how I see it," I said. "Imagine that Tucker Dopple sees Benito's announcement. He probably doesn't know how to get to Castle Rock, right?"

Diamond frowned, remembering. "That's the rocks off the top of Kingsbury Grade."

"Right."

"So he would likely wait in the forest near my office. If I'm alone, he will follow me, thinking I'm going to lead him to Diaz where he can shoot us both."

"If I'm playing Diaz, and I'm with you, he could shoot us both in your office parking lot. Save us the time of hiking to Castle Rock."

"True. But his last two attempts on me backfired. Despite his stupidity, that probably taught him to consider a better way. When he sees me leave, he'll follow."

"I'll think about that," Diamond said. "Meantime, you work out the details with Dr. Benito?"

"I'm on it. All I need from you are times you would be available."

"I have no graveyard shifts for the next, lemme think, the

next six days. So you and Doc Benny can pick your evening. I'll be there."

After Diamond left, I got Benito on the phone and told him about my idea.

"That's perfect. He plans to kill me, stalks me on social media, follows me to Tahoe. Then, when he sees the cop car at your office, he postpones killing me but beats me up instead. It's fitting that I set a trap on the same social media. He stalks me the same as before. But this time, we catch him."

"Not you," I said. "Too dangerous. The cop you met in my office, Diamond Martinez, will be your stand-in."

Diaz did not immediately speak.

"I hate the idea that someone else takes a deadly risk on my behalf," he said.

"He volunteered."

"He does kind of fit my overall look. Better looking, though."

"Especially when your eye is black and blue and green and swollen shut."

"You think that matters?"

It was the first sign of humor I'd heard from Diaz.

"I have some ideas of what you might post on social media," I said.

"I'm ready."

We spent some time discussing the details.

"How long will it take you to post this where he saw your other plans?" I asked.

"My postings usually show up in just a few minutes."

"Can you watch for it and email me a screen shot?"

"Will do."

We hung up.

Benito's email showed up ten minutes later.

The screenshot showed a picture of the lake. Beneath the picture, it said, "Always a great time at Tahoe! Can't wait for darkness tonight when my buddy Owen McKenna is taking me hiking up to Castle Rock to look at the stars. The moon is in its last quarter, so it won't rise until just before dawn. McKenna says the stars will be amazing. And Castle Rock should be perfect because it's at 7900 feet, high enough to have awesome views, but below the current snow line. McKenna says the hike is only a couple of miles, perfect for someone who's only used to low elevation hikes in the Bay Area."

I hit Reply and told Benito it looked perfect.

I called Diamond. "We're on to study the stars tonight," I said when he answered. "Benito has put our meeting information on the same sites where he posted the earlier stuff that Tucker Dopple saw."

"Not too specific?"

"Correct. We didn't put a meeting time on Benito's posting, because we thought that moved a little too close to looking like a setup. However, I think you and I should meet at my office at five-thirty p.m., when daylight is moving to twilight. That will make it easy for Tucker Dopple to hide out in the woods behind my building and watch for us."

"Five-thirty is perfect. It's soon enough that Dopple won't have time to make much in the way of plans or even figure out where Castle Rock is. But it'll give me some time to go scope out the territory. Do you have a vest?"

"Yeah. I'd like to join you, but I should probably stay put so I don't alarm Dopple in case he decides to come and watch me."

"Okay. See you at five-thirty."

EIGHTEEN

As I thought about my plan, I wondered if I was making a mistake not explaining to Street the full range of possibilities. The reality was that I was trying to entice Tucker Dopple into attempting to kill me. But while that outcome was a possibility, I genuinely thought there was a very small likelihood of him succeeding. He'd already brought Benito Diaz to my office thinking he could kill us both, and that didn't work out for him. A few nights later, he fired at me multiple times on Highway 50. With a little help from me, he succeeded only in crashing his car and having to flee on foot into the forest. And this morning, he had the perfect setup and still failed. He probably hadn't tested the tracking on his rifle scope.

I also had the psychological comfort of having Diamond working with me. I'd never known anyone with such a combination of calm intellect and gut-instinct street smarts. When Diamond has your back, you get a sense of invincibility. So right or wrong, I felt I was just putting in another day in the investigation business. Not giving Street advance notice didn't seem like a big deal. And, in fact, it seemed like I was allowing her to have more time without stress.

Diamond showed up at a quarter after 5. He trotted up the stairs with the fast staccato beat of an athlete, and when he walked in my door, he looked a little like Dr. Benito Diaz and a lot like an athlete. If Tucker Dopple was out in the forest watching, he'd assume he was seeing Benito Diaz coming to join me on a stargazing outing.

Diamond's clothes were color coordinated. He wore silver Nikes with turquoise swooshes. His skin-tight shorts were an iridescent silvery green with turquoise accents. His tight stretch shirt was turquoise with silver accents. And his black bullet-proof kevlar vest looked much more like what an athlete would wear for warmth than what a cop would wear to stop a rifle bullet.

"Civvies that tight leave no room for your sidearm," I said.

"Es lo contrario." He lifted his vest to show me a black elastic wrap around his waist, under the waist band of his athletic shorts. It appeared more like a bandage than a concealed carry holster. However, there was a slight bulge at 4 o'clock.

"It doesn't look like you could tuck your wallet in there."

"My Beretta Nano is smaller than my wallet."

"But packs a bigger punch," I said.

"Funny guy."

"I see the barrel is tucked inside your waistband," I said.

"Mexican-carry style for a Mexican," Diamond said. "But the Nano is uncomfortable without the holster."

"I'd think a macho guy like you would like discomfort. Remind you of your hardscrabble youth."

"In principle, sure. But my forty-year signpost is becoming visible down the road. Advanced age makes principles yield to pragmatism. Don't want that gun barrel to abrade my belly."

"I don't think your six-pack abs qualify as a belly," I said.

"Belly is geography. Hard or soft is surface quality. Not much connection between the two."

"Got it. What's next?"

"We head up to Castle Rock. You drive. I want my Nano easy to reach in case this black-hat cowboy takes a shot at us from his horse."

I stood up, pulled my Kevlar vest from the little closet nook. I put it on, covered it with a dark windbreaker, and we left. We looked like two opposite kinds of guys, one wearing billboard clothes to celebrate an exciting Tahoe sports excursion, the other wearing insulated clothes for Tahoe's nighttime weather.

Out in the parking lot, I spoke in a low voice.

"Where's your ride?"

"Left my pickup a block away."

I let Spot into the back seat of the rental Ford, Diamond and I got in, and headed up Kingsbury Grade.

"I did some prep work," Diamond said.

"At Castle Rock?"

"Sí. I found a place in the rocks suitable for stargazing and for drawing a man's fire. There's dark forest down below."

"Which will give him a sense of security," I said.

"Sí. But what's good for us is that it will provide no reflected light back toward the shooter."

"Why would any light reflect?"

"Because I set up a bullet-proof acrylic shield that Douglas County had left over from when the president visited and gave an outdoor talk."

"You often produce the surprise I don't expect. But how is it that a shooter won't be able to see this shield?"

"Same as any one-way glass. We will be on the side that has some light, stars, ambient light reflected from the mountain peaks with snow on them, waning light from the sunset. He will be on the dark side in the forest."

"Like the reverse of the sheriff's office interrogation room. We're in the room with lights, and he'll be in the equivalent of the dark viewing room on the other side of the one-way glass."

Diamond nodded.

"But how do we know he's going to stay in the dark forest? He could walk anywhere around there, right?"

"The spot for us is in a cove of rocks. You have to scramble up some rocks to get there. The only place where one can see people in the cove is from out in the forest. I wedged the acrylic shield into the rocks such that when he sees us, he'll be looking through the shield."

"Is it that invisible?"

"It's pretty impressive. They make that stuff with a non-reflective coating. After I got it in place, I walked out into the forest, and I couldn't see it at all."

"So we get out there first, climb into the cove, then we talk and make noise so he knows we're there."

"It's what I was thinking," Diamond said.

I continued, "Dopple will probably sneak around the forest until he happens into the trees with a view window toward us. He'll find a good place to prop his rifle on a bipod sniper support and then try to pick us off in quick succession."

"When we hear the shot," Diamond said, "we scramble down and give pursuit."

"What's to keep him from running a mile into the dark? We won't be able to see where he went."

"We'll hear him."

"A guy can run without making much noise."

"Not after he gets tangled in my net."

I turned and glanced at Diamond as I drove. We were heading up through Middle Kingsbury, past the entrance to the Chart House restaurant.

Diamond explained. "Because the forest viewing area is relatively confined, I was able to establish a perimeter with screw-in U-hooks on trees. I ran paracord across the ground and pushed it down into the surface duff. At each tree with a hook, I brought the cord up the trunk, looped it through the hook, then back down to the ground. There are maybe seven or eight trees that outline an oval area that is substantially bigger than where a shooter would logically set up his sniper position."

"He won't see the cord and hooks?"

"The hooks are painted dark brown, and the cord is brown. I'm guessing Tucker Dopple is so dim-witted, he could see the cord and not realize what he was looking at. After the boy shoots, he'll grab his gear and skedaddle."

"Skedaddle…" I said.

"Reading up on my American Civil War history. That word was used to describe running away in a fright."

"You really think he'll be afraid?"

"Yeah. Especially when I pull the drawstring and collapse his world."

"Because that lifts the cord up off the ground and he runs into it?"

"Sí. Once he realizes he's been out-maneuvered, he will envision a coming confrontation that he hadn't anticipated."

"These cords you laid out will stop him?"

"Eight hundred-pound test. At the minimum, he trips. We descend on him. It's like when he shot at you in your Jeep. He didn't expect you to turn aggressor and drive into him. It shook him, and he skedaddled."

NINETEEN

Ten minutes later, we'd parked off North Benjamin. I gave Spot a rub, told him to be good, and Diamond and I headed off through the forest as the sky darkened toward night. We stayed on an obvious trail. If Dopple was following us, we wanted to keep it easy for him, and we didn't want him to think we were being evasive. We figured he wouldn't shoot us on the trail for the simple reason that we were moving and it would be a much easier shot if we were stationary, leaning back, pointing our binoculars toward the heavens.

Diamond spoke in a low voice as we approached the rock. Without pointing, he told me where his preparations were.

"Follow me as we approach Castle Rock. That way you won't accidentally kick loose my paracord trap."

"Will do."

The trail to Castle Rock was well graded. It angled gently down and then back up. As we approached, the rock looked as I remembered. It was appropriately named. From some angles it mimics a castle fortress rising 200 feet above the surrounding forest. It reminded me of when Street and I traveled to Italy to search out a diamond connection between Renaissance Italy and Frank Sinatra, who once owned the Cal Neva Hotel on Tahoe's North Shore. All through Tuscany we saw rock projections like Castle Rock. The difference was that medieval builders actually built castles and fortress towns on those rocks in Italy.

After an easy mile, we left the trail and hiked a quarter mile or so to the rocks. Diamond led the way. I wondered what Tucker Dopple would think if he was out in the forest watching and saw a man he believed was Benito Diaz leading the local detective. I decided it seemed natural. Most locals have seen how groups of hikers self-sort. The excited tourists often rush ahead, eager to get to the next view, while their local hosts, who've probably seen the views multiple times, hang back and walk at a slower pace.

Diamond didn't act excited like a tourist. But his clothes would convince anyone he was a flatlander. He even pulled out his phone now and then and took selfies with a glimpse of the lake in the background.

We looped around the rock as we got close.

"Don't be obvious," Diamond said in a near whisper, "but the bullet-proof shield is straight up above us."

I contrived to look around. But I saw no acrylic. I whispered back, "I think Dopple must have found it and pulled it down."

"No, it's there. I can see it."

I was amazed. Maybe it was just that the twilight was so dim, very little was visible.

Diamond called out in a loud voice for the benefit of anyone who might be in the forest listening. "Wow, this place is great. I can already see some stars. Where's the best place to see them from?"

"Up in these rocks," I said in a loud voice. "We're getting close."

After 10 more yards, Diamond turned, looked up at the rock, and started climbing, placing his feet carefully, occasionally using his hands to help pull himself up the rock.

I followed. We both kept moving because we were completely exposed. We came to a ledge of sorts that went back into a small area surrounded by rock walls. A perfect cove, as Diamond called it. It was about ten feet deep and five feet wide, with an opening facing the forest below. A large acrylic sheet was wedged into that opening, filling most of the opening, curved so that it pushed outward and held itself in place, its edges jammed against rocks.

I tried not to stare, but it was an impressive illusion. From out in the dark forest, I couldn't see it. Up here in the cove, with the ambient light from the stars and the remaining orange glow from the sunset, the acrylic sheet was obvious.

"I remember you telling me you were interested in stars," I said in a loud voice, hoping that Tucker Dopple would overhear if he was nearby. "That's why I invited you up to this place."

"I don't know that much," Diamond responded in an equally loud voice. He didn't sound much like Benito Diaz, but I didn't think it mattered.

"But doctors know all kinds of science stuff, right? For example, when I'm out at night, I'm always checking to see where the North Star is."

"Polaris," Diamond said.

"Yeah. What do you know about Polaris?"

"Well, it was used by early sailors. Because it's more accurate than using a compass to find the Earth's North Pole. Of course, it's only useful at night."

I raised my binoculars. "There it is."

Diamond looked at me, not for the direction information, which he knew better than I did, but as part of our theatrical interplay. To be a convincing Dr. Diaz, he needed to inhabit the role.

He spoke in what sounded like a professorial voice. "Even with binoculars, Polaris is still just a dot, like all the other stars. Binoculars just make the pinpoints of light brighter. What's interesting about Polaris is that its position in the sky is changing. As the Earth turns, it wobbles like a top. So Polaris will eventually be in a much different place relative to the Earth's North Pole."

"How long will it take to change position?" I asked, playing along.

"The Earth's wobble is moving pretty fast. In just thirteen thousand years, Vega will be the closest star to north. Thirteen thousand years after that, Polaris will again be the north star."

"You said that even with binoculars, the stars still only look like pinpoints of light. Is there anything that's really good to see with binoculars?" As I asked the question, I wondered if I was making it difficult for Diamond. Did he even have an answer?

"One of the best is in the Orion constellation," he said.

"That's the hunter with three stars in his belt."

"Yes. We're coming up on winter. So Orion will rise in the east soon. Let's look." He turned to the east. "There it is, just coming up." He raised his binoculars. "You'll see that hanging down from the belt of three stars is the hunter's sword, which is a line of four stars. Except the third star down in the sword isn't just a star. It's a nebulae, which is a huge nursery of stars being formed. If you look through your binoculars, you'll see a beautiful grouping of magenta and blue light. It looks small but it's actually twenty-four light years across."

"Meaning," I said, "it takes twenty-four years for a beam of light—the fastest thing there is—to go from one side to the other."

"Exactly. It's amazing, and you can see it with binoculars."

As we looked through our binoculars, there was a sharp pinging snap on the acrylic and the simultaneous crack of a rifle shot.

Diamond had an astonishingly quick reaction. He ran toward the rocks where we had climbed up to the cove. He bent down, waved his hand back and forth as if feeling the air, and got hold of what I immediately understood was the paracord trap he'd laid. As his fingers closed around it, he leaped down a particular set of rocks to a flat area near where we'd climbed up.

As he pulled on the cord, I heard a zinging sound of fine braided cord crossing over rocks and through distant U-hooks screwed into trees. Diamond reached out toward a tree and made a circular motion. It wasn't clear in the dim light, but it seemed as if he was tying off the drawstring line he'd just pulled tight.

Next came a grunt from the forest. "Damn it!" a man shouted. There was a thud like what one would expect when a body trips and falls hard.

"Run," Diamond said. "Help me catch this bastard."

He scrambled down the rocks to the forest floor. I followed, not as fast as Diamond, but fast enough to risk falling or spraining my ankle on the uneven rocks.

Diamond ran through the forest. I followed.

The trees were dark shapes in a dark night. I had no confidence that I wasn't going to hit branches and rip out my eyes or rip off my ears or take a sharp branch in the mouth.

I heard Diamond in front of me. And I heard heavy breathing as if our would-be assassin was just ahead. But everything was dark. I had no idea how Diamond could tell where he was going.

I'm sure he had a flashlight, but he was following the rule of darkness. If you are in the dark, no one knows exactly where you are. The first person to turn on a flashlight can possibly see their opponent. But while their light may not show their opponent's location, it positively reveals their own location.

I heard a grunt and a thud. Then a flashlight flipped on.

A big man was illuminated from behind. He had tripped and was now charging away like a running back, but stumbling, as if trying to get out of the grip of the invisible hands of a tackle. Diamond's cord.

As Diamond ran toward the suspect, he kept his light on the man. I worried that he was going to try to tackle the suspect. The 'fleeing felon' rules gave Diamond legal backing for tackling a man who is considered dangerous and suspected of committing a felony. Diamond also knew that if he pulled his gun and shouted the warning, the man would keep running. As soon as the man could extricate himself from the line, he would be gone.

But I worried that a mano-a-mano confrontation between Diamond and the much bigger man in the dark might end badly. Tackling Tucker Dopple was a questionable move considering Dopple had reportedly bulked himself up in prison and was probably carrying multiple weapons.

I saw the collision as Diamond hit the man. There was a thunking sound, and then they both sprawled. Diamond's flashlight flew and landed in the forest duff. It pointed back toward me, which made it so I couldn't see anything.

A confrontation with a psychopath is always fraught, because the psychopath doesn't have an internal governor regarding the limits of what he should do. He can take out eyes and break thumbs and bite off ears with no sense of restraint.

Maybe I could get there fast enough to help.

I sped up my run. I couldn't see trees and boulders and Manzanita bushes in the dark. I just ran toward the flashlight on the ground.

There was the sound of scuffling as I sprinted toward the light. I scooped the flashlight up off the ground, turned it around, and saw Diamond grappling with the man. The man managed to turn and kick Diamond in his middle. The blow was hard enough to make a sickening whump as boot met flesh.

Diamond fell back. The man ran away.

I wanted to stop and help Diamond, see if he was okay. But I knew what Diamond would say. As I had the thought, Diamond wheezed like a man who'd had the wind knocked out of him, "Get him!"

So I pointed the flashlight at the fleeing figure and ran after him.

The only reason I was able to catch Dopple was that he was still dragging a section of cord that was wrapped around his foot.

As I got closer, I could sense his size. If we got to fighting, my only advantage would come from my previous experience of learning cop-style street fighting, how to pressure joints and break elbows, knees, and shoulders. Those techniques were useful, but Tucker Dopple might know them, too.

So I slowed a bit to match his speed and waited for the right moment to apply a more powerful strategy.

I saw the possibility coming in about two seconds. Dopple was following the clearest path through the forest, which was lit by my light. It was an area of ground that was uninterrupted by boulders and brush. That path led just to the right of a Jeffrey pine. It was a mature tree, not huge, but it had a trunk that was two feet or more in diameter, big enough to destroy the largest of big-rig trucks. I shined my light away from the pine so it wouldn't be too obvious.

I swerved out to the side and then converged back in on Dopple. I hit him hard, adding my mass to his, changing his direction just enough, and we struck the tree at full speed, straight on.

I was cushioned by Dopple's body. The impact was significant, but no big deal for me.

Dopple, however, hit the tree face first. It sounded more like wood-on-wood than a soft-body impact. His air whooshed out dramatically.

He dropped to the ground. There was no tension in his muscles, no movement to resist and cushion his fall. It seemed like a dead body dropping. And maybe it was. I shined the light beam on him.

Dopple lay face down in the pine needles but with his legs turned to the side. If he was breathing, it didn't show. I felt no impulse to get down, check his heart, and maybe start CPR compressions. I'd been tricked by guys like Dopple in the past. They hold their breath, wait until you check if they're alive by putting your ear next to their mouth or touching your fingertips to the Carotid artery for a pulse, then they flash out their hand and crush your trachea. A collapsed throat causes a slow, agonizing death. I wasn't going to risk it just to know if Dopple got what he deserved.

Diamond's voice came through the night, soft and whispered. Another person trying to get air into his lungs. "Hang in there, McKenna. I'll be there to help in a minute." Diamond must have been able to tell from the sounds that the collision had ended badly for at least one of us. He knew the laws of physics that explain why trees always win.

I called back toward the darkness. "Take your time. This guy looks to be thoroughly out of commission."

Dopple lived for a short while, although it looked like he probably suffered brain trauma, among other injuries. He had to be brought out on a stretcher, no small task for six men carrying him over a mile through the forest.

Diamond gave perimeter and evidence instructions to his deputies, who possibly snickered a bit at Diamond's athletic clothes. True to form for a guy who seemed to have no insecurities, Diamond felt no impulse to explain that his outfit was a disguise to appear as a doctor who'd been targeted by the ex-con killer.

The deputies also found Dopple's rifle and wrapped it in a sheet of plastic.

The next morning, I got a call from Doc Lee, whose colleague had been working the ER when they brought Tucker Dopple in. Doc Lee thought I'd want to know that Dopple had died from a ruptured aorta, a result consistent with the magnitude of his collision with the tree.

When I later gave my statement to a Douglas County

Lieutenant, who happened to be Diamond's superior, he asked me how Diamond and I came to be at Castle Rock with a bullet-proof acrylic shield.

I knew three things about crime statements. The first was to tell the truth, because that is how justice is served. The second was to tell the truth, because other people involved, such as Sergeant Diamond Martinez, would be questioned as well and their rendition of events checked to see if they match my rendition of events. The third thing about crime statements is that if you want to affect how the events are perceived—and every person connected to a crime does—the most you can do is to occasionally not volunteer every little thought that comes into your head.

So I told the lieutenant the truth about our sting operation, which was designed to get a known killer to make good on his threats to kill me and a doctor, who was impersonated by Diamond. I explained that the goal was to save the doctor's life and possibly my own by taking that killer off the street. I also told the lieutenant about the bullet-proof shield Diamond had borrowed from county storage.

"You didn't see this operation as entrapment?" he asked me.

"No, because it wasn't. We didn't force the man to commit a crime. We didn't make him live in fear that bad things would happen if he didn't try to kill us. It was a classic sting, nothing more. We presented the suspect with a situation that he could exploit for illegal purposes. Which the man did. When he shot at us, we ran after him and caught him."

"Tell me about the collision with the tree. How did it happen?"

"After the man shot at Diamond and me, Diamond ran after the suspect and grappled with him. The suspect got away. Diamond had dropped his flashlight. So I grabbed it and chased after the man. I could see that the man was running on a path that would take him very close to the tree. I'm certain he didn't realize the danger. After all, he was running in the dark."

"Did you do anything to help cause this tree collision?"

"Well, there's no doubt that having me chase him and close in on him was distracting. So, yes, I played a role in the tree collision."

"How is it that you avoided hitting the tree?"

"I didn't. I was right behind the man. When he struck the tree, I struck him. It was only his body that cushioned me and saved me from injury."

The lieutenant took his time, looking at me, thinking about what I'd said. Eventually, he reached over and turned off the recorder.

I was confident that he assumed I pushed Tucker Dopple into the tree. I was also confident the lieutenant believed that he would have done the same thing. I knew that he was wondering what in his investigation was helped or hindered by the things I'd said or hadn't said. I knew he was also going over the larger issues of justice.

All cops face moral dilemmas. They resolve those dilemmas by revisiting the basics. What is just? What is right? What is wrong? What is in the best interest of society?

It was territory that Street and I had talked about several times. How does one apply his code of ethics? Because Tucker Dopple died as a result of the collision with the tree, I could technically be considered guilty of manslaughter. Yet juries repeatedly find cops innocent of using deadly force in cases where a dangerous felon is fleeing the scene of a crime. So should I volunteer the truth and put the Douglas County District Attorney in the position of having to decide whether or not to put me on trial for my crime? Should county residents be pulled out of their jobs to sit on a jury to debate the legality of my actions?

I've been in difficult situations with regard to ethical dilemmas. This wasn't one of them. Tucker Dopple was a previous murderer, and he tried to murder again. He brought no possible value to society, only stress and threats, violence and misery. Did that mean he had no rights? Did that mean he was fair game to any private investigator who might intentionally cause a fatal accident? No. But it did mean that I wasn't going to lose sleep over his death. In fact, I would sleep better knowing a bad man was gone.

TWENTY

After catching Tucker Dopple, I called Benito Diaz and told him what happened, leaving out the details of how Dopple ran into the tree. He seemed glad to have the threat gone, but he was hesitant.

"I'm sorry he died," Benito Diaz said.

I hadn't told Diaz about Tucker shooting at me and just missing me two different times in addition to his recent attempt on my life and Diamond's life. But it probably wouldn't have made much difference. Benito Diaz and I came from fundamentally different world views. Diaz would save anyone from death at any cost. That was a wonderful motivation, and the world benefited endlessly from people like Benito Diaz. But my experience in law enforcement produced nearly the opposite viewpoint. In my point of view, people who were good were worth saving from death, but not at any cost. I would judge it on a case-by-case basis. But people who were universally bad were not worth saving at all. And when universally bad people died, it didn't bother me. In fact, I thought it improved the world.

I saw little point in telling Diaz my point of view, and I had no desire to change the way he saw things. But I did sum up what had happened. "Tucker Dopple died trying to kill Sergeant Martinez and me. His death is not a loss to society. And his loss takes away a deadly threat to you and Damen."

Benito was quiet on the phone for a long moment. "Yes, that's true. And I appreciate that. Thank you. I didn't mean to sound judgmental. When I went to med school, I took all the Hippocrates' stuff very seriously. First do no harm. And always save any life you can. Always prevent death."

"Understood," I said.

"Is there anything new on Veronica Eastern?"

"Not much. But I'll let you know. I did want to revisit one thing with you."

"Certainly," Benito said.

"When you first told us about Tucker Dopple beating you up and then kicking you into the parking lot when he saw Diamond's patrol vehicle, he had apparently said that he wasn't paid enough to deal with cops."

"I remember."

"When I asked you about it, you thought it was just a figure of speech."

"Right," Benito said.

"Now that it's been awhile, do you still think that?"

"Yes."

"Let me ask another question. What if Tucker Dopple was actually being paid to beat you up or even kill you or me? Can you think of anyone other than Dopple who might want to harm you?"

"No. I've especially thought about patients who might have a grudge against me. Spouses of patients who've died and such. But nothing dramatic comes to mind. The only other violent person I've met was the guy who set up the fraudulent investment business, and when I threatened to turn him in, he beat me up. He went to prison for fraud and assault."

"What was his name?"

"I have no idea."

"What about the name of his phony business?"

"I don't know that, either. I suppose I could look in my old records when I get back to San Mateo. I wrote him a check, but that was a dozen years ago." Benito was silent on the phone.

"I suppose I should let you know that I'm somewhat absent-minded," he said. "I'm so focused on my current patients who are struggling for life that everything else seems small by comparison. And I tend to forget about that small stuff."

"Okay. Let me know if you think of anything."

We said goodbye.

I called Sergeant Jack Santiago.

"Hey, McKenna," he answered. "I heard you and Diamond had an interesting evening last night."

"Interesting... That's one way to describe it."

"So Tucker Dopple had it in for both you and Dr. Diaz because you two put him inside for a long ride?"

"Yeah. One of the Brontë sisters referred to a potential killer nursing a grudge. Dopple took that idea to the extreme."

"You think Dopple had anything to do with the murder of Veronica Eastern in Tahoe City?"

"At this moment, no. But ask me again in five minutes, I might change my mind. There is a weird confluence of people in this case. How about you? Any luck?"

"No. It's like a spaghetti pile of witnesses and potential suspects and not a single good motive. I was just revisiting my notes on all the people near Veronica Eastern when she was killed. I can't find anything to really chew on."

"That's why I'm calling," I said. "The Brontë sisters directed me to their former classmate, Horatio Harris, but whom they call Heathcliff."

"The guy who jumped off the Golden Gate and got brain damage."

"Jumped or fell. When I talked to him, I learned nothing specific other than he's quite focused on airplanes. Says he saw a big biplane flying above Incline Village. Says it was silent. He thinks it means something. Or reveals something. Without anything else to go on, I'm thinking of going back and talking to him. But I thought I should check with you, first. When I asked you earlier about people to talk to, you thought I should talk to the Brontë sisters. I've done that, and I've learned nothing substantial. One of them could be Veronica Eastern's murderer. Or not. So my question is, of the people you've talked to, are there any you think I should focus on?"

I heard Santiago take a big breath over the phone. "The thing is, McKenna, you've been in this business longer than I have. So you know that feeling you get when you're talking to witnesses or even suspects. You come away with a gut instinct that someone might be your killer. Or your gut sense is, no way is this person your killer. Know what I mean?"

"Yeah," I said, nodding to myself.

"I've interviewed all those doctors, one spouse, and one girlfriend. Some of them, twice. And after all of that, I've got nothing. Not even a glimmer. Sure, I could be wrong. Anyone of them might have a bloody screwdriver in their luggage. But I don't sense it."

"I know what you're saying."

"You've talked to the Brontë sisters," Santiago said. "What was your sense of them?"

"Smart, intriguing, clever. Quite full of themselves. But that doesn't lead me to think any of them is a killer."

"Roger that," he said. "Let me know if you learn anything else."

We said goodbye and hung up.

TWENTY-ONE

I sat for a time. I felt becalmed. I had nothing to go on except the repeated mention of flying and airplanes. Heathcliff talked about a large, silent biplane. When I asked him if he had any advice for learning about Veronica Eastern, the woman who'd been murdered. He said, 'Look for the plane.' But he seemed to have no idea why he thought that. He used a vague metaphor of a doctor seeing different symptoms and searching for a connection between them.

Camille had read the Brontë sisters' lips during Benito's party. They had talked about flying. All the talk about flying gave me a growing sense that flying was connected to murder. But how could airplanes connect to a stabbing or shooting murders?

I found Heathcliff in the same coffee shop. I went in the morning when he had told me he was often there. I once again left Spot in the rental Ford, the back seat of which was beginning to acquire a fine coating of short white Dane hairs. Heathcliff was at the same table when I walked in. I got coffee and walked to Heathcliff's table.

I said, "Good morning."

He nodded but didn't speak.

"You only have one cup of coffee. Isabel couldn't make it?"

"No."

I didn't have an idea of why that might be.

"Remember how you told me about seeing a biplane?" I said.

Heathcliff nodded. "Yeah. A big biplane. Silent."

"Did it seem silent because it was flying high? Or was the plane flying low?"

"It was flying high," Heathcliff said. "Five thousand feet.

But that's not why it was silent. And it didn't seem silent. It was silent."

"What makes you think of that number five thousand feet?"

He tapped the binoculars that hung from his neck just like the last time I saw him. "Rangefinder binoculars. There's a readout below the view. It shows the distance to the predominant object in the view."

"Where do you think the plane was going?" I asked.

"Landing, I suppose. No plane can go far without its engine running, right?"

"You think the plane's engine wasn't running?"

"Of course." He was adamant. "It was too big to be one of those gliders that don't have an engine. It was like some kind of airship. So it must have been coasting in for a landing." He frowned. "Is that the wrong word? Coasting?"

"Normally, a plane with its engine off would be gliding. But I think coasting is a good word. Do you have a guess where it was landing?"

Another frown. "Not at all. I'm not a pilot. But it would have to be someplace up on the mountain where it went out of my view, right? Otherwise, why coast in without your engine running?"

"If you were to drive up the Mt. Rose Highway, do you think you could estimate where it might have been heading?"

"Not at all. Like I said, I'm not a pilot."

"You said you saw the plane twice."

"Yes. The first time I saw it was when we had that warm weather. I was out with Isabel. The second time was a week or eight or nine days later when I was riding the Flume Trail. I know because it was chilly and I wore my long pants and sleeves." He looked out the coffee shop window. "Isabel and I had had an argument. So I went out alone. But before I left, I told her I'd die for her. I'd do anything for her. She said she would stay with me always, no matter where I lived, no matter what I was doing. She said she loved me but she didn't always like me. Now I don't know what to do. I don't feel her presence unless we're talking over coffee. But she's not here today. I want to join her. Wherever she is."

"You said you saw the plane from the Flume Trail."

"Yeah."

"Do you mean the local Incline Flume Trail off the Mt. Rose Highway? Or the longer Tahoe Flume Trail to the south up on the mountain above Sand Harbor?"

"The Tahoe Flume Trail. On the cliff edge north from Marlette Lake."

"What time of day did this biplane come?"

"Early in the morning. Both times. The sun was just rising. The first time, we were at the Francis bench. Isabel and me. The plane came from over the lake. It was like an apparition floating into the searing light of dawn. It was high up, and it made no sound at all. I don't think it was a hallucination. It was very real."

"Do you think the plane's destination was the same when you saw it again from the Flume Trail?"

"Probably. But only because the similarities would suggest the same destination." As he said it, Heathcliff seemed to peer inward at a memory. His eyes looked glazed and unhealthy. He still looked like a disheveled movie star, but one who badly needed sleep.

"Could you show me where the plane went?"

He didn't respond.

I said, "Do you remember where you were?"

"Yes. I was walking with Isabel. We'd come to the Francis bench."

"Can we go there?"

He seemed to think about it, then picked up his cup of coffee and drained it.

I waited, not knowing if I should prod or be patient.

He pushed back his chair and stood up.

"I can drive us," I said.

"No, I don't like to be in cars. I like to walk or bike."

"Okay. Shall we bring some food?"

"No. I only eat with Isabel. She doesn't like to eat with other people."

I nodded and followed him out.

He walked out of the parking lot, across the street, then up several blocks. He turned and entered a faint path that led into the woods. There were some houses nearby on large lots. We came to a bench with a fine view through the trees to the lake. The bench was relatively new, and the plaque with the name was shiny gold. Francis Johns. I was certain we were on private property. But it could be that the owner was okay with other people enjoying the same view that Francis had enjoyed.

Heathcliff sat. He closed his eyes, took a deep breath, and let it out slowly. Maybe it was a kind of meditation. Or maybe just a way to connect with Isabel. Or quell the hallucinations. After two more breaths, he opened his eyes and pointed up through the trees toward the sky.

"The plane was up there." He swung his arm around and pointed. "It was roughly heading that way. But I couldn't see well because of all these trees."

"You could see it was a biplane," I said.

He again gripped the binoculars around his neck and made a little gesture. "I looked in my binoculars. That's how I knew it was a biplane."

"It was high enough that you might not have heard any engine even if it was running," I said.

"I told you there was no running engine." Heathcliff sounded irritated. "I have very good ears. The plane was coasting."

"You said the plane was large."

He nodded. "Yes. Very large."

"Do you know much about planes?"

"No. Nothing about planes. Except what a poet would know. Design, wind, floating, soaring."

"I don't want to be difficult," I said. "But if you know nothing about planes, how do you know it was large?"

"I once went to the Fleet Week air show in San Francisco. The vintage aircraft portion had lots of biplanes. They were all similar size. Kind of small. Like they could hold one or two people at most. But this one was much bigger. Like a small ship.

It had multiple windows. It could hold a group."

I stood and looked through the trees at the view, the sky, the direction he had pointed. Street had shown me how my phone had a built-in compass. I got it out, hit the buttons. "Tell me again, please, which way you think the plane was headed?"

Heathcliff sighed with frustration. "I told you I don't know." He gestured vaguely. "Sort of that way."

I sighted where he said the plane had headed. Northeast from where we stood. Or maybe east northeast.

"The second time you saw the plane, when you were bicycling the Flume Trail, was it going the same direction?"

"If I don't really know the direction it was going from here, how would I know if it was going the same direction when I was on the Flume Trail?"

"Good point. The second time you saw it, was it also coasting?"

"Yes."

"Could you describe where it was going?"

He thought about it. "I could draw you a picture."

Heathcliff pulled a pad of paper from his backpack and drew for some time. His marks were not sophisticated like what an artist would do, but they were clear and useful. He explained the drawing at some length, showing me where he was on his bike and where he saw the big biplane.

When he finished, he handed me the drawing and pointed at it.

"Here's the trail. There was a ravine here. A big Jeffrey pine over to this side. This is where the cliff rose up on the right. And here was a big drop off on the left. When I saw the biplane, it was..." He paused, considering. "In the distance, somewhere over here. It was coasting through the trees on this mountain. Or almost through the trees."

"So it was low."

Heathcliff seemed frustrated. "It was low relative to the mountain. But it was high relative to the town of Incline." He paused. "It was going to the right. Like maybe it was going to land over here." He moved his finger to the right and tapped on the piece of paper.

"Can I have this drawing?"

"Yes."

"Thanks." I folded the paper and put it in my pocket. "I'm curious why airplanes are important to you," I said.

"I'm not sure. I don't know why they're important to Isabel, either. She used to say that a plane transcends the ether. I suppose there was something in her past about planes."

"I'm surprised she never said what it was."

"She probably told me. But I lost the memory when I fell. Maybe there was something about planes in my past, too, and that was also lost when I fell."

I remembered that the Brontë sisters said Heathcliff jumped off the Golden Gate. I wondered if it were true. And if so, how did Heathcliff think of it?

"How did you fall?" I asked.

"I don't know. One day I was in my classes. And one day, I was in the hospital. They told me I fell off the Golden Gate Bridge a week before and they'd put me in a coma to help my brain heal."

"I'm glad you survived."

He frowned. "I suppose it was a good thing."

I thanked him for his time and accommodation. "I wish you the best with Isabel. She sounds remarkable."

He looked off. "Isabel and I are together a lot. But not as much as I'd like. One day I'll join her permanently. Then I'll be complete."

TWENTY-TWO

That afternoon, I was having coffee out on my deck. Spot was doing his best sleep imitation, absorbing the sun's heat on a chilly November day.

I thought about Heathcliff's description of seeing a silent biplane. He said it was very large. Like an airship. At the time, I thought it an unreliable description. Biplanes are generally small. Their engines are often as loud or louder than any other planes. And because they are a recognizable shape, people don't generally think of them as an airship. Heathcliff may just be a very creative thinker. The Brontë sisters said he had brain damage from his fall from the Golden Gate Bridge. They said he'd lost his brilliance and could no longer cope with the grueling academics of medical school. Heathcliff himself referred to his hallucinations.

But the plane description had stayed with me since I heard it. I wondered if anyone else had seen or heard of this airship. I'd hit dead ends on my inquiries about the murder of the doctor Veronica Eastern. I thought I should maybe ask around.

The only airport in the Tahoe Basin was in South Lake Tahoe. I called the man I'd rented Cessnas from on occasion. He was out. I left a message. He called back while I was eating lunch.

He said, "The last plane you rented from me got shot full of bullet holes, and I had to replace one of the gas tanks and get some body work done. My insurance company threatened to cancel me and said I should put you on my do-not-rent-to list. It took a lot of talking to convince them you were an innocent victim of a psycho who was shooting tracer rounds at anything that flew by. But as I told them that, I realized that there was maybe something you did that made you not so innocent."

I thought it best not to respond with specifics. "Sorry for the problems. And thanks for the effort. I'm actually calling about something else." I explained what I'd heard about a large silent biplane near Incline Village.

"Strange business you're in, McKenna. Sorry that I can't expand on that fiction."

"You know anyone in the area with a biplane?"

"Nope. There are some aerobatic pilots in Reno who fly biplanes. You've seen them. Bright colors and fancy graphics that look good in airshows. They've come to the South Lake Tahoe airshow, too. But their planes aren't big. Powerful engines, however. They sound big. And as you know, engines that sound big aren't silent. Those stunt aircraft have hopped-up engines that make more noise than a seven forty-seven. Anyway, I don't know those pilots or where they might keep a biplane. Probably in one of those out-lying hangars at Reno Tahoe International."

I thanked him for his time.

I didn't know anyone I could call at the big airport, or at the Truckee Airport, which was the closest to Incline Village. I stood up.

Spot jumped to his feet, looked at me, wagged. He looked alert, which reminded me that his sleep skills included fake sleep, as if that would allow him to eavesdrop on words or motions that suggested a drive. Or donuts.

"What makes you think I'm going for a drive?"

His wag tempo stepped up a notch. He made a yawn, opening the giant mouth wide enough to pick up a basketball. Maybe the sleep act wasn't totally fake.

I stood. Spot trotted down the short outdoor steps and went over to the rental Ford and stood nose-to-rear-door.

I went through my little cabin, reached the key fob off the hook, and went out the front door.

We drove down the mountain to the highway, cruised on by Streets and Camille's condo, and headed north around the lake. I turned off in Kings Beach, went up and over Brockway Summit, and headed down to the Truckee Airport, which sits in Martis Valley, a little southeast of the old railroad town of

Truckee, where the first transcontinental railroad was punched through the Sierra in 1869. The Truckee Airport is out of the Tahoe Basin, but it's the closest airport to Incline Village and a logical place for pilots to go on their way to or from Incline.

I found a place to park, rolled down the windows, told Spot to be good, and got out.

There was an information counter inside the airport. A pleasant young woman who exuded efficiency and intelligence smiled at me.

"May I help you?"

Underneath the kind words was a flavor of impatience, as if she could get some actual work done if she didn't have to interact with people.

"I have a question about biplanes. I'm wondering if anyone in the area has one or flies one out of the Truckee Airport?"

She shook her head. She still looked pleasant, but her mouth tightened in a hint of a grimace as if preparing herself for an extended series of questions and answers.

"Not that I know of," she said.

"Can you direct me to any rental operations that have hangar space at the airport?"

"Sure. We've got half a dozen or more businesses here. Flight training mostly."

"Any of them work with aerobatic pilots?"

The hint of grimace became more pronounced. "I'd try Airshow Advertising. They do banners and skywriting. They might even give lessons. They would know what you need, I'm sure." Her smile grew large and looked phony. "Good luck, and thanks for coming by." She turned to her computer and reached for the mouse.

It was a smooth dismissal.

"Where do I find Airshow Advertising?"

Without even glancing toward me, she kept her eyes on the computer screen and said, "Light green hangar, south of the airport entrance."

"Thank you."

I walked back out to the rental, moving quietly as I got close.

Spot was lying on his back on the backseat. He often slept with all four legs in the air, knees and wrists bent, paws drooping. His head was also upside down, his jowls sagging to reveal white fangs and pink gums. I decided to leave him be.

I tiptoed past and walked out to the light green hangar. There was a sign above the small door that said 'Airshow Advertising.'

I opened the door and went inside.

There was an old plastic counter with an old computer, an even older phone, and a calendar that looked ancient and worn out but depicted the correct year under a photo of a Super Decathlon flying upside down. The place had the sweet smell of aviation fuel. There was a tarnished silver metal bell on the counter with a push button in the center. I tapped it twice.

"C'mon back," came a loud, male voice.

I walked around the counter, through a doorway, and into an open hangar space that contained a bright green biplane with orange graphic stripes. The combination made my eyes flash.

A man wearing blue coveralls was wrestling a new water heater into position near the flex-tube pipes that had, no doubt, run to the old water heater.

I stood in front of the orange and green machine. "What's the biplane?" I asked.

"Steen Skybolt, homebuilt," the man said without looking up from his plumbing project.

"Gorgeous. Build it yourself?"

"Kinda. Three of us went in on the kit."

"Nice. Welded tube fuselage and fabric covered, right? Looks like a Lycoming engine. Power-to-weight ratio must be great."

"You know your birds."

"Not really. I fly a little, but I've never taken a biplane up."

"Interested in lessons?"

"Maybe someday. I'm actually looking for information about biplanes in the area."

The man's pipe wrench slipped off its target and made a metallic clink. "Ouch." The man sucked on his knuckle.

"Can I help?" I said.

"No thanks. I just need to show this beast who's boss." He

put the wrench back on at a different angle.

I said, "A guy in Incline was telling me about a large biplane he's seen that was silent. He said he's seen it go by twice. I asked him to estimate how high up the plane was. He said it was about five thousand feet up. Which is too low to seem silent to anyone who isn't deaf. So I pressed him. Granted, the guy is a little off. But he stuck with the description."

"A biplane that's silent at five thousand feet AGL," the man repeated, using the abbreviation for above ground level.

"Right," I said. "So I was curious what a biplane expert like you would have to say."

The man was rocking the water heater. "Tell you what, I will take some help on this."

I walked over.

"As you can see, this heater is a little shorter than the one I took out. Shorter but wider. So I've got those three patio stones to make up the height difference. Problem is, this heater weighs about the same as a walrus. I'm thinking, if I can rock this beast back and forth, you could toe the patio stones underneath."

"Sounds good to me."

I put my hands on the water heater and my boot toe on one of the patio stones. He rocked. I added to his motion. It took a few tries, but we got the patio stones under it. The fittings now lined up with the flex tubes.

"Okay, you're talking about a silent biplane," he said. "Doesn't make sense to me. Maybe it was a trick of the wind. The sound blowing away from him or something."

"You don't know of any biplanes with quiet engines?"

The man shook his head as he finger-tightened the pipe connections. "That'd be like a quiet race car. You probably know that all the advantages with biplanes in the old days went away with the engineering advancements that produced modern monoplanes. So now, the whole point of biplanes is power for doing aerobatics. With power comes sound. In some cases, the whole point isn't making power at all but making noise. Like a Harley." He made a final twist with the wrench. "Still, it doesn't make sense," he said. The man reached up and opened the water shut-off valves. There was a loud sound of water rushing into the water heater.

The man listened for a bit, then said, "Maybe the pilot was coming out of an aerobatic maneuver and he throttled back the power. From the ground, the contrast can almost seem like silence."

"I bet that was it," I said. "I've certainly experienced the flip side. A plane I hadn't noticed at all, and then the power is suddenly throttled up, announcing the plane's existence. It makes sense the reverse could happen. But the guy who told me about it made a point of saying the plane was a big sucker. And big planes have large, noisy engines." I pulled out one of my cards and set it on a rolling Craftsman tool cart. "If you hear of anything, I'd appreciate a call, if it's not too much trouble."

I turned to leave.

The man called after me. "You probably know the biggest biplane was that Soviet bird. A taildragger. Carries ten people or more. They started making it back in the nineteen forties. The Antonov AN Two. Last I heard, they were still being made up to the early two thousands."

"Rings a bell," I said as I turned back to him.

"'Course, the AN Two has a big-ass engine."

"Which makes a big noise," I said.

He paused. "But I remember reading that it has a ridiculously low stall speed. Less than thirty knots."

"Meaning," I said as I picked up on his meaning, "that the plane can probably be landed with no power at all."

He nodded. "A silent approach. Land into any headwind, it'd be like dropping down in a parachute, barely moving forward at all."

"Interesting idea," I said. "I wonder if there is any registry of AN Two owners."

"Not that I know of." He turned back to his water heater. "Good luck."

I thanked him and went back out to the Ford.

Back home, I opened my laptop and searched on Antonov AN-2. Up came lots of info and lots of pictures. It was a large, ungainly-looking biplane with a 60-foot wingspan and 40 feet of length. The biplane was a taildragger. It would have to be moving down the runway at good speed before the tail would be lifted by air flow. Once the plane was in a horizontal position, it could take off.

In addition to a cockpit with a large mosaic of windows that wrapped around the pilots, the AN-2 passenger compartment had four small windows on each side and one or two doors, depending on the model. The aircraft could carry ten or twelve passengers and was popular with skydiving clubs.

I found there were lots of AN-2 models. Some were for hauling cargo, some were for hauling small groups of people on short-haul transportation routes or on tourist flights. Some models were designed for crop dusting and other agricultural applications.

An interesting bit of trivia was that the Antonov owner's manual claims there is no stall speed. The plane is designed so that, if it slows to less than 30 knots, it pitches just enough forward to maintain a slow forward speed, and then it slowly drops out of the sky. In a power-on landing, the plane can land in only a few hundred feet of runway. But in a power-off approach, the plane can land in a very short space.

Takeoffs were similarly short.

Another feature of the AN-2 was that, because it was able to fly at such low speeds and because it could be outfitted with large tundra tires, it made an ideal bush plane, perfect for flying a group of people in and out of the back country.

As I pondered what I read, a kind of thought experiment occurred to me.

I fetched a beer, went out on the deck, and let my imagination roam.

TWENTY-THREE

Imagine someone who wanted to fly in and out of a place without a normal landing strip. The first thought of many people would be to use a helicopter.

But what if the objective was to come and go without being noticed? A helicopter would be no good because it makes a tremendous amount of noise.

A plane, on the other hand, can glide in with little to no power to speak of. It could land almost as silently as a bird. And what if the runway were inclined? A plane like an Antonov AN-2 would be able to stop even faster if it were landing uphill. Then, once the plane was on the ground, if it were somehow turned around at the top of the hill, the takeoff, going downhill and aided by gravity, might be much shorter than the takeoff distance stated in the manual. Taking off downhill might make it possible to use just a short blast of full engine power to get airborne. Once the plane was in the air, the power could be throttled back to the minimum necessary to stay airborne, and it would fly very quietly.

My idea expanded. I'd once read about the steepest runways around the world. One in Nepal, for example. The inclined runway came down a mountain slope and ended at a drop off. When departing planes took off, the downslope helped them get to airborne speed very quickly. But instead of needing to gain altitude to climb above trees and buildings and such, all the planes had to do was get a few feet into the air. When they went off the end of the runway, the mountain dropped away, and they were quickly hundreds, or even thousands, of feet above the ground.

Landing was done facing the opposite direction, uphill, which slowed the landing aircraft very quickly.

No doubt flying in and out of inclined runways seemed perilous. But there were significant advantages.

It was possible that Tahoe offered many such places where someone could land an airplane that had a very slow operating speed. Some of them could be near Incline Village where the silent biplane was spotted. In fact, of all the towns around Tahoe, Incline Village was the most mountainous of all. It consisted of steep mountain slopes and valleys. There were no significant flat areas anywhere.

But if you were a pilot, why not just fly in and out of the Truckee Airport or the Reno Tahoe Airport in Reno. Clearly that made the most sense.

Unless you were transporting things that you didn't want others to know about.

Like what? People? Drugs? Guns?

So my idea expanded to inclines up high, away from prying eyes. Imagine a high, sloped meadow with a dropoff at the lower end. That could provide a relatively private way to come and go in Tahoe with no worries about patrol cars taking down vehicle license numbers and no airport computers logging arrivals and departures and passenger lists.

Pilots usually filed flight plans with the Federal Aviation Administration. But it was not required for planes being flown using visual flight rules. A VFR pilot could come and go from a remote location, and there would be no record of it anywhere. Unless an observer like Heathcliff was nearby and happened to look up at the right time.

How would it work?

A pilot who wants to glide in and land on an upsloping runway could do it soundlessly as long as the engine was off. The key was knowing the plane's glide ratio. As long as the pilot was on the correct glide slope, the engine could be shut down. With sufficient altitude, the pilot could glide in from many miles away.

But before taking off again, the pilot needs to reposition the plane to the top of the runway and do it without the roar of the engine. How? Maybe he has some kind of winch attached to a tree. It could be battery powered. So he walks up to the tree and winch, picks up the cable hook, and turns on the winch to unspool the cable. The winch could even be controlled by a remote. He hauls the cable down and uses the remote to stop the winch. Then he hooks the cable onto a hook near the rear wheel or even on the rear wheel itself, which, on a taildragger, swivels.

Taildragger planes are not designed to be hauled uphill by their rear wheels. But the plane could possibly be modified to strengthen the appropriate components.

The pilot reverses the winch, and the plane is rolled backwards up the sloping runway.

Of course, Tahoe was not considered a remote location by any measure. But a secluded mountaintop could be effectively remote.

I stood up and leaned over the deck railing. Lake Tahoe was 1000 feet below and looking as blue as a prize sapphire.

I thought about the topography of Incline Village. To the east of town was Diamond Peak Ski Area and a collection of mountains that stretched above the ski runs. One could drive up the Mt. Rose Highway to large stretches of meadows with views of mountains and Lake Tahoe below. But those meadows were too visible to fit my idea of a hidden landing strip.

To the north of Incline Village was a steep wall of mountains leading up to Relay Peak, Mt. Houghton, and Mt. Rose, all between 10,000 and 11,000 feet high. I'd hiked through some of that terrain, and it was filled with crags and valleys and ridges that obscured open views. It stretched for miles, and there could be countless places where a plane could fly in and out, largely unnoticed. And even if a hiker spotted a plane far from any airport, they would likely assume that it was just exploring the mountains.

But there was one thing that would identify a remote location that was used for flying. A plane would be visible when it wasn't in use. Even if a plane was out of sight from hikers, it was visible from above. Most planes are light-colored and stand out from any landscape. Other pilots flying above Tahoe could see planes from above. And there were countless unmanned satellites cruising the heavens taking telescopic pictures of Earth.

How would I find such a plane? By looking through satellite pictures.

Google Earth was the easiest to use.

I brought up a map of the Incline Village area, switched the view to the satellite photo, and started scanning. What a great way to find someone who kept an airplane up in the mountains.

Except that, while the photos of mountains were intriguing and even pretty, it was like looking for a tree in a forest. Every time I saw something that could be a plane, I zoomed in and saw what looked like a group of boulders or some weathered logs. In time, I took a break and got some corn chips and cheddar cheese.

Spot was suddenly alert, his nostrils flexing.

"Later, Largeness. I'm working. My brain needs fuel."

I figured that a plane with a 60-foot wingspan could be seen in a satellite photo if I zoomed in enough. I did a kind of grid search on the screen, moving my eyes back and forth in descending rows.

My search quickly became enormously tedious. My eyes glazed over. I had to sip beer and eat chips frequently. Yet the tedium increased. I did a little calculation on how long it would take to cover even a small portion of the mountains around Incline Village, and I realized I would consume three tons of chips and be 95 years old before I'd completed the task. Except that my boredom was severe enough that it would take years off my life, and I'd never make it to 90, never mind 95. Of course, that was a moot point now that Diamond had predicted my junk food diet would only get me into my 70s.

I gave up, found a picture of an AN-2, and printed it.

I called Diamond and told him I had questions I wanted to run by him. He said he was at a meeting at a brew pub on the South Shore.

"My kind of meeting," I said.

"Yo también. How 'bout you come by?"

TWENTY-FOUR

I found a parking place for the Ford, and Spot and I found Diamond a short time later. He was sitting at an outdoor table, one of three that were arranged around a four-foot-wide, shallow steel bowl with colorful rocks at the bottom. Tall blue and yellow flames from some hidden source of gas under the rocks made an undulating dance in the bowl. Street would, of course, be bothered by the waste in heating up the outdoors, but it was attractive and radiated warmth. A middle-aged woman with spectacularly thick and shiny black hair stood up and was just saying goodbye to Diamond. She turned, saw Spot, and stiffened.

Diamond said, "Akari, I'd like you to meet the dog I was telling you about, His Largeness. Don't worry, he's friendly and a sweetheart to all women. You can pet him."

Diamond rubbed Spot's head as if to show her it was safe.

The woman reached out with trepidation and gave Spot the faintest touch on the top of his head.

"Oh, and this is Owen McKenna, Spot's handler. Owen, meet Akari Tanaka."

"Hi," I said.

The woman gave me a little wave and a formal nod, then turned back to Diamond.

"Arigato, mata ne."

"Sayonara," Diamond said.

The woman left.

"Because you're in your civvies," I said, "that implies you are off duty."

"Why I'm thinking of a drink. But Akari doesn't drink, and I didn't want to seem impolite. But now we can indulge."

Diamond ordered a beer. I ordered a coffee.

Diamond raised his eyebrows.

"I already had a beer."

"Wow, you are one tough, hard-boiled PI."

While we waited, Diamond flashed his hands out as if to slap Spot and then pulled his hands back before Spot could grab them with his teeth. It was a futile exercise. Spot was much too fast. Fortunately, Spot didn't munch down on Diamond's hands. He closed his mouth just enough to show that he was faster.

The waiter brought our liquids. We clicked, bottle against coffee mug.

"How do you know Akari?"

"She's a chemist for Dow Chemical in San Francisco. Came up to Tahoe on a work project, consulting with a Minden company that's working with Tesla's battery factory in Reno. I met her because the Douglas County Sheriff wanted her to give a talk at an emergency responder seminar on safety issues with electric vehicles."

"They have safety issues?"

"Not as much as gas cars, but yeah, cops need to know about the dangers with EVs."

"Such as..." I said.

"Sounds like the main concern is fires."

"Hard to have a gas fire with no gas," I said.

"Right. But Akari told us that if, in fact, an electric vehicle battery catches fire… Look out."

"Bad?"

"Stuff of nightmares. Lithium ion batteries have sophisticated electronics to keep them from over heating. This Minden company is doing tests that involve overheating batteries." He gave me a sly smile. "Apparently, those batteries get pretty exciting when they get too warm."

"How do they heat batteries? Put them in an oven?"

"Maybe. But they probably use methods that might commonly occur. Short circuiting the battery would be one."

Maybe my frown communicated confusion.

Diamond said, "Like when you drop a screwdriver across an old car battery's terminals and that measly twelve-volt power source suddenly produces enough current to melt the screwdriver. The result is a lot of heat and the possibility that the battery kicks out gasses that are explosive."

"Ah," I said. "I'm guessing that lithium ion batteries do that and more."

"Much more. Akari Tanaka said that lithium ion batteries are quite sensitive to heat. If a battery gets hot enough, it can start an exothermic reaction."

"Which means?"

"The kind of reaction that gives off heat. Which makes the reaction more intense. It's a runaway process, and the battery can heat up so hot the lithium metal starts burning."

"Metal can burn?"

"Sure thing. When the burning starts, the battery gets up to something like three thousand degrees or more, and the fire can't be put out."

"Yikes. That's when you wish you carried a bucket of water in your car."

Diamond's eyes went wide. "Actually, it turns out that water might be the worst thing to use in such a fire. Something about a super hot fire with burning metal causes the water to disassociate into hydrogen and oxygen, and they form other compounds, and the whole mess intensifies and explodes the fire."

"Yikes. We grow up thinking water puts out fires. Sounds like you're saying that not only can metal burn, water can burn as well."

"Sí."

"I've heard of electric cars burning up."

"Yeah. The seminar folks showed us a picture of one. Normally a burnt car still has its metal frame. The electric car was just a pile of ash in the street. Three thousand-some degrees is hot enough to burn up other metals that weren't already burning. But Akari says that battery fires are quite rare."

"I hope so."

Diamond gazed off into the distance. "I wonder if Akari likes Mexican food."

"Akari is Japanese, right? You could try making soy sauce

tacos. But that might be the opposite of salsa flavor."

Diamond shrugged. "Opposites attract. Sweet and sour. And we're actually kind of similar. Both immigrants."

"You may be an immigrant, but you know more about America than almost any American."

"I don't know about American social media culture. Posting pictures of yourself everywhere."

"You took selfies in order to masquerade as Benito Diaz up at Castle Rock. You could learn. Post your selfies on one of those dating apps. Women would swipe on your mug."

Diamond nodded as if he were seriously thinking about it.

"You seemed agitated when you called," he said.

"I'm spinning my wheels, but thinking I might find traction with a recent hunch."

"Which is?" Diamond drank.

"The UCSF doctors had a classmate they call Heathcliff."

"The anti-hero in Emily Brontë's *Wuthering Heights*," he said.

"How do you know about that?"

"Went through a Brontë stage some time back."

"Oh. So I met this guy Heathcliff. He went to the same UCSF med school as these other doctors. He told me about a large, silent biplane flying low over Incline Village. And the image is compelling to me."

"How'd this guy get the name Heathcliff?"

"He was born Horatio Harris, but his med school classmates called him Heathcliff. Or at least the female ones did. He's got a look that makes them lose their footing. One of the Brontë sisters gave me his picture."

I got it out and handed it to Diamond.

"I see why these women are so interested. Put him in a group, no one's gonna look at anyone else." He handed back the photo.

"Turns out Heathcliff is wired a little differently from most of us. The Brontë sisters who directed me toward him said he was injured when he jumped from the Golden Gate Bridge. He lost enough brain power that he had to drop out of med school."

"Why did you go to talk to him in the first place?" Diamond was frowning.

"I was pursuing the concept that too many unusual bad happenings in a bucolic mountain landscape suggested they were connected. And when I talked to the Brontë sisters about Veronica Eastern's murder, they thought I should talk to him."

"What do you think it means," Diamond said, "this confluence of med school alums, one dead, one beat up, and one anti-hero who fell off the bridge and is seeing biplanes?"

"I don't know. The Brontë sisters also told me about an autopsy they witnessed in med school. The deceased had been murdered the same way Veronica Eastern was murdered. Makes me wonder if there's a connection."

Diamond drank beer. "Always heard that UCSF Med School was one of the best," Diamond said. He reached over and rubbed Spot, who appeared to be asleep.

"Benito referred to the triplet Brontë sisters when he was first in your office. They also went to that same school?"

"Yeah. And they're here in Tahoe as well."

"But their names aren't actually Brontë?" Diamond asked.

"No. Their last name is Smythe. But their first names match the Brontës. Charlotte, Emily, and Anne."

"I remember that from when Benito Diaz came to your office. What kind of doctors are they?"

"Internists."

Diamond nodded. "I think Brontë is a Greek name. Long way from Smythe. But now I understand the Heathcliff reference. There's a whole Brontë vibe going on."

"Right. The Brontë sisters could barely contain their intrigue about him and their sadness that he got injured during med school. I found him in Incline Village. He's clearly damaged goods. Polite but disconnected from reality."

"Which manifests how?" Diamond asked.

"His girlfriend Isabel died from a fall back during med school. Three days before Heathcliff's fall from the Golden Gate. But Heathcliff still meets her at coffee shops and goes on walks with her, and they have picnic lunches."

Diamond made a slow, single nod. Like all sensitive people, he understood the struggle of people whose traumatic experiences mixed with troubling memories that may or may not be literal.

"For any individual, their own perception rules," Diamond said. "Nothing anyone else says—whether shrink or teacher or cop—is going to change that hierarchy. If a guy has coffee with his dead girlfriend and talks to her in an intimate way, that's all that matters for that guy. Anyone who comes along and says it ain't so is an interloper with no credibility and no value and no meaning in that guy's life." Diamond paused. "His fall from the Gate... Was it a suicide attempt?"

"That's an interesting thing. He doesn't remember. It happened three days after he found his girlfriend Isabel dead from a fall. So it looked like a suicide attempt. I believe the Brontë sisters referred to him jumping."

Diamond was still rubbing Spot's head, giving him hard squeezes more like a massage than a pet. "How'd you find Heathcliff in Incline Village?" he asked.

"The Brontë sisters told me he was reportedly living in Incline, hanging out with Isabel, going to coffee shops and writing poetry. So I went to Incline, showed his picture around, walked the streets, and asked questions. I found him sitting in the corner of a coffee shop. He was at a table with two chairs and two cups of coffee."

I sipped my own coffee, then continued. "I walked over and talked to him for some time. He was disheveled and unwashed, but mostly lucid and well-spoken."

"Lucid even though he was hanging out with his dead girlfriend." Diamond was somber and serious.

"Yeah. He didn't formally introduce her to me. But he spoke of her and gestured toward her."

"Meaning, the empty chair near him," Diamond said as if he wanted to be certain he understood.

"Right. It was as if the only reason he didn't make the introduction was that he wasn't sure she would respond. He said she was like the poet Emily Dickinson, very shy, non-social, almost a shut-in."

Diamond pondered that for a minute.

"Did anyone witness Heathcliff jump off the bridge during medical school?" he asked.

"No. He was seen falling by some men on a fishing boat. They fished him out of the water and thought he was dead. Then they saw him move some fingers. So they pumped on his chest, and eventually he was revived but only barely. After an extended time in the hospital, he slowly got better. But he's still disconnected from reality."

"He talk about anything in particular?"

"Yeah. Isabel and poetry and a large, silent biplane. He said planes were important to him."

"Did he say why?"

"He didn't know why, but he thought there must be something about planes in his past. That's why I wanted your thoughts. He's not a pilot. He claims his interest in planes is only the interest of a poet. The beauty and magic of a machine that can ride the wind."

Diamond leaned back in his chair. "What do you think are the most important things in Heathcliff's life?"

"Isabel, followed by poetry. After that maybe the mystery of lost memories from when he fell. This plane, or some other plane is tied up in one of those lost memories. He said as much himself." I drank the last of my coffee.

"I also found out that one or more of the Brontë sisters are pilots."

"Lotta plane stuff goin' on."

"Do you think that Heathcliff's report of the plane could be accurate considering his disconnect from reality?"

Diamond thought about it. "In the main, yes. I believe that Heathcliff and possibly Isabel had some kind of previous experience with a plane that made this plane seem significant. The fact that the biplane matters to Heathcliff is all that counts from his perspective. But that doesn't mean he actually saw a large biplane over Incline Village."

Diamond sipped beer and looked at the fire saucer.

"What do you mean by that?"

"There's a thing called the availability bias," he said. "Sometimes called the availability heuristic."

"What?" I said. "I've never even heard that word."

"Never mind the word heuristic. Bottom line is that when we're looking for information or relevance or judgment or whatever, if we can think of a potential answer, we're more likely to believe that answer than believe an answer we can't think of but later hear about."

"Example?" I asked.

"You're going about your day. Something you read reminds you of biplanes. So you spend a few moments over coffee thinking of a time when you saw biplanes up close, like at an air show or something. Maybe you even look at biplane pictures online. An hour after thinking about that experience, you and your friend see a plane way up high. Something about its sound is unusual. So your friend wonders what kind of plane it is. You say, 'Maybe it's a biplane.'"

I said, "All because I've been thinking about biplanes?"

"Yeah. You have no information that suggests it is a biplane. All you have is your recent thoughts about biplanes."

"So I begin to think of it as a biplane," I said.

"Right."

"And," I said, figuring out where Diamond was going with his thought, "if I think of the unusual plane a week later, I might imagine it was a biplane."

Diamond nodded. "Think of the availability bias as your brain recalling familiar ideas and ignoring unfamiliar ideas."

"You think Heathcliff did that?" I said. I was the guy who'd spoken to Heathcliff, but now I was asking Diamond about him.

Diamond nodded. "Sí. The biplane was significant to him for some reason."

"Significant because of the availability of a related memory that Heathcliff has," I said.

"That would be my guess."

"I think I know what kind of plane it is." I showed Diamond

the picture I'd printed of the Antonov AN-2.

"Whoa. Big sucker."

"I'm wondering what a big biplane would be doing in Tahoe," I said.

"Drugs?" Diamond said. "Money? They both might connect to doctors. But how could a biplane be connected?" Diamond frowned.

"Drugs are often smuggled. A biplane could carry drugs and maybe do airdrops in Incline Village. Could be some doctors are behind it."

"Makes me think about what else is smuggled," Diamond said.

"People?"

Diamond drank beer. "Can't see Tahoe as a target for human trafficking. Most of the time one hears about people jammed into trucks coming over the border from Mexico or in the holds of ships coming into port from far parts of the world. But I suppose it's possible trafficking could take place in Tahoe. Someone bringing in girls from who knows where. I think drugs make more sense."

"You got an idea who I should talk to about that?" I asked.

"No. But let me make a call."

TWENTY-FIVE

Diamond pulled out his cell phone, tapped a few times. He waited. I could hear the ring from the other side of the table.

"Diamond," came the voice on the other end of Diamond's phone.

"Sí," Diamond said. "Calling about your DEA friend." He paused. "Yeah. Maybe, anyway." Then, "Hard to tell. Got a question about a possible operation involving a plane." Silence for several seconds. "The question is if a particular plane might be flying drugs. Worth trying, I think," Diamond said. He pulled a pen and a pocket notebook from his pocket. He wrote. "Thanks." He hung up.

Diamond turned to me and read from the notebook. "Nadia Solokov. DEA agent in the Bay Area, friend of my buddy Darlene Anderson. Apparently, Nadia Solokov comes up to ski with Darlene. Some kind of escape-the-husbands package at Palisades Tahoe. I think the resort even has a special ticket price."

Maybe I frowned.

Diamond said, "The ski resorts know that women skiers have more moolah than men, so they're going after that market."

"Nice name, Nadia Solokov."

Diamond nodded. "Nadia is in San Francisco and focuses on drugs that get trafficked in Northern California." He handed me the page from his notebook.

"Okay if I call her now?"

"Darlene didn't say it wasn't."

I dialed. It was answered on the second ring.

"Nadia Solokov," a pleasant woman's voice said.

"Hi, Ms. Solokov. My name is Owen McKenna. I'm a private investigator in Tahoe, formerly with the SFPD. I was referred to you by Darlene Anderson, a friend of Sergeant Diamond Martinez at the Douglas County Sheriff's Office in Minden, Nevada. I'm looking into a case involving two people who were murdered. One young man in San Francisco a dozen years ago, and a doctor who was recently murdered in Tahoe. The MO suggests they are connected. I've come across information about an unusual plane flying in the Tahoe Basin. My question to you is if you can speculate about any contraband that might be flown into or out of Tahoe. Especially contraband that might be related to the medical profession."

"Well, now, Mr. Owen McKenna." The woman spoke not with a Russian accent but with a kind of Southern drawl like I'd heard in Kentucky or maybe Tennessee. A Southern drawl that sounded upper class. I could imagine her calling a Thoroughbred race at Churchill Downs. She continued, "That's a lot of rambling far afield from any experience of mine."

"Does that mean you can't speculate on the appearance of such a plane?"

"I know nothing about airplanes. Especially planes in Tahoe. Have you connected this aircraft to any local airport?"

"Not yet."

"I can tell you this," the DEA woman said. "The Drug Enforcement Administration doesn't look much at airplanes except near our national borders. So I'd have a hard time getting excited about planes in Tahoe."

"Because this plane seems out of place in the mountains, I'm wondering if there are any drugs that might make more sense than others?"

"This is a jet?"

"No. A big slow biplane."

"For most drug smugglers, speed and range are critical when coming in from Central or South America."

"But not all drugs come from south of the border," I said.

"Most do."

"So you think my idea is of no account," I said.

Diamond was across from me, leaning back, his hand resting on Spot's big head. Spot was sitting next to Diamond and panting from the steel saucer heat. But as always, Spot liked the heat even if he had to pant to cool off.

Diamond's face was blank. Maybe he expected that I would get nowhere with a big-shot DEA agent in the Bay Area. Whatever the answer, he obviously wasn't surprised.

The woman said, "I wouldn't consider a local, slow plane as a potential problem, bringing drugs into the impoverished, rural backwaters of Lake Tahoe."

Was her sarcasm just her natural edginess? Or was that a verbal slap in the face?

"Well, now that you put it that way," I said. "Maybe I'll just assume it is a new tourist plane, showing people the wonders of the water from the air."

"Maybe you should."

She sounded very put out by my interruption in her life.

"Before you go," I said, "is there any standard situation where the DEA looks closely at planes that go nowhere near the southern border?"

"First, let me emphasize," she said with deliberate words, "we focus on interdiction of opiates and such from the south and the Far East. As for cannabis, the laws have changed, so that is no longer a concern. The only remaining drug is nicotine. Cigarettes are acquired in low-tax states, or from crooked distributors who don't pay for state tax stamps, or from counterfeit manufacturers from overseas."

I was surprised. "Are you saying that there is a lot of tobacco smuggling in the area?"

Did she scoff? Did I hear her chuckling at me under her breath?

"Sorry to bring you into the current world, Mr. McKenna, but—as measured by dollar value—tobacco smuggling is a bigger business than most other drugs."

"Really? What about cocaine and meth and fentanyl and stuff like that?"

"Perhaps you need to hear me say something twice in order to understand?" Her words sliced like knives. "Some estimates suggest tobacco smuggling is as big a business as cocaine, heroin, and meth-amphetamines put together."

"I never knew." I tried to organize my thoughts. "So unusual planes flying in unusual places could possibly have something to do with cigarette smuggling?"

"Possibly," she said.

Diamond looked nearly asleep. Spot had sagged down from his sitting position so that he was now lying in the "ready" position, his weight on both his chest and his elbows. But he kept his head lifted up high so his jawbone could rest on Diamond's thigh. Spot's throat was getting squeezed enough that he was wheezing as he tried to get air. Nevertheless, his eyes were shut, and it appeared that the saucer fire heat had put him to sleep.

"Does the DEA pursue tobacco smuggling?" I asked Nadia Solokov.

"No." The woman sounded very brusque. "In a quirk of governmental capriciousness, the investigation of cigarette smuggling is the exclusive territory of the ATF. You've probably heard what ATF stands for."

"Alcohol, Tobacco, and Firearms," I said feeling properly admonished.

"As a former law enforcement officer, I would think you'd know about the ATF." Her scorn was thick. "If you think you have a tobacco issue, you should talk with them."

"Got it," I said. "Any chance you can refer me to someone in the ATF?"

I heard her breathing. Deep breaths, in and out. Trying to stay calm and keep from yelling at me for having the bad manners to be ignorant and then ask her help.

"Try Special Agent James Rousseau. He's a little slow, but he means well. Four one five, five…"

I interrupted. "Sorry, let me grab a pen." I reached over and took the pen and notebook that Diamond was handing me.

"Okay, I'm ready."

She read off the number.

"Thank you very much for your help, Ms. Solokov. I appreciate the…"

"Goodbye," she interrupted, and then she hung up on me.

TWENTY-SIX

When you get slapped in the face, the best response is to try to ignore it and concentrate on your next move.

"Okay with you if I make another call?" I said.

Diamond nodded. He looked almost as asleep as Spot.

I picked up the phone, and dialed James Rousseau. It rang several times and then was picked up with a breathless "Rousseau, ATF."

I introduced myself and explained how I got his number. "I'm hoping you can answer a couple of questions."

"Shoot."

So I told him what I'd told DEA Agent Nadia Solokov about an unusual biplane that had been seen in Tahoe. I left out the potential connection to doctors. "It may be that I'm onto nothing…"

Rousseau spoke slowly. "But when you see something unusual during your preflight check, you investigate before you release the brakes and push that throttle forward."

That was a strange comment that caught me by surprise.

"You're a pilot?" I said.

"Just enough to get myself in trouble if I'm landing in a crosswind of more than seven or eight knots. But I don't know biplanes much. A guy I know, Bobby Folmer, has a CR Forty Two Falco. And he always talks about his hangar buddy Dick Ryker. Ryker's got a Pitts Special in the next hangar. So I hear biplane stories."

"I don't know that first name you said. Something Falco."

"The Forty Two Falco is an Italian fighter biplane, single seat. Made in the thirties, and was pretty common in Europe during World War Two. Bobby told me a variation of the Falco model still holds the record for fastest biplane ever flown."

"You know your planes."

"Not really. I got my pilot's license flying out of San Carlos on the peninsula, which is where I met Bobby. That's the sum total of what I know about biplanes. Are you currently in Tahoe?" he asked.

"Yes."

"I'm in The City, but I've got to attend a meeting in Sacramento tomorrow. Near the capital. I could meet you there after the gig is over. There's a regular place where the crew likes to get a bump."

"A regular place?"

"Yeah. One of the Assistant Directors for Field Operations is a buddy with the Sacramento Field Agent, so they're always planning stuff in Sac."

"So everyone can go over preflight procedures?"

He made another sigh. "Something like that. Why they can't do it in San Francisco is a mystery. I suppose it's big city envy."

"What's that?"

"It's a Sac thing. It's like they're stuck flying One Fifty-twos, and they imagine the San Francisco guys are up there in Blue Angel fighter jets. But no matter their big league dreams, they're always just going to be the capital city."

"Tell me where to meet you, I'll be there."

James Rousseau gave me an address downtown, close to the capital. He said it was a rooftop bar, so I figured that was outdoorsy enough to bring Spot.

I hung up, then gave Diamond the gist, and thanked him for the phone number for Nadia Solokov. Diamond nodded, and we said goodbye.

The next day, Spot and I got to Sacramento a little early. We explored the Capital Park, looked at the rose gardens and the sculptures, and briefly played fetch when I found a stick underneath one of the giant redwoods.

Unfortunately, of all the working breeds, Great Danes have the least work ethic. They are also acutely aware that people who throw sticks and balls have an ulterior motive of trying to get dogs to engage in needless exercise while the people get no exercise at all. Danes have little tolerance for that double standard.

So Spot's enthusiasm for chasing a stick lasted just two throws. On his third fetch, he picked up the stick—which was three feet long and two inches in diameter—looked at me, and without trotting my way, began to chew the stick up.

I called out, "Spot, I want that stick."

He ignored me and chewed with enough industry to show that he didn't mind jaw exercise.

I raised my voice. "Spot, you're wrecking a prime stick. A guy could do some serious stuff with a stick like that."

But Spot continued to ignore me and doubled down on his mastication. As the stick broke into small pieces, he lay down on the grass, elbows splayed for maximum stick-chewing support, and pulverized the stick into chips.

I walked up. "You should show more respect for the person who provides you with food and hearth and cavernous bed. My stick needs don't appear to make any difference to you."

Spot kept his head down, focusing on his task. He gripped the last portion of the stick between his paws. Teddy Roosevelt's philosophy didn't hold. You can't carry a big stick if you chew it into chips. In a minute, the stick was gone.

"Okay, Largeness, you made your point. Let's go talk contraband with the ATF dude."

We found the bar's address in a hotel a couple of blocks over. The bar entrance consisted of a sign in front of an escalator, which went up to a mezzanine, which had two elevators, which would no doubt take patrons to the roof. There was a bar sign and two well-dressed young men on either side of the escalator. Not bouncers. More like influencers.

"Sorry, no dogs," one of them said.

"This isn't an ordinary dog," I said.

"I can see that," the man said with poise.

Spot lifted up his nose and sniffed near the man's chin. The man's arms levitated a bit. The man's companion took a step back.

I said, "This dog is part of an ATF task force assignment. You can check with James Rousseau, the ATF agent who is inside waiting for us. The dog is looking for sticks. If your rooftop bar were to be patronized by—you know—people in the stick business, you would want to be sure you haven't impeded an official ATF duty dog."

The young man looked both puzzled and worried. "When you say stick, you mean that metaphorically, right?"

I made my face very serious. "Metaphors everywhere you turn."

The man's coworker said, "Let 'em go, Chase. You know that Tony B would freak if he found out you got on the wrong side of a federal agency. 'Cuz then they call the health department and the city inspectors, and who knows what would happen."

The two young men looked at each other. They both made a hint of a nod, then stepped aside.

We walked forward toward the escalator.

Spot looked down at the moving steps. I couldn't remember if he'd ever been on an escalator. But he liked rides of any kind, so I assumed it wouldn't be a problem.

He stepped his front paws onto the moving step, then looked down and back at his rear paws as if to see whether they were also on a moving step.

They weren't, and his front and rear legs were being separated. He walked his rear paws forward. That was better.

He wagged. Then shook his head and jowls. Wood chips flew. One of the men flanking the escalator reached up and wiped a wood chip off his cheek.

At the top of the escalator, we waited for an elevator. When the doors opened, and we walked into the box, most of the other people who were waiting hung back. Was it worth risking your life with an animal that size inside an elevator? A tiny, older woman wearing a purple sequined dress that was too tight was the only one who got on with us.

She put her hand on Spot's shoulder which wasn't much below her shoulder.

"Who's this?"

"His Largeness."

She leaned sideways and hugged him, her arms barely draping the top of his back. "Hi, Largeness."

Spot wagged. He looked up at the red numbers counting off the floors.

"We used to have Great Danes," the woman said. "Two Fawn, one Harlequin, one Black. But the only one this big was the Black. His name was Thor, God of Thunder. He was even bigger than this guy." She smacked Spot on his chest. "But Thor was afraid of thunder. So, on Halloween, when we took the kids trick-or-treating, we used to take a pink blanket and use it to wrap Thor up. Like a pink dress. We called him the Girly Goddess of Pink Thunder. We'd whisper in his ear, 'Girly Goddess of Pink Thunder.' He liked that. He would wag his tail." She leaned sideways and whispered in Spot's ear. "Would you wear a pink dress, Largeness?"

Spot wagged.

"Thor sounds fun," I said.

The woman looked very serious. "He was a drag queen Dane," she said, "back before everyone loved drag queens. Now they'd start one of those groups on the internet. There would be a YouTube channel. Danes in Drag."

"No one gave him grief, a big strong dog dressed in pink?" I said.

"No. Thor weighed two hundred ten pounds and he had fangs like a bear, so no one ever gave him any shit."

"I bet they didn't," I said.

The elevator doors opened, and we were at a glass entrance to a rooftop bar. I held the door for the woman. She waited to let Spot go first. We all walked out on the roof.

The woman walked up to the bar. The bartender immediately nodded at her and reached for a martini glass.

TWENTY-SEVEN

I scanned the rooftop bar for anyone who looked like a cop.

It's a look that is hard to describe but easy for other law enforcement officers to recognize, even if no one is wearing a uniform. Cops in plain clothes still telegraph that they are part of a critical group. They don't act like they're particularly important individually. But they know they're critical. Their group is a kind of societal glue that holds things together and maintains function.

I saw him turn and glance at us. Or, more correctly, glance at Spot.

The man sat alone at a table, his back to one of the two main walls. He faced the crowd, the short wall at the edge of the roof, and the skyline beyond. He was a stocky guy with short brown hair under a baseball cap with Willie Mays' name and a tiny San Francisco Giants logo and the number 24. He had a stiff bristle mustache that protruded enough to make his chin look weak, a look that was accentuated by enough extra weight that his neck wasn't slim. But the most noticeable thing about him was his eyes. They barely showed under the brim of his cap. They reminded me of a raptor's eyes, piercing the air like those of a hawk on a power pole, scanning a field for prey and problems. It was a kind of alertness that indicated he took everything in. The DEA lady might have described him as slow, but I could tell that James Rousseau was aware of everything and everyone.

I walked over. The other patrons stared at Spot, pointing and exclaiming.

In keeping with the cop personality type, James Rousseau didn't react.

"Hi, James, I'm Owen. This is Spot." I held Spot back.

Rousseau nodded, stood up halfway, shook my hand, sat back down.

He had a light-colored beer in front of him, half-drunk.

I sat, had Spot sit next to me. Rousseau looked at Spot but showed no reaction. Cops know how to be cool, no matter what. If Spot balanced a basketball on his nose like a circus sea lion, Rousseau probably still wouldn't react.

A woman with big hair walked up to Spot and started the standard, gushing, hug-and-pet routine. Then she pulled out her phone.

"Let's maybe do the selfie thing later, okay?" I said.

She frowned at me and then walked away. I was such a buzzkill.

A waiter came over, a questioning look on her face. She stood back from Spot.

"A Sierra Nevada Pale Ale in the bottle, please,"

The waiter nodded and left.

"I've tried that Sierra beer," Rousseau said. "Too much flavor. I like to quench my thirst with a lager. Those ales, you practically have to chew them. But a Bud… You can just drink it."

"Yeah. Your ATF gig today go okay?"

He nodded. "It was actually all about what we spoke of on the phone. Recognizing contraband transportation modalities. Their words not mine. If you ask me, a person should just say what they mean. Dressing it up with fancy words just makes it look like you don't have much substance."

"Agreed."

The waiter brought my beer and a glass and set them on the table.

I took a sip from the bottle and ignored the glass.

"Your dog is watching you. It's almost as if he likes beer."

"He loves beer."

"If you gave him a choice between a beer you have to chew and a beer you can just drink, which would he choose?"

"Both."

Rousseau nodded and drank some beer.

"We talked about biplanes on the phone," I said. "Did you

ever hear of a large biplane in Tahoe?"

"Nope." The fast answer didn't go with his other conversation, which was slower.

I pulled out the picture I'd printed and handed it to him. "I think the plane was one of these. An Antonov AN-2."

Rousseau nodded. I thought he'd take the picture. It was an unusual plane, and he was a pilot. But he showed no curiosity.

"Big plane," he said and picked up his beer.

"I can tell you're familiar with the plane."

He shook his head. "No. Never seen one like that."

I said, "When I asked Nadia Solokov, the DEA agent, about it, she said planes are often connected to drug activity. But she didn't think it would be the case as far away from the ocean or the Mexican border as Tahoe is. When I continued to talk about it, she said I should maybe look into cigarettes. It sounded like a way to get me off the phone. Nevertheless, I'm asking you about that."

"Yes, cigarettes are a thing," he said. He sighed as if the subject made him weary. "But connecting them to a biplane in Tahoe is a reach. Probably the biplane you saw is just an aerobatic enthusiast out for a ride." He paused.

I thought, no pilot would do aerobatics in an AN-2.

I said, "Agent Solokov made it sound like cigarette smuggling is a big deal."

"It's true that there is a lot of money involved. But the ATF is a lot more worried about guns and explosives than alcohol or tobacco. The guns coming in now are a whole different kind of thing than when we were kids. Added to that is the new build-it-yourself trend with people buying gun parts online. And the even newer thing is three-D-printed weapons. We can't keep up."

"But that stuff wouldn't be focused on Tahoe."

He shook his head. "No. I can't see how this plane you're wondering about is involved in anything illegal. Sure it could be carrying people or cigs. But I can't see it. Cigs and drugs and human trafficking are more common with trucks. You can cram a hundred people in the back of a big rig truck. Even so, it's hard to make money trafficking people. The coyotes that arrange for their travel charge a lot from the perspective of the illegal aliens who are paying for it. But hauling people is expensive. The only way to make the accounting work is to bring in forty or fifty or more people at a time. And no one would bring them to Tahoe." He thought about it. "At least, I can't imagine people flying illegal aliens into Tahoe."

"There's other kinds of human trafficking."

Rousseau frowned. "You're referring to girls? For prostitution? I hate to think that. But I suppose that could fit with the whole party-night-on-the-town rep of Tahoe. But if the plane is carrying kidnapped girls, that's FBI territory. You should talk to them. I suppose the next thing to do is figure out where this plane comes and goes from."

"How does the ATF learn about planes they might want to look at more closely?"

"There are lots of ways, some of which are secret. But I can tell you that we, and other agencies like the DEA and FBI, all use multiple services, and many are available to nearly anyone. For example, the ADS-B Exchange is one source of unfiltered aircraft tracking info. There are several others."

"Where does their info come from?"

"Lots of places. Flight plans, transponders, airport communications, various published flight schedules. In many cases, airlines and other flight companies put most of their data online for anyone to see. The problem, as you might guess, isn't finding data, it's figuring out how to use it. We've got some young data analysts who help. The best ones are independent contractors, and they're expensive. But, frankly, the work is tremendously boring. We tell them what we're looking for, and they dive in. For example, I could say I'm looking for a biplane flying in the vicinity of Lake Tahoe on such and such days. I would tell him anything I know or surmise about the plane. Likely cruise speeds and flight altitude. Possible airports of departure and arrival. If I knew the model of the plane or any other identifying information, say, part of the registration number, I'd give the analyst that."

Rousseau drank the last of his beer. He waved at the waiter and pointed to his empty beer glass.

He said, "One woman showed me how she uses some kind of algorithm when she's sorting data, but I couldn't understand the process."

"The ATF probably wouldn't be interested in my question unless I had more specific information."

"Correct. Our resources are very limited. Time, money, brain power. But if you come up with substantial information that you think I should consider, I'm available on the phone."

"Do you think pursuing cigarette smuggling is a waste of time?"

He looked like he was trying to figure out a polite way to tell me I was on an unreasonable mission. "Pursuing cig smuggling in the main isn't a waste of time. But I don't think you'll find anything substantial involving a biplane and cigarettes."

"You think Agent Solokov is just trying to get me to go away?"

He shrugged. "Could be. But I'm not sure of that. The numbers would suggest that you could look at any location and at any form of transportation, and you might well find illicit cigarettes. Estimates are that half of all cigarettes sold in California are illegal. The state taxes lost from smuggled cigarettes is something like a billion dollars a year."

"Not exactly small change," I said. "Do you know the places where these cigarettes are brought into the state?"

"Some. Not Tahoe, I can tell you that. And, anyway, half of Tahoe is in Nevada, right?"

"Almost."

"The main entry points to California are seaports, followed by trucks, and then trains. It would be nearly impossible to count the containers on ships coming into L.A. and Long Beach, Oakland, San Francisco, and others."

I gestured at the big city buildings around us. "Even West Sacramento has a seaport, right?"

He gave me a dismissive look. "The Sacramento deep-water channel can fit some big boats, but it isn't a container shipping port. And most smuggled cigs are found in containers. There's also the Humboldt Bay port, which used to be just about forest products, but is now handling lots of imports and exports. You can't do a proper inspection of all those ships. They're all stacked with hundreds of containers. You can look at some here or there, and you see electronics or car parts or textiles. It's hard to know which containers might have pallets of cigarettes stuffed in the back. Or guns and ammunition. And if you should happen to find smuggled goods, who's to blame? Could be the ship's owners have no idea. Could be that even the electronics company, whose container might be loaded with cigs, has no idea. And if you charge someone with smuggling, that's not going to eliminate a hundred other containers on other ships packed with guns or worse. It's extremely difficult to track containers. A crane on the other side of the Pacific stacks those containers on a ship. In theory, there is tracking on those containers. And they're locked. But there's a small industry focused on subverting that tracking and those container locks. In practice, it's impossible to be certain where a container came from. And it's impossible to know if a container has had something added to it."

James Rousseau was tense just talking about it. He had an important job to do, but what I was talking about possibly seemed futile, and frustrating, to him.

I said, "Hard to stop people from trying to get what they want, whether guns or drugs."

Rousseau took a breath and continued. "Trains are easier to track than ships. There are relatively few train companies, and it's difficult for a third party to get cigs on or off a train. Trucks might seem like the easiest transportation to compromise. And trucks come into California at dozens of different places. But we can talk to an actual driver or a loading dock manager. The big trucking companies know where their trucks are at any moment. They know if their trucks are moving or stationary. They have tight controls. As a result, we pretty much ignore the large trucking companies."

The waiter brought Rousseau another glass of beer.

Rousseau drank. He licked foam off his mustache. "Big rig

owner/operators are a different story. They can stop where they want, pick up and deliver third-party loads, and no one is aware. You can fill a big rig with cigs in a low-tax state like Missouri. You're only a two-day drive to California, where taxes are way higher. If you have a place to sell your product, the potential profit is serious."

"Is there no way that California can find those trucks?"

"Actually, we're doing a better job each year. You've probably seen highway cameras, right? On light poles or sign poles or bridges. A bunch of them are public webcams put up by state agencies, and anyone can look at them online."

I nodded. "I've even seen those cameras in Tahoe."

"We've got new software that watches every webcam over every highway coming into the state. The software records the license plate numbers. It separates cars from larger vehicles. When the program sees a truck or van plate more than once, it assigns a higher value to that vehicle. After a certain amount of repetition, that vehicle is investigated. Where it goes. How often it stops. How long it stays in-state. When it leaves the state. Sometimes, we set up a blanket traffic stop. We can't single out a given truck without a warrant. But we can look at all trucks coming through and pay particular attention to a given truck."

"You think trucks are how most illicit tobacco comes into the state?"

Rousseau leaned his head left, then right, a movement that showed he was undecided or else was simply stretching tight muscles. "Trucks are probably how most domestically-manufactured cigarettes come into California. The cigarettes are often loaded near the factory in Virginia or North Carolina, or Florida, or somewhere else along the supply chain."

"Are cigarettes sold in the states ever made in other countries?"

Rousseau made a kind of snort. "Philip Morris claims thirty-eight manufacturing facilities around the world."

"That's the Marlboro company?"

"And a host of others. The situation is similar for other manufacturers. We intercepted a load of Camel brand cigs, and we could not tell where they were made or even if they were counterfeit or not. We contacted R.J. Reynolds, the manufacturer, and got nowhere. The world is awash in cigarettes."

"I thought fewer people were smoking."

"In some places, and to some extent. California has the second lowest rate of smoking in the country, and yet four million Californians smoke an average of more than half a pack a day. That's twenty billion cigarettes per year. That's one billion packs. Of that, half are smuggled into the state. Five hundred million packs."

"Big number."

Rousseau nodded. "No kidding. Let's say we find an illegal shipment of five hundred thousand packs and take it out of circulation. That's just one drop out of a big pot. We'd have to find a thousand such shipments to stop cigarette smuggling."

I was trying to visualize. "How much space does five hundred thousand packs take up?"

"A semi-truck trailer holds a little more than five hundred thousand packs. That's why I used that number as my example."

"So California absorbs a thousand truckloads of illegal cigs every year. Wow."

"Wow, indeed. Kind of depressing for us ATF guys. But the truth is that we view cigarettes as relatively frivolous compared to guns and explosives."

"Makes sense. You said that most domestically-made cigs come into the state by truck."

"Right. And most counterfeit cigs come in by ship because those are manufactured overseas."

"And those come from…?"

"China, mostly."

"So my biplane idea is looking pretty weak. If it's bringing cigarettes into Tahoe, where are they from? And where does this plane land and take off? And where do those cigarettes get taken after the plane lands? And why would someone go to the trouble to smuggle tobacco on a small plane when the potential profits of smuggling by ship are a million times larger?"

Agent Rousseau was nodding emphatically as if to say, 'I told you so.'

"You got any advice for me?" I asked.

He looked back and forth as if trying to decide whether or not to answer. "It sounds like this isn't about a particular crime or a particular suspect."

"No. It's more of a hunch."

"Hunches don't go away, right? So, I'd either figure out how to find that plane, or learn more about what such planes are used for. I think you'll find it's carrying tourists or photographers. Maybe scientists who are studying Tahoe's snowpack."

As I pondered what he said, I thought about Heathcliff's conviction that the biplane was important.

Before I responded, Rousseau said, "Maybe you should ask that cigarette tax guy."

"Who's that?"

"I don't remember the name. Carson something. Or maybe Carston. You've probably heard of him. He's been written up in the media for his campaign to reduce smoking, especially among kids. He's some kind of rich art collector who gives back to the community by working to improve public health by getting people to quit smoking. His approach is to lobby politicians to raise cigarette taxes to discourage cigarette purchases."

"Has he had success at that?"

"Apparently."

"How would I find out his name?"

He pulled out his phone. "There's a guy I can call."

He dialed a number. "Mack? Rousseau here. Looking for the name of the cigarette tax guy." Pause. "Right. The guy who tries to convince states to raise tobacco taxes to help discourage kids from taking up smoking." Pause. "Okay, I'll wait."

Rousseau held the phone near his ear while he used his other hand to drain the last of his beer.

I heard a voice coming from his phone.

"Patrick Peterman?" Rousseau said. "Okay, thanks. Talk to you tomorrow."

Rousseau clicked off. "Did you get that? No wonder I

couldn't remember Patrick Peterman. It's almost exactly the same as Carston."

It takes a very dry sense of humor to say that with a straight face.

"Yeah. Patrick Peterman. Any idea where he lives or works?"

"L.A., I think. Or maybe it's San Diego. Google his name with 'cigarette tax promoter' and he'll pop up."

"Thanks, James." I pushed back my chair and stood up. "I appreciate the help."

He made a small movement with his head. "Call if you have more questions."

We shook hands, and I left. As Spot and I walked along the bar, we passed the woman in the sequined dress who'd hugged Spot in the elevator. She slid like liquid off her bar stool and once again wrapped one arm around Spot, all while she continued to hold a martini. It was like a reunion between life-long friends.

I kept hold of Spot's collar as I thanked the woman for her companionship. As I pulled Spot along, he turned his head back to look at the woman, a new love in a list so long no one could keep track.

TWENTY-EIGHT

The ATF Agent James Rousseau had mentioned a guy whose mission was to get states to raise their cigarette taxes as a way to discourage smoking. Patrick Peterman. Rousseau thought he was in SoCal.

When I got back to Tahoe, I looked up the man, found a phone number, called. A very efficient-sounding young man answered and told me that Mr. Peterman could speak to me at 1:00 p.m. the next afternoon at his office in Half Moon Bay. Okay, not SoCal.

The next morning, we left at 6:30, giving us six-plus hours to make a five-hour drive to the Pacific Ocean. The weather was clear and the roads were dry, always the critical components of any easy drive over Sierra passes. At the top of Echo Summit, as the temperature dropped to 12 degrees, Spot pulled his head in from the window. Fresh air in his nose and ears would have to wait until we dropped down to the Central Valley and its palm-tree weather.

We hit the valley floor just as rush hour was beginning to ease up. Although Sacramento is nearly 100 miles inland from the ocean, it sits only a few feet above sea level. Dropping over 7000 feet of elevation and into the valley air mass raised the temperature to 65 degrees, well into the Great Dane happy range. Spot resumed his position with his head far out the window, causing stares from all other drivers, an ego reinforcement he'd learned to expect.

There are numerous routes through the Bay Area to Half Moon Bay. The most beautiful is to cross over the Bay Bridge or the Golden Gate and head down the coast.

But I chose a route that's sometimes faster, heading down the East Bay on 680 and crossing over the bay on 92 and the

San Mateo Bridge, a highway that takes you up and over the coastal range and dumps you directly into Half Moon Bay.

California's Pacific Coast has two classic presentations. When the ocean air mass pushes toward land, you get heavy dull gray sky and water with a fog bank as the backdrop. But when a high pressure system above land pushes clear air out to sea, you get an improbably blue spectacle that holds its own against ocean blues all over the world.

Today was one of those very blue days, and driving the curving highway down toward the beaches provided delightfully distracting views.

I remembered a dog-friendly beach. We had just enough time to let Spot burn off some energy.

He ran this way and that. And after he'd met a couple of dogs and investigated a small pile of kelp and tasted the salt water, he decided to do a run along the water. It takes him a bit to get up to speed, but soon, he was screaming along the undulating line of foam, his paws splashing into an inch or two inches of water. A quarter mile down, he turned and came back. On his return trip, he got very brave and angled closer to the surf, charging through as much as six inches of turbulent water at a time. Because his paws are very large and he weighs a lot, it was a little like when a truck hits a deep puddle. Spot's high-speed run kicked up a water curtain that obscured vision. A German Shepherd had decided to run alongside. But the smaller dog got soaked by Spot's spray and veered away.

Spot came to an abrupt stop near me and stood facing me, his legs spread a bit for balance. He walked his front paws down so that his chest was nearly on the ground but his butt was still in the air, his back impossibly arched and his tail still wagging. I sensed the shake coming, and I took several steps back. But I was too late. Spot straightened up and put on a water-shedding shake that was like I'd suddenly stepped into the shower. I got thoroughly wet.

Still wagging, Spot looked at me as if he expected that I would think he was great for getting me all wet.

"Yes, you're very impressive," I said. "You can make me look completely unprofessional in the space of three seconds."

We went back to the rental Ford.

Patrick Peterman's office was located in a wide, three-story building that was backed up to the bluff. The building was a modern box covered in reflective silver blue glass. From the outside, one couldn't tell how many offices it contained. But those offices would have a great view of the ocean.

The lowest level was a windowed parking garage with vehicle entrances on each end. I pulled in and parked in a spot with the Ford facing the windows. The view out the windows was better than what movie stars get in their Beverly Hills mansions.

The suite number I was looking for was 2D. Second floor. I took the steps two at a time and hustled down to 2D. The glass door had gold lettering.

Patrick Peterman

The Live Longer Live Better Foundation

I made a double tap on the door, then pulled the door open. I walked into the office and found myself facing a wall of glass that looked out at the ocean. The room appeared to be a reception area and secretary's office made elegant by landscape paintings framed in gold. Through an open door to the right, I could see a refined room with large leather furniture. On the far wall were built-in bookcases with hard-bound books. Between the bookcases were more paintings with elaborate gold frames. Both of the rooms were decorated in forest green and maroon, with golden accents. The carpet was thick wool and dark green. The leather furniture was deep maroon. The walls were covered in some kind of nubby maroon fabric. The portions of roller blinds that were visible at the top of the windows were dark green. But because the sun was high to the south and the room faced west, the blinds were up to let the brilliant blue Pacific light flood the space.

The reception desk was mahogany. A pair of desk lamps were gold.

Behind the desk was a man in his mid-twenties who looked like an Elvis impersonator who was color coordinated to go with the Pacific outside the windows. He wore a light-blue suit that had little decorative panels of glossy blue satin fabric on the chest. His black hair was swooped up in a pompadour. He had deep blue eyes, great teeth, and blue rings on both little fingers.

He looked up from his computer.

"Good afternoon," I said. "I believe we spoke on the phone. I'm Owen McKenna, here to see Patrick Peterman."

"Yes, of course. Let me tell him you're here."

He picked up his phone, waited, and said, "Mr. McKenna is here to see you, sir." Pause. "Okay."

"He will be with you shortly. You may wait in the library." He gestured toward the open door and the room beyond.

"If you don't mind, I'd like to look at your paintings up close."

"Yes, of course."

I stepped over to one that was a spectacular painting of a mountain scraping the sky, less filled with detail than an Albert Bierstadt or a Thomas Moran, but nearly as dramatic.

There was an engraved plate on the bottom of the frame. 'Simplon Pass by John Singer Sargent, rendered by Tamara Cattaneo.' I knew Sargent to be the foremost 19th century portrait painter. I'd never heard of Cattaneo.

I turned to look at another painting, a landscape of water. In the distance were old churches with domed tops. The churches seemed to shimmer through a mist. It also had an engraved plate. 'Le Grand Canal by Claude Monet, rendered by Tamara Cattaneo.'

"Do you know art?" the man asked.

"Not especially. These are very nice."

"Mr. Peterman is really into art," he said with dramatic flourish. "He's always talking about how artists are... what's his phrase? Something about how iconic cultural inflection points are always marked by an artist. Sometimes caused by an artist."

"Mr. Peterman said that? That's a very insightful comment."

"Mr. Peterman is all about insightfulness." He glanced at the other door in the room, a door that was closed. "He'll be with you shortly."

I understood that he had work to do and I should let him get back to it. I walked through the open door.

The library was grand and impressive. The framed paintings were less dramatic than the ones in the reception room but were still beautiful. One was of Paris at night with the Eiffel Tower in the distance. The brick streets and horse-drawn carriages were wet with rain. The engraved plate said, 'City Reflection by Emile Kowalski.' There was no 'rendered by.' Maybe that meant it was an original.

Nearby was a painting of a jungle landscape with towering trees above a lush understory of plants. A stream coursed through the picture from the rear left corner, tumbling over a moss-covered ledge. I was about to look away when something caught my eye. Nearly hidden in the moss was a lizard of some kind, green like the moss. It looked like the geckos I'd seen in Hawaii. This painting also had a plate with title and artist and no 'rendered by.'

In the bookcase next to the painting was an 8 X 10 frame sitting upright on a miniature easel like a plate stand. The frame contained a photo that showed a jungle setting not unlike the painting with the camouflaged lizard. I picked up the photo frame and turned it over. On the back was another photo, nearly identical. Except that this one showed a Big Foot-type creature in the jungle. It took me a second to realize that it was a man wearing a kind of shaggy green suit like what military snipers use to camouflage themselves. I looked at the front of the photo again. I realized the camo guy was probably hidden in the front jungle photo and revealed in the back photo.

"Those ghillie suits are something, aren't they?" a voice said. "Total camouflage."

I turned and saw a man in a brown suit that was quite formal looking and custom-tailored. He was about 40, a bit over six feet, and had sparse hair, brown mixed with bits of gray, parted on the right and combed to the left. He was trim almost to the point of being skinny.

He looked at the photo I was holding. "That is a friend of

mine, ex-military. He has a contracting company that specializes in espionage. When the CIA needs surveillance on foreign government operations, they'll often send my friend's guys in. What a hugely different world from mine."

"Mine too," I said. "They actually wear these suits?"

"Yes, it's a weird world." He leaned toward me and reached his hand out to shake.

His grip was strong.

"Patrick Peterman," he said. "Pleased to meet you."

I introduced myself and told him I was interested in the world of cigarette taxes.

Peterman gestured toward one of the big leather chairs. "Please sit."

I sat, and he moved to a chair opposite me. As he sat, he pinched the creases of his pants and pulled up at the knees, a technique to prevent the fabric from being stressed. He wore elegant brown loafers made of fine, polished leather. They had little tassels. They looked expensive and very much not American. Italian maybe. His socks were thin fabric and stretched up under his pant legs so that no skin showed. He was a picture of elegance and wealth.

I glanced out the windows. "Nice view. Nice office. Nice paintings, too. That landscape in your reception room… I only know Sargent as a portrait painter. But that landscape is spectacular."

"Yes. He was a master. I connect to him on several levels."

"The title plate says, 'rendered by…'"

"A replica painted by a young woman who will be famous in her own right in another decade or so."

"Is that common? Replica paintings?"

Peterman nodded. "I've learned from my artist friends that copying paintings is a proven study technique. In fact, artists actually call them 'studies.' You can't spend much time in art museums without noticing young artists sketching famous paintings. I've been told that if you go the full distance and try to paint an entire painting to be exactly like the original, it is a marvelous way to learn."

"Like a forgery?" I said.

He smiled at me. "The difference between a forgery and a comprehensive study is purpose. Artists have always learned by studying the masters. It's not much different from up-and-coming quarterbacks watching clips of Joe Montana or Tom Brady and copying their moves. Or baseball pitchers practicing Randy Johnson's sliders."

"Are you an artist?" I asked.

"No."

"You said you connect to Sargent."

Peterman grinned. "You know something of Sargent?"

I didn't know much, but I'd learned the advantages of getting people talking about their passions. "I only know that I love his paintings."

He nodded. "Both Sargent and I were born to families that were comfortable if not wealthy. Sargent's father was a doctor. He was able to take his family and live and travel in Europe. But like me, Sargent knew he would only have significant resources if he earned them himself. He was not content to live off a small allowance."

"The similarity in yours and Sargent's background was financial?"

"More than that. Sargent's mother struggled with mental illness. My mother did as well. To make things worse, she was a heavy smoker and died of throat cancer."

"Sorry to hear it. And your father?"

Peterman looked a little embarrassed. "My father wasn't a doctor like Sargent's father. He was a televangelist, which, never mind what you think about religion on TV, is a very good business model."

I could feel myself frowning at a distasteful subject. "A good business... I've never thought about preaching on TV as a business."

"The new world has taught us that every subject can be studied for possible ways to monetize it. And there is no greater subject to monetize than God."

TWENTY-NINE

I said, "I've never thought about monetizing God."

"No, most people haven't. So I'll give you a quick primer. TV is the most viable way to monetize the business of God," Peterman said. "I saw how it worked as I grew up. You study inspirational sermons. Then you write a bunch of them and practice giving them. When you have some degree of polish, you start a church and bring in TV cameras and provide a video feed to local TV stations for free. Once some of them take you on, you promote your church as the church run by the guy on TV. And as you know, everyone wants to see someone who's on TV, if only to know what all the fuss is about. As your audience grows, you expand your physical location. Word gets out, and people flock to see you. Some people do as the Old Testament says and tithe ten percent or even more of their income. Some merely give generously as the New Testament says."

"Just like a regular church?" I said.

"Sort of. But the TV audience can be huge compared to the people who physically come to the church. And the people who watch you on TV often respond when you break for announcements that exhort the glory of God. Sending in money, after all, is supporting the holiness of God."

"Where does the money given to televangelists go?" I asked.

"In the case of my father, it went in small measure for upkeep on the church and in large measure to his personal expenses, which included a thirty-passenger yacht and a wine cellar that was almost as large. Another significant portion of incoming dollars went to all the high-priced call girls he had on speed dial. Eventually, some of the most committed members of his flock learned about his non-biblical life. They publicized his indiscretions. Everything fell apart, and he took his own life. Fortunately, years before that, he'd set up a small investment account for me. I adjusted the portfolio, shifting assets into growth stocks, and grew it into a good sum. That is what allows me to collect art and do good works for the public."

Peterman crossed his legs. "Despite my background similarities with Sargent, I have none of his genius. And where his upbringing had the feel of aristocracy and a focus on education, mine was tawdry. Our fathers made some money, and our mothers suffered."

"Understood," I said. "I was referred to you by an ATF agent named James Rousseau. He said you work at reducing smoking, and that's what I'm interested in."

Peterman gave me a quick half-smile. He looked a bit embarrassed.

"I try to give back. I would have loved to be like Sargent and make beautiful art. I even went to art school for a time and studied the basics. But I didn't have what it takes. So I've supported and shepherded several good artists. I think I've made a difference in their careers. But I've done more good with public health initiatives. My work in reducing smoking is the best thing I've ever done."

"The ATF agent, Rousseau, said you know more about cigarette smuggling than most and that you could answer my questions."

"I'm happy to answer any questions, if I know the answers."

"I'm investigating reports of a large biplane flying in and out of Tahoe. It appears in the area around the north end of the lake. There's no airport there. So I'm wondering what its purpose is. It's probably just a sight-seeing plane, carrying passengers from Reno or something. But I haven't been able to find any information about that. So I wanted to know if there was any other possible purpose. Rousseau thought that Tahoe is not a place that would have any use for smuggling. But when I pressed him, he said that smuggling of cigarettes was a big business in every corner of the state. He said I could get more information from you. So I'm here to ask. What do you think?"

Peterman crossed his legs the other direction and leaned back in his chair. "Cigarette smuggling is primarily done with ships and, to a lesser extent, with trucks."

It was what Rousseau had told me.

"I can't imagine why a smuggler would choose to use a small plane," Peterman said.

"It's not a very small plane. It can hold ten or twelve people."

"Oh, I see. One could certainly carry a lot of cigarettes in a space that size. But what would be the motivation? A truck could carry so much more. If you're going to go to the effort to smuggle cigarettes, why not choose the approach that could make you millions instead of thousands?"

"So it doesn't make sense?"

"I don't think so." Peterman looked out at the ocean. "If a cargo ship comes across the Pacific, almost no one pays any attention. If a big truck comes into the state on a freeway, who's going to notice? But this plane you mention, it flies into Tahoe, and people see it and talk about it. It makes enough of an impression that you are going around asking questions about it. You live in Tahoe, right?"

"Yes."

"And you drove all the way to Half Moon Bay to ask me about it."

"I get your point," I said. "If that plane is part of a smuggling operation, it's not very secretive."

"Right. I would think that smugglers give a lot of thought about how to do their job without attracting attention."

We sat in silence for several seconds.

I said, "I'm curious about your efforts to raise taxes. How did that come about?"

"It goes back to when my mother died. The cause of death was listed as esophageal cancer. But the root cause was her smoking. I found myself thinking about that a great deal."

He paused as if considering what he was about to say.

"As you probably know, the federal and state governments

have been engaged in a drug war for decades, and they've had very little success. But cigarettes are unique among drugs in that they're sold over the counter in millions of places. They are also unique in that states have developed a successful way of taxing tobacco by requiring tax stamps to be affixed to each pack of cigarettes. That way, retailers know that the state tax has been paid."

Peterman seemed more relaxed than before. I could tell that this was a subject in which he was well versed and was comfortable discussing.

"What I learned long ago—and I should hasten to add that many others before me also recognized—was that, when any given state raised their cigarette taxes, the smoking rate went down. It wasn't a huge drop in smoking. But it was significant."

"How do the people who study this know it was the actual smoking rate? Couldn't it just be that people bought fewer legal cigarettes but still smoked the same amount and made up the difference with illegal cigarettes?"

"That was always the question from way back. But there are many scientific ways of determining actual smoking as distinct from cigarette purchases. I don't know the details, but very smart people have verified the methods of determining smoking rates. I guess it has something to do with statistics and such. Of course, it is likely that the transport of smuggled cigarettes rises when taxes go up. But a sizable portion of smokers don't have access to smuggled cigarettes. Or if they do, they would worry that they might get caught buying smuggled cigarettes and get in trouble."

Peterman took a breath as if he'd learned that pausing at that point in his speech was an effective way to make a point.

He continued, "I should back up and point out the obvious, that smoking is linked to all manner of health problems. A sizable portion of all smokers die from smoking-related diseases. So when the smoking rate goes down, it saves lives. What the actual number is doesn't matter much. To save even one life is important. To save thousands of lives is huge."

Peterman gave me an intense look as if to add emphasis to

his point.

I asked, "Do most people believe these statistics?"

"The experts do, yes. A statistician who works in this area once told me that their motto is, 'Believe your instruments.'"

"Like believing the facts they uncover and not hearsay or myths?"

"Exactly." Peterman was nodding his agreement. "So I decided years ago that if I could help inspire our legislators to raise cigarette taxes, I would be doing a significant public service. I talked to experts and met legislators. In California and other states. I realized that most states viewed cigarette taxes as a pain-free way to raise money. But I was looking for a pain-free way to reduce smoking and improve public health. They were two different goals that happened to use the same mechanism.

"The first time one of the states where I was lobbying raised taxes, I was ecstatic to find out that smoking rates went down in just the first year. It was a small percentage, but that still indicated that many people quit smoking."

"Glad to hear it," I said.

"But I need to reach more ears with this information," Peterman said.

"You've got the ear of James Rousseau, the ATF agent who referred me to you. He's the one who also told me that cigarettes are the most smuggled drug."

"I didn't know those ATF agents paid that much attention to cigarettes. I realize they are tasked with tobacco enforcement. But I would guess that they're much more concerned with guns and such."

"That's what Rousseau told me. But he pays enough attention to cigarettes to mention them and to mention you as well. He didn't have to look you up. You loom large in their world."

Peterman raised his eyebrows. "Whenever I'm around law enforcement types, they mostly act like I'm a lightweight. A mere art collector. As if what I do doesn't really matter."

"But it does matter, right?"

Peterman took a deep breath. "I think so. The statistics say so."

"And they should believe their instruments," I said, grinning.

"Right." Peterman's face darkened. "The truth is, by many measures, my own especially, I've largely failed. California's taxes are only two dollars and eighty-seven cents a pack. I helped get them to that level, but I can't seem to get them higher. Two eighty-seven is much higher than some states. But my goal is to get taxes up over four dollars a pack, which would be closer to New York and Connecticut or the District of Columbia. If we could raise them like New York state, I could only imagine how much smoking rates would drop and life expectancies would go up."

"If raising cigarette taxes is such an effective way to reduce smoking and improve public health, why don't states all raise their tobacco taxes?"

He made a sad grin. "It's always the same reason. Many laws that are good for society don't get approved. The tobacco companies give politicians huge amounts of money. The politicians are in bed with those companies. They owe them, so they don't cross them."

"Back to my original question. Do you have a gut sense about whether cigarette smugglers ever use small planes?"

Peterman tilted his head, thinking about it.

"I suppose it's possible. But I doubt it. There's just too much money in using a large truck instead."

I stood. "Thank you for your time. It was generous of you to talk to me, and you've been very helpful. You do good work, and I wish you continued success."

Peterman stood, shook my hand again, and I left.

THIRTY

On my drive back to Tahoe, I thought about what Peterman had said, which echoed what ATF Agent Rousseau had said, which also echoed what DEA Agent Nadia Solokov had said.

They all pointed out that smuggling cigarettes by plane made no sense. A plane couldn't carry a fraction of what a truck could carry. And planes call attention to themselves. Biplanes, especially. My whole thought experiment about how a pilot could fly in and out of the mountains was flawed by lack of a realistic motive.

Nothing about my case was turning out like I expected.

I thought the unusual events in Tahoe would be connected. The murder of the doctor in Tahoe City would connect to the ex-con who wanted to kill Benito Diaz and me. I thought the strange past of UCSF Medical School students, one of whom died in a fall but seems to live on as a ghost, and another who almost died but is focused on a strange biplane, would connect to everything else.

I caught the ex-con only to find out he likely was an outlier disconnected from everything. The Brontë sisters had told me about Heathcliff and his twin fixations on his dead girlfriend Isabel and planes. But that had come to nothing but speculation.

I'd asked Heathcliff about it, and all I'd gotten was a sketch of a ravine. He gave me lots of details about where he saw the plane and which way he thought it had gone. But it didn't tell me anything about the crimes I was trying to solve.

After I got home that evening, made some dinner for Spot and myself, and called Street to check in, I realized that, even after meeting with ATF Agent James Rousseau and the cigarette tax guy Patrick Peterman, I had nothing to pursue.

Except Heathcliff's sketch from his last bike ride.

It was an amazing lack of information. I might as well take a break and go to Hawaii.

Or, I could get my bike out from under the deck and go revisit that most spectacular ride of all: The Flume Trail.

In the middle of the night, I had a spell of sleeplessness, brought on by the experts telling me that my idea about the big biplane made no sense.

I pushed away the thoughts, telling myself I would reconsider in the morning.

The next morning, I sat on my deck, looked at Heathcliff's sketch, then looked up at the mountain ridge that stretched up the East Shore of Tahoe. The mountains went from Genoa Peak just east of my cabin toward Mt. Rose far to the north. While my deck had the world's greatest view of the lake, it was impossible to discern anything about the mountains behind my cabin.

But along that ridge of Tahoe mountains was the Flume Trail. Popular with mountain bikers, the Flume Trail was a thousand feet higher than my cabin. Like many mountain bike enthusiasts, I'd ridden the Flume and admired its astonishing views of the lake below. Perhaps it was time to revisit the Flume. Maybe I could find the ravine that Heathcliff had sketched. If so, I could get a sense of where the plane had gone. If it had nothing to do with the mysteries I'd been investigating, it was still a beautiful ride.

My phone rang.

"Owen McKenna," I answered.

"Hi, this is Benito Diaz. I don't mean to be presumptuous, but I wonder if we could possibly meet and talk."

"Certainly. Where are you?"

"At a restaurant not far from your office."

"You have a rental car?" I asked.

"Yes."

"Why don't you come to my cabin. I'm only a few miles to the north."

He agreed, and I gave him directions for how to look for the winding mountain road a mile or so north of Cave Rock.

Fifteen minutes later, Spot stood up from his position at the corner of the deck. He tilted his head left, then right, listening to sounds below the threshold of human hearing, then trotted down the short steps and walked out and stood next to Camille Dexter's pickup camper. I knew that Spot could hear the flight of a butterfly the next county over. But he didn't respond just because there was a faint sound coming from down on the highway. He only responded when someone was coming to see us. How he knew, I had no idea. In time, I too could hear a vehicle. But I had no idea it was destined for our cabin. Sure enough, a red Subaru turned into my little drive and parked next to my rental car.

Benito Diaz got out.

Spot was much more gregarious than he'd been in my office. Perhaps partly because he'd already met Benito. But mostly, I thought, because Benito had gotten cleaned up. The scent of blood was gone, and with it, Spot's wariness about potentially facing more human death, something that is very upsetting for dogs.

Spot walked up to Benito and turned sideways to him as Benito gave him a rub. I saw Benito take a step back, and I realized that Spot had leaned against him, a Great Dane trait that shows the dog is very comfortable with you.

I waved, and Benito walked to the deck stairs rather than the front door. He came up, and we shook hands.

It had been several days since Benito came to my office. His eye was still swollen and looked scary enough to frighten children. But it was no longer sealed shut. He could probably see a narrow range with it.

He looked across the lake. "I see why you live here," he said. "Amazing view."

"Have you been out with your doctor classmates?"

"Yes. As you know, several came to my party. But our get togethers have been very subdued. Veronica's death threw the whole mood into the dark. We're still going through the motions. The Brontë sisters have been especially adamant that we do what Veronica would want, which is to try to have a good time. So we all went to a show last night. Who knew a country singer would have high-heeled dancers."

I smiled. "The showroom producers seek to entertain."

"They did," Benito said.

He turned and looked down at the lake 1000 feet below us.

"I was looking at almost this exact same view online in an article about the Flume Trail," he said.

I nodded. "The Flume Trail is just to the north of here. At a higher elevation. One of the most spectacular bike rides there is. It's especially nice considering it is easily accessible, and it doesn't take great skill to ride it. I'm actually planning to go up there tomorrow, assuming we don't get any more snow. But last I checked, the weather looks clear."

"I imagine it to be a great way to get exercise."

"That's true, but no more so than other bike rides. The reason I'm going is to track a plane of all things."

Benito looked confused. "That sounds unusual."

"It is. But I talked to the man the Brontë sisters call Heathcliff. You may know him as Horatio Harris. He was briefly enrolled in the UCSF med school."

Benito nodded. "Yes, I know Heathcliff. He jumped from the Golden Gate."

"Right. He doesn't remember the circumstances. So when I looked into the death of Dr. Veronica Eastern in Tahoe City, it made sense to talk to the various doctors who'd come to Tahoe. Heathcliff isn't a doctor, but he was originally in your class. So I spent some time tracking him down. He's delusional to some degree. Acts as if his dead girlfriend is with him. Maybe he believes it, I don't know. He has coffee with her."

"You mean, he sits down with two coffees as if she's with him, but he's alone?"

"Yes."

"I don't know much about psychiatry," Benito said, "but my doctor perspective on unusual behaviors is to consider if they might serve a useful purpose and if they don't cause any harm. If so, they are probably benign and do not need any kind of intervention. They might even be considered good behaviors for the individual."

"What could be a useful purpose for Heathcliff's delusions?"

Benito took his time. "Stability. Comfort. A way to process his thoughts by talking them out with his phantom girlfriend."

"Like when I talk to myself to try to figure something out?"

"Yes. I think exactly like that."

"Do you think these delusions might morph into something else? Something less benign?"

"You don't mean…" Benito stopped himself.

"Yes, I probably wonder about all different possibilities. Up to and including murder."

Benito looked shocked. It was a moment before he spoke. "I have no idea if Heathcliff would have delusions that would motivate violence. But they maybe could."

"Does it sound to you like a person who has a kind of phantom girlfriend would get worse? Or better?"

"If his delusions are caused by a brain injury that is static, maybe they don't change. If they are caused by a brain injury that is slowly changing, maybe his behaviors slowly change. Maybe his brain health improves. Maybe his unusual behaviors lessen. All one can do is watch. The brain is a marvelously plastic and malleable organ. We used to think that nerve cells weren't good at healing. Now we know otherwise. Injured brains are capable of incredible adaptation. Even if Heathcliff says or does things that seem outlandish, I would deal with him as if he has no delusions at all."

"Will do. Anyway, Heathcliff has a thing about airplanes. At first, I thought he was a pilot. But he's not. He said planes are important in his memory. Yet he doesn't know why."

"Interesting," Diaz said. "A latent memory of some kind, yet he doesn't understand the origin."

"He said the doctors who treated him thought he was going to die from the injuries caused by his fall. But he survived and the most lasting effect was that the fall erased some memories.

People talk to him about events in his past, and he has no recollection of them. And he has delusions and hallucinations."

"When you've talked to others such as the Brontë sisters, has anyone suggested why planes might be important?" Benito said.

"No. I asked him about it. When he saw a biplane flying over Incline Village, he had no idea why it seemed important. He has spotted the plane from town and also from the Flume Trail. There's no reason a biplane would be flying very low in the area. There is no close airport. Common sense would suggest it's probably a delusion."

"Like the delusion that his dead girlfriend is joining him for coffee?"

"Right. Either way, my cop sense tells me I should check it out. Multiple unusual occurrences are sometimes connected."

"You mean, like Veronica Eastern's murder."

I nodded.

Benito seemed to think about it. "Is it a crime to fly a biplane very low?"

"Not generally."

Benito paused longer. "When doctors are looking for certain symptoms that might suggest a disease, we sometimes see something unusual. It maybe doesn't seem related to what we're looking for, but we nevertheless put some effort into figuring out what this unusual thing is."

"Are you saying a doctor's hunch is like a cop's hunch?"

"I think so, yes."

"I'll go up on the Flume Trail, and I probably won't see a thing. So I won't know if Heathcliff is dreaming up planes. But who knows? Maybe I will see something."

"When I read the article about the Flume, I wanted to ask you about it."

"You want to ride the Flume? You're welcome to come with me."

"I came here to ask you about that. My nephew Damen wants to ride it. He, too, saw pictures and read about it. He's so stoked about it that it would be hard to keep him away."

"I know it's none of my business," I said to Diaz. "You're the doctor. But you mentioned the downside of Damen getting a possible injury."

"Right. Hemophiliacs are always at risk of bleeding. The risk for people with his version of the disease is serious. So maybe I could ask you about the Flume Trail."

"Of course."

"Is it a hard ride?"

"Not at all. Anyone in good enough shape to ride up a long trail at high altitude can do it."

"Is it the kind of ride where people often fall?"

"I don't think so," I said. "The original flume aqueduct carried water from Marlette Lake. It went north for several miles along the mountainside and then dumped its water into a tunnel that went through the mountain to the east, out of the Tahoe Basin. From there, the water went down to Washoe Valley and was eventually pumped up to Virginia City for use in the mines. The thing about aqueducts is they have to be level to do their job. When they took out the flume a hundred years later, the trail that was left was substantially unchanged. Nice and level. There are some places where the trail is eroded. In most of those places, we get off and walk our bikes twenty or thirty feet until we get back to good ground. Some people might describe that as challenging, but the truth is that the challenge is to your psyche if you're afraid of heights. There's very little physical challenge. And at the end of the trail, you don't go through the old tunnel. You just cruise down a gravel road to lake level."

Benito nodded.

I looked at his black-and-blue eye. "I would be as concerned about you as Damen. You're pretty banged up."

"I'm past the worst. As long as I don't jar my head, I'm okay. As for Damen, I try to catalog the potential risks for any activity that Damen pursues. My constant struggle is Damen's appetite for physical activity. Perhaps it would be more accurate to say 'his demand' for physical activity. In that way, he's a typical thirteen-year-old boy. I've been fairly successful at steering him away from things like skateboarding and water skiing, horseback riding and motorized minibikes. And, of course, contact sports. Statistically, there's nothing worse for hemophiliacs than playing football. But if I were to try to keep him too coddled, he'd sneak off to do dangerous stuff on his own."

"Makes sense," I said.

"He has been really pressuring me to go mountain biking. He even bought a used mountain bike with the money I pay him to do yard work. We've done four gentle rides in the Bay Area. Now he wants to graduate to the Flume Trail."

Benito took a deep breath. "Maybe I'm not judging this right. But it's hard for most people to understand what the world looks like through the lens of hemophilia. So I made an agreement with Damen. I'd let him go mountain biking as long as I approved the trail. Nothing technical. No boulder jumping. No tricks. No acrobatic riding. Just comfortable trails where riders are unlikely to get injured. They can have thrilling views, like the Flume Trail. But easy riding. And from what I understand, that describes the Flume Trail, right?"

"Yeah. To some extent, the dropoff on the edge of the trail is scary enough to slow riders down and make them even more careful. And there are some narrow, eroded places. If a person did fall off, it could be bad. But I don't think it's a big risk for someone who's competent on a bicycle."

"Damen has no fear of heights. And he's naturally athletic, so the dropoff won't bother him. The good thing is, he's not especially inclined to be a daredevil. I research the locations, talk to locals like you, and I go along with him. And I set an example for protective gear. Helmet, knee pads, elbow pads."

Benito lowered his voice as if someone were listening.

"Without telling him, I carry a small medical bag in my pack. In the unlikely event he should get injured, I'm right there."

I sensed a hesitation in his voice. I said, "Is there anything you are afraid to ask?"

"No. I'm just being thoughtful. And I try not to be too influenced by my belief that if I say no too often, he'll take risks anyway but simply not tell me about it."

Just the idea made me tense. "Would you like me along for the ride?"

"Would you? Yes. Definitely! I'd especially like it if you went first along the trail. And if you see something coming up that you would warn other people about, then I'd like you to call back and warn us."

"Okay."

"One more thought," Benito said. "While Damen isn't a daredevil, he is a natural show-off. You probably saw him playing the piano at my party. If other people are around, he's inclined to lose his focus on the ride in favor of performing for others nearby…"

"We'll go alone," I said. "Just the three of us."

"Thanks," Benito said. "I'm excited. I know Damen will be, too. The Flume Trail will be the highlight of all the trails we've ridden."

THIRTY-ONE

The next morning, the weather forecast looked good. It had been a warm fall, and our only significant snowfall had fallen at higher elevations, so the snow cover was still mostly above 9000 feet. Because the Flume Trail was around 8000 feet, it would be clear of snow except, possibly, in shadowed ravines or in heavy stands of trees.

Because it was November, the tourist shoulder season, and we'd be riding in the middle of the week, there would be very few other riders. Perfect conditions.

Even if I'd wanted to bring Spot, dogs are not allowed on the trail, so I left him with Street, Camille, and Blondie. As always, he was happy to be the only male among females.

We brought lunches and water in my pack and just a few supplies in Benito's pack. He kept room for his medical bag. Benito said that Damen would carry his own water.

Because the Flume Trail ride is 14 miles one way, the most common approach is to set up a shuttle. We left Benito's rental up at the Tunnel Creek parking lot in Incline Village.

We tied the bikes to the roof rack of the rental Ford and crammed in for the ride down the East Shore. Damen was all eyes, looking at the lake and then peering up at the mountain above us to the east.

"The Flume Trail is up there, right?" His voice almost croaked with excitement.

"Yeah. Way up. If you had binoculars and a lot of time, you could maybe spy other riders going along the side of the mountain."

"Is it like being on the edge of a cliff?"

"No. It's just what you'd imagine if you found a nice deer trail along the side of a steep mountain. Not very wide, but nice and level. The views are something."

Benito spoke. "You'll have to pay attention, Damen. No rubber-necking as you ride."

"Uncle Benny, you worry too much! I'll be careful."

We pulled off at the Spooner Lake Campground and found a place to park. Benito made a show of putting on his protective gear. Damen probably thought it was excessively demonstrative, but I understood Benito's goal.

Once on our bikes, we took it slow. From Spooner, it was a few miles and a thousand-foot climb up to Marlette Lake. Damen led most of the way.

When we got to the spectacular overlook above Marlette Lake, Benito spoke casually. "I see the trail goes down a bit and then disappears over by the far side of the lake."

I said, "It goes through the trees and then pops out on the Flume Trail, which is almost two thousand feet above Lake Tahoe. From there it's several miles of the greatest views in the world."

"I can't wait!" Damen said. He had one of his feet on his bike pedal, ready to fly.

Benito asked what was obviously a leading question. "Owen, is it always clear where the trail goes?"

"Usually, yes. But sometimes there'll be a washout. I'll go first in case it's confusing."

"Sounds good," Benito said.

I had no doubt that Damen understood that Benito wanted me to go first for safety reasons. But if he didn't like that, he didn't seem bothered. I pushed off and headed down the slope to Marlette Lake and the entrance to the Flume Trail. I pushed away all thoughts of the pop star Glory who'd been killed up here a few years before. I'd eventually found justice for her, but others had died before I managed to wrap up the case.

The trail was dry, the mid-November air at 8000 feet was cold, and the sun was hot. Perfect.

I slowed as I went around the curve where the trail ran next to Marlette Lake. Just as promptly, the trail left the lake and went through the forest toward the edge of the mountain. The path curved again, and I was suddenly on the Flume Trail. The mountain dropped off to my left as I headed north. My bike tires were on a sandy, rocky path two feet wide. To my right, the mountain rose up. But to my left, it fell away, a serious drop to the water. The slope down wasn't a cliff, but it was steep, and in places it consisted of sand and sliding scree. If you sat on the ground where there weren't a lot of trees and slid down on your butt, you might go a long way before you could stop.

Far below, the highway that followed the lake shore was a skinny dark-gray snake curving this way and that to parallel the inlets and secret harbors that made up the East Shore. A few white-hulled boats dotted the azure water. Maybe they were large, but they looked tiny.

A good strategy for riding the Flume is to ignore those beautiful views and concentrate on the trail. When the view becomes too grand to ignore, then it's time to come to a stop, and do your staring while you have two feet on the ground instead of on bike pedals.

I took such a stop as we approached a ravine that looked something like the one Heathcliff drew. I turned my bike a bit sideways and blocked the trail so that Damen wouldn't fly by.

Damen came up behind me and stopped. "Wow, this is so cool," he said, as Benito pulled up behind him.

"I'd love to live here," Damen gushed. "You can go mountain biking and snowboarding and paddleboarding. It's perfect!"

"Someday," Benito said.

I pulled out the Heathcliff sketch and compared it to the ravine before us. It didn't look very similar.

"Is that the sketch that Heathcliff gave you?" Benito asked.

"Yes. He was bicycling The Flume Trail when he saw the biplane. He sketched the area where he was when the plane appeared." I folded the sketch and put it back in my pocket. "Let's continue on. There are some good lunch spots not far from here."

I started off. I tried not to turn our ride into a speed race, but I went fast enough that Damen would likely be happy. After a mile or two, I pulled over at another ravine. Damen and Benito followed.

"Looks like a good lunch spot?"

"Awesome," Damen said.

We found a comfortable place to sit on a fallen tree trunk where we were off the trail and yet still had the great view below us.

Benito had gotten us deli sandwiches and two bags of chips, one for me and one for the two of them to split. As Damen tore into a chip bag, Benito said, "Not too many chips."

"C'mon, Uncle. You eat donuts."

"Yes, and they are bad for me. But my job is to keep you from getting habituated to junk food. When you're old like me, you can make your own decisions."

It was an unusual statement coming from a single man in his late thirties. But he was a doctor, and his comments, although unusual, made sense.

Damen said, "So I'm not supposed to get used to eating chips, but you want me to get—what's that word—habituated to playing the piano."

"You like playing the piano."

"Yeah. But I hate piano lessons as much as I hate not being able to eat what I want. None of my friends have to take lessons. They just play, you know, for fun. I would like lessons if we had a nice piano, like that grand piano in our rental house. That would be awesome. Our little piano constantly has that one key that goes out of tune. Even if I play something perfectly, it still sounds bad."

Benito turned to me. "Damen is very good on the piano. Now that he's played the grand at the rental, he wants us to get a grand instead of our little spinet."

Damen was nodding. "A grand is pretty awesome. Music just sounds better on a grand. Ask Nanna. She says the same thing. You should listen to her and get me a grand piano."

"Someday, maybe," Benito said. "Someday." It was his second use of the word while talking to Damen. Benito turned to me. "Nanna is our neighbor in San Mateo. We've sort of adopted her as Damen's grandmother."

"I met her at your party," I said. "Nice lady."

"And she's a musical expert," Damen said. "Used to play violin for the San Francisco Orchestra. If she gave piano lessons, I'd like them."

"She's the one who put us onto the rental house where we're staying," Benito said. "She owns a vacation home next door, so she knows the neighborhood."

Damen ate his lunch at a speed more like a dog than a person. He was done when Benito and I were still halfway through.

Benito was embarrassed. "I tell Damen that it's good to eat more slowly. For digestion, for enjoying a good conversation, for savoring a view."

"I might be done with lunch," Damen said, "but I'm still enjoying the view."

Fifteen minutes later, we were well down the trail. When the path curved in a long narrow S, we came to a ravine that looked like the one in Heathcliff's sketch.

THIRTY-TWO

I came to a stop and pulled out Heathcliff's sketch. Damen pulled up next to me and Benito next to him. They leaned over and looked at my sketch.

"It looks like this very spot." Benito said. "That tree is just like the one in the sketch."

"The man they call Heathcliff drew it," I said.

"From our med school days?"

"Right. He said this is one of two places from which he saw a large biplane.

"Can I see the sketch?" Damen said.

I handed it to him.

He held the sketch up and out in front of him. He moved it left and right. "This is definitely the place. What are we looking for?"

"Pretend you're in the center of a clock face and noon is north. We're plotting an airplane course from ten-thirty straight east."

"Oooh, cool. Like a treasure hunt. Ten-thirty is easy. Ten-thirty from noon is forty-five degrees. But we need to verify north." He pulled out his phone, pulled up a compass, and pointed his hand to north. "Now the compass will show us that forty-five degrees is northwest, otherwise known as ten-thirty." He looked down at his compass, then pointed at the mountains to the northwest.

"The problem is," he said, "to know the path of a plane heading east, we'd have to know how far away the plane was when it appeared at ten-thirty. If it was five miles away, the plane's course would be a lot different than a plane that was a hundred miles away."

"Smart kid," I said, glancing at Benito.

Benito was grinning.

"The plane was seen from this very spot," I said. "And the person who saw it said it was very low as if flying through the tallest trees."

Damen was studying the distant mountains. "Then I would guess it first became visible to the right of that building on the lake."

He pointed toward what looked like a small building miles away.

"That's what used to be called the Cal Neva Hotel in Crystal Bay."

"The one Frank Sinatra used to own," Benito said.

Damen turned to Benito. "Who's that?"

"A singer. We saw him in that movie *Von Ryan's Express*."

"Oh, the old guy. He was a singer?"

"Yeah. And he owned a record company."

"Really? He didn't look like he could sing. He looked more like a banker or something. Like he had a job counting money."

"Based on his music earnings, he probably spent a lot of time counting money."

Damen was looking from the landscape to his phone. He tapped on his phone and got a map of the area. "There aren't a lot of trees near that building. So if the plane was in the trees, it was quite far back from the lake." He looked again at his phone map and zoomed in. "Probably around here." He pointed on his phone.

"A topographical map would show us the slope." He tapped the map to reveal the terrain. Damen turned to me. "What altitude would a plane be at if it flew in the trees?"

"Maybe two hundred feet above the ground. And the ground near the Cal Neva Hotel would be about sixty-four hundred feet. But the plane was later seen to fly above Incline Village, which would put it at eight thousand or eighty-five hundred feet. The observer said the plane was flying roughly level."

"Okay. We find the eight thousand-foot topo line and follow

that over to the mountains behind that building."

Damen zoomed some more, then dragged the map back and forth. "Got it." Damen's tone had a delightful confidence. "Your plane probably appeared here. This ground is high enough that a plane at eight thousand feet could fly in the trees. From there it took an easterly course to this point above Incline Village. But the mountains get higher, especially to the north. So either it had to climb a bunch, or it had to turn, or it had to land."

"Damen, you are a genius at this stuff."

He made an embarrassed grin. "It's just basic logic."

"Can you email me a screenshot of this?"

"Sure."

I gave him my email.

"Okay," I said, "let's ride the Flume."

Before I could take the lead, Damen sped away.

"Damn," Benito said. "I wanted to get in front of him. Oh, well, he seems to have good control."

"He'll be fine," I said.

We rode, much faster now with Damen in the lead, and we got to the end of the Flume Trail fifteen minutes later. As Benito and I approached Tunnel Creek Road, we saw Damen standing there, off his bicycle, leaning against a tree, looking very casual and accomplished.

"That was so awesome," Damen said. "I want to do it again."

"We will," Benito said. "Another day." Benito sounded weary, but also relieved. No doubt he'd been worrying that Damen might fall off his bike. It was comforting to know Damen got through it okay.

"Okay. I forgot to get a selfie. I'll just take one over there. Watch my bike?"

He carried his phone back to the trail, scouting good locations for a view. He snapped a photo, then called out, "Uncle Benny, I want a pic with you and Owen. There's a place over here where there's a better view."

We left our bikes and walked back down the trail fifty yards or more. Damen was in the distance, stepping into a good photo position at the edge of the trail, when his shoelace caught on the low branch of a young pine sapling. He lowered down on one knee and was reaching to free the shoelace when the gravel under his knee seemed to crumble. He started to slide down the slope, moving at a good rate. Like a natural athlete, he lay on his stomach and spread out his hands and arms for stability as he slid. He slowed. But then his other foot hit a large rock and sent him rotating crossways to the slope.

I started running. Benito followed.

My first thought was that Benito would be worried sick that Damen might get hurt. But the slope was not very steep. It made a gentle S curve like a ski run. Damen was sliding at a significant rate, but his speed didn't seem to be increasing as he slid left, then right, then went out of sight.

When I got to the point on the trail where he started sliding, I stepped down onto a slope of gravel and loose scree and did a kind of controlled stepping descent, sliding an extra foot or two with every step I took. I knew that Benito would follow me.

The slope tilted to the left. With every step, the slope propelled me farther to the left. I tried to compensate by angling my steps to the right. I went past a house-sized boulder. To the side of that was a small cliff. The slope then tilted to the right. I thought of sitting down on the slope and sliding on my butt. Maybe it would be faster, but I didn't think so. The fastest way would be to body-surf the gravel and scree not unlike how Damen slid down. But that would give me the least control. I decided to stay with my deep stepping.

After another curve, Damen came back into view. He was farther down than I anticipated, maybe 75 yards below us, still sliding with his arms spread out, still doing a slow rotation like a sky diver in freefall.

Below Damen was a group of Manzanita bushes, a kind of plant that was very strong. I was glad to see the Manzanita because there would be no way Damen could slide past them.

Damen slid into the bushes and came to what looked like a comfortable stop.

I still rushed down the slope as fast as I could go.

As Benito and I got closer, Benito called out.

"Are you okay? Damen? Okay?"

"Yeah, Uncle Benny," he called out in a loud voice. "I'm fine. I got a little poke in the arm, but no worries."

I felt myself breathe a big sigh.

Damen pushed up onto his hands and knees.

Benito saw the blood first.

He shouted, "Damen, you're bleeding."

"No, I'm not," Damen's shout came back. "I'm fine." He looked down at himself, then raised his arms. "Oh, yeah, I guess I am bleeding." Now his voice didn't sound so strong.

THIRTY-THREE

I got to Damen first. The bleeding was from the inside of his upper arm. His shirt was torn where a sharp Manzanita branch had caught the fabric. Apparently, some pointed broken branch had stabbed into the inside of Damen's upper arm a few inches below his arm pit. As Damen lifted up his arm, the blood spurted. It was a brilliant red, arcing flow, pulsing with each heartbeat.

"Oh, Jesus!" Benito shouted as he rushed up. "This a brachial artery wound. That's bad. Damen, lie here. On your back. Turn this way, wounded arm uphill."

Damen was already moving sluggishly. My uneducated sense was that he was already suffering a significant loss of blood.

Benito unzipped his pack and pulled out his medical bag.

"What can I do?" I asked.

"Call nine, one, one. We need a rescue up here. Helicopter or whatever they've got."

Damen tried to say something, but his words were mumbled as if he were very cold and shivering.

Benito said, "Tell them we've got a punctured brachial artery and the victim is going into hypovolemic shock. We need help very fast." As he spoke, he was cutting away Damen's sleeve and rigging up a tourniquet. The blood coming out of Damen's arm was voluminous. The ground was already splashed with lots of red.

I got out my phone. There was no cell reception.

"Benito, I need to know if your phone has reception."

He tossed it to me. It had no cell reception. I scrambled over to Damen, who seemed mostly unconscious.

"Damen's phone," I said.

"Right rear pocket," Benito said.

I got it out.

"No reception on any of our phones," I said. "We're in a cell shadow. The phones are no good to you without reception, right? You can't use them for any medical purpose?"

Benito shook his head.

"Then I'm going to take all three phones upslope until I get reception on one of them."

I turned and started running up the mountain.

Benito called after me. "Please hurry, Owen. Damen's going to run out of time."

I pounded with my legs, lifting my knees high, powering up the slope.

Benito's desperate voice called up the mountain after me, his voice plaintive, pleading. "Hurry, Owen! Please hurry."

Was he crying? I couldn't tell. In his place, I would be.

My feet slammed down onto the scree, sinking in, sliding backward. Over and over. It took forever to make progress going up.

I scanned the mountain as I went. Maybe I could get a cell signal if I went to the side. Even in deep scree, traversing across a mountain is much faster than climbing up. But there was nothing about the shape of the mountain folds that indicated whether one way or another would be better for cell reception.

Generally, cell coverage is better the higher you go. Maybe I could go both sideways and up at the same time. But what if I came to a spot where cliff rocks blocked my passage? Better to slog up the way we came down than risk getting trapped and being forced to retrace my steps.

I checked all three phones. No cell signal. I kept charging up the slope. One and a half feet up for each leaping step. One foot back. Sometimes two feet back.

My mind went to Benito's task. What could he do other than apply a tourniquet? Put his thumb directly over the wound? Maybe he'd already tried that. Benito had served with Doctors Without Borders. That must have put him in stressful situations where you learn emergency medicine.

All I knew was that when I glanced at Benito as I left, he was covered with blood.

Maybe there were certain techniques to keep a person's heart beating. Maybe there were drugs to raise blood pressure.

I kept seeing the image of him working over Damen. His movements were fast, more frantic than I've seen other doctors. But as a geriatric oncologist, Benito didn't practice trauma medicine or whatever they call it. This kind of event would be a shock to him. Adding to the stress was his relationship to Damen. When a loved one is at risk of death, even the most science-focused doctor gets rattled and maybe falls apart.

I was breathing so hard, I couldn't keep up my pace. I slowed slightly and concentrated on breathing.

I checked all three phones again. Nothing.

We had cell reception when Damen pulled up the map on his phone. So I knew there was a signal higher up the mountain. But how long would it take me to get there?

I focused on breathing and stepping. Breathe and step.

I didn't know how much time had gone by when I finally got a signal. Too much time, certainly.

Damen's phone showed a signal first. I dialed.

"Nine, one, one emergency. Please state your name and address…"

I cut the dispatcher off. "Owen McKenna. I have an injured hemophiliac boy named Damen Diaz. He's punctured his brachial artery. He's down below the north end of the Flume Trail. Just south of Tunnel Creek Road and two hundred yards below the trail. I need medics and a helicopter medevac ASAP. Sergeant Lori Lanzen of the Washoe County Sheriff's Office can vouch for me."

"Hold on, please. It'll just be a minute."

"It can't be a minute! The boy is going to die unless you turn heaven and Earth upside down and get medics up Tunnel Creek Road and a chopper up here for a cliff rescue. IMMEDIATELY. Do you understand? The BOY IS GOING TO DIE!"

"I've got rescue underway, sir."

"Tell them the boy's uncle is a physician. He's on the scene and trying to stem the blood loss. He says the boy is suffering hypovolemic shock. I will wait where the Flume meets Tunnel Creek Road and direct rescue personnel."

"Please stay on the line."

"Will do. I'm still hiking up the mountain."

I huffed and puffed and continued my slog up toward the Flume Trail. Having gotten through to emergency rescue didn't ease my brain or the burning in my thighs. I couldn't stop thinking about Benito and what must be going through his mind. He was so careful about Damen's hemophilia and the risks of riding a bike, and now the boy was possibly going to die from an injury when he wasn't even on his bike. I didn't know much about medicine, but I knew that if you sever the brachial artery, you'll likely bleed out and die. It kills nearly everyone, hemophilia or not. Benito must be going crazy. And I had no way to tell him help was coming. He wouldn't know until he heard sirens and a chopper.

After what seemed like an eternity, I got up to the Flume Trail. I turned and ran to the intersection at Tunnel Creek Road.

"Rescue personnel are en route," the dispatcher said.

What followed was the longest ten minutes of my life. When someone is dying and the rescue time matters, the anguish is beyond description.

I paced. I huffed. I grunted. I ran down the trail as if I might see something I hadn't seen before. I charged over to where we'd left our bicycles. I grabbed mine as if to ride it. What was I doing? Where would I ride it? I let it fall back against the others.

I started jogging down Tunnel Creek Road. But what if the helicopter came over the mountain from the east? I ran back up the road. I bent over and pounded my fists on my thighs.

Damen wasn't my nephew. He was just a kid who ended up on a bicycle ride with me. But in the short space of time since he'd gotten stabbed in the arm by a branch and started spilling blood over the mountainside, he'd become hugely important to me. As I waited forever for some first responders to show up, I wanted to scream.

Then came a siren.

It was faint at first, and I wondered if it might just be a cop making a traffic stop on the highway two thousand feet below. But the siren grew, and I let a little hope creep into my darkness.

It took another eternity for the siren to grow loud enough to make me believe it was coming around the last curve on Tunnel Creek Road.

And then it was there. I waved my arms. The rescue ambulance scraped gravel coming to a fast stop.

The passenger door opened and a medic jumped out. "Injured boy?"

The driver's door opened and the driver jumped out.

"Yes. Follow me. The boy's down a scree slope. He caught his shoe on the trail, and he slid down until he was stopped by Manzanita bushes. One of them punctured his arm and brachial artery. It will be very hard to come back up, carrying him on a gurney. I think he's got to be choppered out. Bring whatever you need for that. There's a lot of blood loss, so you will want whatever you need for that. And bring your radios. There's no cell signal down there."

The two men opened the back door and pulled out a gurney and some other gear.

We ran along the Flume Trail until we got to the place where Damen slid off.

I deep-stepped my way once again with the two young medics following and carrying their gear. It took longer than I remembered, probably because I was so stressed. It must have been an hour since Damen's accident.

As we got within sight of Damen and Benito, I didn't understand what I was seeing. They were both there, but Benito was down on the ground near Damen.

I kept charging down the slope, stepping and sliding, stepping and sliding. Soon I was near. What I saw didn't make any sense.

Then it made a great deal of sense.

Damen was lying in the same place as before, across the steep slope, on his back, his arms out, wounded arm on the upper side. As before, there was blood everywhere. A lot of blood. Much more than before. Damen's sleeve was cut away. There was a tourniquet at the top of his wounded arm, right up against his armpit. But the tourniquet had been loosened. The bicep on Damen's wounded arm had a large blood-soaked surgical bandage on the inside. Lying on the rocks was a needle and a piece of thread. It was as if Benito had done a field operation to try and stitch up the punctured artery.

On the inside of Damen's elbow on the same arm was an IV needle taped in place. Attached to the needle was a long plastic tube filled with red blood. The plastic tube went up the slope several feet to where Benito lay. Benito had a similar IV hookup, and the tube from Damen led up to Benito's arm.

Benito obviously knew that Damen was going to die from loss of blood. So Benito cut into Damen's arm and did some kind of emergency artery repair to stop or at least stem the flow of blood out of his wound. Then Benito set up a transfusion. He no doubt knew that their blood type was compatible. So he connected their veins with a tube and IV needles. He positioned himself above Damen so that gravity would make his blood flow into Damen's arm. Depending on how much blood Damen had lost and how much was still leaking out of the stitched-up artery, Benito's blood might make enough difference to prolong Damen's life. And if medics could get Damen to the hospital soon enough, maybe it would save Damen's life.

I squatted down next to Damen and placed two fingers on his neck. His carotid artery had a weak pulse. He was still alive. As I touched his neck, he moaned.

I scrambled up the slope to his uncle, who was motionless and looked very pale. I spoke in a low voice next to his ear.

"Benito, the medics are here. A chopper is coming. Damen is alive! You saved his life."

Benito didn't respond. I leaned my ear next to his mouth. I couldn't sense any air motion. I touched two fingertips to his carotid artery. I couldn't feel a pulse.

"Guys, we have a cardiac arrest!"

One of the medics checked the pulse, then opened a bag and

pulled out a defibrillator machine. The other readied transfusion materials. In the distance came the rapid staccato thwop of an approaching helicopter.

I spoke next to Benito's ear. "Stay with me, Benito! You saved Damen. Everything is going to be okay!"

Maybe I sensed Benito stir. Maybe I just hoped for it.

"C'mon, Benito!" I gripped his hand and squeezed.

It seemed like Benito's mouth was moving. Again, maybe I just wished for it.

I bent down with my ear next to his mouth as the medic ripped off Benito's shirt and readied the paddles on his chest.

Before they hit the electrical trigger, Benito tried to speak. His voice was just a hint of a whisper. But the words were clear to me.

"He kindly stopped for me." Then Benito's lungs made a kind of rattle and were still.

The medics hit the button. Benito's chest jumped. They did it again. His chest jumped again. And again, many times.

I held onto Benito's hand as they made a futile effort to restart the life of a man who'd already given all the blood he had to his nephew.

The helicopter arrived overhead making a tremendous noise and blast of air.

The two medics had been conferring about Benito. One of them mouthed some words that couldn't be heard over the roar of the chopper. The other nodded.

They turned to Damen, who was mumbling but mostly unconscious. They got him strapped into the gurney, hooked it to the line lowered from the helicopter, and he was raised up to waiting medics in the chopper. Then they rushed him off to the hospital.

The medics who'd arrived by ambulance stayed with me and Benito's body.

Eventually, the helicopter returned, and we sent Benito into the sky.

THIRTY-FOUR

I didn't know the fate of Damen Diaz. Any normal person who tears open a brachial artery is lucky to survive. When it happens to a hemophiliac, the odds drop precipitously. I spent several hours at the Reno hospital.

Street and Camille came down to pick me up.

I pulled up a chair and sat close and across from them in the hospital lobby and told them the basics. They were kind and caring. I kept getting up, walking to a nurse's station and asking for an update on Damen's condition. A doctor finally told me to go home. The message was clear. Stop asking questions. It won't help his chance of survival.

Street and Camille had brought the dogs, meaning that once again Camille sat on my lap in Street's VW Beetle. I didn't mind. It felt nice to feel her companionship so close to me.

Once I got to Street's I tried to be useful by making phone calls. I first called Nanna Hansen and told her what happened. She was horrified. We struggled on the phone while she tried to comprehend the situation. Eventually, after many tears and exclamations and questions, she calmed a bit. I got the sense that she was as competent as people come. She assured me that Damen, if he survived, would be taken care of. I called Diamond and explained what had happened, then made a tentative plan for retrieving Benito's rental car and our bicycles.

I called Doc Lee and talked to him. He knew the physicians at the trauma center in Reno. He said he'd make sure I got the news as soon as they had a solid update.

My cell phone rang that evening. A Dr. Ramirez told me that Damen Diaz was stabilized and semi-conscious, and if he made it through the night without major bleeding episodes, he would probably survive. A surgeon had reinforced the field surgery Benito Diaz had performed on the Flume Trail. The man said that Damen Diaz's injury was not typically survivable in the field. His type of brachial artery damage would usually result in death in less than five minutes with a person who did not have hemophilia. A person with hemophilia faced worse odds. But Benito Diaz's surgery on the artery, his application of hemostatic agents, and his transfusion with his own blood had been done with great skill. He saved the boy's life against great odds. The coming night would likely tell if their treatment with additional hemostatic agents and surgery would hold.

I thanked him profusely and hung up.

After dinner at Street's, we sat in front of her fire.

We talked about Damen Diaz, the subject segued to Grandpa Charlie, and, eventually, Camille brought it back to Damen.

"If a boy almost dies, and then his uncle dies, in some ways that's worse than when a grandpa dies," she said.

I nodded. "I watched a young boy's life flicker and slow and come close to stopping," I said, my eyes suddenly wet. "Damen Diaz has a big personality. I could see why Benito was so attached to him, never mind their relationship."

I wiped my hand across my eyes then reached over and put one hand on Street's leg and the other on Camille's leg.

"Remember what you told me," Camille said.

"What's that?"

"You said the friendship of another person can make everything better. Street and I will always be your friends and make it better." Then she took my hand, drew a circle on my palm, and closed my fingers.

I took her hand, lifted it to my face, and pressed it against my cheek. "Yes. Thank you, Camille. You and Street make it better."

THIRTY-FIVE

The next morning, Diamond had delivered my rental Ford to the lot at Street's condo. Spot and I left Street and Camille and Blondie and headed up the mountain. I had a kind of death hangover thinking about Benito Diaz giving his life for Damen. I thought it would help to follow my standard routine, so I had coffee out on my deck. Spot sprawled out to absorb the maximum amount of the sun's heat on a chilly November day.

I called the Reno hospital to check on Damen's condition. He was still stable. I asked to talk to him. They said he was sedated. I got the feeling it was only partly for his artery healing and partly for his emotional adjustment to the death of his Uncle Benito.

I asked the hospital to keep me informed, then hung up, and tried to think of something useful I could do.

I thought again about Heathcliff's description of seeing a silent biplane. He said it was very large. Like an airship. At the time, I thought it an unreliable description. But after I'd learned about the Antonov AN-2, I knew that, compared to a common biplane, it was an airship.

I thought it time I go hunting for a big biplane.

I once again pulled up some maps on my computer. Using different levels of zoom, I printed out several maps of the Incline Village area. I made an X where I believed the Francis bench was, the place where Heathcliff went with Isabel.

Next, I thought about what Damen had said up on the Flume Trail. His idea of where the plane might have come from suggested a different location. I put two more Xs on the map as my best guess based on Damen's analysis.

I also assumed that Heathcliff was correct that the biplane was gliding, which meant that the engine was either shut down or was at what pilots call 'flight idle,' which simply means the engine is turning enough to run the generators that produce electrical power but producing no appreciable forward thrust. At 'flight idle,' the AN-2 might seem silent from 5000 feet below.

My task was to guess where a gliding Antonov AN-2 would land if it came over the locations marked with Xs and was flying 5000 feet above the ground.

I didn't know the glide ratio of the plane. But I could guess that like most planes without power, it wouldn't go far. I knew that the glide ratios on some planes were very long. But looking at the photo of the AN-2, it was clearly a boxy shape, a design appropriate for hauling stuff. There was nothing especially aerodynamic or sleek about its design. I was confident that it did not have a great glide ratio.

When I Googled it, I got no definitive answer.

So pick a number out of the hat, McKenna. What is a typical low glide ratio? Eight or ten feet forward for every foot of drop. 5000 feet of altitude above the ground was almost a mile straight up. A mile up would possibly let the plane glide eight or ten miles forward, if the ground it was heading toward was the same elevation as the lake.

But my entire notion of the plane landing in the mountains above Incline Village meant the landing site was probably up high. In that case, the plane couldn't go far.

I drew a circle around both of the X marks I'd put on the map. The circles showed a range of three miles. That dramatically reduced the territory the biplane could reach by gliding alone. But as I reconsidered searching this reduced territory on the computer, I realized I still couldn't do a thorough search in any reasonable period of time.

I had to revisit the investigator's oldest technique. Gumshoe footwork.

I marked on my map the various neighborhoods a coasting Antonov AN-2 might have flown over. Then Spot and I drove back to Incline Village.

When a single man wanders through neighborhoods, people get wary. But I carried a clipboard and took Spot with me. He makes people forget that I could be a bad guy.

I knocked and rang doorbells and spent an inordinate amount of time answering questions about big dogs and letting people pet him and take selfies with them crouching down next to him. Occasionally, I was able to ask questions about my task.

"Sorry to bother you, ma'am, but I'm from the dog-hearing sensitivity forum. You've probably seen the reports on CNN and Fox News. Anyway, you probably know that dogs have hearing that is a hundred and seventy times more sensitive than our own. And of course, we've demonstrated that neighborhoods with low sound levels in the range that dogs hear are much safer neighborhoods. So we're mapping neighborhoods nationwide to produce a canine hearing sensitivity report. When we're done, we'll have maps that rate neighborhoods for sound just like those maps that categorize neighborhoods for crime rates."

At that point, I always grabbed Spot's ears and made a stage whisper that could be heard 100 yards away. "Isn't that right, Spot? You need quiet neighborhoods in order to do your job of protecting us."

He always wagged, and then smiled for more selfies.

"Anyway, we got a report of planes flying above this neighborhood. And we're hoping you can confirm this report and tell us where the NANL falls on a scale of one to ten."

"I'm sorry," the person would say as they caressed Spot's head and hugged his chest. "The NA what?"

"Oh, sorry. The Neighborhood Aircraft Noise Level. On a scale of one to ten."

After I asked the question, most of the people said they hadn't noticed. Some said it was definitely a one or a two. One person said that the airport was all the way down in Reno, so how could he be expected to notice aircraft noise up here in the mountains?

After an hour of door knocking, a man scrunched up his face at my question.

"The, uh, Aircraft Noise Level might be zero sometimes. But it might also be an eight or a nine at times. Depending on."

"Depending on what, sir?"

"Depending on if an aircraft engine only roars for a minute or less. Does one minute count in your analysis? Or does it have to be longer term sound?"

"Well now, that's a very good question. I can see that you have an engineer's perception of sound impacts."

"A pilot's perception of sound impacts," he corrected. "Thirty years with the majors. The Pacific route, mostly. San Francisco to Tokyo. We always dealt with sound issues at airports. But never at the neighborhood level, so you've piqued my interest."

"This one minute sound you mention... It comes from an airplane?"

"Of course. That's why I brought it up. Someone revs an old radial engine for short periods. It's quite a roar. I'd guess a nine cylinder. Probably a four-blade prop from the vibration it gives off. It reminded me of a B-Seventeen Flying Fortress practicing for an air show. But what I heard was a single engine, so it couldn't be a B-Seventeen."

"And after this roar goes for a minute or so, then what?"

"It drops down to a low buzz and stays that way for several minutes. Then, if there's very little breeze, you can hear the engine RPMs come back up."

"The roar returns?" I asked.

"Yes, but the plane is far away. It's the damnedest thing. Like someone is coming up from Reno so you can't hear them. As soon as they get over the pass above Incline Village, the engine roar is huge. But then it cuts out. It's as if once they get past Mt. Rose Summit, they cut the power and glide into Incline Village down below. But where they go is a mystery. There isn't an airport here. I figured the plane must have floats, and they're heading for the lake."

"Well, that's very interesting. When you first hear the roar, where would you place it on the one-to-ten scale?"

"Like I already said, it's an eight or nine. It's a loud sucker, let me tell you."

"Have you ever seen this aircraft fly overhead?"

"No, and I wonder why."

I looked at the paper on my clipboard. "There's a place on this where I'm to note where the sounds come from. Can you tell me the direction?"

The man stepped out past Spot and went halfway down his walkway. He turned and pointed up and behind his house.

"Perfect, hold that position," I said. I got out my phone—with much more finesse than when I talked to Heathcliff—opened up the compass feature, and noted that the direction he pointed was north. I scribbled on my clipboard. "And the time of day?" I said.

"Morning. Seven a.m., once. Nine a.m., and ten-thirty. All three times I've heard it. The last time was just a couple of days ago."

I scribbled on my clipboard, then looked back up at the mountain behind his house. "I'd be curious to hike up there and possibly see this plane coming over the summit."

"Me too. But I've only heard the plane three times. The rest of the time there's nothing. And, for what it's worth, I hiked up there when I was much younger. It's very tough territory. Very tough."

I looked back at my clipboard. "Okay, I'll make a note. And I'll check this box that's labeled 'intermittent.' It's important that we attach a time frame to these sound assessments."

I turned to him. "Thank you, sir. You've been most helpful. You can know that the future neighborhood mapping for dog hearing sensitivity will benefit greatly from your observant help." My words were not quite the truth, but my appreciation was genuine.

When I got home, I looked at the maps I'd previously printed, found the neighborhood where the pilot lived, and noted the location of his house. I drew a line from his house going north. The line intersected the other line that showed where Heathcliff had seen the plane.

I spread out the drawing that Heathcliff had made showing the ravine on the Flume Trail and his estimate of where the biplane had gone relative to the trail. It took some careful measuring on Heathcliff's drawing and my map, taking into account my notes. But I was able to plot some new points on the map and draw a new line.

Eventually, I had one map with three lines. One was Heathcliff's estimate of the plane's movement from when he looked up from the bench in Incline. The second line was Damen's estimate of the plane's movement when he was up biking the Flume Trail and looking at Heathcliff's notes and drawing. The third estimate of the plane's travel came from the pilot who'd never seen the plane but had heard its engine roar and then go silent.

The three lines I drew on the map didn't converge at any single point. But they all crossed each other and made a triangle of sorts up in the mountains above Incline Village. The triangle ranged from one to two miles on a side. The topo lines showed the area as very rugged, like the pilot had said. They also showed that the area ranged from 9000 to 9500 feet of elevation. Which meant approximately 3000 feet above the lake, very similar to my thought experiment.

Of course, none of it meant much. And the area encompassed by the lines was high enough and rocky enough that it would be extremely difficult to search. But that triangle intersection of lines seemed to me like gold on a treasure map.

THIRTY-SIX

As I planned how I might explore the mountains above Incline Village, it seemed like it could be a long hike. Because Spot loves hikes, and because he's happy to carry his dog pack with food and water, I planned to take him with me the next morning.

I wondered whether to invite Street and Camille. Street loved hikes as well, and she could go longer and farther than I could. But Camille had just turned nine. She was a strong, fit kid, and she could probably go a long way on a maintained trail. But I didn't think it was appropriate to take a child that young on a bushwhacking trip through the mountains with no clear idea of how far and how long the hike would be.

According to the topo map and also according to my recent talk with the pilot, the area where I was going would be tough. It looked like it might involve scrambling over lots of rock.

The next morning I stopped at Street's just after dawn. While Spot and Blondie engaged in their new pastime of shadow boxing with Camille, Street and I drank coffee, and I told her the basics of where I was going and explained that I planned to be back by evening. I told her I'd leave my phone on vibrate but that I imagined cell coverage might be sparse or even nonexistent.

Street wished me luck, kissed me, I said goodbye, and I left.

I drove up the East Shore to Incline Village and turned up the Mt. Rose Highway, which climbs to 9000 feet before dropping in switchbacks down to Reno.

I had a full range of hiking supplies in my pack and in Spot's pack. Lots of food, water, clothes for both warmer and colder weather. My maps fit into my belt pack along with a spare flashlight and my phone, which was charged. My folding knife remained in my pocket.

By 8 a.m., I'd parked up on the high meadow that stretched off to the sides of the highway. My plan was to hike a few miles over to the area above the neighborhood where I'd canvassed and where I hoped to learn about what the retired airline pilot thought was the occasional roar of a plane that he'd never seen. It would save much effort not climbing up from below.

The dried meadow grasses were crispy with frost. Spot ranged out in front of me, his pawprints standing out as green/brown shapes among the white ice crystals that coated the grass. As is typical of dogs, his track meandered this way and that, nothing like purposeful carnivores such as coyotes and mountain lions whose tracks are much straighter lines. Dogs explore and investigate and have fun. Coyotes and mountain lions are focused on finding their next meal, and their path shows that focus. Bears are omnivores, and their tracks show more exploration. But they don't develop the carnivore's focus on finding meat because they can eat almost anything, including grazing on grass like the deer they occasionally eat.

Although the frozen grass was slippery, it was easy to hike through. At the far side of the meadow, the forest quickly rose up a steep slope. I'd memorized the general topography, and I had a general idea about which way to go, a route that involved minimal cliffs and outcroppings and escarpments. Minimizing outcroppings didn't just make it easier to hike, it made it more likely I might come upon the kind of land where a bush plane could land and take off.

As soon as I started up the slope, the territory no longer matched what I'd memorized from the map. I got out my phone compass and studied the maps. Spot came running back to see what I was doing.

"A little navigation, Largeness. Nothing more." He stuck his nose on my map, leaving a wet mark. "Go back to exploring. Lunch is two or three hours away." He got the message and headed off through the trees, sniffing out the transgressions of squirrels and other critters that hadn't gone into hibernation despite the cold.

Topographical lines are great for comparing a map to a real-life setting. You see a steep southern slope on a map and match it to a steep southern slope in front of you, and you know where you are.

The problem was, the southern slope in front of me was shallow, and the closest steep slope faced southeast.

So I made a kind of reconnaissance loop that gave me some elevation gain and a view in two directions. I decided I hadn't taken into account sufficient magnetic declination for the area. Like all compasses, my readings were off, attracted to the Earth's magnetic pole, which was a lot closer to Hudson Bay than the geographic North Pole. I reminded myself that a north heading on the compass in Tahoe was actually 13 degrees to the east of true north. But the government cartographers used true north on their maps instead of false north. Accurate maps meant I had to take north on the compass and turn counterclockwise the amount of a narrow slice of pie in order to find true north.

Once I got my bearings straightened out, I resumed hiking. Spot joined me, headed off in a new direction, came back to me five minutes later, then charged off anew.

Most of an hour later, I came to the major tough country the retired pilot had told me about. As I made my way upslope, I began to think that I'd overlooked an important point.

Anyone who flew a plane into a rough mountain area would probably want to have land access, in and out. It could be a nearly-impassible Jeep road, but there would probably be some kind of dirt road. If a pilot were transporting contraband, it would be even more critical to have ground access to load or unload the plane.

One could come in by snowmobile in the winter, but a plane couldn't land unless it had skis for landing gear.

I went up a boulder field and across a slope. I had to angle my boots to grip with the edges of the soles.

Spot did better than I did, but that was to be expected considering he had twice as many feet on the ground, and his feet came with nails. Canine studded snow tires.

I entered a steep thick forest that had endured an avalanche within the last ten years or so. The forest was littered with tree trunks all piled facing down the slope, large trees that had snapped off like twigs as a monster avalanche came down. I had to climb over some logs, duck under others, and two times I simply started over and tried to find a new route through the forest. Then I came to a wall.

The rock wasn't smooth and vertical like in Yosemite, and it wasn't more than 200 feet tall. But it was a wall nevertheless. The rock was granite, with hard and sharp edges. I couldn't find a way around it, and neither Spot nor I could climb it. So we retraced our steps a quarter mile or more and headed in a new direction. We eventually came to a very steep slope of boulders and broken rock. My maps suggested I was below the wall and above the neighborhood where the pilot talked to me. My only choice was to attempt to go across the slope like a skier traversing sideways around a mountain. But unlike the ease of movement a skier has on snow, I felt like an ant climbing up and over rocks, then descending down between slabs and giant boulders, then climbing up once again. I was certain I climbed and scrambled the better part of a mile, but when I got to a vantage point where I could look back to judge my progress, it seemed I'd only traveled 50 yards or so.

After three hours of rough hiking, we stopped for lunch. I looked around and decided there was no trail and no human nearby. Yet when I looked at my phone, incredibly, I had a cell signal, an often rare experience in the Tahoe mountains. I must have come up high enough to be within line of a cell tower, however far away.

I slowly tapped out an email to tell Street of our progress while I ate bread and cheese and apple and chocolate chip cookie and Spot ate bread and cheese mixed into the dog food sawdust chunks, and we each drank a canteen of water.

Twenty minutes later, we resumed hiking, forcing our way through steep slopes of timber and rocks. Despite looking at my maps, I had no confidence about my location.

I had friends who had GPS apps on their phones. They were able to view their position on a map based on satellite signals. My Luddite impulses had always resisted such modern technology. But my resolve to only navigate with 16th century skills was eroding. Magellan didn't get all the way around the world using dead reckoning. He used the stars and a sextant. NASA doesn't put spacecraft on Mars using a sextant, they use stars and atomic clocks and many computers. Yet here I was using a paper map and a compass. I found myself thinking that it worked for Lewis and Clark. Yet the world had moved on past those explorers. Past me, too.

After another hour of hiking, I had no view, no clear sense of position, and every direction seemed impassable. I paused to rest. That's when Spot's ears perked up. I paused and looked at the direction his ears were turning. When I turned to face that way, I heard a vehicle.

THIRTY-SEVEN

The sound possibly came from below me. But I wasn't sure. When you're in the mountains, sounds can be deceptive. You think a sound is from the north, but it turns out to be from the south and bouncing off an unseen rock wall behind the trees to the north. Based on the low volume, my vague sense was that it was a couple of hundred yards away. It sounded like a Jeep or a truck grinding along in low gear. I stepped down the slope, trying to move quickly.

The vehicle sound had a variability that demonstrated it was moving. But it didn't seem to change position. It must have been farther away than I'd first thought. The sound rose to a slight crescendo, then the driver up-shifted, the engine pitch lowered and softened, and the vehicle's sound faded away into the forest. I couldn't even tell which way the vehicle came from or which way it went away.

Because I didn't know where the trail was, it may have been futile to try to find it. But the sound of the vehicle was a clear indication that someone was traveling through this part of the mountains. If I could find the road, I could possibly find a person. Maybe a smuggler. I worked my way down the slope to a forest area that wasn't so steep.

There was no point in checking my compass heading, as there was no visual landmark to follow. All I had was dead reckoning. Try to walk straight toward the area where I thought I heard the vehicle.

Five minutes later, I found the trail. It was just two vague ruts. They curved around a thicket of trees and meandered through the forest. If I hadn't heard the vehicle and started looking for the trail, I might have hiked right across the trail without realizing it was there.

The trail perfectly traversed the slope, neither rising nor falling. I had no idea which direction to go. Either direction might eventually crawl up to a view spot or down to a sheltered valley, or even to a hideaway meadow where a bush plane could land. Or the dirt trail could descend two or three thousand feet to a residential neighborhood in Incline Village.

With no obvious best direction to go, either was as good as the other.

"Hey, Largeness. You wanna go that way?" I pointed. He looked. "Or that way?" I pointed the other direction. He looked. He turned his ears one way, then the other. He seemed more focused on the second direction.

"Okay, the second direction is more interesting." Someone else would think it was like flipping a coin. But I'd learned to pay attention to a dog's focus. A dog's senses were many times more sensitive than a human's.

We began hiking along the rutted trail.

Off-road Jeep trails sound intriguing in concept. Put the top down, range over the mountains. Search out impressive views, never-before-seen petroglyphs, get a photo of elusive wildlife, mountain lions, bears, elk.

The reality is that off-road trails can be brutal, twisting and lurching, filled with potholes, blocked by fallen trees. Driving them would be as slow as hiking them. Maybe slower, if you had to cut up trees to get through.

The wheel ruts were deep in places and non-existent in others. Rocks projected here and there. Many of them were sharp enough to cut my boot soles if I wasn't careful. Any vehicle that drove the trail would need heavy off-road tires.

The trail went through forest that was so dense the sun's position was obscured, and I had no perception of where I was. I periodically looked at the compass to check my direction. After several hundred yards, the trail curved as if it were going in a circle. In time, the trail climbed up a rise, and I got a slight view. I could see a small meadow with rocky ridges surrounding it. The middle of the meadow was interrupted with rock projections. No place to land an airplane.

I walked on for another ten minutes and saw that the territory was even less promising for a potential landing spot. I rechecked my compass and got a sense of where I might be on the map. Unfortunately, it was a vague sense. But the topo lines were all close together, indicating steep slopes over a wide area. Certainly, that corroborated what little I could see through the forest. So Spot and I turned and headed back the way we had come.

I decided to give it twenty minutes to see if I got a clearer idea of my location. If not, I'd abandon the trail and strike off through the forest based on my map rather than following a trail.

I retraced my steps to the point where I'd first found the trail. After another few hundred yards, the hiking became easier. But the viewing did not. The trees had branches so dense I couldn't see more than ten yards in any direction. As before, the trail curved, small S-turns followed by large arcs, which came to abrupt stops as the path headed up the slope. The trail switch-backed, headed up a steep section, reversed direction and continued up. After some distance, it reversed again.

I came to an opening in the forest. It was a relief to be out of dense tree cover if only for a short distance. I was on a slope with low Manzanita brush. To one side of the slope was more forest. To the other was another rocky ridge. Beyond the rock ridge was a more distant ridge. I knew that the trail I was on might head off into the mountains for ten or twenty miles, never to take me anywhere a plane might land. The rock ridge, however, promised a potential view.

I left the trail and headed across the slope toward the ridge. Spot was nowhere to be seen. But I'd learned over the years that even if I couldn't see him, he could keep track of me. I had decent vision, and that was all. He had excellent vision, superlative hearing, and an olfactory that was beyond comprehension. Ten minutes after I'd last seen him, he appeared in the forest, a nonchalant look on his face as if to say, 'Why look surprised. I've known where you were this entire time.'

The slope I was crossing was interrupted by lots of

underbrush.

Depending on elevation and moisture drainage, Manzanita grows from three feet tall to twenty feet. It is quite beautiful with rich green, succulent leaves and shiny mahogany-colored branches. The branches are extremely hard wood that grows in a dense tangle as if its purpose is only to provide cover for little birds, of which there were many, an unusual sight in Tahoe in late November.

When Manzanita grows in interconnected bushes, it is often impenetrable to humans without a chain saw or a bulldozer. Most smaller animals would also have trouble getting through it, thus making it a haven for birds who want to escape predators, whether furry carnivores or the feathered variety. Raptors couldn't fly through Manzanita any better than coyotes could crawl through it.

I had to weave my way around individual Manzanita bushes. When I came to a large group, I had to retreat and find a new path.

Eventually, I got to the rocky ridge.

I'm not an accomplished rock climber. But I can scramble on all fours. I found a route up a narrow ravine where the rock was fractured and small trees had taken root and had grown into stunted two or three-foot-tall saplings. In a couple of places I had to wedge my boot, find handholds, and tug myself up. Prop a knee here, an elbow there, feel for a new lip on which to hook the edge of my boot sole and do it without looking down, then pull up some more. After I'd started up the ravine, Spot came up behind me. I thought he would have trouble. Compared to dogs like Belgian Malinois that can nearly climb trees, Great Danes are no gymnasts. But Spot dug in his nails and scrambled up behind me with no delay. All Wheel Drive with off-road tires.

After five minutes of scrambling up sloped rock, I came to what seemed like a top edge of the rock. I reached my hands up to new grip points, then pulled up. My head slowly rose above the top of the rock, and I could suddenly see a large, sloped meadow.

The lower edge of the meadow stopped abruptly as the

ground fell away. A miniature version of the inclined airport in Nepal.

I turned to look toward the upper part of the meadow. It too came to an abrupt stop. Not because it fell away, but because it was backed by a rock wall that was fronted with thick brush.

I got one knee on the top edge of the rock, and scrambled up, then stood up.

Spot was still below on the rock slope.

"C'mon, boy, piece of cake for you."

I got down on my knees and reached down. He had all four paws spread, nails digging in. He looked left and right. He didn't need my help, but he was happy to accept it.

I got my fingers looped into his collar. "Easy up, hound dog," I said and pulled.

He came up and over the edge.

"Good boy," I said, but he was already ignoring me and exploring the meadow.

I looked across the meadow. It was perfect for what I had imagined. Sloped. Dropoff at the lower edge. Large. Yet secluded with a cliff at the upper end, a rock ridge to one side, a forest to the other side.

The only problem relative to my hope was there was no plane nor any sign of a plane.

I unfolded my topographical map. I looked to see where my current location might be. It was not obvious. I could see two prominent high points about a half mile away, one to the north and one to the east. Not major mountains. But steep-sided promontories. Unfortunately, the topo map showed four or five areas where the topo lines were close to one another, signifying steep slopes. It was an example of how a view from the side made a high point look dramatic. Whereas a view from above, as on a map, revealed there were multiple high points, with some hidden behind others.

I realized I was somewhat lost. Not in the big picture. I had my compass. I could head south and continue until I came to the Mt. Rose Highway. I also found two or three places on the map that could be other plane-friendly meadows. But I could not pinpoint my location on the map. The GPS crowd would be laughing at me.

I walked down toward the lower end of the meadow. The ground, which likely had some give in the summer, was mostly frozen hard. Its grasses were flat and looked lifeless. The early snowfalls had, no doubt, compressed the ground and its plants. But the meadow sloped to the southwest. So the afternoon sun would melt any snow along with the morning frost.

As I walked across the meadow, I thought it was perfect for an inclined runway on which to land a bush plane. Although it was short, it had a substantial slope, perfect for slowing a plane landing uphill and helping speed a plane taking off downhill. When I got to the low end, the ground fell away at a 45-degree angle or more. Farther out, the dropoff got even more dramatic. No obstruction at all. If you could get a plane airborne by only a few feet, the moment it went off the end of the meadow it would be well into the air, because the ground dropped away fast and steep. Once your plane was several hundred yards out, it would be more than several hundred yards above the ground. A pilot could throttle back the engine, pitch the plane down at a steep angle, and let the downward glide add to the plane's speed with no engine roar at all.

From the low end of the meadow, I turned and walked up the slope.

After hiking through thick forest and steep scree slides and Manzanita tangles, the meadow was easy hiking territory.

When I got near the top of the slope, I paused and looked around. I'd seen nothing new of interest. All the meadow lacked was any sign of use by a plane.

I reconsidered the visual landmarks and looked again at my map. I picked out the likeliest places where we could be. Then I planned how I would hike to explore other possible airfields.

"This way, boy," I said, turning. We walked off to the side of the meadow, entered the forest, and headed toward another area on the map that looked promising.

As I fumbled my way through thick patches of trees and then through another boulder field, I thought again about the concept of using a biplane the way a bush pilot would. What would be the point? What would make the effort worthwhile?

I revisited my meetings with Heathcliff, a man who seemed gentle and kind despite his obvious delusions. His fixation on his dead girlfriend Isabel seemed benign. Could it be otherwise? And his report of seeing a big biplane above Incline Village was unusual, even if that part of his thoughts seemed rational and level-headed.

I wondered what was the likelihood of such a plane existing? Was I crazy to be focused on a delusional man's report of a big biplane? And, whether it existed or not, what was the reason for Heathcliff's fixation on planes? I thought it was probably connected to an experience he had before his girlfriend Isabel's death, and before his supposed suicide attempt. He'd said that he didn't know why the plane seemed important. That suggested something in his past.

The forest opened up, and I saw another open slope in the distance, not too steep, and with not too many Manzanita bushes blocking my way. According to my map, I might get to my next area of investigation more easily by heading up that slope.

Spot followed.

As I hiked uphill, I considered a different thought process. I wanted to ignore Heathcliff and figure out a scenario that would explain the existence of the biplane and its pilot flying above Incline Village.

I thought of the potential purpose of a biplane in the basin. There could be several innocent explanations. For example, a pilot with a large biplane, probably flying out of Reno, could possibly make good money doing tourist flights up over Mt. Rose Summit, into the Tahoe basin, around the lake to scenic spots such as Emerald Bay and then back. A trip like that would take two or three hours. By charging $500 per person and taking ten passengers, the revenue would be $5000 dollars per trip. In addition to the sightseeing and photo opportunities with all the windows, the biplane itself would be an attraction to people who were interested in unusual aircraft. Add in the thrills of flying low over the mountains and looking down at the palaces of billionaires, even I would be interested in such an adventure. Why take a ride in a Cessna when you could experience a one-of-a-kind trip?

No doubt, the expense of operating an AN-2 plane would be significant. But I thought that the revenue would be worth it. Careful scheduling might allow for two trips per day, doubling the daily revenue. But if it were for tourists, it would be advertised. I would have heard of it.

The concept of innocent purposes of a large biplane could be extended to other uses. Perhaps a company specializes in entertaining corporate clients. Instead of typical corporate perks like renting one of Tahoe's yachts for a company event, they could rent a large, slow plane.

But none of those possibilities explained the plane flying silently, either with its engine off or on 'flight idle.' And none of the possibilities explained what the retired airline pilot had heard, a sudden roar of a plane's engine followed by unnatural silence.

So the question was what kind of contraband would be suitable for flying in by plane? I didn't think it would be guns. They are very heavy. You wouldn't be able to put many in a plane without going past the weight limit of what a plane can carry. Same for explosives. And, unlike guns, the demand for illegal explosives was relatively small. There was always a demand for alcohol, and tax-free libation had been a smuggler's choice from the beginning. But liquids were heavy. Any plane smaller than a cargo transport would not be worth the trouble. Better to take your chances bringing product in by truck. Smuggling contraband in a plane would only be appropriate if it were relatively lightweight. And the only thing I could think of that was lightweight was what the DEA and ATF agents had already said. Cigarettes.

I came to a game trail and followed the paths of deer for awhile. Then the trail seemed to fork at a heavy stand of fir. I had to duck and push branches aside to get through. Spot ran up from the right, disappeared into the forest, then later ran up from my left. He was getting a lot of exercise. He'd sleep well tonight.

I remembered that the ATF agent said that half of all cigarettes in California were illegal. I couldn't remember the exact dollar amounts, but he said that bringing cigarettes in from lower-tax states, whether acquiring them from manufacturers or distributors, could produce a financial windfall in the range of two dollars or more a pack.

Up ahead was a rocky slope, boulders and scree and outcroppings and small rock cliffs. I called out, "Hey, boy, I'm heading up a rock-strewn slope."

I thought I should revisit the question with the ATF agent. I pulled out my phone. No reception, of course. Any mountain resident who's checked the cell phone carrier coverage maps knows that the carriers are scamming their customers. Sure, there's coverage in a given area, but only if you hike or drive to the correct high spot. But what can you do after you've bought your phone? You can't call and complain, because you can't get a human. You'll only get a voice recognition robot that doesn't recognize your words. 'I'm sorry, I didn't understand that.' The synthetic voice may as well say, 'That Wappa Wabbit.' At least then we'd be entertained.

Five minutes of hiking later, I got a signal.

THIRTY-EIGHT

I found a rock to sit on with a view of distant mountains and a tiny slice of lake. Somewhere out there was a cell phone tower beaming radio waves my way. I looked in my contact list and found ATF Agent James Rousseau and the ATF's Sacramento number.

I dialed and got Rousseau's voicemail. I remembered that Rousseau answered my last call directly. It made sense that I'd get his voicemail if he were on the line and not picking up incoming calls.

So I clicked off and spent some time searching out an office number for the ATF in Sacramento. Five minutes later, I was dialing again.

"Alcohol, Tobacco, and Firearms," A young male voice answered. "How may I direct your call?"

I knew if I just asked for Rousseau, I'd be directed to his voicemail.

"My name's Owen McKenna. I'm a Tahoe investigator. I have a follow-up to my meeting with Rousseau in Sacramento a few days ago."

"I'm sorry, James Rousseau is out. I'll connect you to his voicemail."

"Wait," I said before he could hit his button. I was trying to remember Rousseau's specific words, which might give me credibility. "Agent Rousseau and I were talking about looking into illegal cigarette transportation modalities that involve Tahoe. I believe it's critical to get him some information immediately. Can you do that? Call him on his private line and pass on some info?"

The man hesitated. "I, uh, can't because he hasn't come into work these last couple of days."

"Oh. He didn't mention he was taking time off."

"He wasn't. At least not that we knew of. But when you say you are in Tahoe, I would think he was contacting you."

"Me?" I said. "Why?"

"Because he said he was running up to Tahoe to check something out. It wasn't a break. It was work. He said he'd be back later that day. Now you mention Tahoe right after he mentioned it. So I imagine you are both working on the same thing."

"Have you tried his private line?" I asked.

"Mr. Feinstein did, yes. He left messages on both Jim's cell and his landline. But Mel—that's Mr. Feinstein—hasn't heard back."

"In the past when Agent Rousseau is gone, does he check in now and then?"

"Absolutely. Mr. Feinstein runs a very tight ship. Anytime an agent is on a field trip, they are required to check in twice a day."

"How long ago was this when he said he was going to Tahoe?"

"Let me think. Two days… No, three days ago. I remember because Mel—Mr. Feinstein was having his weekly meeting."

"Can you please give me Feinstein's voicemail? I'd like to leave him a message, too."

"Sure."

At the beep, I explained who I was and why I was calling.

When I hung up, I had a disturbing thought.

THIRTY-NINE

ATF Agent James Rousseau had talked to me at length about cigarette smuggling. It seemed to be his opinion that smuggling cigarettes into California by plane, while possible, was impractical. I don't think he thought a plane could carry enough cigarettes to make it financially worthwhile.

And he should know because he revealed he was a pilot, and he spoke from a pilot's perspective. He also knew something about biplanes because he had a friend or two who kept a biplane at the San Carlos Airport.

Could it be that Rousseau wanted to give me a subtle push away from the subject because he was actually smuggling cigarettes on the side? As an ATF agent, he would know better than anyone how to run a smuggling business.

And why had Rousseau suddenly gone AWOL from work? Was he going to Tahoe to close up his smuggling business? Did he think my focus on a biplane was an indication that I would uncover details of cigarette smuggling that could be linked to him? Did he go AWOL from his job because that was an easier way to get time off without having to put in a request?

Spot came running up, no doubt wondering why I was parked on a rock when there was so much to be explored. I rubbed him, and he trotted off.

When I'd previously seen Agent Rousseau, he suggested I speak to Patrick Peterman, the cigarette tax crusader who was trying to raise taxes in an effort to reduce smoking. He'd given me statistics that indicated that states with higher taxes on cigarettes had lower smoking rates than states with lower cigarette taxes.

I didn't have his number in my contact list. But I could probably find it with a search. I remembered that his office was in Half Moon Bay and had spectacular views of the Pacific. The address and phone number showed up on the Google page. I was pointing to the screen on my phone as the info came up and, to my surprise, my phone automatically dialed the number. Maybe I should have been delighted, but instead it bothered my inner Luddite to think that you can't even hover your finger over information without the phone trying to be "helpful" and dialing, whether you want it to or not.

A man answered. "Welcome to Live Better, Live Longer," he said. I recognized his voice from when I visited before. I could visualize his blue suit with the artistic blue satin patches.

"Good afternoon, this is Owen McKenna calling. I had an appointment with Patrick Peterman several days ago at your office. I wonder if I could ask him a quick question."

"I remember you. You were studying our paintings. Mr. Peterman was so pleased that someone cared about them. He thinks no one ever cares about art."

"I'm not the only one who cares about art." I managed to stop myself from launching into a tour-guide lecture about the dozens of major art museums in California.

"Well, anyway, he was glad. I'm sorry he's currently in a meeting. But I think he's almost done. Do you mind holding a minute or two?"

"That would be fine, thank you."

He put me on hold, and I gazed at the mountains and the little slice of blue lake that showed in the notch of two intersecting slopes.

Three or more minutes later, I was about to hang up, when there was a loud click as someone came on the line.

"Patrick Peterman, here. Sorry to keep you waiting, Mr. McKenna."

"I'm sorry to intrude without an appointment. You will recall me asking about cigarette smuggling and whether it could be done with an airplane."

"Yes, I remember."

"I have another question."

"I'll do my best," he said.

"I'm wondering if you've ever come across ATF employees who were smuggling on the side?"

"Now there's a messy subject. I should probably just say, no comment." He made a little embarrassed laugh.

"I'd understand if you did," I said. "But if you're willing to comment, I promise it won't be on record. You need not mention any names or specifics. A simple yes or no would suffice for my current investigation."

He didn't respond.

I waited.

After a long silence, I added, "I'm very discreet. Like you, I'm not on a witch hunt, just a better society. I won't name names." As I said it, I knew that, depending on the circumstances, it might not be true.

After another wait, he said, "Yes."

"Just to be sure I understand, you mean yes, you've come across ATF employees who you believe were smugglers?"

"Yes," he said again. "But that's all I'll say. Good luck. And please don't get me killed." He hung up.

I stood up from my rock perch.

"C'mon, boy," I called out, not seeing Spot but knowing he would hear me.

I started walking back toward the general direction of my rental Ford. A hundred yards later, Spot trotted out of the forest, came close to me, then headed back into the trees.

As I hiked, I pondered the implications of Patrick Peterman's statement that he'd known of ATF employees he thought were in the smuggling business.

It could of course be false. But it would possibly explain Agent Rousseau's sudden trip to Tahoe and his absence from work. He knew the cigarette business. And he possibly understood smuggling better than anyone. It would also explain my vague sense that he seemed a bit suspicious when we'd spoken. Some of his responses came a bit too quick. Others a bit too slow. The combination gave me a sense of calculation on his part.

But if he was smuggling cigarettes in a large biplane, I was still no closer to finding it or learning about his actions.

I stopped and checked my map.

As I resumed hiking, I thought about everything I'd learned from my meeting with Agent James Rousseau. But there wasn't much to think about.

Next, I went over my conversations with Patrick Peterman, cigarette tax crusader, art collector, son of a televangelist who committed suicide after he got caught in sexual and financial indiscretions. Peterman seemed like a classic case of a man compensating for his father's embarrassments and his mother's death by cancer. He threw himself into doing good by trying to reduce smoking rates.

Additionally, the process of creating a well-appointed office and collecting art for it added sophistication to a life that must have been dogged by darkness.

I thought about his art. Originals by little-known artists and studies of masterpieces.

I thought about his careful speech, good diction, articulate comments, qualities that went with art collecting. Some phrases stood out. Words like, "I know a statistician who says to always 'believe your instruments.'" A good rule in confronting the science of statistics.

But it was also a pilot's mantra when flying by instruments.

Never go by your gut feeling. Focus only on what the instruments reveal.

Was it likely that Patrick Peterman would remember such a line if he'd only heard it from a statistical analyst? Or did he remember it because he'd heard it in flying circles? Had Peterman been in the military? If not, he had friends in the military. He'd explained about the photo of his ex-military friend in the ghillie camo suit. The suit that can hide anything.

That thought actually brought me to a stop in my hiking.

Spot was nearby, and he stopped when he saw me stop.

I stood there in the forest, not looking at the mountains or the sky. I was only looking inward, remembering the inclined meadow Spot and I had just visited, the meadow that would be a perfect place to land and take off in a bush plane, the meadow that showed no sign of a plane.

But what if it were hidden by a type of ghillie suit? Was that even possible? Some kind of big ghillie blanket that could be pulled over a plane?

When a killer stabbed holes in the roof of my Jeep some time back, I pulled a tarp over it to keep water out until I could fill the holes. The tarp was relatively small. And it was lightweight compared to what it would have weighed if it had piles of shredded camo fabric stitched to it. But getting it over the Jeep was still work. I worried that my tugging would tear it.

A big airplane was an entirely different thing to cover. But there was probably a way it could be done. I wanted to get a fresh look at the meadow where I'd seen no plane.

I checked my phone. I still had reception. I dialed Street.

She answered, "Are you and His Largeness having a glorious, Sound-of-Music hike in the mountains?"

"Nearly. But I'm calling to request a favor if possible."

"Camille and I are debating the pros and cons of home schooling versus public school. Important stuff, but we're not too busy."

"Maybe this favor I'm asking could add fuel to the debate."

"Okay, we're listening."

"We are listening?" I said.

"I listen with my ears. Camille listens with her eyes, watching my lips. And because she can't watch your lips, she has to do twice the comprehension work, inferring what you said by listening to my response. Listening with her eyes. I could hook you up to the TTY voice transcription machine, but I'm on a different phone. And we haven't finished the TTY setup, yet. In the meantime, what favor do you want?"

"I'm hoping you can log onto a criminal-records website that I use and look up two men."

"Sure. I assume I would need your login and password?"

"Yes." I gave them to her. "One man is named James Rousseau, and he's an agent with the ATF."

"Alcohol, tobacco, and firearms?" she said.

"Yeah. He lives in the Bay Area and apparently works some of the time out of the ATF's Sacramento office."

"And the other man?"

"A guy named Patrick Peterman. He's a well-to-do art collector in Half Moon Bay. He has some kind of non-profit called Live Better, Live Longer. His main focus is to lobby states to raise their cigarette taxes in an effort to reduce smoking. All I know of his background is that his father was a televangelist who spent church money on boats, wine, and girls and committed suicide when he was found out. And his mother died of throat cancer brought on by smoking."

"From your request, I'm guessing these men might not be as honest and true as Abe Lincoln?"

"Most of what I've learned suggests they're both as honest as the next guy. But if they aren't, it could explain some things that Heathcliff said about a big biplane."

"Call you back?" she said. "We'll look on the computer?"

"Please." We disconnected.

I paused our hike and took another look at my maps. Although I couldn't imagine that the meadow we visited had a hidden plane, I was considering going back to it. A ghillie suit can hide anything. A plane was huge compared to a soldier. But all that meant was that a ghillie suit that could hide it had to be huge.

I took another look at the map to find other potential meadow areas. There were several. But none of them was worth visiting until the primary meadow was reinspected.

I also didn't want to move until Street called back. There was too much risk of losing cell reception.

"Hey, Spot," I called out to the forest. "You ready for a post-lunch snack?"

Almost immediately, I heard breaking twigs and crunching branches. Spot appeared in less than a minute, wagging, looking like a kid anticipating a hotdog.

I'd long ago figured out the appropriate technique for packing Spot's food. Put the plain dog food in his pack. The trick was that I carried the aroma enhancer in my pack.

I opened Spot's pack and poured some tasteless, aroma-less dry food into the folding dog bowl. From my pack, I got out the enhancement goodies, a zip-lock bag with diced chicken and a little bottle with chicken bouillon. I added some to his food, then stirred.

He ate it very fast, then used his tongue like a big wet towel to wipe down the inside of the bowl. I emptied a water jug into his bowl. He drank it, then looked at me.

"All done," I said, shaking my head. I'd just finished my sandwich when my phone vibrated.

I hit the button and Street said, "Agent James Rousseau has no record. I also looked on some social media sites, and he appears to be a regular guy. Photos show he has a taste for beer and the kind of drinking contest where you down shots before your beer. He occasionally leaves comments on a blog site about the San Francisco Giants. It seems like he has season tickets and is passionate about them. He's also a pilot of some kind. Likes to fly around the Bay Area. He takes photos and uploads them to sites like Instagram.

"As for your man Patrick Peterman, he used to be called Pat Palmer. Palmer ran an investment scam. Apparently, one of his investors caught on and challenged Palmer."

"That would be Benito Diaz," I said. "He told me about it but couldn't remember the man's name."

"Then you know that Palmer beat him up. He was caught during the assault, and the cops learned about the fraud. He went to prison on multiple charges, financial fraud and assault and battery, a total of ten-to-fifteen."

"I'm guessing there's more," I said.

"Yes," Street said. "Camille wants to tell you. She's practicing her phone skills with this new TTY machine, which we just got hooked up."

"Just so I understand," I said, "when I talk, the machine recognizes my speech and prints out the words on the screen. And she…"

"She reads it and can either type back to you and the machine translates text-to-speech so you can hear it. Or, she can talk directly to you. She'd rather do the talking because she's insecure about her typing speed."

"She's just a kid. How could she possibly expect to be a fast typist?"

"That's what I said."

"Okay, I'm ready, Camille," I said.

Her high-pitched voice was strong and clear and had remarkably little of the deaf accent.

"Mr. Palmer grew up in Bakersfield," she said. "His mother was a my... migrant farm worker from Mexico and she died in a car accident. His father was a homeless alco..."

I heard Street's voice saying 'alcoholic' in the background. How that helped a deaf person learn pronunciation, I didn't know. Maybe Camille put her fingertips on Street's throat to feel the vibrations? Or maybe she just watched Street's mouth and lips?

"Alcoholic," Camille said. "He died from..." She sounded out the word. "Al-co-hol-ims." Then she corrected herself. "Alcoholism."

I remembered telling Street about Peterman's background. I said, "So the whole televangelist story was made up. Same for the mother dying of cancer. He made the story purposely tacky to be more believable. Quite clever, actually. This guy is something."

"No kidding," Street said.

"And his story about getting money from his father was brilliant. No one ever questions someone's money when they claim an inheritance. Did you see anything about this Peterman/Palmer guy being a pilot?"

"No."

"Thank you, Camille. Thank you, Street. This is very helpful."

"One more thing," Street said.

"What's that?"

"Camille and I were searching pictures connected to UCSF Medical School. Camille spotted one with a group of students from a dozen years ago. It was one of those standard group shots with three rows of people. Camille noticed it because in the front row were the three sisters named Smythe. The ones known as the Brontë sisters.”

“Identical triplets stand out wherever you see them.”

“Right. The caption listed first initials and last names of all the people. In the back row was a young man who looked like a movie star. A troubled movie star. He was the only person in the group who wasn’t smiling. His hair was kind of unkempt, with a curl that came down his forehead. He telegraphed discomfort. Not physically uncomfortable. Psychologically uncomfortable. The caption listed his name as H. Harris.”

“That would be the man called Heathcliff.”

“That’s what I thought. Another person in the photo was a man listed as P. Palmer.”

“What did he look like?”

“The kind of guy who is often overlooked. Plain in every way. Small eyes. Round head. Big ears. Short thin hair combed carefully to the side.”

“This is an interesting connection. Pat Palmer was in UCSF Medical School,” I said.

“It appears that way,” Street said. “At least until he went to prison on the fraud conviction. What’s your next move?”

“I’m going to a place where this man might keep a biplane.”

“In the mountains near Incline?”

“Yeah.”

“Spot is coming with you?” Street said.

“Yes. Nothing to worry about.”

“Say hi to His Largeness,” Camille said in her high sweet voice.

“Will do,” I said. “We should be back by dark. Love you both.” We hung up.

For a moment I thought about hard-boiled fictional detectives. They would grunt and hang up a phone without even saying goodbye. Their mood would be gruff, their attitude tough, their demeanor brusque. A tough guy like Philip Marlowe would not say, ‘Love you both.’

What a softie you are, McKenna.

FORTY

It took twenty minutes of fast hiking to get back near the inclined meadow we'd already found and walked across. Nothing had changed. But I moved more slowly as we approached. The meadow looked the same, a potentially perfect place to land a bush plane, especially one with no stall speed that could land when it was practically already stopped.

On this second visit, I paused at the rocks near the meadow's edge and took a long look at the surroundings. I got out my binoculars and scanned the territory. No sign of anyone. And, certainly, no sign of any plane.

I decided to walk up to the upper end of the meadow, just to imagine where someone would put a plane in position for takeoff, if, in fact, anyone did try to land a plane on the meadow.

I thought of keeping Spot from running around, just in case someone was close enough to see us. But there was no sign of human presence, so there was no point in restraining Spot.

It seemed surreal to be in an isolated, deserted meadow in the mountains, a place where no one would likely ever come.

Spot wandered like before, ranging out in front of me.

When he got to the bushes and undergrowth in front of the rock wall that rose up, he paused, then walked along with his nose to the ground.

Something made me stop and watch.

Spot was walking in a straight line.

Dogs do nothing in a straight line unless they're following a scent line that is straight. I walked up and looked closely.

The trees in front of the rock wall comprised a mini forest 100 feet on a side. They were closely spaced. They were fir. So their branches hung down like a big curtain. The undulating bushes below the branches were nearly opaque. I touched one as I walked nearby. It didn't give me the resistance I expected from a bush. I touched another. It moved. So did a nearby bush. I shook it. A bunch of bushes moved. I lifted up on a bush, and an entire section of bushes responded. They were all interconnected with each other. I tugged on a small fir branch and brought it up to my eyes. It had green needles. But as I looked closer, I realized they were very good fakes. It reminded me of the silk flowers in the supermarket. Even when they were positioned next to the real flowers, it was hard to tell them apart.

I kneeled on the ground and lifted and pulled and tugged. I saw strong, dark-green cords that made a mesh. The bushes and branches were attached to it. I inspected the bushes up close. They were made of fabric as well. It was a giant ghillie suit wall. I stood up and walked along it, peering, pulling, trying to see through it.

Eventually, I figured out that there was a kind of roller up above. I recalled that I once saw a swimming pool cover that retracted on a very large roller that was 30 feet long. This was like that. Only there were two rollers, end to end. Together they spanned sixty or seventy feet. The rollers were dark green. They were mounted on something about fifteen feet above the ground. It was like two giant roller window shades next to each other. If one understood the mechanism and knew where the lifting crank was, the illusionary bush wall could be rolled up.

I walked along the rustling fabric bushes until I came to a vague corner.

When I looked up, I could sense a building that was fronted by the ghillie suit fabric wall. I poked my fingers through the fabric bushes. I hit a hard, metallic surface. It appeared to be a metal building painted green and brown in a camouflage dappling. At the top edge was more brush and grass. Maybe it was fake. Or maybe it was a real sod roof. The giant roller shade was mounted on the edge of the roof. The power of the illusion was impressive. I'd managed to walk up to a large building and get within a foot of its walls and still not see it. If Spot hadn't walked the straight line of a scent he smelled, a smell that probably seeped from the lower edge of a door, I might have wandered around just feet from the building and never realized it was there.

The building was obviously designed to conceal something big, probably a bush plane, but I still couldn't see how to get inside the building. Was there a plane in there now? I couldn't tell. I stood there, staring, amazed at the illusion.

I turned around and looked back toward the meadow, sloping down and away. From this perspective, I got a vague sense of wheel tracks, a sense that only came to me now that I knew it wasn't just an untouched meadow. The tracks were very slight impressions in the meadow grasses. Whatever plane used the meadow must have had what are called tundra tires. Big, wide, bouncy tires that enabled bush planes to land on rough territory. The tracks spread apart and wavered. The pilot must have taken care to vary his takeoffs and landings so his tracks wouldn't become embedded in the same place in the meadow grasses.

A distant raptor screamed "Keee-arr!" A ground squirrel, perhaps worried by the bird, emerged from behind a rock and sprinted to a distant hideaway. A late season beetle buzzed and made an ungainly landing on a fake bush just inches from my head. It took several seconds before the beetle could fold its wings under their hard protective covers. I thought it an awkward process until I realized how cool it would be to have wings in my backpack, waiting for the next time I wanted to fly. But most amazing was that the beetle was as fooled by the ghillie suit wall as I was.

Even knowing the building was there, it still was nearly invisible, perfectly camouflaged in the shadows of the cliff wall that rose up on the upper edge of the meadow. The trees at the base of the cliff helped obscure the lines of the building.

I walked sideways and back. The side of the building had no ghillie suit disguise. Instead, the dark wall had been covered in moss and lichens and other forest detritus that had somehow been attached to the wall. There were also large pieces of ragged bark. They reminded me of the way Native Americans had protected their shelters, only these chunks of bark were only for camouflage. The wall was well disguised. Although one could clearly see the wall up close, from a distance it would blend into the natural vegetation. The nearby trees obscured the building such that no one could see the side of the building without walking directly up to it.

I stepped up on a large boulder so I could see the sod roof. The sod was partially covered in pine needles that had probably rained onto it for years.

There were no openings in the wall, no windows.

I walked around to the back of the building, which was very close to the rock cliff. There was a single door. Like the wall, the door was disguised by tree and bush debris that had been attached. The door had a hasp and padlock, both painted dark brown. The idea of security for a nearly-hidden building in a remote part of the mountains seemed redundant. Maybe it was to help keep bears out. Then again, I was here. Other people might come here, as well. Especially if there was a Jeep trail nearby.

I stepped back to get a better look at the rear of the building.

I sensed something in my peripheral vision. I turned and saw that my new position brought another building into view.

I darted into the protective shade of the sod roof and slowly peeked out. The other building was a cabin, this one also with a sod roof, but this building was made of dark log walls. While the big building had a few trees overhanging its rear side, the smaller cabin was completely enshrouded in a thicket of trees.

The cabin was hidden well enough that it didn't need a ghillie covering or any other items attached to it to be well hidden.

A hiker could walk within a few yards of both buildings and never see them. And the sod roofs and overhanging trees of both buildings would make them invisible from above. They were nearly invisible on the ground. I'd had no idea there was private land up in this part of the mountains. It hadn't shown up as such when I'd done my online search of the area.

I looked at the cabin. There was no movement or sound.

Spot was nowhere to be seen. Which suggested there wasn't a strong recent scent of another person. Nevertheless, I decided to wait a few minutes.

I thought of a time I'd once gone wilderness canoeing in a lake district in Canada. When I'd paddled my canoe up to an island in the wilderness to pitch my tent and camp, I realized that there were thousands of places in the world where one could hide. And the best way to stay out of view wasn't to buy a thousand acres and build in the center of it. It was to not buy any land at all, don't get into any database, and live on public land in a place where no one went.

That was easy in the wilderness.

But it was also possible in the middle of civilization as long as you avoided the paths where people traveled.

I heard a noise? A thud. Where was the source? I couldn't tell.

I decided to wait longer.

I remembered reading about a challenge an NYU professor gave to his students. He said he'd camp in Central Park for one week, and he challenged them to find him. They never did, because they searched in the normal places people search, likely hideaways not far from the standard paths and roads and walkways. But the professor hid in plain site, camping in a roof attic of one of the park's buildings. Even in one of the most crowded cities in the world, if you go where no one else goes, you remain hidden.

Tahoe is one of the most visited places in the country. But the place I'd just found was far off the well-traveled paths.

When there was no sound for fifteen minutes, I began to think I was probably alone. I peeked out again, looking for a vehicle of some kind. There was nothing I could see. I especially wanted to get a glimpse into the big building with the padlocked door next to me. If there was no vehicle in it, whether the driving kind or the flying kind, that would add to the sense that I was alone on this mountaintop.

I moved along the back wall of the building, which also had no ghillie covering because it was close to the rock cliff that rose up behind it. There was some kind of dark, narrow opening a dozen feet up on the wall. Maybe a boulder had fallen off the cliff above and struck the building, bending a piece of the sheet steel that comprised the building's skin. If I could get up to that opening, I might be able to look inside.

I looked around for a way to climb up the building's wall. There were no easy rocks to move and use as a step stool. I went around the far side of the building. Still nothing. I walked into the group of trees near the cliff. A large branch had broken off one. I reached for it and tugged. It was hooked on one of the trees. I reversed direction, pushing it the other way. It seemed to come unstuck. I pulled again, weaving back and forth, and got it free from the trees. Like all tree branches, it was deceptively heavy, maybe 80 pounds. As I pulled it away, I saw three cigarette packs on the ground. They did not look very weathered as one might expect. But weathered or not, they were curious items to be so out of place in the mountain forest. It was a strong hint that my suspicions were correct. An ATF agent and a cigarette tax crusader with a pilot's license and the use of a plane could make serious money bringing cigarettes into California.

I got the branch turned around and tipped it up against the building, leaning at a 30-degree angle from the ground to the wall near the sheet metal opening.

I put one boot on the branch and pushed. The branch sagged, but it held. With one hand reaching down to the branch and the other against the camouflaged metal wall, I got both feet up on the branch. The branch bounced and slid down a bit. But I was able to move about six feet up it. I took my hand off the branch and gripped the ribs of the wall with both hands. Rising up another few inches, I looked into the narrow opening, a space that turned out to be created by a damaged seam between two of the metal sheets that made up the wall.

At first, it appeared that the opening did not penetrate through the wall. But as I stared at the dark opening, I started to sense a little light. The building was very dark inside, but I could see a few spots where light leaked in through tiny openings in the walls or even the sod roof.

I tried to hold my position with one hand while I used my other to turn my backpack so that it was on my front. The zipper was difficult to manipulate one-handed, but I got it open a few inches. I reached inside, felt for my flashlight, pulled it out, and shined it in the opening.

The flashlight didn't seem to illuminate anything. I angled it back and forth and tried shifting my head to change where I was looking. There. A little bit of flashlight beam was visible. It hit metal roof trusses. The light showed the bolts that held the trusses together. I'd seen these kind of buildings on farms as well as at airports. They were the kind of trusses that were assembled from lightweight angle irons. It was a labor-intensive type of truss, but one that didn't need heavy steel posts and beams. This type of building could be assembled from pieces brought up the mountain in a van or a pickup. The building could be assembled on dirt, the heaviest members resting on portable concrete piers.

I moved the light. Moved my head. Now the light beam hit something close to me. A large vertical panel. Dark green. Or brown. I shifted the light. I couldn't see anything. Moved it again. Another vertical panel. No, the same vertical panel. I realized what I was seeing. It was the vertical stabilizer and rudder of an airplane. A large plane. I aimed the flashlight forward. There was a horizontal line. Two of them.

I was looking at a large biplane. An Antonov AN-2.

"If you move, you die," came a man's voice, an angry whisper, almost a hiss.

FORTY-ONE

I started to turn my head.

"I told you not to move! I'm not going to miss with this twelve gauge."

I stopped moving. I hadn't seen his face. But I recognized the voice. It was the man I knew as Patrick Peterman, whose previous name was apparently Pat Palmer. I heard running noises. Spot coming at speed.

"The dog is mine," I said preemptively. "He won't hurt you. You don't need to hurt him."

"Tell him to back off!"

I called out, "Spot, no! Don't jump." Then, in a lower voice, "May I get down off this branch so I can hold my dog?"

"Slowly. Keep both hands visible. No sudden moves. No tricks. I didn't get where I am by being a pushover. My own death doesn't mean much to me. Your death means nothing."

I got down off the branch. "Spot," I said. "C'mere, boy."

He was midway between me and Peterman, looking back and forth. "Spot, come." I took slow steps toward Spot and took hold of his collar.

Spot had lost his exuberance. He could tell the mood had turned serious. He looked up at me, worry on his brow, then looked at Peterman.

Peterman cradled the shotgun in his left arm. His right hand was on the stock, finger ready on the trigger. If he fired the gun, he wouldn't miss. At this distance, I'd be blown nearly in half.

Peterman seemed different than before. Replace the business clothes with jeans and sweatshirt, cover the combed hair with a knit ski cap, switch out the pleasant, thoughtful art collector face for an aggressive look, and I barely recognized him.

"You almost fooled me, talking on the phone a few minutes

ago and making me think you were at your office in Half Moon Bay," I said.

"My secretary knows the drill. He explains that I'm almost done with a meeting. It gives him time to set up the call forwarding to my cell phone. If I've got reception, it's a good ruse for anyone who calls."

I nodded.

"Take off your pack," he said.

I shrugged out of it.

"Let it drop to the ground."

I dropped it.

"Slowly take off your shirt and drop it on the ground."

I did as he asked but left my T-shirt on. He no doubt wondered if I had a concealed carry holster under my arm or in the small of my back. I lifted up my T-shirt and turned so he could see.

"I'm not armed," I said.

"Lift up your pants, one leg at a time. Slowly. Prove to me you don't have an ankle holster."

I lifted my pant legs.

"Now reach into your pockets and empty them. Drop the contents on the ground. Now pull the pockets inside out. Very slowly."

I did as he asked, dropping my keys and pocket knife and cell phone on the ground.

"Unbuckle your belt, pull it out, and drop it. VERY slowly."

I pulled my belt out and let it fall.

"Drop your pants so I can see if you've got a weapon near your groin."

I did as he asked.

"All the way down to your knees. Okay, pull them back up. Now take off your boots and kick them to the side."

I did as he said. It was an effective way to hobble a man, making him remove his boots and making it clear that you're willing to shoot him with a shotgun if he makes the slightest move.

"Step away from your gear."

I took slow steps back, scuffing the dirt and duff with my stocking feet.

He bent down, picked up my folding knife and cell phone, and put them in his pocket.

"Okay, walk around to the back of the building."

I walked slowly, feeling every little twig and stone, a sense of physical threat almost as dramatic as the shotgun at my back.

Peterman followed me.

When I was in front of the padlocked door, he tossed a key on the ground. "Unlock the padlock."

I reached down and picked up a large key fob made in the shape of an airplane.

I fitted the key in the lock, turned it, pulled the padlock off so the door was unlocked. I hooked the padlock back in the hasp so it hung freely. The key and fob still hung from the padlock.

"Open the door. Slowly."

I pulled it open. The bottom edge of the door caught on the ground. I lifted it and used my toe to push an obstructing stone to the side.

"Reach inside to the right. There's a light switch. Turn it on."

I did as he said. Six big lights came on above, bright bulbs inside of shiny, parabolic reflectors.

The lights revealed the huge biplane. It was just as I imagined except that, instead of the light colors I'd seen in photos of AN-2 biplanes, it was painted in dark camouflage colors. Forest green and tree-bark brown and gray. Even with the lights on, it was hard to see inside the building. The dark camo paint job made the plane seem ominous, like an evil apparition. The man must have had some kind of off-grid solar/battery electrical system that could light the hangar and maybe keep the plane's batteries charged. I hadn't seen any solar panels, but they were out there someplace, probably mounted under a flimsy camo net that would disguise them from pilots above yet let enough light through to produce some electricity.

"Inside," the man said.

Still holding Spot's collar, I walked inside.

Because the plane was a taildragger, the fuselage pointed up at a steep angle. The huge engine with its four-bladed prop loomed up by the roof trusses. I was standing on the right side of the plane.

There were four round windows between the upper and lower wings. Behind the windows was a space and then another window.

"Go around to the door on the left side," the man said.

I walked behind the plane's tail to a door with a window in it.

"Open the door and pull out the stair step."

I did as he said. I looked inside the open door. The cargo hold was about six feet tall, a dozen feet long and about five feet wide, very similar in size to a modern, tall cargo van.

I leaned into the door opening. The plane's cargo area had two large cages made of heavy wire mesh. There was about 18 inches of space between the cages and the door of the plane, enough for a thin person to get inside and maneuver to the front where there were two steps up into the cockpit.

Each cage was about five feet from front to back and a little less than four feet wide. Both cages had a wide folding door made of four narrow sections similar to bifold doors on some closets. The doors could be opened without needing a lot of space for movement. The cages were like the mesh compartments inside a plumber's van or an electrician's van. They made it so no equipment or supplies could accidentally fly toward the driver or, in this case, the pilot. With the cage doors open, it seemed like there was a lot of room to move around the cargo area.

"See the coils of line hanging on the starboard wall?" Peterman said. "Take one of them and set it on the airplane floor near the door. And don't even think of throwing the line at me. This shotgun has a hair trigger. If I barely think about the trigger, it goes off."

I did as told.

He picked it up and looped the coil over his shoulder.

"Now take another coil and tie the line to your dog's collar. I did as he said, tying a line to Spot's collar.

"Now put your dog inside the rear cage."

"C'mon, boy," I said. I stepped up the little step-stair into the plane. "Into the cage." I tugged on Spot's collar and walked him into the wire mesh compartment. Crumpled in the far corner of the compartment was a baseball cap. Orange and black, with the number 24. It had the San Francisco Giants logo and the name Willie Mays. Where had I recently seen such a cap? Of course. It was worn by ATF Agent James Rousseau at our Sacramento meeting.

"Now shut the cage door so that the line from your dog's collar comes out under the bottom of the cage door."

I did as he directed, but first rubbed Spot along his neck.

Spot looked very confused as I shut him in the cage.

"Don't worry, boy. Everything's going to be fine."

Spot's eyes went from me to Peterman.

"Slide the cage door latch over and down and swing the safety hook through the hasp."

I did as told, noting that the latch and hook were cleverly designed so that the wire mesh door couldn't be opened from inside the cage.

"Now step back outside the plane."

I stepped out.

"See those fuel tanks in the corner of the hangar? On the other side of them are concrete blocks. Get two of them and put them in the plane."

The man studiously kept the shotgun pointed at me as I walked over and picked up a block. It must have weighed 80 pounds. I thought of throwing the heavy block at him, but he would surely shoot me. It's hard to miss with a shotgun. And the block was too heavy to throw well, anyway. It could only be lobbed toward someone, giving time enough for the target to step away.

I carried the block to the plane and set it inside the door. As I set it down, it made a loud scraping noise on the metal floor of the plane.

"Now pick up the end of the line that's attached to your dog's collar. Tie the line to the concrete block. Very thoroughly. I know knots, so don't try to trick me with a fake knot."

I put the line through the opening in the block and tied it off with a square knot.

"Next block," Peterman said.

I again stepped out of the plane, got another concrete block, and set it inside the plane.

"Stop there, facing away from me." It was the perfect time to spin and grab him. But I felt the cold curve of the shotgun barrel on the back of my neck. With his free hand, he tossed the coil of cord he'd been holding. It landed on my stocking feet. "Wrap it around your ankles, pull it tight, and tie it," he said.

I did as he said, tying my ankles together. He was smart to get his prisoner to tie himself up.

"Hands behind your back," he said when I was done.

I put my hands back, he looped another cord around my wrists. The man had good coordination. With one hand, he held the shotgun on my neck while he used his other hand to tie my wrists.

He pointed toward the door in the aircraft. "Get inside the front cargo cage," he said.

I hesitated and considered how few individual movements remained before we were in the air, and he was opening the aircraft door, tossing the concrete blocks out into space, then opening the cage doors and bludgeoning us until we got pulled out the door by the 80-pound blocks tied to us.

Unfortunately, I had no idea of how to interrupt the process when he had a shotgun to my head.

"Up the steps and inside the door," the man said. He sounded impatient.

I needed to delay him. "My ankles are tied."

"You can hop up the steps."

I hopped over to the steps and then jumped up the first one.

I saw two more cigarette packs on the floor of the plane. For a moment it seemed absurd that Spot and I were going to be murdered over cigarette smuggling. But I remembered what the ATF agent told me. Cigarettes were the most widely smuggled drug in the country, exceeding by dollar value nearly all other drugs including heroin, methamphetamines, fentanyl, and others. And Agent Rousseau's baseball cap in the mesh cage suggested that he had died just a day or two before, by the same method the man was going to use to kill Spot and me.

"It's a perfect cover," I said as I lingered on the steps. "The more you got politicians to raise cigarette taxes, the more you increased the demand for your business. Smuggled cigarettes. Everyone thinks you're working hard to increase deterrents to smoking. The reality is you're just feeding the profit of your smuggling business. What's the cigarette tax difference between Nevada and California? No doubt enough to make a lot of money for every load of cigarettes you fly from Nevada into California. How does it work? You load them here and then fly them where? California's a big state."

"You got part of it. I load them at an isolated ranch in Idaho," the man said. "That's where the taxes are really cheap, two dollars and thirty cents less per pack than the taxes in California. For every load of sixty thousand packs I bring in, I make almost one hundred forty thousand dollars in tax savings alone. But I don't fly them to California. Too many bureaucrats in California are doing data analysis on air traffic. Instead, I fly them from Idaho to this little mountain hideaway on the Nevada side of the lake. Then I haul them by four-wheel-drive van down a dirt trail to the lake. I know a guy who lets me keep a boat at his place in Crystal Bay. From there I take them across the water to a place near Rubicon Point on the California side. I've got a farmer's market vendor who picks them up and drives them down to the Central Valley. He makes ten times as much money hauling my cigs down from Tahoe as he does hauling strawberries up to Tahoe."

"More customers for cigarettes than strawberries, huh?"

The man made an exaggerated nod. "Where do you think the demand is? Nicotine or health food? Stockton and Modesto and Fresno and other points south are great places for unloading cigs. People there hate the Bay Area and L.A. politicians for making their lives more expensive. So they love buying cheap cigs without tax stamps. I've developed a whole network. The beauty is that the ATF agents are always looking for vehicles crossing the state line. They use highway webcams at all the border entry points to identify vehicles that come into California. So a simple plane trip and then a boat ride across Tahoe solves that problem. The local work vans and pickups that don't go between states never get checked."

It was exactly as ATF Agent Rousseau had told me. They focus on ships and big rig trucks coming in on interstate highways.

Peterman obviously loved bragging about his money-making arrangement. He had no worry about revealing information to me, because I'd be dead soon.

"So you have no problem getting the cigarettes driven down to the Central Valley towns," I said to keep him talking.

He chuckled. "The ATF thinks they're so clever, but they don't have a clue. My farmer's market driver even avoids the agricultural inspection station on the South Shore. And in the summer he goes over Carson Pass to Mormon Immigrant Trail."

"A nice road that's closed because of snow for half the year, but no cops in the summer, right?" I said.

"Yeah. It drops down into the heart of the Central Valley. The key to all smuggling is you never drive over a state line. Of course, flying is different." He made a little chuckle as if he couldn't help being amused by his cleverness. "Get in the cage."

I hopped up the last step, made some movements as if to obey his demands, but didn't get into the cage. I said, "But even after you fly cigarettes down from Idaho, you still have to find retailers who can move the product to customers."

"They're everywhere. Especially the truck stops. I split the tax savings seventy/thirty. Seventy percent for me, because I do all the work. I get most of my cigs from a distributor before they ever buy Idaho tax stamps, so it works out to even more money for me. And no one is checking this stuff up there. Idaho is just a bunch of ranchers pretending to be a state." His boastfulness was adolescent.

He continued, "And even though my retailers don't pay California tax, they usually charge their customers closer to the amount that cigs are supposed to sell for in California. So their customers save a little, and the retailers make a huge profit. It's a win for everybody."

"Yet you get lauded as the champion of anti-smoking."

I could almost hear him grin behind me.

He prodded me with the shotgun. "Into the cage," the man said again.

I bent my head and shuffled into the cage. It smelled oily as if the metal mesh was coated with a sheen of oil. I got inside it.

"Face away."

I turned.

"Back up to the front cage wall."

I turned sideways and moved until my hands and wrists hit metal.

He went around to the other side of the cage's front to hook a finger through the cord around my wrists and pulled back hard until I my hands were next to the mesh wall. I could feel him manipulating the cord behind my back, tying me to the cage wall. Then I heard a zip tie ratchet tight around my wrists. It was much tighter and more constraining than the cord had been. There was the zipper sound of another tie. Despite claims to the contrary, it's very difficult to break a zip tie. Two is nearly impossible. I was now completely under his control.

I tried to think of an approach that might give me some kind of small hope, but nothing came to mind. And in the process, I felt a tug on my socks. Too late, I realized he'd looped a line around the cord holding my ankles. He ran the line along the floor out the cage door, then shut the door. The latch slid, the hook lowered, and I was locked in the cage.

Peterman pulled the line from my ankles over and through the opening in the concrete block and tied it off.

While my wrists were still tied to the cage wall, he ran

another cord from my wrists and snaked it out through the gap between the bottom of the cage door and the floor. The man grabbed the line, stretched the loose end over to the concrete block, looped it through one of the holes in the block, and tied it off.

Now that I was thoroughly tied to the concrete block, both wrists and ankles, he untied me from the cage wall. I could move around, but I was always attached to the block that would eventually drag me to my death.

When the time came to drop me out of the plane, he would put the plane on auto-pilot, step down into the cargo compartment, open the outer door, and toss out the concrete blocks. The blocks would fall until they jerked tight on the cords from both my wrists and ankles and the cord to Spot's collar. Then he'd open the mesh cage doors, one at a time. With my wrists and ankles jerked hard by an 80-pound concrete block dangling from the plane's open door, I'd have a very difficult time using my legs and feet to keep from being dragged out the plane's door. The man would have no trouble kicking me in the face until I stopped resisting and was pulled out into space, there to fall to the lake and be dragged down under fifteen hundred or more feet of water to the bottom, never to be found. And after me, Spot would be his next victim.

No one would ever be able to prove we died at Peterman's hands. And even if someone saw us fall, there would be no bodies to recover and use as evidence. Lake Tahoe is so deep, it keeps its secrets forever.

I had no idea of how I could escape my predicament. The zip ties were so tight on my wrists that I was unable to do anything with my hands.

I looked over at Spot. His eyes looked very sad. Dogs understand gloom and darkness. And they pick up the mood of their owners. He didn't understand the details of the fate that awaited him, but he did understand that we were both tied up in cages and had lost all control.

I had to try something. But I didn't know what that could be.

FORTY-TWO

"You said death doesn't mean much to you," I said to Peterman. I was hoping that getting him to talk would slow down the process of killing us.

"I spent some time in prison," he said. "When you're inside, you see how many prisoners get murdered. You learn that life is expendable. We all die. The only variable is when."

"And all you do is create a mystery about that variable." I tried to sound sarcastic. He responded as if I was being earnest.

"I don't care about mystery," he said. "I just right the wrongs. Fix the mistakes. Solve the problems."

"What prison did you serve your time in?"

"What do you care? A prison is a prison. Pelican Bay, if you want to know."

The words hit me hard. That was the prison where Tucker Dopple spent 21 years for the murder of Benito Diaz's mother.

I tried to figure it out, but it wasn't clear.

I took a long shot.

"It was at Pelican Bay where you met Tucker Dopple," I said. Maybe Peterman would have no idea who I was talking about. Or maybe he would.

"Who would think I had anything in common with that cretin," he said. "But Benito Diaz put both of us in prison," Peterman said. "Having common ground with Dopple helped me learn about prison life. One of the rules inside is you collect favors and you distribute favors. Favors are currency. I figured out early on that Dopple was dumb enough to fall for any ruse I floated by him. So I made him my buddy, bought his friendship with favors. I helped him write rap lyrics. I listened to his complaints about how unfair life was. He told me his plan was to kill you and Benito Diaz when he got out. So I told Tucker I also wanted Diaz dead. I said I'd pay him five thousand to take out Diaz. Tucker was so excited. I had one of my friends on the outside funnel five hundred dollars into Dopple's account. I told Dopple that I'd used a special deposit security code that made the bank take off a zero on the statement, so that significant deposits don't get special attention from the IRS. I told him it was a security technique known only to a few selected customers with large bank balances. When Dopple and I went to the prison library and looked up his account on the computer, he saw my deposit, five hundred dollars on his bank statement. I looked on the screen and found some inconsequential glyph in the corner of the screen. I don't know what the symbol was for, but I pointed to it and said that the symbol meant the security technique had been activated on the bank statement. So that what looked like five hundred dollars was actually five thousand dollars."

"He believed that?"

"You obviously have no idea how stupid these guys are. So once Dopple thought I'd put five thousand in his account, I practically owned him. And he believed everything I told him. He had to, right? After all, why would I lie when I'd already given him five thousand dollars."

"He became your private henchman."

"That was the idea. But you screwed that up. Getting Dopple fired up about killing you was easy because you were an ex-cop. Getting Dopple fired up about killing Benito Diaz was even easier because not only did Diaz's testimony put Dopple in prison, but Diaz was a rich doctor who had everything. Envy is a powerful motivator."

I wanted to keep Peterman talking.

"Benito Diaz was a nice guy. Why would you have a problem with him?" But as I asked the question, I remembered that Diaz had told Diamond and me that he got beat up by an investment manager who Diaz was going to turn in for fraud.

"He invested in a business of mine. Then he brought the District Attorney down on me for an inflated fraud charge. I told Diaz I had a plan to cover the losses. I told him he could trust me. But he didn't believe me. He was one of those teacher's pet kind of guys. I hate guys like that. He put me in prison just like he put Tucker Dopple in prison. So Dopple and I made our plan. I even gave Dopple extra expense money, and I let him stay at my condo in Incline Village. I knew where to steal a car, and I put Dopple on that."

Peterman was so calm telling me his story, that I got more unnerved. I looked over at Spot, locked in the rear cage of the plane. His sadness enraged me. But I didn't know what I could do about it. I kept him talking.

"Then why the mystery about Heathcliff? Why is he so fixated on your big biplane?"

Peterman went silent for a moment.

"Heathcliff is a dead man," he said. "He was suicidal. So I helped him. He tried to change his mind at the last moment. But that's just a sign of being weak and feeble-minded. If you're going to kill yourself, make the decision, and then follow through. He was up on the fence, vacillating like a freaking wimp. So I helped him be strong. He hit the water and died. That creature they brought back to life is a zombie."

"He doesn't seem like a zombie to me. His fantasy world is very much alive. He was having coffee with his girlfriend. In some ways, even she seemed alive."

"Isabel is dead! Heathcliff stole her from me! She was mine. If I can't have her, no one can!"

I heard what the man said, but I wasn't sure of the meaning. "So you helped Isabel fall, too? You pushed her? Just like you pushed Heathcliff off the bridge? A woman you liked fell for another man, so you tried to kill them both?"

"She was mine," he said again. "No one takes what is mine. Not Horatio Harris. Not you." The man leaned toward the cage, his eyes glowering. He spoke in a whisper. "They all drooled over that man. It was disgusting when they started calling Harris by the name Heathcliff. It was the Brontë sisters who started it. All this crap about his big dark eyes and thick wavy hair and his moody poetry. And then Isabel got pulled into his aura. It was disgusting! I was the hard worker. The relentless worker. I was the reliable one. I sacrificed everything for her." The man was breathing hard, his anger intense.

He continued, "When we were in college, I was the one who coached Harris on how to pursue pre-med classes and prepare for medical school. I was a year ahead of him. I deserve credit for him being accepted into medical school. But did he ever thank me? No. He was so consumed by his dreary pessimism and his stupid poetry.

"And I was the one who introduced him to Isabel. Isabel and I thought we could both help him. Why? Because he was so damn helpless. One day he said he wanted to try flying a plane. He thought flying a plane would make him seem like a real man. He thought flying a plane would be the greatest thing. He knew I was a pilot. I volunteered to take him up. He was scared like a little boy. Eventually, Isabel convinced Harris it was safe to go. So I took him up. He could see that I was a pro, that I knew what I was doing. I showed him the basics. But it was a joke. He couldn't do the simplest of things, maintaining a bank or even a constant altitude or heading. Even a child can do those things after five minutes of instruction. But Harris was like a kid who can't ride a bike. I've never seen such incompetence. That's when I realized that poets were simply people who can't do anything else. They realize they can pass off their failed lives as part of the mystique of the introspective, tortured poet. Horatio Harris was a loser who relied on his looks and his parents to get him through life."

The man stopped talking.

I said, "What I don't understand is why Heathcliff was so focused on you."

Peterman scoffed. "That guy is so gomered, he doesn't even know who he is."

"But he saw this biplane," I said. "He knew it was important in some way. He just can't remember why."

Peterman made a snorting sound. "I'm in his subconscious because I can do all the things he can't. I'm a pilot who could have inspired him. He was a failure. I even inspired the Brontë sisters to do like me and solve the problems in their lives."

"Ah, you don't murder. You just solve problems," I said.

He looked at me with a kind of disgust as if he couldn't imagine how I was so stupid. "Society doesn't right the wrongs. Society is stupid. Society looks the other way. Another student, Jason Dahtberg, thought he could beat up and rape med school girls and they wouldn't turn him in for fear that being raped would damage their reputation and mess up their doctor careers. He raped Emily Smythe, one of the Brontë sisters. When she fought back, he hit her in the face with a shovel.

"But I'm a decent human being. I right the wrongs. So I talked to them about it. I explained that Jason would never be caught and tried. He used a condom and he wore gloves. There was no DNA, no evidence beyond what Emily saw of him in the night. And she was afraid to talk because Jason's daddy was a defense attorney. She'd heard how that man ripped rape victims apart on the stand. I explained that they could correct the situation themselves. They'd studied anatomy. I told them what they needed to do, how they could run a screwdriver into his heart. I was the one who showed them the logic. Live in fear the rest of your life, or solve society's problems yourself. I gave them the roadmap and the courage. Then the sisters took him out. Lured him to a meeting and fixed the mistake. It was an easy choice. Take out a bad guy and make the world a better place."

"You believe in vigilante killing."

He looked at me in the corner of my cage and shook his head. "You're hopeless. You don't get it at all."

"Is killing me a vigilante killing? Of course not. Killing me is first degree murder. And you're doing it because I've caught you in your crime. Same as ATF Agent James Rousseau caught you in your crime."

"You're going to die anyway…"

I finished his thought. "And all you do is adjust the time variable of my death. What about the doctor who died in Tahoe City? Veronica Eastern?"

"I don't know the details about that. But I know she was a bad person. Veronica Eastern was a drunk."

The man shook the door of the cage as if to see that it was shut solid. Then, satisfied that I wasn't going anywhere, he left the plane.

I heard a grinding sound like a garage door opener. But the garage door didn't move. After a time, the grinding sound stopped. Then another motor started up. This time the front of the hangar building started to rise up, folding in half as it moved. I realized that the first motor sound came from raising the ghillie camo curtain.

Now the huge door—four times as wide as a normal garage door—made loud cracks and moans as it rose. Light flooded into the building, through the cockpit windows of the plane and through the cargo door and windows.

Peterman walked out of the hangar and disappeared from view. He was probably going to grab some supplies. He hadn't planned on finding me. But now that he had, his schedule had expanded to include a sudden flight and another murder of a man and a dog. No doubt that required some additional items.

I tried to shift my focus away from that stressful thought to assess the plane and the space where I was tied. If I were to have any chance of fighting my would-be killer, I needed to know my surroundings.

But there was almost nothing to see.

I looked toward the opening that led up to the cockpit. Because the plane was a taildragger, it sat at a steep angle with the nose high and the tail low. There were two steps up to the cockpit level. Adding to that, the design of the plane put the cockpit up high relative to the cargo area. From my position, I could see some of the cockpit windows. But I couldn't see anything out those windows beyond the blindingly-bright sky.

I looked around my mesh cage prison. There was nothing except one of those safety lights that are designed to automatically turn on when the power supply goes out. There was a small red LED light that indicated it was getting power.

I'd never flown a plane large enough to need safety lights. But the principle made sense. If you lose power in flight, or even after an accident, a safety light could show you the way out of a smoldering aircraft.

There was some detritus on the floor. Two Post-it notes. Another cigarette package. A Bic pen that had been stepped on and was smashed into plastic splinters.

There was nothing else of note.

I heard a noise. Peterman was back. He came into the plane, squeezed past my cage and stepped up into the cockpit. I could see his right shoulder as he sat down in the left seat and made a sound like releasing the parking brakes. I thought I'd read that this plane had pneumatic brakes, but those would only work if the electrical systems were on and the compressor was running. There must have also been mechanical brakes for when the engine was off.

He came back out of the cockpit, walked through the cargo compartment, and went back out to the ground.

I heard sounds from the rear of the aircraft. A groaning sound. The plane started rolling.

I realized he was running the winch, letting out cable so the plane could roll forward, downhill, out of the hangar. His method of dealing with a sloping runway was just as I'd thought it would be.

By looking out the small side windows, I could see that the plane was moving out of the hangar into the bright sunlight. When the plane was fully out of the hangar, the winch stopped. He came back inside, went up into the cockpit and set the brakes.

Once again, he went outside. I heard some noises and then the winch sound. He'd disconnected the cable from the rear of the plane and was retracting it back onto the winch wheel. Next, he shut the hangar doors behind the plane and lowered the ghillie curtain over the hangar. He re-entered the plane, shut the door, and went back up into the cockpit.

Normally, a pilot does a preflight check, going through a long list of items to make sure everything was in good shape. The checklist included such things as inspecting the wings and other surfaces for any potential damage and even checking to make sure there was sufficient fuel in the gas tanks.

Peterman did none of these. Either he was cavalier about being thorough and safe or he was distracted by the task of murdering me.

He turned on some breakers and switches. I heard gyros and fuel pumps spinning up. Maybe a trim motor or flaps motor. There were some clicks and a knob turning as if he were setting the altimeter. Maybe he turned on his transponder or other radio, but I doubted it. He wouldn't want anyone to be aware of his craft, location or speed or otherwise.

Eventually, I heard the heavy sound of the starter motor grinding. The huge engine turned over slowly, the giant propeller blades doing a slow rotation in front of the engine. It sounded labored as if it were a struggle. But I knew that a 9-cylinder, 1,000 horsepower engine took much power to start. It ground around very slowly for several seconds. There was a pop. Then another pop. Then came a rough string of rat-a-tat sounds as the engine tried to fire. Suddenly, it caught, though the engine was still coughing. As I looked toward the cockpit and out the cockpit windows, I could see the prop spin into a blur.

The engine was tremendously loud. No doubt Peterman had ear protection. I had none. I would have plugged my ears but my hands were zip tied behind my back. The entire plane shook with intense vibration.

The man throttled back the engine to the dull roar of idle. I tried to discern his actions as he prepared to do the runup, the process of speeding the engine to full power and doing last minute checks.

There it came. The engine roared. The plane shook as if to come apart. But we didn't sit still with the brakes on for him to check the engine operation. Instead, we rolled down the sloped runway. He was taking off without doing the standard checks. A rogue pilot on a rogue mission.

The plane bounced and jerked, rolling faster and faster. The tail of the plane lifted up so the plane was level. Suddenly, the roll went smooth. I looked out the small windows. We were airborne. And then, in the most unusual flying experience of my life, the barely flying plane went nearly silent as he throttled back to idle. I could see that we were still just six or eight feet above the ground. Then the ground dropped away at the lower end of the grassy meadow that was his runway. The plane was airborne but still going slow, losing altitude. But the ground fell away fast, and we were quickly hundreds of feet above the ground, angling down at a steep glide angle. We gained speed not because of engine power but because we were plunging through space down at a steep angle. But the cliff below us dropped at a steeper angle.

It was as I'd speculated. The man was letting his downward flight bring him to cruising speed. As we dropped down in altitude, the ground dropped away even faster. We got higher and higher above the ground. Eventually, the man throttled the engine back up. Not enough to roar, but enough to begin to provide some lift. We half flew/half glided above Incline Village 2000 feet below. Then we were out over the water of Lake Tahoe.

FORTY-THREE

The takeoff pattern with the quick burst of power and then throttling back matched what the retired airline pilot told me. He said he'd heard a roar of a plane as if it were taking off, and then the roar went away. Now I had experienced that very thing.

Lake Tahoe from above is a spectacular sight, bluer than any body of water I've ever seen. But I was distracted by the pilot's mission to dump us overboard.

When he was far away from land, he gradually brought up the throttle to cruising power, leveled out, then began a gentle climb. He had no reason to gain altitude in order to drop me overboard. It must be that he simply wanted to be less noticeable from the ground. Higher altitude means less engine noise on the ground. Less engine noise means less chance that someone is looking up when a plane disgorges its passengers. And if someone should happen to see plummeting concrete blocks dragging a person and a dog to their death, the higher the plane was, the less likely anyone could give a clear description to the authorities.

Since he had throttled up, the engine noise was deafening. Without ear protection, I couldn't think clearly.

I tried to focus on how I might fight back when it came time for him to toss me out. But the essential problem was that, with my hands tied behind my back and attached to a heavy weight, and my ankles bound as well, there was little I could do. Dumping me out of the plane would be like dumping a heavy duffle bag. And if I were able to resist, he could disable me with kicks. If I could surprise him with any kind of fighting prowess, he had the last resort of a shotgun.

I needed to find a way to cut the zip ties on my wrists. Urban legend claims that you can break zip ties with certain techniques. As a former cop, I knew that urban legend is nothing more than entertainment for 12-year-old boys. And even if a circus strongman could break one zip tie, two would be too much for any creature smaller than King Kong.

If I could find a sharp edge on the mesh wall, I could back up against it and possibly rub the plastic zip ties against it.

I made a circuit of my little prison cage. At each questionable metal edge, I turned around so my back was against it, and I tried to feel the place with my tied hands. There was nothing sharp. I got down on my knees and made another circuit. Nothing.

When I stood in my little cage, my head had to be bent over because of the limited height. So I sat down on the airplane floor. Sometimes a different perspective helps. I looked around at my enclosure. Because we were now flying in brilliant sunshine above the reflective lake, Spot's and my cages were very well lit. But there was still nothing to see. The cages were made of panels of metal mesh. Although they were coarse, they weren't rough. There was nothing sharp enough to cut zip ties.

The only other item was the safety light, which was small and had no sharp edges. There was no way that I could see to use the light as a weapon.

Or was there?

Safety lights had batteries. Rechargeable batteries for those times when the power goes out. The light comes on and then, when the power comes back on, the battery recharges. What had Diamond said about rechargeable batteries? Hazards he'd learned about from Akari Tanaka? They were often lithium ion batteries. They were very safe under most conditions. But then Diamond launched into an explanation of potential problems. What did he call it? Exothermic reactions. I couldn't remember the details. But I recalled that under some conditions, lithium ion batteries could overheat. And if they overheat enough, they can produce a runaway reaction where the battery lights on fire, burns hot enough to combust even the metal, and can't be put out, not even with a bucket of water.

What if I could get the safety light battery to overheat? Even if it didn't produce the exothermic runaway fire, could it get hot enough to melt my zip ties? And how would I get it to overheat? Diamond said that shorting out the battery was one possibility. I knew that batteries can be shorted out by simply putting a wire across both the positive and negative terminals. In an electrical short, a large amount of electricity would flow across the terminals. Batteries are meant to provide small currents for long periods of time, not large currents for short periods. With a large current discharging the battery, it would heat up. How hot, I didn't know. But it seemed worth trying. The worst that could happen was that the man would catch me doing it and shoot me to stop it. But I was going to die anyway. Another "worst" effect might be that my overheating battery might start a fire. But that was also no big deal considering my circumstances.

With my head bent, I hobbled over to the corner with the safety light. I turned around and tried to reach it with my tied hands. It was too high. I couldn't tell how far off I was. Maybe if I bent over and lifted my arms back and up farther, my hands could reach a little higher.

I tried, but my fingers only touched air. I bent more. Nothing. I tried rotating my shoulders, stretching and flexing to make my hands lift higher behind my back. My fingertips brushed the plastic of the safety light. I made a little jump. My head hit the ceiling. But I sensed that I was almost able to grab the light. I bent my head farther and jumped again. Grabbed again. For a moment I got a decent grip, but the plastic was slippery. My fingers slid off.

I tried lying down on my back to see if I could reach it with my feet. Too high.

I tried standing up and raising my knee. It didn't come up high enough to touch the light. But what if I jumped?

I made some practice moves, bent my head, and then jumped, lifting my knee as I went into the air. But my knee wouldn't go high enough to hit the light.

But what about my elbows? Even with my hands tied behind my back, I could still raise my elbows.

That wasn't high enough, either.

So combine a lowered head with a raised elbow and a jump. I did a little test jump. Not very close. Again. I hit my head for the second time, but I got closer.

In a normal situation, the pilot could hear the thumping sounds I was making. But the biplane's engine was so loud, he didn't notice.

I wondered if I could get my elbow any higher if I leaned sideways as I jumped? Or could I simply flex my arm more to get my elbow to the proper height?

I bent my head as much as possible, and leaped.

My elbow hit the safety light hard. The light flew off its mounting bracket and hit the opposite side of the mesh cage. It made a lot of noise. But I didn't think that Peterman could hear it over the engine noise.

But he could see.

Planes don't have typical rear-view mirrors like cars. But the pilot could still sense movement in his peripheral vision and turn around to look through the cockpit door and see what was happening behind him.

I quickly got down on the floor, nearly sitting on the safety light to block it from the pilot's vision.

Fortunately, the man didn't turn around.

I looked at the light. It had a clear plastic front that was now cracked and splintered from the blow of my elbow. The sides were opaque white plastic. The back was against the floor. Presumably, the safety light could be opened to reveal the battery, or batteries. I couldn't see how from my perspective.

So I scooted around, felt for the light with my bound hands, turned it over behind my back, so its back side was facing up. Then I rotated back around so I could look at it.

The light was like two cupped shells clamped together, one shell clear plastic for light to shine through, one shell white. There was a tight seam between the two pieces of plastic. I saw no obvious catch that would disconnect the two pieces from each other.

Rotating again, I felt the pieces and tried sliding a fingernail between the two plastic pieces. I got a little movement, pulled harder, felt my nail rip, and the piece popped apart. I let the pieces sit on the airplane floor, rotated again, saw that there were two batteries of the double A size. They weren't the standard supermarket variety, but bright yellow rechargeable types. Lithium ion.

I spun once again, grabbed the light, and, working by feel alone, pried at the batteries and got one of them out of the housing. Now what? I obviously hadn't thought this through. In order to short out the battery, I need to make a metal connection between the two ends. Not the simplest task without the normal use of my hands. If, in fact, shorting the battery made it heat up to a temperature that was hot enough to melt a zip tie, I needed to be able to handle the hot battery. I needed some kind of a pincer to hold the battery and direct it against the zip ties. The pincer would need to be relatively impervious to heat.

The zip ties were against my skin. How could I maneuver a very hot item against the zip ties without burning my skin off? The whole concept seemed impossible.

But I was going to be dead soon, so I might as well try. If I burnt my wrists while managing to stay alive, it would be a small price to pay.

My first task was to short the battery. I needed metal to connect the battery ends to each other. Just because I was surrounded by metal didn't make the problem any easier.

There were places in the corners where the cage was assembled with nuts and bolts. At each bolt, the mesh had been bent in order to make a gap so the bolts could be inserted through the mesh. It looked like I might be able to insert the battery in one of the spaces created where the mesh was bent.

I gripped the battery, scooted back to the corner of the mesh cage, and felt around for the gaps near the bolts. When I felt a gap, I slid the battery in. It scraped on the mesh, went in an inch or so, and stopped when it hit more mesh.

I turned around and looked. The battery looked secure and projected out an inch. It looked like the negative terminal at the rear of the battery was pushed up against the wire mesh wall. In order to short out the battery, I might only need to get a wire of some kind to go from the mesh wall to the positive terminal.

But where would I find a piece of wire? I examined the space, looking for an errant piece of wire. There was nothing.

I realized that the safety light might have some wire inside the housing. Without being able to touch it with my bound hands, I looked closely at the inside of the light. Sure enough, there were two fine wires attached to a miniature circuit board. I rotated, got a grip on the wires, and tore them free.

Rotating again, I took one of the wires and wrapped it around the metal mesh near where I'd inserted the battery, mesh that would have a continuous connection from the negative terminal of the battery, and hence be an electrical conductor. Working by feel, I touched the free end of the wire to the positive terminal.

I heard a pop and smelled burning insulation. I dropped the wire, turned around, and got a look at it.

I don't know much about wiring, but it was easy to see that the wire had melted. The current from the battery was too much for such a fine wire, and it burned through it. I needed a much heavier gauge wire to properly short the battery.

The plane suddenly lurched. I heard the pilot yell, "Damn you, jerk, watch where you're going, dumbass!"

The plane banked left, then right, then settled back to a steady course, its roar undiminished.

It reminded me that the skies over Tahoe are not barren. There are plenty of aircraft. Not that it would do me any good. But if law enforcement ever attempted a forensic flight examination connected to my disappearance, maybe they would get a report about a camo-painted Antonov biplane. Maybe they could find the owner. Maybe, just maybe, they could find my DNA inside the cargo cage.

I glanced out the little windows. I realized I was looking southwest. The cliff face of Mt. Tallac stood tall and close and loomed over us. Fresh snow dusted its face and whitened the famous cross. I knew the mountain summit was 9700 feet. Judging by the mountain's height above us, I guessed we were flying at about 8500 feet, or a little over two thousand feet above the water. That was far enough to make my body very difficult to see when I fell from the plane.

I renewed my visual inspection of the cage, looking for some way to short out the battery. Look along the mesh wall. Left to right. Do it again a foot higher. And again. Move up and continue.

I found a damaged section of wall where something heavy had struck the mesh.

About a foot above the airplane floor, a portion of the damaged mesh projected from the wall of the cage. A small chunk of the mesh triangle had torn and stuck out. Could I tear that piece free?

I duck-walked over to that part of the cage, turned my back to the wall so my hands faced the wire mesh, and moved around until I found the damaged mesh with my fingertips. I tried to bend it. But metal mesh is tough stuff. I pushed on it as hard as I could with my thumb. The bent mesh gave way a bit. I got my bent forefinger behind it and pulled it back. Pushed again with my thumb. Pulled it back a second time. Did it flex a little more easily?

I repeated the process, back and forth, until it felt like my finger and thumb would fall off. I was buoyed by the awareness that the mesh was fatiguing. Some kinds of metal get easier to bend the more they're flexed.

At each point when I was about to give up, I sensed that bits of the metal lacing were giving way. Soon, a piece of the mesh simply fell away.

I got the piece of mesh in my fingers and scooted back over to where the battery protruded from the mesh wall. After taking a good look at its position and the broken piece of metal mesh that I held in my fingers, I turned around facing away from the battery, felt my position, and then pressed the metal mesh up against both the mesh wall and the positive terminal of the battery, hoping to make a short circuit from the battery's negative terminal to its positive terminal.

At first, I sensed nothing. I held the mesh piece firm. A burning smell wafted through the air. The smell became more acrid. I knew that heat from a warming battery would gradually get transmitted to everything near. But I thought that the mesh piece that I held would be slow to warm to a point where I could no longer hold it.

As the burning smell increased, I saw my first visual glimpse of smoke coming over my shoulder from behind. The mesh in my fingers was now very warm. I pressed harder.

Smoke swirled around my face. It was difficult to breathe. I kept pressing the mesh piece against the battery. My fingers started to burn. I didn't know when it was appropriate to drop the mesh and press the zip ties up against the battery. I wanted to pull the mesh away and try to press it against the zip ties, but I worried that the mesh would cool too quickly and I'd lose my temperature momentum. My guess was that getting the battery itself to heat up was where I might get enough temperature to melt the zip ties.

I kept up the pressure.

Soon, the mesh piece was too hot to hold.

I had it gripped between my right thumb and forefinger. I used my left fingertips to grab onto the end of my right sleeve. I pulled the fabric and got it positioned on the metal mesh like a miniature hot pad on a hot griddle. The thin fabric gave me a little extra time. But the mesh continued to heat up. There was a new smell of burning clothes and then, burning flesh. Finally, I could take the heat no longer. I dropped the metal mesh and tried to press my wrists and the zip ties up against the hot battery.

Instantly, my wrists burned as if my skin were being branded by a red hot poker.

I flexed my hands to put extra pressure on the zip ties. Nothing happened.

I pressed harder, unable to see, working blind behind my back, but trying to push the ties against the hot battery. I had no idea if my hands were in the best position to bring the zip ties in contact with the battery. Nor did I know if there was enough heat to melt the zip ties. I only knew there was plenty of heat to brand my flesh and burn through to my tendons and bones.

"What's that burning smell?" the pilot shouted back from

his high perch up in the cockpit.

I yelled as loud as I could, hoping he'd hear over the roar of the engine and through the muffling of his headset. "I think it's coming from the engine!"

I pressed my wrists harder against the battery, enduring pain like red hot charcoal against your skin, gripping one hand with the other in an effort to make a twisting force that might break a melting nylon zip tie.

The pilot got out of his seat and stepped down into the cargo compartment. Maybe he'd engaged the auto-pilot mechanism. Maybe not. He was not carrying the shotgun. A good sign. He assumed I was rendered useless by the binds on my hands.

"The smoke is here!" he shouted. "In the cargo hold!"

I kept my back against the corner of the mesh cage. My hands were still against the hot battery. Blocking his view. I twisted my wrists harder than ever.

"I saw smoke coming down from the cockpit," I shouted. "Maybe the engine is on fire!"

"It's not! I think you're doing something to make the smoke!"

The pain from my burning flesh was excruciating. I flexed my hands and wrists as hard as I could, driving my elbows outward to put maximum pressure on the zip ties.

The man reached over and swung a big lever on the outer airplane door, unlocking it. The door came in and slid back on a curved track. The wind roared, but not as loudly as the engine. The door was held open and back by the wind pressure. The plane was now open to the sky.

Peterman kicked at the concrete block that was tied to Spot. The block skidded out the door and fell. The line to Spot's neck snapped tight, and Spot was pulled toward the door of his cage.

"Time for you to make your last leap!" Peterman turned to me and shouted. He unhooked the cage door latch, opened it up, then grabbed the concrete block, to which I was still tied, and flung it out the open airplane door.

FORTY-FOUR

As I watched the block disappear and fall away, I felt a dread that was unlike anything I'd ever known. The lines to the block snaked out of the door as fast as a whip. One line led directly to my wrists behind my back, the other to my ankles. I braced myself, feet out, gritting my teeth against the coming jolt as much as against the pain and smell of my burning flesh and the melting of plastic. I tensed every muscle in my body and made one last burst of effort to pull my wrists apart.

The zip ties broke.

The line from the concrete block to my wrists snapped tight and then went loose as it and the zip ties flew out from behind my back, flashed through the air, and shot out the open aircraft door. The concrete block dangling from the plane was now only connected to my ankles.

Peterman looked astonished. I didn't give him a moment to react. I dove through the cage door, simultaneously trying to raise up my arms and burnt hands, which seemed rigid from being pulled behind my back for so long.

But Peterman was quick to recover. He jumped sideways to the rear of the open door. I kicked at him. He dodged like a practiced fighter. He was younger than me and obviously fit, and I was hampered by being too tall to easily move in the short cargo compartment. I had no time to assess the extent of my wounds. But the pain was searing. The man grabbed at my arms, caught one, and swung me around as if to throw me out the open door. But the door was small, and even though I fell to my knees, I managed to get my arm out to slam against the airplane wall next to the door.

My ankles were being pulled toward the open door. I twisted and turned to the side. The line to my ankles seemed to tighten.

With every movement, I was being inched closer to my death. Unable to stand, even in a bent position without tripping and falling, I was reduced to wrestling on the floor.

I glanced around the space, desperate to find something to grab. But what I saw instead was the view out the cockpit windows. The plane was in a gentle banking turn. And the cliff face of Mt. Tallac was coming into view in front of us.

Peterman grabbed at my pants. I raised my arm and gave him an elbow punch on his thigh, the point of my elbow splitting his thigh muscles. He gasped and grabbed his leg with both hands. I took hold of one of his hands, pulled it to my abdomen, and rolled. He screamed as his elbow broke with a loud snap. I was now behind him. I faced Spot's cage. My poor dog had been pulled by the concrete block so that his head was at the cage door. He wasn't being badly hurt. But he was trapped. I had a sudden memory of what the Washoe woman, Nettie Moon Water, had told me. The life of a bad man was not as valuable as the life of a good dog. Spot's plight renewed my energy to fight.

I put an arm around Peterman's neck to put a choke hold on him. But he bent his chin down and bit my forearm.

In a world with carnivores that have large sharp fangs, we often overlook the power of a human bite. The pain of his teeth sinking into my arm was as bad as the burning of my flesh. It felt that he was going to remove a mouthful of flesh.

I got my other arm around his head and jerked as if to snap his neck. His teeth came off my arm. He went limp. I made the universal mistake of relaxing my grip.

He suddenly twisted and rolled. He kicked at me. His foot hit my hip, but I was already turning so that his blow glanced off. I got my arm around his ankle and put a leg lock on him. The concrete block pulling me to the open door was now pulling him as well.

I levered down with enough pressure to break his ankle. He struggled, writhing on the floor in the small space. His hand was under him as if in his pants pocket.

My body turned as I focused on my leg lock. The view out

the cockpit was clear. We were now flying directly toward the face of the mountain.

Peterman jerked his hand out of his pocket. He held my pocket knife. He pressed the lockback button, and the blade snapped open. Before I could pull away, he stabbed at my leg. It was an angled blow into my calf muscle, going deep into the flesh. It burned like it was red hot.

He pulled the knife out and raised it to stab a second time. I knew that the lockback catch had broken some time ago. The knife was still sharp and useful, so I hadn't thrown it away. But if the knife was used at the wrong angle, the blade would fold back into the housing. I'd stupidly continued to use the knife, always reminding myself to make certain I applied pressure in a manner to keep the blade extended. Maybe now it could be used to my advantage.

As Peterman stabbed down a second time, I turned in a way that would cause him to put pressure in the wrong direction.

It worked. As the point of the blade jammed into my knee cap, the knife folded, severely cutting into his fingers. He screamed and dropped the knife.

His blood sprayed as I got a leg lock on his neck. Holding him in place, I picked up my bloody knife and used it on the cord that was taut from the pull of the concrete block dangling out the open door of the plane. I got it cut, and the cord flashed away. I continued to keep my leg lock on Peterman's neck while I stretched my arm out and cut the cord that was pulling Spot to the cage door. As that cord also snaked out the door, Spot pulled back from the cage door and shook his head.

I next cut the cord that had tied my ankles and made a loop and a slip knot that I could use around Peterman's body to secure him to the cage wall. While I manipulated the line, I kept my leg lock on the man's neck. For safety, I poked the end of the line through the wire mesh of the cage and tied a quick half-hitch in it, thinking it would help restrain him as I secured him in position. But as I loosened my leg lock on his neck, he tried again to leap away from me.

I grabbed his ankle and put leverage on it. His body hit the floor of the plane. He rolled, reached out with his good hand, and tried to stick his thumb in my eye.

I shifted away, saving my eye, then grabbed his hair and used it to slam his head toward the outside corner of the cage. His neck struck the metal and I felt two snaps that were loud enough to be heard over the roar of the engine. Trachea breaking in his throat?

Peterman must have realized he'd lost his battle with me. He turned and scrambled fast on hands and knees to the open door and threw himself out to his death.

I glanced up toward the cockpit. The rock face of Mt. Tallac filled the window view. I couldn't tell how far away we were, but it was clear that we were only seconds from crashing into the cliffs.

I leaped up through the door to the cockpit and pulled myself into the left seat.

There was no time to consider how best to act. We were racing at full speed toward the snow cross on the cliff face of the mountain. Our collision was just a few seconds away. There was rock everywhere. Without really thinking about it, it seemed that the only possibility for not crashing was to go left and up and head toward the ridge that stretched from the summit down toward Cathedral Lake.

I didn't know how to fly this plane, or any plane this big. And I didn't know how to disengage the autopilot. Maybe it was like cruise control on a car, and any additional inputs turned it off.

I grabbed the yoke, turned it a good way to the left and pulled it back.

The plane shuddered as it pitched up and rolled to the left. I stepped on the left rudder to aid my sudden banking, climbing turn. Reducing the throttle would slow our approach to the cliff, but I wanted as much lift as possible to gain a few more feet of altitude. I pushed the throttle forward all the way. The engine roared even louder.

There was a banging noise from back by the open door that I didn't understand. Maybe my sudden, major bank caused a mechanical problem. But I ignored it.

The plane was buffeted by the turbulent airflow of the wind coming over the mountain and down the cliff face. I wanted to pull back harder. But even a plane that is designed not to stall at slow speed can lose all lift in mid-air if it is angled up enough to have its belly facing the direction it's traveling.

I tried to follow a pilot's universal, dispassionate goal of focusing on not over-reacting as the plane hurtled full speed toward the rock. Fly the plane. Don't overreact. Stay calm.

I glanced at the airspeed. 130 knots and increasing. Fast enough that there would only be small pieces of wreckage left after we crashed.

Altitude: 9200 feet. High enough that the tourists in town wouldn't notice much when they gazed up at the most dramatic mountain on the shore of Lake Tahoe. From town, it would simply look like some debris had been sprinkled by the gods.

The plane seemed to scream as it raced toward the rocks. The banging back by the open door intensified, then stopped for a moment. Then resumed. The ridge I was aiming for didn't look like it was getting any lower.

I went through my safety mantra. Stay calm. Hands light on the controls. Fly the plane, don't fight the plane. Be an aerial artist. Ride the air like a raptor. Explore the nuance. Find the zone where the plane is most like a bird.

Airspeed: 140 knots.

Altitude: 9300 feet.

The rock ridge grew larger.

I shouted toward the back, words that sounded good but I didn't believe. "We're almost there, Spot! Hang in there, boy! We'll be home free in a bit."

Airspeed: 145 knots.

Altitude: 9400 feet.

More banging.

I could see that we weren't going to make it. The big plane wasn't powerful enough or spry enough. Or maybe I wasn't enough of a pilot…

What else could I do? Nothing but fly the plane.

The ridge was only 200 or 300 feet in front of us. We were flying at over 200 feet per second. The ridge was too high to clear.

Keep flying the plane.

A narrow notch appeared on the ridge. Farther to the left. Was it low enough and wide enough to fly through?

I couldn't tell.

Keep flying the plane.

As we got closer, I could tell the notch was too narrow to handle the plane's 60-foot wingspan. But what if we banked very steeply?

I turned the yoke all the way to the left and gave the plane some more left rudder. Our banking turn got steeper until we were nearly on edge. I realized that despite turning toward the notch, we still couldn't make it. I wanted Spot with me, but he was still trapped in the cage.

Then we made it to the notch.

We raced through with the plane on edge. The left wingtip was no more than a few feet from the bottom of the notch and the right wingtip was pointed toward the sky. The belly of the plane was close enough to the rock that I thought we were going to rip off the landing gear.

Then we roared through the notch, past and out the other side of the ridge as the back of Mt. Tallac dropped down toward the Crystal Range in the distance. I leveled the plane out, then pulled back on the throttle. I took some deep breaths, then put the plane into a very gentle turn to bring it around and back out over Lake Tahoe.

I didn't know how to set the auto-pilot. When the plane was level, I took my hands off the yoke. The plane seemed to hold its course. I climbed back down out of the cockpit. The banging noise on the plane continued. I hung on to handholds on the wall as I looked out the open door.

Peterman was still there, hanging by his foot, flopping in the 130-knot wind. It took me a minute to figure out what had happened.

Apparently, when Peterman tried to jump to his death, he

didn't realize that, as he'd made his crawling motions, his left foot had gone into the slip-knot loop, and it tightened around his ankle. He'd fallen only a few feet from the plane before the slip knot tightened on his ankle, stopping his fall to the lake. The cause of the banging I'd heard was obvious. His head was severely bloodied from his body being continuously smashed against the plane's fuselage.

I hoped the plane would continue to fly itself as I struggled long and hard to pull on the line and haul Peterman's limp body back into the plane. He still seemed to be alive. He was unconscious, but his lungs were heaving and his right hand twitched in a kind of tremor.

There was nothing I could do for him now other than what I would attempt to do for Spot and me. Land the plane without crashing it.

I got the open door shut and locked. It was only a small relief to no longer have the roar of the wind because the roar of the engine was still crushingly loud.

I opened the cage that held Spot, hugged him and rubbed him. "Come up to the cockpit, boy," I said, although I imagined his ears were also numb.

As we moved through the narrow passage to the cockpit and stepped over Peterman, I had the thought that he might regain consciousness. I'd seen too many movies where the hero wrongly assumes the bad guy is dead and the threat is gone. So, I took the time to put him in the front cage, tie his hands behind his back, and shut and lock the cage. I stepped up into the cockpit and slid into the left seat.

"C'mon, boy," I shouted, trying to be heard over the engine roar. I tugged Spot into the space between the two cockpit seats. He stood with his front paws on the cockpit floor and his rear paws two steps down and back in the cargo compartment. His head was 12 inches from mine, and he seemed to look out the cockpit windows at whatever I looked at.

I gave him a long hard hug, then focused on flying the plane.

There were several boats out, white shapes against the blue

water. The M.S. Dixie sternwheeler was cruising across the water. Cars crawled along the highway and climbed up the switchbacks near Emerald Bay.

It was a peaceful placid evening with people enjoying the mountain beauty as sunset approached. If anyone glanced up and saw the big old biplane rumbling along in front of the face of Mt. Tallac, no one was aware it was flown by a wounded, bleeding pilot who'd never been in such an aircraft. And they wouldn't have pictured a killer in the cargo hold, bloodied from a fight and suicide attempt.

I set my sights on the runway at the South Lake Tahoe airport and then got on the radio to explain to anyone listening that I knew little about what I was doing, but that I'd like some South Lake Tahoe or El Dorado County cops to meet my plane and pick up an unconscious killer, assuming we didn't crash and burn.

FORTY-FIVE

While I'd managed to avoid crashing the plane into the cliffs of Mt. Tallac, I had no clue about how to land a plane as large as the AN-2 biplane. I especially didn't know how to approach a landing with a giant 9-cylinder, 1000-horsepower engine. For a brief moment, I thought that I could maybe use the radio to get connected to someone with experience landing the airplane. But that was as unlikely as finding someone in Tahoe who knew how to dock a supertanker.

I figured I had no choice but to apply the basics. Try to approach on a 3-degree glide. Explain to other traffic that I was entering the landing pattern on the final leg. Slow as I approached, although to what speed I had no idea. I had backed off the throttle and slowed our current cruise to 120 knots. But that didn't help me know what was a good landing speed. My impulse was to think that if a Cessna Skyhawk lands at 60-70 knots with full flaps, then a big plane like the AN-2 might land at 70 knots or more. But would that be with full flaps? I didn't even know where the flaps control was.

Then I remembered that an AN-2 had no official stall speed. That implied that if I got too slow for an ideal touchdown, the plane wouldn't, in theory, pitch over nose first and auger in. Supposedly, the plane would maintain its attitude and just drop down onto the runway, do a slow crash landing, and possibly be okay.

The sun was sinking behind Mt. Tallac and shooting orange rays across the mountains. The snow cover on the taller mountains, Freel Peak, Jobs Sister, and Jobs, caught the light and glowed a warm rose orange.

I pulled back on the throttle to slow a little more, and I focused on the instruments, the altimeter, the attitude indicator, and the air speed. As my speed dropped off, I finally found the flaps control and set one notch of flaps to give me more lift when the time came to land. Looking out the window, I could see the flaps down on the lower wing.

Spot watched my hand each time I took it off the yoke. When I regripped the yoke, he pushed his wet nose against the back of my hand. Dogs know when their owners are under stress. If it's major, dogs will emote. Spot was making whimpering sounds that were loud enough for me to hear over the engine. He turned to look directly at my face, then looked back out the cockpit windshield.

I pointed the plane toward the South Shore, which was three or four miles away. We droned on through the darkening sky, sinking in altitude, aiming for the South Lake Tahoe Airport.

I backed off the throttle some more. You can't land if you're going too fast.

When I reached to set a second notch of flaps, Spot once again planted his nose on my hand when I put it back on the yoke. It was as if he wanted me to watch the road, not fuss with instruments and controls.

The second notch of flaps caused a portion of the upper wing ailerons to droop down, possibly increasing lift as the plane slows to a near standstill. The plane was buffeted by the increased drag, but I assumed the gain in lift would help as I slowed further and approached the tarmac.

I didn't know when or how much to flare. I didn't know what the "ground effect" would feel like on a big biplane. I didn't know how best to steer a taildragger. I didn't even know about braking such a large, heavy plane.

But the South Lake Tahoe runway was long and wide, so I assumed that once I was on the ground, I could cut the power and I'd coast to a stop.

There was some radio chatter as I approached, but I ignored it and concentrated on keeping the plane straight and level.

Earlier, out on the lake, I'd seen the wave motion glimmering in the approaching twilight. The pattern indicated the wind was out of the south. In order to land facing south, into the wind, I would come in on Runway 18. I didn't feel competent enough to do any kind of airport flyover or even enter the pattern on any leg except final. So I announced that news on the radio and hoped it would work. I also explained that I was bringing in a man named Patrick Peterman AKA Pat Palmer, the murderer of ATF Agent James Rousseau and possibly several others. I explained that Peterman was gravely wounded, and I requested that someone inform law enforcement and call an ambulance for the wounded man onboard. I also repeated my request that they send cops out to meet our plane.

I knew that later, I could explain that a decade ago, Palmer had murdered a woman named Isabel DeMille by causing a deadly fall. And after that, he tried to kill a man by throwing him off the Golden Gate Bridge, a man whose given name was Horatio Harris but was known to a bunch of Bay Area doctors as Heathcliff.

As I got close to the airport and entered the pattern on the final leg, Runway 18 was largely shrouded in twilight. But I could see that the wind sock showed that I was indeed coming into a slight breeze out of the south. Fortunately, there was very little crosswind, because I had no idea of how to put the big plane into a crosswind slip.

I looked for the plane's landing light or lights, but couldn't find it among the huge number of switches and gauges. I forced my eyes back and forth and up and down, doing a kind of grid search in the cockpit. But it eluded me. It should have been obvious. It probably was obvious. But we'd have to land without a landing light.

When I came over the runway threshold, there was no longer enough light to clearly see how I was doing. But when I saw the white threshold lines flash beneath us, I felt I was too high on my glide. Nevertheless, I was committed. I had no skills for any kind of a go-around. I had one shot. I told myself that I was doing fine. I even took my right hand off the yoke and gave Spot a rough rub.

"We're fine, boy. A beer and dinner awaits. We'll be on the ground in moments."

I put my hand back on the yoke. Spot planted his nose on my hand one more time. He still whimpered.

Then the wind sock swung around. Instead of pointing north toward me, it pointed to the east. The big plane was still pointed south, but it started to drift to the east. In five seconds, I was no longer over the runway. I realized I'd acquired a sudden crosswind of five or six knots. That wasn't a death sentence, and I'd be fine if I were in a familiar small plane. But a crosswind was a serious problem considering this plane was the size and weight of a big truck, and I didn't know what to do. I remembered my initial research on the plane. It was expressly stated that the plane was not designed for landing in any but the lightest crosswind.

I tried the basic response. A little right rudder, a little right bank, and a little throttle.

I didn't like my chances. But I didn't have much choice. I understood from basic flying that if the left wheel made contact first, the wind would get under the right wing, lift it up, and maybe flip us over. What would come after that could range from a destroyed plane and an awkward exit to an explosion and fire that would incinerate us.

Turning the yoke to bank was easy, even though I didn't know how much. Same for boosting the throttle. But I fumbled the rudder when my right foot slipped off the pedal. The plane was already going so slow, and it had so much weight, that it didn't seem to respond. You need airspeed to get a proper push against the surfaces. So I gave the plane a little more throttle.

As I had the thought, the air seemed to grab the rudder, and the plane did a sudden yaw, swinging to the right, pointing toward the terminal. Spot made a pronounced cry as if he understood flight principles, when, in reality, he was simply responding to my stress.

I gave the plane more throttle, even though it seemed as though I should be cutting the throttle to get us down on the ground. The engine roared, and the plane's speed became a touch more pronounced. It drifted back over the runway. That seemed a good time to cut the throttle all the way back while I held my right bank far longer than seemed appropriate. I tried to pull back on the yoke and flare at the right moment, but it seemed to have no effect. We were banked enough that I thought the right wing tip was going to be the first part of the plane to contact the ground.

But the right wheel hit the tarmac before the wing tip did. The plane made a giddy swing to the right. As it rotated clockwise, I leveled the wings and gave it a little left rudder. Out-of-focus light-colored objects moved in front of my face, and I realized they were my white knuckles on the yoke. The left gear hit the tarmac hard. The plane turned back to the south. We bounced and rumbled, and the plane made groaning sounds as we once again moved down the runway in the direction I'd originally planned.

We slowed. Then, in a brief moment, we were pointing up toward the sky. I inhaled in shock and then realized that we were going too slow to get airborne. With our slowing speed, the tail had merely dropped down until the rear taildragger wheel hit the tarmac.

I leaned to the side, trying to get a glimpse of the runway edge and the taxiway. Now I remembered seeing taildragger pilots weave side to side. They were simply looking out the side windows, trying to see where they were going while their planes were pointed up toward the sky.

I gently toed down on the brakes. The right one grabbed harder, which turned me back to the right. We bumped off onto the grass. The plane bounced and shuddered. Then I was suddenly back onto smooth tarmac as I rolled onto a taxiway. I came to a stop, set the brakes, and cut the engine. The huge prop shimmied as the big blurred circle became less blurred and then resolved into four long, motionless blades. I knew I wasn't stopping in the right spot, but I was tense and light-headed, and I wanted out.

I eased backward out of the cockpit.

I limped on my wounded leg past my bloodied passenger in the cargo cage, opened the door, and was stepping down out of the plane and pulling Spot with me into the night as a cop car raced up and stopped with a scrape of tires on sandy pavement.

Its light bar was flashing, but its siren was off.

A man and a woman jumped out.

"Owen McKenna?"

"That's me. The guy you want is Patrick Peterman. He's tied up inside and severely wounded. Head trauma, I think. I'm happy to answer basic questions, but after you haul the prisoner off to the hospital, I should catch my own ride to the ER fairly soon to get some repair work done."

As I said it, an ambulance raced up and made a fast stop. Two paramedics jumped out. I repeated myself to them, and they ran to the plane.

The woman cop looked down at where my pants were soaked with blood.

"Oh, man, you're losing blood at a serious rate. And your hands are all messed up. They look burnt!"

The other cop came out of the door of the plane as the paramedics went in through the door.

"The other guy's bleeding, too," he called out. "One of his fingers is near cut off. What happened? You guys fought? Christ, there's a bloody knife on the floor! This guy attacked you with his knife?"

"Actually, it's my knife. He took it from me in the mountains above Incline Village."

"If he got your knife at Incline Village, then how'd you get in this plane? There's no airport in Incline Village."

I looked back at the plane. "Not a normal airport, no."

As the cops climbed into the plane to help the paramedics deal with Peterman, I held Spot's collar and hobbled with him away from the plane. We made an uneven meander into the night. We paused in the dark, both of us trying to find some lessening of the tension of the last hour.

The plane was a big dark hulk looking mysterious like it was out of a black-and-white noir movie from the fifties. The lights on the cop car made blue and red staccato flashes in the mist that swirled around the big plane.

I bent down and gave Spot a hug. "We made it, boy."

I took long deep breaths, and it seemed like Spot did, too.

FORTY-SIX

Street and Camille and Blondie came and picked Spot and me up at the hospital. At my request, they brought some towels so that I could keep blood off the seat fabric. Even though I'd been bandaged in multiple places, there was still blood weeping, and my clothes had blood on them. The bandages on my hands were goopy with some kind of light colored liquid that was soaking through from the hot battery burns. The doctors had said my charred hands would ooze pus for a long time.

Spot squeezed into the back of Street's VW Beetle along with Blondie. I sat in the front, with Camille on my lap. I kept my bandaged hand over my kneecap where I'd been stabbed, and I directed her legs away from my calf where they'd put in multiple stitches to close up the main wound. The arm that Peterman had bit was my worst wound of all. The medical people were concerned about an infection, so they were extra vigorous about cleaning it, stitching the muscles back together and then the skin. I kept that arm away from Camille so that she wouldn't accidentally cause me to grunt with pain.

As Street drove, we had the predictable conversations about the flight, how it came to be and how it resolved. Street's concerns and gasps accompanied my explanations. I edited my comments here and there because of Camille's presence even though I didn't imagine she could read lips much in the dark. Camille knew I had a dangerous job, but there was no point in making it melodramatic.

I showered at Street's condo, and Spot and I ate enough chicken chili to feed an NFL team.

Later, I told Street, "It was a long day. It feels good to be back with you and Camille."

"She tells me this place is beginning to feel like home. Glad you feel good about it, too."

"Gooder than I can say."

"I'm trying to teach Camille proper grammar."

"I'll be the goodest role model for that."

Street gave me a little punch on my shoulder, one of the few places where I hadn't been injured.

Spot and I stayed at her place with her too-small bed. But when I lay back and she put her head on my shoulder, I forgot about the suicidal murderer hanging by his ankle from the plane while it flew at 130 knots, his head banging against the outside of the AN-2's fuselage, and I slept.

The next day, Diamond once again fetched my rental car from up on Mt. Rose meadows, and I took Spot home and drank excessive amounts of coffee while I researched on my computer, made multiple phone calls, and paced my deck, trying to puzzle out a case that had multiple people dying in unconnected ways.

I had made a few connections. Tucker Dopple and Patrick Peterman had both been sent to prison because of their connection to, and anger about, Benito Diaz.

Peterman had told me about the man who'd raped Emily Smythe and attacked her with a shovel. He explained that the man had died at the hands of the Smythe/Brontë sisters.

But I still didn't know why Veronica Eastern was murdered.

The only hint of where to start searching was that both Patrick Peterman and Benito Diaz had said she had a drinking problem.

With most searching, you Google names and events and anything else that might produce a useful lead. Most of the time you hit nothing but dead ends. I learned bits and pieces about Veronica Eastern's past, her schooling, her work. There was nothing of substance. But when I put her name in a database that searches for criminal records, I found out she'd been arrested three different times for drunk-driving accidents.

In the first accident, she hit and killed a homeless man in San Francisco's North Beach neighborhood. The police report said the man had been sleeping on the street. The report suggested that an alert, sober driver would have swerved to miss him. Veronica Eastern did not. Although she failed the breath test, the District Attorney declined to prosecute her for DUI or manslaughter.

In the second drunk-driving incident, a bicycle courier was riding between two lanes of one-way traffic in the Financial District. He was going with the traffic and apparently obeying the law. He suddenly swerved to go across one of the traffic lanes and was hit by Veronica. The bicycle courier was severely injured and was put on life support, where he remains in a vegetative state to this day. Witnesses blamed the bicyclist for reckless riding. Again, Dr. Eastern failed the breath test. She paid a large fine for driving under the influence, lost her license for a year, and was ordered to attend DUI school. As before, the DA declined to prosecute her for injuring the bicyclist.

I wondered about the DA not wanting to shut her down. There was no clear answer. But I found a YouTube video someone had posted which mentioned that when Veronica Eastern was in college, she lived with her aunt in Oakland. When I searched on that aunt, I found out she was a close friend of the governor and was also a trusted member of his staff in the governor's office. Was it possible that influence flowed from the governor's office to the San Francisco District Attorney?

In the third traffic accident, Veronica Eastern drove at excessive speed through San Francisco's Outer Sunset neighborhood, not far from where Dr. Eastern had her clinical psychology practice.

There was a group of kids playing in the street. Dr. Eastern struck one of them, a 10-year-old girl, and killed her. Witnesses said the girl ran across the street without pausing to look either direction. Veronica Eastern was again given a breath test and failed. She was prosecuted for driving without a license and for Driving Under the Influence. She paid a very large fine for all of her transgressions and spent one month in jail. Again, she was not prosecuted on any charge relating to the child's death. But there was an ongoing civil lawsuit over the wrongful death of the 10-year-old girl.

Eastern was clearly a woman who had a major drinking problem, major judgment problems, and major financial problems as a result. She'd risked everything in life because of her poor judgment. I wondered if Eastern's transgressions could possibly provide motive for her murder in Tahoe City. But I couldn't find anything to suggest it.

I poured more coffee, took it out on my deck, and looked down that the lake.

As I sipped coffee and stared at the mountains of the Crystal Range 15 miles to the west, I thought about Camille, a vital child almost the same age as the girl Eastern had killed with her vehicle. Such a loss would be as soul-crushing as any a family could experience. It would possibly drive friends and relatives of the victim into a murderous rage.

I went back inside and looked up the victim.

Her name was Olivia Johnson Warnell, and she attended a public elementary school nearby. Olivia's father James was an accountant at a bank downtown. Olivia's mother Abigail was a nurse at a hospital near UC San Francisco.

The cliché in real estate is that location is everything.

In the murder business, location is also everything.

I focused on Olivia and Abigail. Type in a search term. Hit enter. Scroll down for anything that might hint of related information.

Twenty minutes later, I'd learned that Abigail was a nurse at St. Catherine of Siena Hospital, not far from UCSF. Twenty minutes after that I learned that Anne Smythe of the Brontë sisters had admitting privileges at St. Catherine of Siena Hospital. After another hour, I found a blog that mentioned the memorial held for young Olivia Johnson Warnell. The blog listed the donations that people in the community had made to a non-profit that serves children. One very generous donation was listed as coming from Dr. Anne Smythe, godmother of Olivia Johnson Warnell.

Rarely does an investigator get a more dramatic bell to ring.

FORTY-SEVEN

The next evening, feeling even stiffer from my injuries and various stitches, I squeezed myself and Spot into the rental Ford and met the Brontë sisters at their vacation rental home in Kings Beach. It was a calm evening with a brilliant swath of red in the southwestern sky as the sun set behind Mt. Tallac, the mountain I'd nearly crashed the plane into two evenings before.

The sisters were packing up, readying to leave for the Bay Area the next morning.

We sat in the living room. The bright floodlight ceiling cans were turned off, and the only light was from craftsman-style wall sconces that were turned down low. The mood was so subdued, it was almost as if they'd anticipated the reason I wanted to see them. Even Spot was somber. He sat near me and didn't show his standard social enthusiasm.

We sat on the Scandinavian living room furniture. There was no rapid-fire dialogue as before. No rush to finish each others' sentences.

"Two evenings ago, the man I knew as Patrick Peterman tried to kill me in his biplane, the plane Heathcliff saw." I said.

"Back when we started med school, we knew him as Pat Palmer," Anne said. She revealed no surprise at what I said. Probably they'd already heard the news. "Of course, Palmer couldn't stay in med school when he was convicted of fraud and went to jail."

"Right. Pat Palmer is now attached to machines that breathe for him, pump nutrients down a feeding tube in his nose, and monitor his heart, which persists in making a feeble beat despite the blunt force trauma that destroyed his brain. They're looking for someone with the authority to tell them to turn off the machines. Peterman originally intended to murder me and my dog by dropping us out of his plane into the lake. He'd attached concrete blocks to us."

The sisters all glanced at Spot, horror on their faces, feelings I don't know if they'd ever experienced regarding people.

"When Peterman realized he wasn't going to succeed at killing me and that I was going to bring him in on a range of charges including the murder of an ATF agent, he tried to kill himself by jumping from the plane. That was another thing he didn't succeed at. He got his foot caught in a rope and spent a long time dangling outside of the plane, banging against the fuselage as I flew the plane, trying not to crash.

"But before that, he told me a story about a young San Francisco man named Jason Dahtberg and his defense attorney father whose specialty in court was eviscerating rape victims, making them look promiscuous, destroying their reputations, and getting heinous criminals like his son off. Peterman claims to have coached you all in how to kill Jason Dahtberg. He gave me multiple details."

Emily Smythe glanced first at Charlotte and then at Anne.

I continued. "Patrick Peterman also said that, while he didn't know the details of the circumstances of Veronica Eastern's crimes, he knew she'd been charged with driving drunk multiple times. Apparently, Peterman's own pursuit of solving problems, as he referred to murders he's committed, had made him interested in other people who've taken the law into their own hands.

"In my research, I learned that one of those times when Veronica was driving under the influence, she hit and killed a man in San Francisco, a crime that may not have gotten much attention because the man was homeless.

"Another time, she hit a bicycle courier, and he has been in a coma ever since.

"And just a year ago, after having already lost her license for driving drunk, Veronica ran over and killed a ten-year-old girl in the Outer Sunset neighborhood. The girl was Olivia Johnson Warnell.

"Eastern failed a sobriety test at the scene. But for whatever reason, she was never charged with manslaughter. It certainly looked to me like malfeasance on the part of the justice system. But then I learned she's got a powerful connection to the state political machine."

I paused. The sisters looked very uncomfortable, as I expected they would.

I continued, "A little more research revealed that Olivia Johnson Warnell was the daughter of Abigail Warnell, a nurse at St. Catherine of Siena Hospital, where you, Anne, have admitting privileges. In reading about Olivia's tragic death, I saw a posting that listed memorials for Olivia. One of those memorials expressed appreciation to Anne Smythe for a sizable charitable donation to a non-profit that supports children at risk. And it referred to you as godmother to Olivia.

"When your goddaughter died from being hit by your former classmate Veronica Eastern," I said, again looking at Anne, "it must have been an extra tragic blow."

Anne looked very serious but didn't speak.

"It seems clear to me that Veronica Eastern was a woman who clearly needed to be physically taken off the street. It's my guess that you sisters succeeded in doing what the legal system failed to do. Having done so means you've possibly saved the lives of future potential victims of Veronica Eastern's drunk driving."

The three women showed a mix of worry and what seemed like righteous indignation. What was left of their lives was potentially going to be destroyed. But they knew they had reasons for their actions, and those reasons were as far from trivial as you can get.

I continued, "As an officer of the law, it is my responsibility to alert people in law enforcement to your likely participation in these crimes."

I took a deep breath. "My phone call to the authorities would start a series of developments that, at the minimum, would make your lives overwhelmingly miserable. If I called up the DA's office in Placer County, which is where Tahoe City is and hence where the recent murder of Veronica Eastern took place, and if I gave them the info I've learned, some young attorneys who want to make a reputation for themselves would put a lot of effort into creating a case that would ruin your lives. Same for the San Francisco DA. At the maximum, some or all of you would possibly be indicted on either or both murders. If charged and convicted, you could spend much of the rest of your lives in prison. Please understand that I'm not judging your crimes, although perhaps I should. But that's not my intention at this point. The law intends to bring criminals to justice. It doesn't spend a lot of effort on understanding any claims of justification for crimes, never mind the failures of the current system."

All three sisters were moving, shifting, fidgeting as they contemplated their futures.

"There is also a personal aspect to this. My friend Jack Santiago is a sergeant with the Placer County Sheriff's Office. He and I have an understanding that we share all information pertinent to each other's jobs. In other words, separate from my legal responsibility to report your crimes to the authorities, I have a personal responsibility to uphold and honor my friendship with Jack, a man who has helped me many times in my work.

"So my question to the three of you is this: As I consider what information I should share with those to whom I'm obligated by law and honor and friendship, do you want to tell me anything before I make those calls?"

They each looked down as if in introspection.

We were all silent for a minute. Spot turned his head toward me, no doubt wondering about the silence. I gave him a pet.

After another minute, Charlotte finally spoke: "In Shakespeare's *Merchant of Venice*, Portia says, 'Though justice be thy plea consider this, that in the course of justice none of us should see salvation.'"

Charlotte looked at Emily and Anne, and then at me: "We've discussed this hypothetical concept at length because… We're interested in such things."

She seemed to choose her words carefully. "We know that not showing mercy to a killer would mean lowering one's self by some measure. Maybe by a great measure. But the quality of mercy would be very strained in a situation such as this."

Anne said, "We feel that in a harsh world, there are some personal judgments that retain value despite any critical scrutiny of society that would say otherwise."

Finally, Emily spoke. "I'll put it in simpler terms. I would make no apology for killing a villain who would attack and destroy women. If society did its job, society would take the same action. But society often doesn't do its job. This isn't because society is exercising the quality of mercy. It's because society doesn't have the mechanisms in place to even consider the quality of mercy. I could write a dissertation on the value or lack thereof of a legal system designed to find justice but which fails its design criteria. When a man such as Jason Dahtberg attacks a woman as one might attack a pile of offal and then, when the woman fights back, cleaves the woman's head with a shovel so viciously that he leaves her for dead, that's a man who should be put down by whatever means available."

I looked at her long and hard, my eyes following the faint scar that still traced diagonally across her forehead, through one eye, and back to her ear. Her statement, like Charlotte's, was designed to be hypothetical and admitted no involvement. If I'd recorded her words, and played them to a jury, they would find no admission of guilt, nor could they infer as much.

I said, "I've sometimes wondered, if I had a God button and could push it to make particularly evil people vanish, would I use it?"

Emily held my look and then eventually nodded. "Yes, you would use it. Anybody would except those who cling to a system that values form and process and arbitrary rules over basic right and wrong."

After another half hour of talk, I had implications and inferences. But I had no actionable information.

I thanked the sisters for their time and drove away thinking about the Hippocratic Oath. Did the focus on saving lives extend to eliminating those who take lives? Certainly, taking some lives can save many others. With the exception of ATF agent James Rousseau, each person who'd been murdered had killed, some more than one person, so it could be argued that those deaths directly saved lives.

That night, after Camille went to bed in Street's guest room, which was gradually being converted to Camille's own room with all of the appropriate components that a 9-year-old girl would want and should have, I sat with Street on the couch in front of her gas fireplace. Spot was on one side, Blondie on the other. Earlier, Camille wanted us to use her new Wonder Woman drinking glasses. So Street poured some wine in them, and I told Street about my talk with the Brontë sisters.

"They are unrepentant in their murders of the rapist attacker and the drunk driver who has killed two-plus people?" Street said.

"Correct. They admit nothing, but they rationalize hypothetically."

"Do they explain their actions in any way?"

"Yes, they do. Their explanation is kind of intellectual, and I don't remember the details. But they quoted Portia talking about the quality of mercy in Shakespeare's Merchant of Venice, and they talked about how, despite the potential value of mercy, it's not deserved in this situation. They think these people they've killed don't even deserve the opportunity to be charged with a crime and then tried, unless society could guarantee real justice."

"I know Portia's quote, and I agree," Street said.

We sat and watched the fire and sipped wine.

I said, "Now that I've told you this, do you think I should pass on what I know to Sergeant Santiago of Placer County? Or the San Francisco DA?"

"No. Separate from whether or not they should be prosecuted and incarcerated, you have no concrete evidence that you can report."

I thought about it. "Like the Brontë sisters, you don't believe in justice as defined by our laws?"

"In concept, yes," Street said. "In practice, not so much. It's like your code of ethics," she said. "You've said that there are times when your ethics require a course of action that runs counter to the law. I assume that's still the case."

"Yes, it is. It was even a factor in my statement to Diamond's boss regarding the death of Tucker Dopple."

This time, Street paused. "It's like a dichotomy with clear differences between the two sides. I suppose it would be a trichotomy, if that's even a word. Do I believe in the principle of law? Yes. Do I believe I should be able to break the law in certain situations? Yes. Do I believe others should be able to break the law? Mostly, no."

I started laughing. "My girlfriend, the anarchist. It's a good thing you don't have super powers."

Street held up her Wonder Woman glass. "Maybe I will now." She drank wine.

I smiled.

We watched the fire.

After a period of silence, Street said, "I know it shouldn't matter in this situation, at least in an intellectual analysis. But I'm curious. Did Veronica Eastern have family? Children or other dependents?"

"I agree it shouldn't matter. But I wondered that, too. So I looked into it. She didn't. She was married and divorced years ago and had no children or family that I can find other than an aunt who is a close friend of the governor and an employee in the governor's office. Eastern apparently lived with the aunt for a time when she was in college. I surmise that the aunt still cared for her and possibly placed some phone calls on Veronica's behalf when Veronica found herself in trouble."

Street made a slow, single nod. "Veronica Eastern was a doctor, like the others, right?"

"Not a medical doctor. She started out in pre-med, got accepted to UCSF Med School, then switched her career plans to pursue a Ph.D. and become a clinical psychologist. She remained friends with her med school classmates and was invited to join them here for their Tahoe reunion."

Street made a little twitch that told me she'd had a thought. "It was probably the Brontë sisters who invited her. Which was the sister whose goddaughter was killed?"

I nodded. "Anne Smythe."

"And which sister was attacked by the man in San Francisco?"

"Emily Smythe."

"And you think they and their other sister Charlotte have done these murders together?"

"Probably. Their responses to me implied they think and operate as a unit in these regards."

Street nodded. There was more silence.

After a time, she said, "I've often thought of my father and the depth and breadth of his evil. When he attacked me, it wasn't nearly as severe as what happened to Emily Smythe. And yet I came away with a similar feeling to what she had. He needed to be eliminated. And because he wasn't, and he is serving a life sentence in prison, he may in fact one day get paroled. He would be a very old man. But the thought still terrifies me. I'm not saying that society should show no mercy to people who are convicted of crimes. And I'm the first to acknowledge that many innocent people are convicted of crimes they didn't commit. But I know what my father did, just as Emily Smythe knows what her attacker did. I understand her actions even if I couldn't do what she did."

We sat in silence for several minutes.

"Not exactly a clean wrap-up to a long day," I finally said. "It leaves a messy trail of thoughts for a person to digest as they try to sleep."

"As you said once," Street said, "life is messy."

"But I still love you, messiness be damned."

"I'm glad," Street said, turning her face to mine. "Very glad."

EPILOGUE

Nanna Hansen, the woman who was Benito and Damen Diaz's Bay Area neighbor and who owned the vacation home next to the rental house they'd rented, left a message on my office machine. Damen was coming home from the hospital tomorrow. Nanna said that Damen wanted to see me.

I called back.

We exchanged some pleasantries. Then Nanna said, "I heard that you got kidnapped by the man who originally ordered Benito's death, and he took you up in a plane, where you managed to get the upper hand."

Obviously, she'd spoken to Diamond or maybe Commander Mallory of the South Lake Tahoe PD.

"Yeah. It ended up working out okay. I just wish it had turned out better for Benito."

"I've learned that if a person faces a substantial risk from— let's say—the east, death will come from the west. That's what happened to Benito, right? A couple of ex-cons planned to kill him, and instead he dies trying to save his nephew."

"Yes. How is Damen?"

"In most ways, he's pretty much the same kid who went bicycling on the Flume Trail with you and Benito. The same exuberance, the same enthusiasm. He does have some sensory and motor deficits in his arm. But he acts as if it's no big deal. The doctor told me that Damen has a big personality, which is good for healing, but only if he doesn't stress the surgery site on his upper arm. He sleeps a lot, which apparently is a normal response to this type of trauma. With luck, he'll be back to normal in a couple of months."

"Good to hear. How is he taking the loss of Benito?"

"It's obviously hard. But he appears to be doing well. On the surface, at least. I've spent a fair amount of time in the hospital. I've seen him go quiet and dark for long periods. Sometimes he tears up, but he won't talk about it. I don't push him. I give him space, and often he'll drift off to sleep. When he wakes, he's much better. I don't know how well you know kids, but kids are remarkably resilient. I'm guessing Damen will come through this okay."

"That's great that you are there for him."

"Benito probably didn't tell you this, but he asked me long ago if I would be Damen's designated stepparent if Benito got incapacitated. I said yes."

"A good choice on Benito's part," I said. "Very giving of you."

"Anyway, I'm hoping you and your family can come over tomorrow evening. Nothing fancy. But I'll serve some finger food. And there's probably still some beer in the fridge."

It was the first time I'd had someone tell me to bring my family. It was a seismic shift in my world. The lone-wolf detective part of my life seemed to be over. If you have a girlfriend and add a kid into the mix, you have a family.

"Thanks for the invite. If Street and Camille can come, I'm sure they'd love to join me."

"And your cop friend, Diamond," she said. "I've heard about him. He sounds quite… interesting. And your dogs. Damen said he met your dog at your office and, to use his word, your dog was awesome."

Nice to hear Diamond and the dogs were considered part of my family as well.

"Thanks, Nanna. I'll pass the invite on to Diamond and the dogs as well. Thanks. Where should we come?"

"The vacation rental house where you already attended Benito's party."

She gave me the time, we said goodbye, and hung up.

The next evening, Street, Camille, the dogs, and I showed up in Street's VW Beetle. I was stiffer and more sore than I had been the previous day. It was difficult for me to get into Street's car, even more difficult to get Camille onto my lap.

Nanna met us at the door. I held Spot's collar. Camille held Blondie's leash. Blondie seemed tentative. She hadn't been in many houses. Nanna let us in, paused to take a long look at Spot and Blondie, gave each of them a pat on their heads, then walked us over to where Damen sat in the big living room, not far from the grand piano.

"Hi, Mr. McKenna... Oh, I remember, Owen. Sorry that I'm just sitting here. I'm not supposed to get up and charge around."

"Hi, Damen. I hear you're doing very well."

The boy had a thick bandage on his upper arm. His arm was in a sling of some sort with an elastic strap that went across his chest and around his back. It appeared the purpose was to immobilize his arm.

"You remember Street and Camille from the party," I said.

"Yeah. You guys are nice to come here and hang out before Nanna and I go back to the Bay Area."

"Happy to."

"Please sit," Nanna said.

Street and Camille stepped over to a huge leather couch and sat. Blondie sat next to the end of the couch, close enough that Camille could lean over and pet her.

I held Spot back as I handed Damen a package that I had just received via next-day delivery. I didn't want Spot to be rambunctious and bump Damen's arm.

"Wow, what's this?" He opened it up and held up a mug that said 'The Flume Trail, Lake Tahoe.'

"Hey, this is cool! I'm going back, just so you know. I'm going to ride the Flume again."

"I'll come with you if you'd like," I said.

Damen was very smooth. "Only if you bring Street and Camille."

They grinned. "Count us in," Street said.

Nanna had gone to the kitchen. She came out with a big tray of food, crackers and cheese and some kind of roll-ups in mini tortillas.

The doorbell rang.

"That's probably Diamond," I said. "I'll let him in."

"Am I late?" Diamond said when I answered the door.

"Fashionably."

I showed him in. Diamond was carrying a flat package wrapped in paper. When I introduced him to Damen, Diamond said, "Hey, dude, I hear you rode the Flume." He handed Damen the package.

"More presents? We haven't even met!" He took the package and started unwrapping it.

"Your reputation as a mountain biker is almost as dramatic as your reputation for airplane flight path analysis," Diamond said, referring to what I'd said about Damen figuring out airplane paths from up on the Flume.

Camille was paying very close attention as Damen unwrapped Diamond's present. No doubt she didn't know that guests sometimes show up with gifts. By the time Damen got his package unwrapped, she was bouncing on the couch.

Damen unfolded a shirt and held it up in front of his chest. Now I understood. It was a long-sleeved, dark-blue T-shirt with a light-blue moon painted on it. In front of the moon were some filmy clouds.

Under the moon were hand-painted words.

'I Kicked Butt On The Flume Trail'

In the lower corner, it said, 'Camille's Tahoe Moon.'

"This is cool," Damen said. "I've never seen a shirt like this. Where'd you get it?"

"There's a local company called Camille's Tahoe Moon," Diamond said. He winked at Camille. "They started out making hand-painted scarves. Then they branched out into custom-painted shirts. When I called them yesterday and told them I needed a special gift for tonight, they got it done really fast."

Camille was looking from Diamond to Damen, reading their lips. Her grin could have lit a dark moon.

"Fast is good," Damen said. "But what's really great is their artist. Talk about talent…" He paused talking and looked at Camille who was now kneeling on the couch, bouncing and leaning back against the upholstery.

"Wait, your name is Camille," he said. "Did you paint this?"

She nodded.

"No way! Wow! I'm impressed! Thank you so much. You should come over here, and Nanna can take our picture together with the shirt."

Camille looked at Street. Street nodded.

Camille walked over and stood next to Damen's chair. Nanna and Street both took pictures.

"I'll be back to mountain biking soon. I'll wear this shirt. I'll be playing the piano again, too."

"Oh, that reminds me," Nanna said. "I have some news. When Uncle Benny saw how much you liked this piano and this house, it got him thinking. Then you apparently told him you would love to live in Tahoe. So he bought it."

"Bought what?" Damen asked.

"This house. And the piano."

Damen frowned. His frown morphed to shock. "Uncle Benny bought this house so we could vacation here?"

"Yes. Vacation here, maybe spend summers here, maybe move here someday."

"Oh, wow, I can't believe it."

"Yes, it was a sudden decision on his part. But I know the people who owned it before. They agreed to sell it to him. He was very excited to do it."

"But now he died," Damen said. "Doesn't that, like—I don't know—change everything and make it so the house still belongs to the previous owner?"

"No. He'd already been in touch with the insurance agent and the bank, and he already signed the paperwork with the title company. So the house is now..." Nanna's voice caught. She swallowed. "The house is now yours, Damen."

Damen's eyes teared up. "Uncle Benny was always so nice. Now he did this super nice thing. I don't think I will be able to live up to this gift. Uncle Benny was my best friend. I don't even have friends who would understand such generosity."

Camille walked over next to Damen and lifted up his hand.

He watched her but didn't resist.

"We'll be your friends," she said. She used her finger to draw a circle on Damen's palm. Then she closed his fingers.

About The Author

Todd Borg and his wife live in Lake Tahoe, where they write and paint. To contact Todd or learn more about the Owen McKenna mysteries, please visit toddborg.com.

A message from the author:

Dear Reader,

If you enjoyed this novel, please consider posting a short review on any book website you like to use such as Goodreads and Amazon. Reviews help authors a great deal, and that in turn allows us to write more stories for you.

Thank you very much for your interest and support!

Todd

Made in United States
Troutdale, OR
10/03/2023

13366086R10195